TETHERED

BY

DECEPTION

KATHERINE SCHEIRER

Tethered by Deception

Copyright © 2026 by Katherine Scheirer

Cover Art by Katherine Scheirer

Illustrations by Canva & Katherine Scheirer

All rights reserved.

No portion of this book may be reproduced in any form without written permission from the publisher or author.

Any unauthorized use of this book to train generative artificial intelligence (AI) technologies is prohibited.

This is a work of fiction. Places, names, character descriptions are the product of the author's imagination. Any resemblance of any persons, living or otherwise is purely coincidental.

Print ISBN #: 978-1-0693908-2-0

eBook ISBN#: 978-1-0693908-3-7

TO THOSE WHOSE
BLINDFOLD
HAS BEEN REDUCED TO
ASH.

Foreword
Trigger Warning

This book deals with mature themes. As such, please review the following to decide if this story is suitable for you.

Blood, gore, and general violence

Forced confinement and imprisonment

Torture – physical, emotional, sexual, and religious

Fundamentalist cult behaviour

Sexual harassment & sexual themes

Child abuse and forced indoctrination (mentioned)

THE WEST
THE FALLEN CITY
SACRED CANYON
NIMA'S VILLAGE
RUINS
VILLAGE
RUINS
VILLAGE
PORT TOWN

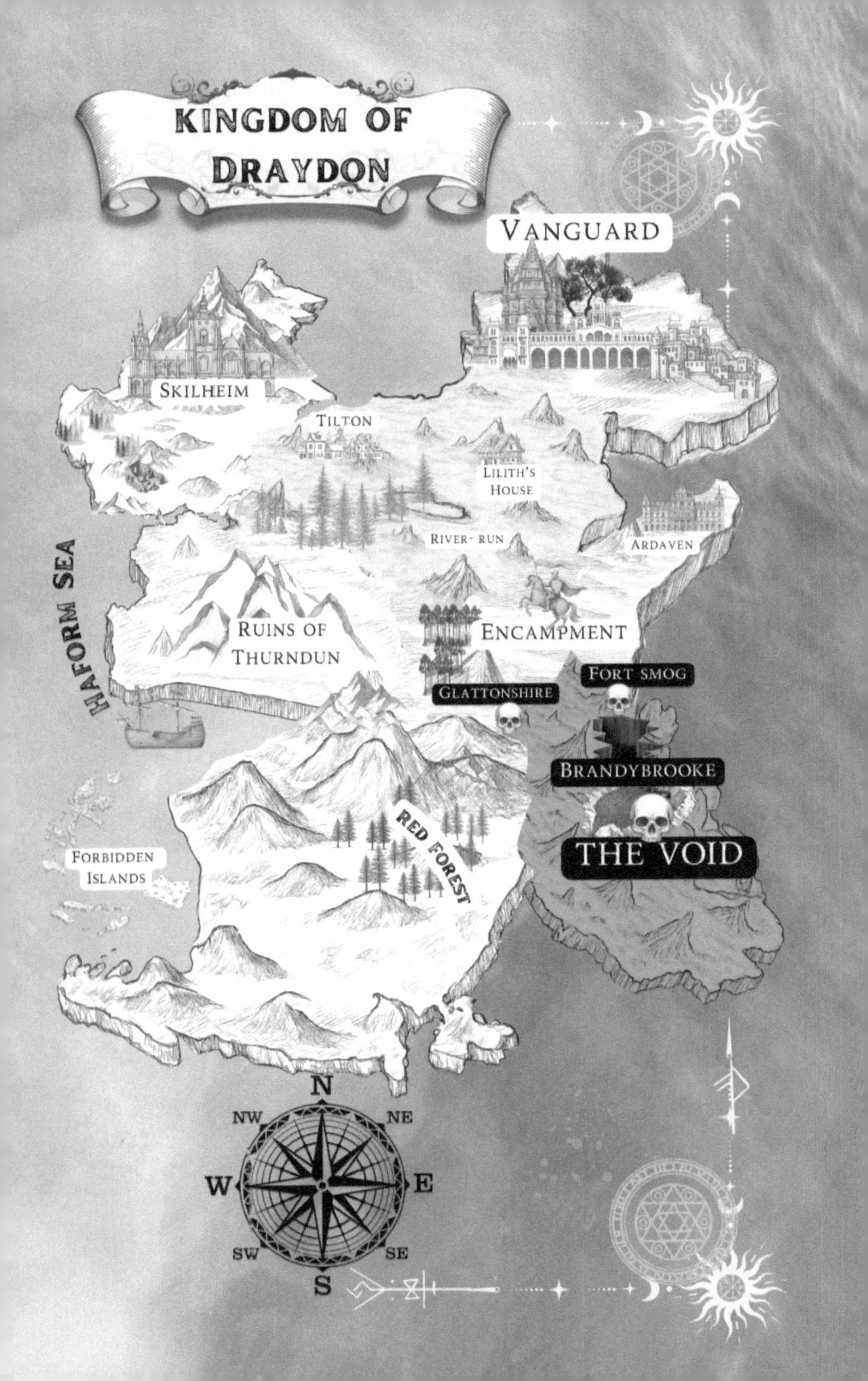

KINGDOM OF DRAYDON

VANGUARD

SKILHEIM

TILTON

LILITH'S HOUSE

RIVER-RUN

ARDAVEN

HAFORM SEA

RUINS OF THURNDUN

ENCAMPMENT

FORT SMOG

GLATTONSHIRE

BRANDYBROOKE

THE VOID

FORBIDDEN ISLANDS

RED FOREST

N
NW NE
W E
SW SE
S

PROLOGUE
LAND OF THE DYING

Demetrius

How long had it been since he had seen light? A long forgotten sensation of a warm blaze from the sun caressing one's skin? There was heat in this realm, leaking between the hardened scorched ground, yet it gave no comfort. There was no way to trap its warmth, no way to hold it to one's body. Hues of orange and red were the only colours coming up from the depths of the centre, so far down that it was out of reach and acted as a reminder that this place was volatile and merciless.

Volcanic ash had made this place inhospitable, blanketing the sky in infinite darkness. At first, it was difficult to breathe in the thick air, but then he learned how to adapt, adjusting his body to function and survive. The hot breeze was so dry that no moisture lingered to make the environment tolerable. It was a perfect place to keep condemned souls, where despair and hopelessness thrived.

Shards of thin obsidian rock crunched beneath his feet. The land was barren and unyielding. Nothing grew here, but that is why they had selected this place for their purpose. It was his recommendation, after all, which caused them to select this realm. Among all the worlds under their authority, this was the one that no one wanted to claim. It was a perfect prison, and he didn't regret his decision.

The creatures that were sent here were beyond salvation; they were beyond giving another chance. New souls were sent here to perish and be tormented until death claimed them. They were monsters that should never have existed, ones that only welcomed destruction and would threaten mass extinction. They had been called many names: devils, demons, nightmares, beasts of the underworld, and world-enders.

How long had he been trapped here? Betrayed by those whom he held the closest: his family. Had it been a hundred years or a thousand? His rough hands gripped his weathered sword, its once-shining lustre having long since faded, as had his once-brilliant ivory armour. His sword's edge had countless nicks and was blunted beyond repair, yet in its prime condition, it was a glorious tool. Its curved blade and rounded, white crystallized hilt were perfectly balanced. This sword was an extension of his arm and claimed the lives of countless enemies. Once, it shone so brilliant, it would blind those who opposed him. What a shame that it was now reduced to this useless trophy. Nothing could be replaced unless he killed one of the prisoners. And he had killed many, but nothing could compare to his trusted sword.

In a prison full of predators, only one could claim the title of the alpha. Initially, he had focused on survival, getting through one day at a time, in the hope that someone would come for him. Perhaps they would free him in a moment of regret.

He did not deserve this cruel existence.

After the first dozen years, that hope dwindled, and a new goal took its place. He was the one who helped force these creatures into this confinement, and now he lived amongst them. There was only one way to carve out a life here and that was to become their king. With every swing of his blade, he rose another step in their hierarchy. It cost him dearly. With every swing of his blade, he lost a piece of his sanity. They hunted him until they learned that even by himself, he should be feared.

Time moved in a consistent flow. He would rest in the darkest corners of the realm, moving about the shadows until he came across something. The creature would either submit and retreat or he would purge it from existence. He had thought himself a superior being until this rigid schedule of living in continuous fear had shaped him as one of them.

Time seemed endless for a monster like him.

An immortal that learned how to live without sleep, to live without enough food and water. He lived in a hunger that could never be satisfied, and a thirst that could never be quenched.

In the beginning, he sustained from the rotten-tasting flesh from some of these monsters. He learned which ones were more palatable, though most of them weren't. The reptilian creatures had long since vanished from the lands; they were the easiest prey and the weakest of the prisoners locked up. After their fall, he was reduced to starvation. It took a century to reach the top of the hierarchy, where only the truly despicable ones remained.

No, that wasn't true.

There was one that everyone feared. One that truly deserved much worse than this place. It had squirrelled itself somewhere out of reach, and no one went looking for it. The sounds of rushing wind were the only evidence that this beast existed. It thrived in the darkness when most were weakened. It was the original monster of this realm. It created this world, this place of ash and darkness.

His armoured knee dropped to the ground, and he ran his hand through the sharp shards. Behind him, hidden under the black veil, came an echo of a call. A challenge. Tightening his grip on the hilt of his worn sword, he caught a glimpse of his reflection in the tarnished silver. He was used to seeing his once bright white hair, permanently stained black from the soot. He gasped, taken by surprise. He was expecting eyes that were his usual iridescent light turquoise, but staring back at him were beautiful greens. Her eyes. Most of the distinct features of her face were a faded memory, but he remembered her eyes. Green as the lush ground. A gentle glint of a woman who was graceful and ethereal. She was too kind to live amongst his people, and they took advantage of her. Only a few had seen her fierce side, the fire that raged in her soul. He rubbed the pad of his thumb with his finger, struggling to remember what she felt like. He had once called her soft, but couldn't recall what that meant. He had forgotten many things, but one thought drove him forward: the promise that he would find her again.

The call of challenge became louder as he rose to a stand, brushing the dust off his broken armour. There must be a way out of this godsforsaken cage, and he would sacrifice whatever he had left to escape.

Blood dripped off the tip of his blade into the ground, lost to the black. He huffed as he took a step forward, the lying carcass of his challenger discarded behind him, a warning to others that this was his territory.

He lost count of the years that passed.

It was by luck that he was near enough to see the flare of light on the horizon's edge. Something that didn't belong. Immediately, he ran to the source, the last threads of hope beaming to life as he came upon the wisp of power that didn't belong in this world.

He forced his fingers through the light. It felt like he was pushing into dense mud. A laugh escaped him, revelling in the sensation of something new. A spasm of pain passed through his body, draining his power. Realization dawned on him, as he understood the sacrifice he would have to make in order to tear open this fragment of promise, a way out. He gave as much immense power as he could summon, pulling apart the seams of this doorway. His physical body had transformed into a husk, but he had given up enough that the rift was just wide enough so what was left of him could pass through. The sword he had cherished all this time, now discarded as one last offering to the cage.

A sharp coldness tore at his spirit as he dug what was left of his fingers into the crumbling earth; that scent of soil made him giddy. The feeling of humidity hitting his flesh snapped his last bit of his rationale.

"Find her!" His voice felt scratchy as he called out. He drifted in and out of consciousness, thinking of green eyes.

Boot steps thudded closer. Someone heard his plea. He had given his vision to the rift, but he could sense a familiar power approach. One who was unlike himself, but a being that once lived alongside him.

A hand reached towards him, and he used what was left of his power to shift once more. His energy, his soul, attacked the oncomer, invading his body. Possessing him.

He had made it out of that hellhole, and now he would stop at nothing to fulfill that promise. She would be somewhere, and he would find her.

Once freed from the cage, he lived behind eyes that were not his, passing from body to body until he found the right vessel. No longer was he a powerful being crafted for slaughtering the most vicious creatures. He survived by lingering in another's mind and learning about this realm. Then came a time when a vessel called to him, a child destined to die at birth, but who now served as an opportunity for him to properly enter this world. One he could entirely control as if it were his own.

White hair was born midnight blue. Hands that had not seen battle felt buttery and soft. But not all features were created as something different from what he had looked like before. How strange that his eyes resembled the same iridescent blue hue? How odd that his flesh developed similar scars, as if the pain he suffered tainted his soul. Some things could not be wiped clean.

"Demetrius, are you ready?" his mother came up to stand behind him, dusting off his fine navy jacket. "It's time you head off." Queen Isolde was the picture of refinement and royalty. Her silky blonde hair was in an elegant updo, but he did not resemble her. He had the tell-tale sign all direct royal blood shared; his hair signified his lineage. A prince.

"I hear this will be the largest intake of students your school has ever received." Gossiping was the most favourite pastime of the queen.

"So I heard."

"Who knows, you may meet someone to your liking." The queen's latest fixation was trying to find someone to secure the bloodline.

"You know, if you had committed this determination to finding a way to seal the Void, we would have been saved by now."

The blonde woman let out a practiced, jovial laugh. "Let's hope your future wife enjoys your humour." She moved to the nearby door. "Anyway, your father is feeling unwell. He sends his wishes for safe travel." She patted her son on the shoulder and left.

Once outside, Demetrius took a deep breath, filling his lungs full of fresh, clean air. Never again would he take such things for granted. This was his second chance. Every bite of food he took filled him with hope. Things that were simple he saw as a luxury: walking through the forest, feeling blades of grass through his fingers, taking a bath, and changing his clothes. These things were all so meaningful after a lifetime of having nothing, and it annoyed him to no end when someone felt entitled to these comforts.

Acting was easy to develop. He knew how to behave, to mask the real demon inside and only show those around him his carefully curated version of what they expected of a prince. With every spare chance, he searched for her with no luck.

The more he exposed himself to others, the more he grew to despise these people. Their life was run and dictated by a system of entitlement. Generations were blessed with inherited wealth and titles, leaving few to rise up the ranks from nothing, and those who were at the lowest tier of society endured the constant pain of survival. Every passing year, his plan developed, morphing into something sinister. He would be their savior, their divine retribution that equalized the playing field, and make this realm his.

He was not selfless, for fate would deliver her to his side. She would be his gift, his obsession.

The Knowing One declared the promise that his path would find hers. He would just have to be patient, and after centuries of waiting, patience was ingrained in his soul. When fate intertwined their lives once more, she would never leave his side. Only then could he turn the tide and turn his attention to revenge. There would be no corner in the universe that they could hide. Their suffering would only be too sweet, and he would not show mercy.

Before climbing into the carriage, he looked to the sky. Maybe this would be the year.

"Your Highness, we are ready to head to Skilheim," a servant gingerly called out.

"Yes. I'm ready," Demetrius replied, taking a seat. He smirked in anticipation. This would be amusing.

PART ONE

Chapter I
The Last Article

A Name Forgotten

By Beatrice Bane

No one would have suspected that the turning point of society came from the rise of a seemingly normal child. It wasn't a king or noble that had taken over the minds of every household and changed the future of our children. It was just a boy.

Born to a house nestled in the very drudge-infested back alley of our own city, Vanguard. His father served as a foot soldier for King Amadeus. His team was one of the last to help secure the borders to the fallen lands. Much like others, he came home with tales of what lay hidden in the Void. And like many others, this family turned to the Holy Words for guidance.

By age fourteen, his family had joined a group of fundamentalists, devoted to the last scriptures of the old gods.

Though his family turned pious, the boy was commended by teachers and neighbours alike as highly intelligent and critical, as an observer that was always listening and thinking. Strangely enough, he was always surrounded by classmates. It was as if he had a magnetism that attracted all folk, placing them all under his spell, his charismatic presence. It was a gift that when he spoke, people would drift closer. He was not a talker, but when he preached, his words provoked emotion, making those around him feel special.

When the boy was just sixteen, the streets of Vanguard were ravaged by the spotted plague, which killed thousands. His community was wrecked, sparing few who were trapped in grief and desperate for guidance. He used what was left of his religious group, eleven other boys around his age, now orphans, and traveled to the mass gravesite, proclaiming that this plague was an act of the gods, a warning to no longer turn a blind eye on what was happening in the south. It was at this moment he formed the Apostles of the Reckoning.

In two short years, his group published a short book, *Heart of the Abyss,* a distorted medley of broken scripture from the Old Gods with critical assessment of how society has fallen. His ideas were vague enough to invite interpretation, but they also held a magnetic draw. In truth, he disguised thinly veiled threats as promises of salvation. A way to seek redemption by serving their real master, the one that controlled the Void.

By his mid-twenties, he had shaped his vision of the Apostles. Eleven of his "brothers" had been taught to wear the white robes of purity, showing a carefully crafted version of their ideal: a unified brotherhood where they were equals amongst themselves.

Now, they rule Vanguard, the jewel of the kingdom. Through fear they have forced the practice of other religions out of the city. Through obedience, they control the market and trade, ensuring that the upper echelon of the city receive the best. Hand in hand with the nobles, they have severed aid going to the encampments. Our sons and daughters, who are sent to face the oncoming darkness, do so with limited supply. They desire to weaken us, the everyday people. The people who are trying to survive. They try to force our young to learn their ways, and without protest, they are eradicating our history.

Why are we staying silent while they burn our books, our knowledge? Why are we allowing them to shape the minds of our children? How much are we willing to sacrifice before we realize they have sunk their claws into our backs? They have chained us with their false words, and we have become their puppets.

Since the queen has invited the Apostles into her house, fifty two houses of nobility have aligned themselves with the new religion. Seduced by greed, they have instilled their own as apprentices; the grey robes that shadow their masters in white.

Thousands of refugees flood the city, while those who have lost their beliefs, their way of life, are desperate to leave. We are trapped, and they have created the perfect breeding ground for oppression.

The royals have abandoned us.

So I ask you to open your eyes. See the truth of what is unfolding in our city, our kingdom. We need to stand against those that want to oppress us further. I speak to those that realize it's not too late to remove the claws of injustice: become the beacon of hope for the hard workers of this kingdom. Drive out those who wish to climb the ladders from the backs of our hardships.

The gods have given us this land, our home. We will not give it away so freely. No longer will the manacles of darkness prevail. You are the hands that shape our future. You are the eyes of truth.

Though I will disappear, let my words spark fire in your hearts. Let my words burn away the blindfold that they have placed over your eyes.

CHAPTER 2
PRINCESS OF THE NIGHT

Felicia

Felicia stirred. She felt cold and clammy as she looked around in the dark. Tiny droplets of water trickled steadily down the rough stone wall, echoing in the room.

The Apostles left her on the damp stone floor, but they removed her bindings and her gag. Her long white nightgown was stained from blood that wasn't hers and clung to her skin. She couldn't breathe, it was like she was suffocating from an invisible force. Her breath came out in short and shallow pants. The walls felt like they were closing in—a feeling she had experienced before.

Her mother had locked her in her room for days as a child, and she suffered panic attacks frequently, with only her brother to calm her nerves. He would whisper through the door, walking her through ways of calming herself. *Breathe in and out, slowly.* Repeated it again and again until her sobs stopped and the weight on her chest subsided. His calm voice filled her mind again, soothing her.

Just breathe, Felicia, in and out, just like you used to. She could swear she saw him in the shadows of her cramped cell. Madoc. He smiled at her, his unruly golden hair flowing to his shoulders. *You need to get up. Find a way out.* Her sanity was clearly holding on by threads, but instead of fighting it, she embraced her hallucination.

She crawled slowly around, trying to get her bearings. The rough stone scraped along her fingertips and hurt her knees, but she was too weak to stand. Whatever tonic they forced her to swallow not only suppressed her ability to reach her mana but also drained whatever energy she had stored. Her body was shaking from the strain of moving around. Just as she was going to give up, her fingers grazed something wooden. She felt upwards and pushed herself onto her feet. Her hand traced the surface of a rough wooden door, finding a small circular window with bars. She looked over her shoulder to where she had seen her brother, but now she was alone.

"Lilith?" she asked the darkness, her voice weak and raspy. She listened for any movement and heard a tiny groan in the distance. It was too dark outside her cell to see anything.

"Hello?" said a weak voice. "Felicia?"

"Lady Thalassa!" Felicia called out hoarsely, resting her face on the door. "Are you hurt?" Every breath felt like her lungs were on fire. She had never been without her mana to this extent; it shocked her how weak she felt. Her legs quivered, then buckled, and she fell to her knees.

"Am I hurt?" Lady Thalassa's small voice was barely audible. "My mother is dead, they've stripped me of my powers, and my brother betrayed me." Sounds of faint weeping filtered into Felicia's cell. Felicia closed her eyes; the sounds of crying made her head throb.

Felicia let out a little groan and slumped against the door, her consciousness fading in and out. If only she could rest a little, maybe she would have more strength to figure out what was going on. Darkness enclosed around her as her breathing settled into a deeper rhythm. She drifted into a memory.

Her body snuggled deeper into the comfy mattress, as she pulled the soft cover over her arms. These comforts felt like a blessing, different to the ones she experienced for the last several months at Skilheim. Quality sleep. She could hardly remember the last time she was able to fully relax. After their confrontation in the throne room, she was sure her night would end in bloodshed, but she never looked a gift horse in the face.

A creek sounded around her as multiple hands grabbed her all at once, holding her down. Her eyes bolted open to see the shrouded faces of men dressed in a grey version of their masters, the Apostles. Two of the white robes stood on either side of her, leaning over her face. They smelled of incense and body odour. She opened her mouth to scream, but a hand quickly smothered her mouth. Straining against them, they tightened their grip and pinched her skin.

One of them reached into their pockets and pulled out a glass vial with a dark green liquid in it. Felicia's eyes flared wide as she realized what they were intending. One of the Apostles pinched her nose as the other uncorked the vial and pushed it between her lips. She pressed her tongue against its opening, refusing to take it. After a few seconds, she struggled to breathe and started wiggling to get out of their hold. Her saliva started to drip down her cheeks as she held out as long as she could, but the green liquid made its way down her throat. The Apostle, holding her nose, let go, making her gasp at the rush of air. The effects of the tonic were immediate; her muscles relaxed once more, and she felt the pull of darkness overcome her.

Another memory filtered to the forefront of her mind.

She was dragged to the throne room, her feet scraping along the floor. Her head rolled to the side as her eyelids blinked open. Everything was a blur, but she could make out the greenery of the large oak tree that stood behind the white throne. Someone was seated in it, a figure shrouded in shadows.

She grimaced as she recognized who this was despite the shadows; her intuition had always been keen. Prince Demetrius. She had sensed a disturbance whenever she was in his presence, as if the air was thicker around him. An intoxicating aura of energy simmered under his skin, making those around him either be pulled in by his attraction, or avoid him from fear.

She should have listened to her fear.

The shadows pulsating out of him dissipated, and his image cleared, allowing her to make out his form. He sat with an air of refinement, wearing a black suit more suitable for a funeral than one befitting a person of his title. He smiled at her with his piercing blue eyes, but as he blinked, darkness enveloped them. It was just for a flickering moment, but she was sure it was real.

Her head rolled to the side, feeling the weightlessness of something missing. Her mana. How did Lilith manage all these months? It was different, though, because at least Lilith had some magic; she was completely drained. An absence of her nor-

mal connection to the earth, of a life force circulating through her. She pulled against the bindings around her wrists and grunted against the gag in her mouth. She wanted to scream, to curse them, to cry and claw at the Apostles. The tightness of the cloth gag mixed with saliva only amplified her anxiety. The tightness in her chest grew rapidly, as her panic flared. A throbbing ringing pulsed in her ears, muffling the sounds of those around her. It felt as if her senses were muted.

Prince Demetrius moved to stand as someone else was being brought in—a figure she recognized immediately: Lilith. Dressed in a long black tunic, her hair was a disheveled inky mess falling around her face. A bitter resentment settled in her stomach as Felicia understood what had transpired between the prince and her friend. She had warned Lilith that something felt off with him. Guilt crept up her spine, knowing that she could have voiced her concerns more aggressively. She should have pushed for Lilith to see reason. She should have listened to her intuition. Her brother had warned her that her perception was only a gift if she had the courage to act on it.

Looking around her, she could see the body of someone else, another woman. Lady Thalassa. She, too, wore a long white nightgown, a twin to the one Felicia had borrowed from her. Lady Thalassa stirred from her drugged slumber. Her eyes locked with Felicia's, wild fear wracking through them. Felicia's fear was much more controlled. A lifetime with her mother, the general of the king's army, had desensitized her from her current condition.

She looked back to the prince, seeing his mouth move. The prince was saying something; if only she could focus on his words.

Felicia looked to Lilith, who was battling her own state of con-fusion, her attention transfixed on the speaker.

Another voice broke through the ringing: Sir Erikson. "What is the meaning of this, Your Highness?" he yelled, as he was dragged in with Mistress Rhodes and Lady Tessa. They all looked like they had taken a beating. Some of the guards were covered in gashes and bruises of their own.

Lady Tessa locked on her daughter's presence, and they shared a look between them. Although no words were spoken, her mother was trying to comfort her. Both of their eyes were glistening.

"It's okay," Lady Tessa mouthed to her daughter. She looked at Felicia, sending the same feelings of motherly comfort to her.

This would not end well.

There must be a reason why they were specifically targeted.

Prince Demetrius spoke once more. "I said I would root out the pests, and I plan to. It is time I take the throne and free myself from this tiresome charade." He seemed fully relaxed, as the shadows grew around him. This was the negative energy that she had felt in the Ruins of Thurndun. At the end of their journey, she was starting to curse her intuition. Lilith was so sure that he could be trusted. She was a victim of his obsession. Felicia had wondered why the prince took such an interest in Lilith. In almost every occasion that he was with her, Felicia caught the quick glimpses between them. He viewed Lilith with possessive eyes, as if she was his prey. He had paid little attention to anyone else; they were all just pawns in his game. She saw this and said nothing. Felicia didn't want to accuse someone of such high status without being certain, and that doubt had failed her.

He stood before the throne and ran his long fingers through his midnight blue hair. A look of wild abandon transformed his face, making it seem like he was in a state of euphoria. "Look at you all," he spoke with a dark, unearthly voice, "The confusion on your faces as you try to figure out what is going on. Is this a ruse? Is this a game? You are too quick to trust and too eager to follow. Deep down, you wanted this: you looked to me to lead you."

That dark voice, so similar to the one that had been tormenting her sleep. A voice that was haunting her dreams, whispering about the approaching darkness. It showed her a warning of what was to come. Mistress Rhodes was yelling at him, but her words were lost as the dark voice rumbled once more.

With a smirk, the prince's icy blue eyes turned to a solid onyx. The Apostles crept closer, surrounding them. She had barely noticed their presence alongside the prince's. Of course, they were working together. He was their master. How long had he planned this? How long had this shadowed king walked amongst them? And for what?

Felicia turned to face Lilith. She was the prize. It was as if the roots of the prince's shadows crept closer to Lilith. They stared at each other in a silent conversation. Felicia and the others were mere spectators.

It felt as if death hovered around them. Something dark and menacing was about to transpire and she was unable to do anything. Lady Thalassa's body was quivering beside her. Yet, Felicia remained oddly calm. Tears were cascading down Lady Tessa's cheeks, as the Apostles dragged her to stand over her daughter. Craning her neck, Felicia looked at Mistress Rhodes. She, too, looked calm, but her eyes held a different expression. She knew that this would end in bloodshed. An acceptance of her fate.

The sounds of someone new approaching startled her, and she could tell by the scent that this person was someone she knew. Silver. His silver hair framed his face in a disheveled mess. It was not that long ago, she had seen him being taken deeper into the palace in search of a healer. What happened between then and now? How was he able to stand and walk as if nothing happened? He wore the same tattered clothes he had when they moved through the Ruins, the white of the cloth soaked with a mixture of dried blood and black ooze. His skin, covered in a sheen of sweat, seemed paler than normal. He walked in front of Felicia, his eyes matching the obsidian darkness of the prince's.

The bonds of their friendship had grown last year. To her, he walked the fine line between friend and something more. They met on a few occasions late at night, in a long-forgotten passage hidden at Skilheim. Their passion was quick, a mutual physical outlet, but they were in no rush to place feelings. Quick-witted and sarcastic, Silver countered her introverted self, who liked to silently observe. However, there were glimpses of who he really was. She told him once that he reminded her of a sly fox, always up to something.

She squirmed as she tried to get to him, grunting his name against her gag. However, his gaze remained emotionless. Unhearing. Was he aware? Was he lingering deep down, past this eerily dark facade? His name passed her lips once more in a whisper, a near-silent plea. She tried to reach him, her hand brushing against his ankle as he pulled out something long and glinting—a knife.

"No!" she cried out. Did he know all this time of the prince's plan? She knew Silver held the prince in high regard. His family

and their friend, Taran, were weaved among the royals. She watched him bring the knife to Mistress Rhodes.

Then, blood. So much blood.

It sprayed on her, bathed her hair, and soaked her white nightgown. She heard the bodies drop behind her. Silver stood at her back; she couldn't feel the heat that usually rolled off him. Was she next? She desperately wanted to twist around, grab that knife and slit his throat. But she was frozen in fear. Her mind was yelling at her to move, to do something.

All she could do was wait.

Hands seized Felicia and carried her away as she set her rage on the two who caused so much despair. She shouldn't blame Lilith, but she was here because she followed her. Lilith screamed and bucked against the hands of the Apostles as they took out the vials of green tonic. Lilith pleaded and begged for forgiveness, and the sounds of the prince's laugh echoed in the throne room. Felicia twisted and glared at the shadowed prince.

"I'm going to kill you!" she choked out, as an Apostle yanked her gag down and forced the green liquid down her throat. She swore her revenge against the prince, Silver, and the Apostles, cursing them as her consciousness succumbed to darkness.

Felicia, wake up! Madoc's voice rang loudly in her ears. Tingles shot up her arm which she rested her head on. It felt numb and lifeless, similar to how she felt, as she hauled herself upright and massaged her limb. The sounds of a woman's voice called out to her.

"Hello?" called out the stranger, with a voice Felicia couldn't recognize.

"I can hear you! Who are you?" answered Felicia. She pressed her ear to the door's window and waited for a few seconds. "Hello? Can you hear me? I'm Felicia. We've been taken by the Apostles. Do you know where we are?"

The woman coughed, then replied, "I'm Ivy. We're under their temple."

Their temple? Were they still on palace grounds? Felicia tried to press herself closer to the door. "The Apostles, what are they planning?"

Ivy weakly replied, "I've heard the sounds of them. It sounded like they were singing. I don't know. They haven't taken me out of here." Ivy's coughs sounded wet and wheezy.

"Have they done anything to you?" Felicia was thinking the worst. She sat in silence, waiting for Ivy to answer, but she could only hear the faint sounds of Lady Thalassa crying and water dripping. "Ivy?" she called out again.

Ivy's frail voice answered, "They beat me. Everything hurts, but since you came, they don't come for me." Her voice cracked. "I'm sick. I don't know how long I've got left."

Felicia didn't know what to say to Ivy; no words could help her. If anything, Ivy's words filled her with dread.

"How long have you been here?" Felicia asked Ivy.

A moment of silence passed, but then she heard the wheezy voice speak once more. "I can't tell. Weeks, months—it feels like my life has passed in this cage."

Felicia knew the Apostles had slowly worked their way into the palace by the invitation of Queen Isolde. That was how long ago? She thought of the news articles, which mentioned them shortly after her start at Skilheim, so at most six months had passed. This poor woman could have been the first soul down here.

"What happened? How did they get you? Tell me everything, every little detail." Felicia needed more information. She wanted to know what kind of enemy she faced.

Ivy cleared her throat and replied, "I was working the streets. It was warm out. The nights were only just starting to cool down, but I didn't need a shawl or anything to fight the midnight air."

"By working the streets, you mean..."

"Selling myself. I'm not ashamed. Some of us weren't lucky enough to be born with security, a home. I was a child raised in one of the brothels, and I accepted my fate long ago."

"I didn't mean to sound judgmental. Please, tell me everything."

"They started skulking around our streets only recently, spreading their holy presence to the furthest reaches of Vanguard. The place I worked for was seen as a high tier establishment. We were Vanguard's 'Princesses of the Night.' The mistress of the house carefully selected our customers, mostly nobles with deep pockets. A few of our customers were influenced enough to see their light. But those who knew only darkness could sense a kinship hiding in those sinister white robes. Their covered eyes never lingered on our bodies, but rather they sought our souls." Ivy released a raspy laugh. "Too bad for them, we had given those up long ago. They were compromised beyond repair."

Ivy paused, her breathing laboured. "At first, the Apostles chose to pressure our customers, cutting off our means of survival. Stupid fools. Lust outshines their holiness. It's not their fault that they've turned their backs on true worship: the one that happens between a woman's legs. You'd be surprised at how many other priests, different from the Apostles, have succumbed to our temptation. Behind closed doors, they gave into their wildest desires. They were all the same. Yet, the Apostles never gave in; it was like that part of them died."

Felicia took an immediate liking to Ivy. She seemed intelligent, despite not growing up in privilege, and that said something about the strong will of her character. "There is no denying that they are extremely disturbing. Who knows, maybe they complete a ritual and have their bits cut off."

Ivy gave a little laugh. "It would not surprise me. We noticed that the lower tiers of street workers had started to disappear.

At first, we thought it was an angry customer, but then they left us a message, inviting us to their new house of worship. They left it in a pool of blood. We were smart enough to stay away, and our mistress established stricter rules. Their warning had done its duty and scared almost all of us off the streets. We moved further into the underbelly of the city, making our transactions hidden. We created a watch system to safeguard each other, but there was a rat. Someone sold us out. Told the freaks of our new operations." A string of coughs interrupted her story. "I told my mistress that I was done, and so I called in every favour that was owed to me in exchange for shelter. It worked until the favours ran out and I had to survive alone. The nights had become bitter, but to be honest, it wasn't too bad. The hunger, though, wore me down faster than the cold. It always does. I had no choice but to turn to what I was best at."

"That's when they took you."

"The hunger had dulled my senses. I'm usually quite good at keeping alert. They had their own goons beat me to a pulp."

"'Goons'?"

"They've been actively recruiting ever since they got here. Unlike the Apostles, these guys are in grey robes. They aren't held to the same standards as the Apostles. They are still more men than inhuman creeps. They still fall for their basic desires."

Felicia had met some of these 'goons'; they were the ones holding her down while they force-fed her the green tonic. While the Apostles were held to the expectations of being holy messengers of the Void, the grey robes were given more freedom to exploit the civilians and do the dirty work for their masters.

Ivy broke into another fit of coughs. She needed some medicine, and soon. "That's when I woke up here, in this fine dungeon. I figured out there are over a dozen of us here, based on the different screams. They take turns teaching their apprentices how to convert us 'wretched souls,' and punish us until we're black and blue. They asked me questions: my name, my age, where I came from, and who my parents were. They wanted to know if I have any magical abilities. I willingly told them everything, but that didn't matter. The beatings still came. They've been more aggressive lately. They even brought in that reporter, Beatrice Bane. I guess they weren't fans of her recent articles. "

A loud clunk reverberated through the dungeon, followed by footsteps. Whoever was approaching was heavy on their feet, their keys jingled, and their robes dragged behind them. Whimpering women and children cried out as the person passed their cells. A small voice of a child crying for their mother drifted to Felicia, whose fury filled her weak body. They had children here. Would the prince know about this? Of course, he would. They were his puppets; their actions would not go unnoticed by their master. Despicable. The rattle of keys stopped in front of her cell.

"Move back!" yelled the person standing on the other side of her door. Felicia didn't move. "You will not receive any food or water if you do not comply. Move back!" The promise of their food and water held no interest for her. They could have tampered with it, added the suppressant to it. She was better off not eating, allowing her body to pass whatever they gave her.

"What do you have planned for us?" Felicia asked the stranger. Was he an Apostle or one of their apprentices?

"Now, you are at our mercy. The master has given you to us." His voice had no inflection, no emotion that a normal man's voice would have.

Felicia leaned her weight into the door. "Who is your master? What does he want? He's from the Void, right?"

"Our master is the reckoning this world needs. He is our absolution after centuries of warfare. We are not worthy of him, and yet he will guide us to a new beginning."

Felicia made a sour face. They sounded deranged, but for the first time, she could detect some emotion behind their words. They believed wholeheartedly that he was their saviour. However, a saviour coming from the Void itself raised a few issues. For starters, was he the one breaking the barrier? If so, he could be the key to closing it.

Not to mention, Felicia thought, *the prince cares very little for the people around him. The only one he cares for is Lilith. Everyone else is expendable, including us.*

"What would this new beginning look like for us?" questioned Felicia. Really, she was testing the waters. She wanted to see how willing this person was to tell her their plan. Rage consumed her at the thought of everything she had done and lost. Rage towards the prince for betraying not only them, but the kingdom. Rage at the loss of her powers and her helplessness.

"We can discuss this further if you just open the door and let me in," answered the man. She really had no idea if it was a white-robed Apostle or one of their followers, but she took a gamble and believed it was an Apostle.

She shouted curses at him. "I don't think I'll be doing that. You've stripped me of my mana, your master has betrayed me, and there is no chance that I'll be civil. " Felicia's tone was snarky, just to see if she could get a rise from him. "Even if you manage to pry your way into here, I'll make it my personal mission to give you a slow death. I will smile as I tear your tongue from your body, I will laugh as I take out your eyes, and I promise you and your little gang that you all will suffer for what you have done."

The Apostle's breath stuttered slightly. His response had a faint edge of anger laced through it as he said, "You will learn what happens to smart-mouthed girls, child. You will learn to repent your ways."

A faint smile was on her lips as she countered, "Here I am, and yet you are not allowed to touch me, like the others, am I right? You can't do anything without *his* consent. If I were to get injured here, he would know. That's why *you're* outside my door and not one of your grey-robed apprentices. I am too valuable to him."

"You are of value to him for now, but circumstances can change. Now let me in."

"Or what?"

"Or you will starve. We have been told to keep you alive and unharmed, but if you die by your own hand, then so be it."

"Won't my death, even by my own hand, go against the wishes of your master? How about you give me my mana back and then maybe I'll go easy on you."

The Apostle waited a moment; his breath came in steady, but Felicia knew she had ruffled his feathers. Footsteps retreated to the next cell. Lady Thalassa screamed as her cell door opened. Felicia yelled for him to stop, but her words fell on deaf ears. This is what would come from disobeying them; they would find her weaknesses and exploit them.

Lady Thalassa struggled and fought with the Apostle; the sounds of a fist hitting flesh echoed in the dark until the screaming stopped. The intruder grunted, and the sounds of dragging slowly faded until the cell became silent once more. Clearly, she had not received the same orders to keep her safe and untouched. Even though she was furious at Lilith, Felicia should thank her for this protection. Or was it due to her mother being the general?

"Where are they taking her?" Felicia called out, to no one in particular.

"I do not know. They usually don't take us out of here. She is the first. May the gods protect her." Ivy's voice sounded distant. Scared.

Felicia lay down, her back against the cell door, and closed her eyes. Her stomach growled in the dark. At least she could lick the damp walls if her thirst drove her to it. She let out a deep cry of frustration as her tears spilled over her cheeks.

Where was Lilith?

CHAPTER 3
A SCORNED WOMAN

Lilith

Warm fingers moved across her forehead, tucking a loose strand of hair behind her ear. She shifted her face and went to roll over, murmuring to herself. The comfortable mattress dipped as she felt someone sit beside her. Demetrius? Images of a knife crossing over Mistress Rhodes sprang to the forefront of her mind. Was it a dream?

Stirring, she lifted her hands to rub her eyes; noticing she was no longer tied up, but the skin on her wrists was red and sore. Her eyes adjusted to the morning light as she turned to face the presence on her bed. The prince sat beside her with his black eyes, watching her carefully.

This was no dream.

She gasped and sat up quickly, scooting her body closer to the headboard and then cradling her knees in to protect herself. Looking down, she was still wearing his black tunic, something she had borrowed after they had sex. Now it was covered in specks of dried blood. Not hers.

Her body felt dirty. Memories of his touch lingered everywhere, and she felt a slight soreness between her legs, a reminder of what she had willingly offered to him. She was a fool. How much had she lost when she lowered her guard? There was an emptiness, where energy once flourished. It hollowed in the pit of her stomach. When the absence of her powers had finally hit her, she'd let out a primal scream of pain and sorrow.

"Give it back!" she screamed at him. She started to lunge for his throat, but some self-preserving part of her forbade her to move. Her muscles seized, exhausted from everything that had happened. "Give it back!" she trembled. Everything shook as she held herself back, but also cursed him for what he did. "How could you?! You've taken everything from me!" Bile rose in her throat as she leaned over and dry heaved. He took her mana, he took her body, he took her freedom. Not only that, but he had murdered her teacher, and killed people that were kind to her. Her thumbs rubbed the palm of her hands, feeling the grime lingering on her skin. Her thoughts brought her back to the moment of Mistress Rhodes' death. Could the stain on her flesh fully be washed off, or was it now ingrained with her tainted soul? Their death was her fault.

He cocked his head and gave her a smile. "Your fear smells wonderful, especially when it's mixed with my scent still lingering on your skin." The tears that Lilith was trying to hold back finally spilled over. This was too much. She felt his presence draw closer and looked at him through bleary eyes.

"What do you want from me?" Her voice was meek. She felt defeated, and with her powers once more suppressed, she was useless and at his mercy. "Just kill me and be done with it. Why are you doing this to me?"

He moved with otherworldly speed, lightly squeezing her throat with his hand. He leaned in and whispered with his deep, low voice, "I want you to cry and beg for my mercy. I want you to admit that I own your body, your soul, your every desire. You live and breathe for me. I want to break your will, punish you for tormenting and consuming me. Condemning me to a lifetime in that godsforsaken realm." He squeezed her throat ever so slightly tighter, while she frantically tried to pull herself away from his grasp. Her nails dug into his hands, scratching deep into his skin, making him bleed. The tips of her fingernails were painted red with his blood. Yet, he never raised his voice nor winced.

"Part of me wants you to know the pain that I've felt, trapped in an endless existence, never being able to move or touch, never being able to quell eternal hunger." His lips touched the tips of her ears as he continued. "The other part of me still relishes your presence. It's maddening."

"Please." Her voice sounded ragged. She surrendered to his touch. Her body found stillness, realizing how useless it was to fight back. The dark edges were closing in around her vision.

Lilith gasped as he released his hold, slumping forward on the bed. She sputtered, grasping her neck while sweet air rushed in. Curling in on herself, she rested her head on the mattress. What nightmare had she woken up to? She closed her eyes, tears forming in the corners once more, as she told herself to hold it together. After this never-ending string of disastrous events, she was starting to believe she had horrible luck. She was losing the will to fight, to keep trying, and to stay hopeful that she could turn things around.

"Lilith." He enunciated every syllable of her name. "I'm sure you have questions." His fingers softly touched her back, so she sat upright and pushed his hand off, glaring at him.

Her mind was still processing what had happened, but she had questions.

"Who are you?" She knew he was Prince Demetrius, but something else dwelled behind those obsidian eyes. An enigma she had yet to understand. Out of fear and hurt, she kept her eyes downcast, focused on his lips. It was all she could bear.

The prince grinned, "I'm afraid you're going to have to figure that one out by yourself. If you're asking what to call me, just go with the name you've used so far, though the title has changed. 'King Demetrius' has a nice ring to it."

Lilith gasped in shock. "Did you kill your father?"

"'Father' is a loose term. King Amadeus lives for now. Until the coronation at least; then we shall see."

"Is the prince still alive? Within you, I mean. Does part of him still exist?"

"He and I have been one and the same since his existence, so there's no need to concern yourself about him. I am surprised you haven't asked a more personal question."

She ignored his statement. "You crawled out of the darkness. Are you in control of it? If you were to die, would the darkness go away?"

The prince squinted his eyes, carefully considering his answer, "As much as I would like to claim myself the mastermind behind the Void, I am not. My death would not change its existence. However, I sacrificed much to become their king, and what lurks in the Void falls within my dominion."

"So you could have stopped that thing from attacking Silver and me?" She thought back to that day, when he was so adamant about leaving those who fell behind. Her mind raced. Why go to so many lengths? "You could have spared him? Gotten those creatures to fall back? Why?"

The prince paused, then replied, "I could have. I was not ready to show my hand, so I played my part, and as a result, I was able to learn more about you. Though I am still unsure if you are really that selfless or if it is an act."

"But you could call the darkness back? Save those that are trapped inside? You could free them?" Her eyes gleamed with hopefulness.

He laughed. "And why would I do that?"

Lilith looked away from him and closed her eyes; a deep sorrow grew within her heart. He was a monster, a shameless creature of the Void. His words rang through her mind: "Their lives were meaningless, a blip in your path. You will become my queen. My wife. My mate." *Mate.* She thought to herself, *How could this be my mate? My equal? What does it say about me?*

"Your people are not just from the Void; you are the heir to this kingdom as well. Would you just let everyone in this world perish? Have you not come to care for a single person since you became one of us?

Demetrius inhaled sharply. He looked like he was truly considering her words before replying, "There are some that I tolerate, but it doesn't matter in the end. They are mortals and their lives will pass in the blink of an eye."

"I am mortal. My life will soon be over, and you'll be stuck here with no one but those creatures. If you do nothing, you will turn this place into the realm that you were so desperate to escape."

He let out a menacing laugh. "You think you can change me? You have no idea how far I've fallen." For some reason, his sentiment made her pause. She figured he must have some tortured past, but for the first time, she didn't care for his excuses.

"What, no more questions?" He reached forward to brush his fingertips along her cheek. Sensing his intentions, she shifted her face over, rejecting his advance.

With closed eyes, she asked her next question. "My powers—are they gone forever? What about Felicia? What did you do to my friends?"

She felt his presence become distant and opened her eyes to find him disappearing into nothing, with sounds of faint laughter fading as he left. She cried and screamed, begging him to come back, yelling, "Please, give them back to me! Please!" She cried as she struggled to calm down. Her mind was unravelling, tormented by what had happened.

She didn't know how much time had passed before she was able to settle. Curled on the bed, she didn't have any fight left in her to move. Her eyes wandered around the space. This room was his. It brought back so many memories of that night, before his betrayal. She didn't want to think of that night. The calm, light green walls and ornately arched windows seemed less fitting for a man, or creature, like the prince. She wanted to burn it all down. Everything. She wanted to see this place fall to destruction.

Spurred on by the idea of finding something useful, she made her way to the wardrobe and rummaged through his things. Throwing the black tunic off to the side, she grabbed a fresh sweater, hidden in the back of the wardrobe, as well as, pants and a leather belt. Her body felt sluggish and completely drained.

She moved ever so slowly towards the oversized tub in the adjoining room and turned it on. As she waited for it to fill, she caught a glimpse of herself in the mirror. Her ghastly reflection displayed her exhausted state. Her usual warm, light brown skin had turned a blotchy, pale, greyish hue, and under her eyes were dark circles. Moss-green eyes stared back at her, haunted by recent events. Her eyes widened as she recognized the colour; it was the same green as the walls in the bedroom. Too many things had happened for her to think it was a coincidence. How long was she his obsession? Would he go to sleep thinking of her?

Fury raged through her at her own stupidity.

She walked to the tub and slipped in, turning off the faucet as the water reached the rim. Thoughts of taking her own life flitted to the forefront of her mind. She couldn't do this anymore. It was too hard, and she had suffered too much. Her hands shook as she contemplated her own end, bracing her hands on the edge of the tub as she slipped further into the warm water. She could just end it now and finally find peace. But then what would happen to the others, to her family and her friends?

Tears escaped once more as she sobbed from frustration, knowing that she had to keep going. She had to keep trying for her brothers and for Felicia. Her thoughts jumbled up in her mind, as she tried to make sense of how things had gotten to this point. Every second of every day since she arrived at Skilheim played over and over, again and again. At what point did she fall for him? When did she become blind and hand over her trust so easily? She had sworn that, after what Lord Elwin did, she would never place herself in a situation that made her vulnerable, and yet look at her now. Her eyes glazed over as she stared at the white walls of the washroom, devoid of any emotion. She was beyond heartbroken; she felt empty inside.

The water had turned cold long ago, and the orbs had flickered to life in place of the fading sun. Mechanically, she reached for the soap. The crisp pine scent made her nauseous, but she lathered herself up, scrubbing her skin until it was raw and red. No matter how much she scrubbed, washing off the specks of blood and the memory of what she shared with the prince, she felt his touch on her skin. She scrubbed her nails into her skin, wishing she could just peel it all off. A frustrated cry escaped her, and she chucked the soap across the bathroom. It was all her fault. The choices she made, the trust she put in the prince, all led her to this situation. Her naive optimism caused only heartache.

After drying, she dressed herself in the fresh clothes. They were still his, but at least they didn't smell like death. At least the fresh clothes didn't carry the scent of what transpired between them. At least they weren't covered in the blood of those she cared for.

She stared at the black tunic on the floor and slowly picked it up. She grabbed two sides of the front and tugged, drawing in as much strength as she could muster. The satisfying sounds of material tearing made her shudder. Again and again, she tore the tunic into pieces; it was all she could do. So badly did she want to engulf it in her flame, to see it crumble into ash. If only she had her powers.

Where were Felicia and the others? Taran should have arrived days ago, and where was Silver? Silver. He had betrayed her, too. Maybe he couldn't control himself? Maybe Demetrius was in control and commanded Silver to kill Mistress Rhodes and the others. Or, maybe he was a pawn from the start and knew everything.

She went to look out the window, stretching on her tiptoes to find any clues or see if what happened last night caused any commotion, but she only saw the almost pristine garden. She could see trees in the distance, no houses or buildings from this angle. Just a warped lifeless tree amongst a sea of blooming flowers. Where were they keeping the others?

A knock at the door made her jump. An Apostle entered cautiously. It was the same one that stood at the centre of his group, the one that spoke to the prince. She could remember the shape of his mouth. His hood shielded his eyes, but he gave her a relaxed smile. The curve of his teeth, the irregularities, and smile lines were features that Lilith had memorized.

"Good to see you are awake. Here." He carried a tray with a plate of food and a goblet of water. Over his arm was a dress. Lilith didn't move or reach to help him, so he placed the items on the small table in the lounge area and started backing away.

"Please. Where are my friends? Are they here? In this part of the palace?" Her words came out in a rush, "Why? Why are you doing this?"

He let out a soft breath. "My child, you are a guest. A special one at that. Where you are does not matter, only that you are where you're supposed to be."

"And my friends, the golden-haired woman and the prince's sister?" She waited for his reply, scrutinizing every word.

"Their lives are of no concern to you. You should rest. He wants you to relax." He started to back away again, moving to the door frame.

"Wait! Who is he?" She started to walk carefully towards the Apostle.

He smiled at her, reaching close to the door. "He is our King. Our salvation. Your salvation." The door slammed closed, and she heard the sounds of keys rustling, locking her in.

"Wait! Come back! I need to know what happened to Felicia. Please, tell me what you want from us." She rushed to the door and slammed her fist on the wood over and over again, yelling and begging wildly. "I can't do this. Please."

She looked at the door, listening to the footsteps fade, until she was alone, and turned to face the items on the table. The ebony black dress was made of the finest silk. From the back of the dress, an image of a silver-winged beast weaved up the skirt. She traced the beast's silver feathers to its head which she imagined would stop midway up her back. It felt buttery soft and slipped through her fingers as if it were crafted of air. She could see herself in this dress, the wide neckline showing off the top of her cleavage, and the flowing beast on the skirt trailing behind her, making her look like a dark queen. Grimacing, she pushed the dress off the table.

The plate on the tray was piled with steaming vegetables and seasoned meat. Her stomach growled at the sight, but she eyed it suspiciously. Her body felt empty. Lost was the familiar tingling of mana running through her veins. Its absence gnawed at her, driving her mad. Again, she blamed herself. No matter what powers she was capable of, she was weak and defenceless. Too quick to trust, too easy to manipulate. Others were too quick to play on her naivety and rashness.

She sat on the plush couch and hugged her knees, hot tears trailing down her face. Images of blood spraying onto her friends, Felicia covered in blood, the prince's black eyes, the touch of his hands everywhere, all played over and over in her mind. Again and again, she watched the blade drag across Mistress Rhodes' throat. She replayed every encounter she had with the prince, every gentle caress, every hint of the evil that dwelled in his soul.

When did the change occur? Felicia noticed a change in his character while they were in the mines, but did it start there? Or was it there from the start? Who was in on this? Sir Tornbury? Lord Helmer? Danai? She waited, grinding her teeth, diving into her feelings of hate and letting her rage fester.

CHAPTER 4
SERVING A PLATE OF TEMPTATION

Lilith

It was not until the morning light rose, shadowed by clouds, that she heard someone come back. An Apostle picked up the untouched food and spied the silk dress on the floor. She had only nodded off on the couch for an hour or two at a time, unable to relax enough to sleep soundly.

"I see that you have neither rested nor eaten anything. You realize this is a pointless endeavour; you won't be able to fight him."

"I don't want to fight him. I want my powers back, and I want my friends back." She nodded her head at the plate. "If that's all you came here for, you can take it and leave."

The corner of the Apostle's mouth twitched, the first flash of emotion one of their kind genuinely displayed. Instead of going to the untouched plate, he tilted his head and smiled.

"The master wants you downstairs to dine with him. You will come along and behave." His tone was measured and gentle.

Lilith clenched her jaw. How dare he speak to her like a child! How much power could he possess? The corner of her lips turned up as she gracefully walked right up to the Apostle, looking like a docile woman. She said sweetly, "Lead the way." The Apostle looked at the black silk dress, but before he could utter any more insults, Lilith sternly commented, "I'm ready now. Go ahead and show me the way."

The Apostle moved slowly to the door, as if he recognized her falseness, but was curious enough to see what would happen. Outside her door, there was a grey-robed man waiting for them. His hood was up, but she caught a flash of his eyes before he tugged the hood lower. She smirked, knowing she saw most of his face clearly. He looked at her with such hate. He was thin, and his cheeks were hollow, but there were no rough attributes. His skin looked too fresh, too pristine.

"Have your robe fixed," the Apostle commented, though there wasn't a hint of dissatisfaction in his tone. He started to walk down the hallway towards the main staircase. The corner of the grey-robed man's lips turned down in embarrassment.

Lilith couldn't help herself as she followed beside the Apostle, hollering back to the grey robe, "I can see why you'd want your face covered. You're a noble. I can tell by your skin, and that arrogant look in your eyes." She turned to face the Apostle. "Looks like this one needs more training to hide his emotions."

"We all started in his place."

"Has he figured out yet that I am one of his masters now?"

"You are not our master."

"Am I not? You see the prince's obsession with me. With one word, I could have you killed." The grey-robed man pounced forward, striking her across the cheek.

"You are nothing but filth," the grey-robed man spat at her.

Lilith laughed, uncontrollably. Both at the situation she was currently in, but also at the ridiculousness of the challenges that cursed her life.

The Apostle stood in front of her. "We are not to harm her. You will bear the responsibility of your actions." He turned to face Lilith. "Enough taunting him."

She was completely beside herself, laughing as she said, "Oh, I'm not nearly finished. I can't wait to hear what the prince says."

The grey robe lifted his hand to strike her once more.

"I said, enough!" It was the first time Lilith heard the Apostle raise his voice, and it gave her so much satisfaction. They underestimated her because they had taken her powers. But they forgot how strong she had become after months of brutal training.

Humiliated, the grey robe ignored his master and lunged for Lilith, a predictable move she knew the noble would make after she attacked his pride. She easily dodged him, positioning herself behind the Apostle. With a swift kick to the back, the Apostle toppled to his knees, giving her just enough time to turn on the grey-robed man, rushing him with a kick to the head. He braced his hands to his face, as Lilith attacked with a series of hooks and jabs. She was conserving her energy, so her strikes weren't powerful, but all she needed was an opening.

Since this morning, she had felt the return of her mana tingling through her veins, and she was working at burning off whatever suppressant she had been given. It felt like that time with Danai, on their failed trip to Tilton. Her powers were a hint, a sliver of what they were, but that was enough. She had her answer to the question of whether her powers were permanently removed.

Their mistake.

With what she had stored, she backed her next strike with most of her magical energy. The grey-robed man edged closer to the banister. Just a bit more. Using a thrust of air element, his body collided with the railing, lost balance, and was sent tumbling to the floor below. Before she could hear the satisfying thud, the Apostle had regained his position and blocked her path, his arms ablaze with fire. Swiftly, he struck out, hurling rapid blasts of fire at her.

"I guess you're ignoring your order not to harm me," Lilith smirked.

She shielded herself and formed an earthly blade of sharp stone. They moved in a quick succession of strikes and counters, a familiar dance Lilith was trained in. She admitted he was more agile than she expected. He was deft with his assault, and it was evident that he had some training. However, even though she was weakened, starved, and suppressed, he was no match for her.

She quickly got the upper hand, dodging his hits and moving in for the final blow. The tip of her knife dug into his skin as she grabbed him from behind, pulling his beloved hood down. His appearance was similar to his apprentice, a former noble now turned cultist. His blonde hair, striking features, and bright blue eyes would have made him popular with the ladies, but his personality was his downfall. It would be all too easy to end his life here and now, but she needed information.

"Where are they keeping the golden-haired woman that came with me?"

The Apostle grinned. "She is safe... for now."

The tip of the blade nicked his neck, releasing the smallest droplet of blood. At least she knew he was not some hidden demon. His blood trickled red like hers. He was not under the Void's influence.

"Where?"

"She is where we can provide the utmost care."

Lilith's mind raced, deciphering his words. Somewhere where they have complete control. The Temple, it must be. "And Silver? Taran?"

"The silver-haired man is one of *his* servants. He is unreachable even to us."

She felt a new presence shift around her. A livid-looking prince formed in front of the Apostle. There were no traces of summoning magic, so how was he transported here? Lilith held her grip on the Apostle tighter, digging in the blade further.

"Hello, dearest," said Lilith, her voice dripping with bitter sarcasm.

Demetrius grinned like a fool as he replied, "Lilith, Lilith, Lilith. Go ahead. Finish him."

The Apostle struggled against her grip as she tried to see a way out. If she slit his throat, that would be one less Apostle, but it would cost her the only leverage she had. *Too bad we aren't surrounded by those robed assholes,* she thought. *They would finally understand that they mean nothing to him.*

His voice rang through her mind. *Tick tock, Lilith. Go ahead.*

She smiled back at Demetrius, backing slowly down the hallway. She could already hear them coming, feel the vibrations of their approach through the flooring.

"Be a good little puppet and stop fighting me," Lilith whispered to the Apostle. For once, he showed uncertainty. Hearing the truth, that he dedicated his life to someone who cared so little for him—the truth must have jarred his rationale. His "divine" purpose.

They came to a stop as Demetrius stalked her. From behind, the others had found them. The rest of his Apostles.

"Do you care so little for this one's life? Are you unwilling to bargain? Or should I end his life like you had suggested?" *Come on, Demetrius, don't you want to play?* A mix of white and grey robes surrounded them, watching them. *Do it, Demetrius. Tell them they are worthless.* Lilith's eyes sparked in challenge. This was not a fight she could win, and there was no way she was getting out of here unscathed, but if he were to encourage her to end this Apostle's life, it could have but two outcomes: perhaps they were willing to die for their master, or perhaps this could spread the seed of doubt through this cult. Would he risk losing favour with his worshippers?

Demetrius paused, ran his eyes down her body in assessment. Then he did something she never expected. He bowed to her, his eyes once more trailed slowly up her body as he rose. With a smile, he turned and disappeared. She had won this challenge. Surrounded, she had no choice but to let the Apostle go. He fell to his knees as she looked at the others.

She leaned down, whispering to the fallen Apostle, "See how he bowed to me? You are worthless."

She rose to meet the eyes of the surrounding Apostles. "There's no need. I know my way back to my room. Good night, puppets." Lilith didn't spare them a glance. She made her way back to her cage with no footsteps sounding behind her.

Once the door to the room closed, she released a ragged breath and leaned against the door. This would never end for her. He was going to such lengths for *her*, but at least the Apostles knew their place.

A dark figure materialized in front of her, placing his hands on either side of her face.

"You're in a playful mood. I like it when you play dirty."

Her heart was thumping, but she composed herself carefully. "Playful is not the mood I would describe myself feeling. More like hurt, angered, betrayed. Pick one."

"You feel anger towards me now, but you will see that I am not your enemy. If anything, I'm the only one that sees you for what you are. You don't need to pretend to be something you are not."

"What am I pretending to be?"

"Fragile. Feeble. Weak. Pick one."

"But I feel weak. You have made me weak."

"Please. You think I could make someone like you weak. You are denying your own strength and resilience." He leaned back, opening one hand to call forth an item. A book. "Here, a reward for your tenacity."

Lilith spotted runes dotting the cover. She wanted to read it, but she eyed him suspiciously. "Why are you giving this to me?"

Demetrius held the book out to her. "I once promised to help you rid yourself of those runes. You can start with this, and once you're done, I'll give you another." She took the book from him, savouring the feeling of worn leather beneath her fingers.

Her eyes met his gaze. He watched her with such intensity, it made her blush despite herself. "You must be hungry after today." He held his hand out for her.

"I won't risk my mana being suppressed." She could distract herself from her hunger pains by curling up with this leather-bound tome. A growl from her stomach filled the awkward silence.

He sighed and went to sit on one of the couches. "Suppressing your mana is temporary. There are too many pieces of this carefully constructed puzzle coming into place, and your wrath risks my plans."

"You would not be dealing with my wrath, had you not betrayed me."

"You may feel that way, but this is the only way. Out of all of the possibilities, years of speculation, this path will be the fastest way to reach my goal."

"And what is that?" Lilith edged closer to him, wanting to know his secrets.

"To force their hand and have them show themselves. Too long have they been hiding from this realm." His face turned dark as his thoughts turned serious.

Lilith watched him as his gaze went distant, fixed on something or someone else. She was confused at his explanation and mulled over his words. Who were Demetrius' enemies? Another growl from her stomach brought Demetrius out of his trance, just as a knock on the door had Lilith jumping.

"Perfect timing." Demetrius walked past Lilith and headed to the door, opening it wide enough to be handed a tray. He laid the tray holding a steaming plate of savory meat and potatoes down on the small table. "You have a choice."

Saliva was pooling in her mouth as the smell of the food wafted closer. She could imagine the taste of the creamy potatoes and buttery tender meat. A neatly arranged assortment of vegetables was covered in rich sauce. The temptation made her fidget as she held her ground, looking at Demetrius with defiance.

"So be it." Annoyed, he refused to look at her. "Since you are so set on making enemies, I will check in on you periodically."

For the rest of the day, no one bothered her. She covered the plate with a shirt she found in the wardrobe, hoping it was one of Demetrius' favourites. The hunger pains were settling deep within her stomach, and the energy she just used to fight the Apostle made her feel weaker and more exhausted. She couldn't bear the idea of laying down in bed, so she made herself comfortable on the couch, reading through the text of the book. At some point the runes blended into one another, as her eyes closed against her will.

CHAPTER 5
AN HONEST ANSWER

Lilith

She woke once more in the damned bed. If this was some sort of strategy to win her over, he was failing miserably. Considering she fell asleep on the couch, there was only one possible way of her ending up in this bed, and that was Demetrius.

The warmth of her mana flowed through her veins, which comforted her. At least he had not forced her to take the suppressant. She glared at her runes. If only they would disappear entirely, she would stand a chance against freeing herself and the others. She looked at the closed book on the couch. So far, it had revealed nothing about rune curses or how to undo one.

Her stomach felt devoid of any hunger, even though she had not eaten for a few days. Her head was spinning as she walked to the bathroom slowly, and she almost missed the figure sitting in the lounge area. The couches had been rearranged so that a small, white, round table with two white chairs now occupied one of the corners overlooking the garden. In one of the seats, Demetrius was casually reading a scroll while eating from a selection of foods. From the intensity of his frown lines, she could tell he was in a horrible mood. Taking a scan of him, she noticed his unkempt hair, and his normally pristine attire, now untidy.

"Since you refuse to eat with me downstairs, I had arranged something to be brought up here so that we may enjoy our morning together," he said, as he put the scroll down and gave her his undivided attention. His stare bore into hers.

A snarky response was on the tip of her tongue, but she found herself unable to say anything. It took such effort to put one foot in front of the other that she had to brace herself on the back of the couch. She heard a growl coming from the corner, then warm hands found her to hold her steady.

"You are such a contradiction. One moment you're threatening to kill me, the next you're helping. I don't understand," whispered Lilith, slightly delirious. She couldn't tell if this was part of a dream or if this was actually happening.

"You are right. I am tormented by you. Even now, I don't know whether I should put myself out of my misery or worship you." He swept her into his arms and walked over to the table.

Lilith let out a little yelp, more confident that this was indeed a dream. She basked in the warmth of his arms. Abruptly, he placed her on the seat across from his. His furious expression made her second guess her confidence.

Once she was seated, he sat across from her, his hands clenched in his lap. His voice sounded almost like a growl. "I am tired of trying to force your hand. You win. Eat. I will not tamper with your food. Your mana is useless anyway, while you're still bound."

Lilith scowled at the mention of her runes, then stared longingly at the food. Her eyes wandered over the golden breads, the vibrant glazed fruits, and the savoury smell of tender meat in the bowl of soup. Then she looked at the cutlery, a spoon, but no knife or fork. She smirked in her mind, knowing they feared her enough to remove potential weapons. The thought of what she could do if she only had a butter knife thrilled her. Her fingers raised to find the silver spoon, but paused.

"Why should I eat, if only to prolong my fate?" She silently cursed herself for denying her hunger once again, her eyes looking anywhere but at the food.

Demetrius smirked, "You haven't changed. Still as stubborn as ever."

"What do you mean?"

"You'll find out soon enough. I will leave. You need to eat. No one else will bother you for now. Here." He placed a stack of books next to the food.

"Wait. It's been ages since I've spoken with my brothers and my father. They'll come looking for me."

"In time. I've sent a messenger with a scroll. Your father knows you are here, and he most likely has told your brothers. He thinks you are here with me. Helping me unravel the secrets behind the Void."

"I doubt he will just accept your word. He will want to speak with me directly."

Demetrius went around the table and leaned down to kiss the top of her head. "You sent the letter. Well, to be clear, I forged your writing."

Lilith scoffed, and leaned away from him. "He'll know it wasn't me."

Demetrius let out a laugh. "You underestimate how well I know you. You mutter when you read. You hate not immediately being good at something. I know that you're incredibly loyal, sometimes you say things you don't mean when you're hungry, and above everything, I know you feel our connection. I don't have to read your mind or hear your thoughts to know your little quirks, though it does help."

Lilith was speechless. His love, no, his obsession, ran deeper than she thought. Part of her loved hearing how much he noticed, but mostly she was scared of his devotion.

"Nothing to say?" Demetrius teased her. She remained quiet, contemplating her next move. "Fine. I will let you enjoy your meal."

Demetrius didn't stay around to hear Lilith's response; he just left her with the pile of food and books. She didn't keep track of how long she stared at her plate, her stomach sounding its gurgling protest.

Eventually, she brought the savoury broth to her lips and drank. The warm soup heated her soul, with a blend of vegetables, herbs, and spices; it sent her taste buds dancing. Her first bite of the mouth-watering flake of meat just about sent her over the edge of pleasure. She couldn't help but inhale the contents, stopping only to swallow and breathe.

Almost immediately, her stomach clenched; it was too much for her starved state. Too much, too fast. She barely made it to the washroom to empty her stomach in the toilet. It was worth it, though. The comforting feel of her mana still ran through her veins, evidence that he was true to his word and didn't try to suppress her.

Returning to the table, she carefully ate some bread, eating at a much slower pace. In the battle of wills, she had won this round. She flipped open the book she was reading last night, skimming over the contents.

Time and loneliness became her enemies. After completing the first leather bound tome, she picked up another, rubbing her eyes. Why was she here? Her thoughts sent her anxiety into a spiral. He wanted her for some reason. Specifically her. She recalled that entry from the diary, a mysterious voice calling from the dark, *Find Her.* Was that person looking for her? How? That was fifty years ago. She wasn't even alive yet. Earlier, Demetrius had implied that she was always so stubborn, *'you haven't changed.'* Could that mean he knew her from a long time ago? 'What-if' scenarios went rampant in her mind. It was useless to speculate, at least until she had more evidence.

Right now, her focus should be on trying to escape. These books he gave her distracted her from her desire to try anything. He knew her well. Instead of wasting the day reading, she had to figure out the layout of the palace. Much like Skilheim, a palace of this size would have secret passageways. If only she could explore outside her room.

With that thought in mind, she went to the windows and looked at the almost pristine garden carefully. A dark-haired guard, wearing silver armour, walked slowly through the pebbled pathway. Counting in her head, she waited for fifteen minutes before the guard turned around to return. For hours, she observed the comings and goings of those who milled about the outer perimeter; she would have to do this for several days until she learned their routine.

Taking a step back, she examined the fine arched frames of the windows, looking for a way to create an opening, but to her dismay, they were sealed.

Since Demetrius' room at Skilheim held a secret passageway, she thought to examine the rest of this room closely. With some luck, maybe she would come upon a secret hinged doorway. Dragging her fingers along the walls, she walked the perimeter of the room. After her third time carefully inspecting the green wallpaper, she tilted her head and looked at the large wardrobe. The back of it was mounted oddly to the wall. Usually, there was a tiny gap between the wardrobe and the wall, but this one looked as if it were built from the wall itself. The white oak panels were ornately carved, making this piece seamlessly blend in with the rest of the palace. It looked as if it were purposefully built.

"Show me your secrets," muttered Lilith, excitedly.

Opening the wardrobe doors, her shoulders slouched at the seemingly normal interior. Demetrius' clothes were neatly arranged with precise organization. She smirked as she roughly shoved the clothes to the side and saw the outline of a hidden door. The seams between the door and the back panel almost looked invisible to the eye, but she could make out, in the upper and lower left corners, thin silver hinges. Her hands reached out to feel the smooth wood, and with a light press, she heard the panel click. It sprang forward just a hair, but it excited her with renewed hope.

The sounds of footsteps came from outside, startling her, as she quickly scooted the clothes back in place. Just as she closed the door to the wardrobe, Demetrius strolled into the room.

"Why, hello," he said with a smirk. Clearly, he was in a better mood. His eyes were icy blue, making him appear more human.

"I thought you said no one else would bother me," she retorted, casually stepping away from the wardrobe to walk towards the window in the bedroom. She built a mental fort against him, shutting him out, though she felt his gentle caress linger across her mind.

"I will have clothes brought here for you," he stated as he nodded to the wardrobe. "In the meantime, how about we go for a walk?"

"Here I was, thinking you'd keep me hostage in your room." Lilith glared at him.

"I could. It would wear you down faster. No matter." He shrugged and walked off. " If you are content to be here, we can stay." Demetrius looked out the window.

Lilith's eyes widened, and she eagerly stepped towards him before her words came out in a rush, "No, I would like to leave this place." She walked past him into the lounge area to make for the door. She noticed all the food laid out for her had disappeared.

Demetrius quickly grabbed her arm, "Before I let you out, I need to remind you that it is useless to try to escape. There is no place, no shadows that you could hide in, that I won't come looking for you. You are mine."

She hated that her heart raced at his words. Though his possessiveness was overbearing, she couldn't help but blush. A small part of her felt good to be desired. No one had obsessed over her the way that he was unabashedly displaying. It thrilled her—she would never admit this feeling to anyone.

Trying to conceal the rush of emotions, she turned her face from him as she spoke, "I will be on my best behaviour."

A lie.

Demetrius took a step towards her. "Will you now?" He tilted his head and watched her profile closely. With a smug grin, he continued, "Well then, good girls will be rewarded."

She whipped her head towards him as shock hit her. Her face turned a beet red, making Demetrius let out a genuine laugh. For a fraction of a second, everything that had happened melted away, and she stood in awe of his beauty. That giddy smile on his lips and the crease of his eyes, as they beamed with joy. This is why she fell for him. This was why she surrendered to him. Now, she wanted to wipe that smile off his face for what he did to her. His betrayal cut her too deep to forgive. Snapping out of her trance, she walked past him to the entrance of the room.

"Lead the way." She could behave, for now. Curiosity edged her as to what reward she would receive. If it was sexual, she would not be opposed to murdering him with a spoon she'd hidden in her pants pocket. He opened a door and led her down the familiar hallway.

The Queen's Wing was as immaculate as the gardens. Large, opulently carved arched windows overlooked a courtyard that was decorated with small iron tables and chairs, surrounded by an abundance of flowers. Unlike the windows in her room, these ones were propped open, allowing the sweet aromas of the flowers that bloomed around them to drift in.

They passed another door on the side of the windows. Confusion hit her as she took in the unassuming door.

"If this is the Queen's Wing, where is the queen's room?" Lilith asked. Looking behind her, she figured there must be at least half a dozen rooms in this wing.

"She is at the end. The king's room is beside hers. The rest are meant for their children, but as she only had me, they mostly use these rooms for esteemed guests."

"But you have siblings?"

"Half-siblings, like Thalassa. Born by His Majesty's consorts. They are not true heirs and are not permitted to stay in this wing." They had reached the grand staircase and started to descend. The white marbled stone felt cool to Lilith's fingertips.

"From my interactions with you and Lady Thalassa, it seems like you care little for your siblings." Lilith could not imagine her life without her brothers. The months they spent apart while they studied at Ardaven were lonely and depressing.

"You are right, I don't consider them to be of importance to me." Demetrius stopped on a step in front of her, turning to face her so that his lips were just mere inches from hers. "You, on the other hand...You are of the highest value." He continued descending the stairs, rounding the landing and asked, "Why are you so interested in my life?"

Lilith continued her steps, walking around him. Her reply was barely audible, "I don't know. Maybe I want to learn more about my enemy." She wanted to know more about him. Her excuse was to learn more about her kidnapper, but really, she couldn't help herself from wanting to know everything about him. It infuriated her that he consumed any part of her thoughts. She should hate him. *I do hate him.*

"Amusing," he muttered as he matched her pace. He steered her through the lower hallways that jutted out from the building. She recognized the stone pillars carved as a tree trunk. Everything was pristine, even with the abundance of plants growing around the pillars.

"Where are the others? Taran? Did you turn him like Silver?" This was eating at Lilith's mind. What had happened to the plan? She was there at the meeting in the library before they set off to Thurndun. Narticia, Taran, Fang, and other students had all agreed to travel here.

"What if I told you they knew who I am? Would you still care?"

Somehow, she didn't believe they would know. "I consider some of them my closest friends. I'd like to know, even if they've betrayed me."

Demetrius considered his next words, "They arrived before us and were instructed to make for the encampment. My dear cousin is with them, safe. For now. Though I could call him back." This was just another threat to keep her in line.

"And Silver's fate?"

"You mean you still care for him even though he killed Mistress Rhodes?"

"*You* killed Mistress Rhodes. Her death is entirely on you, as you gave him no choice. How could you murder her? She cared for you."

"No. She cared for *you*, and her presence here was a threat to me. If you had not made us go back to the encampment, she would not have met with us, and her life would have been spared. She came here because of you, and I knew she would have fought to free you. No, we couldn't have that." The conversation became heated as their mutual anger was nearing a tipping point.

"You didn't have to kill her. Why not take her to where you're keeping Felicia?"

"The Apostles could never handle her." Demetrius rolled his eyes.

"You don't like the Apostles, but you need them. Why do you give them so much freedom?"

"Their usefulness is running its course. I need them to rise as King. The quickest way to influence the masses is through either hysteria or religion. And what better religion than one that serves me?"

"How exactly did you get them to form their beliefs?"

"Charm and charisma. I have a magnetic allure that some find hard to resist."

Lilith rolled her eyes, sensing he had just told her a lie. "I'm sure it had nothing to do with the promise of power that you enticed them with. Look at how far they've come. How much they have taken over the palace. What will they take from you next?

Demetrius stopped walking, facing her with a smile of delight. "Ha! I see what you're trying to do. You are trying to make me tell you where Felicia is."

It was indeed her intention. Lilith growled, "You and your Apostles have told me enough." They were keeping her at the Temple. The new house of the Apostles.

Swiftly and with poor planning, Lilith blasted him with a bolt of lightning. Since she had her powers back, she had yet to release her mana, so a large blast rocketed into Demetrius.

Completely caught off guard, his body sailed backwards and crashed into a pillar. The stone broke against the force of the blast and crumbled beneath him. He was struggling as his muscles seized from waves of her electricity.

Not wasting time, she bolted through the halls and found a door leading to the outside. In the distance, she could see the corner of the consorts' building and, further back, the Temple. Several guards and some grey robes were patrolling and when they finally noticed Lilith running through the open space, she pushed mana through her muscles, allowing her to rush past them. The sounds of her name being yelled and footsteps chased after her. A loud horn sounded around her, calling in reinforcements. She hurled a blast of fire at the crowd behind her, wishing for just a bit more time. They saw her incoming attack and dodged, but lost their advance.

"Do not harm her!" The Apostles called orders into the erupting chaos.

The Temple became larger and larger; its curled-tipped roof and large beams of rich brown wood were almost within touching distance. The smell of that nauseating soap invaded her nostrils. It was a scent she hated because she knew Demetrius was near.

Demetrius suddenly appeared in front of her, making her crash into his chest. "I thought you were going to behave, *my goddess.*" Immediately, her presence shifted from outside to back in his room.

"How should I punish you?" he asked her.

"What did you expect? You really thought I would behave? You should spare yourself the trouble and let me go." Lilith huffed.

"Your smart mouth will not save you now." He held her in a twisted grip, forcing her to face outwards towards the room entrance. In front of her materialized Silver. His pale silver hair was a mess, and his skin had turned greyish with black veins growing up his neck. He stared lifelessly at Lilith.

"Silver!" cried Lilith, struggling to get out of Demetrius' hold. "Please, help me," she begged.

Silver held out a long dagger, one that Sir Tornbury had given them for the trip, the one that slit Mistress Rhodes' throat. He held up the dagger in his free hand.

"Cut them off," ordered Demetrius. Without flinching, Silver brought the blade to his hand and sliced through his first finger. Lilith screamed and tried to look away, but Demetrius used one of his hands to grip Lilith's chin, forcing her to watch. Black blood oozed out of the cut; the finger toppled carelessly to the floor. Silver made no sound, no signs of distress as he brought the knife to his second finger. The blade seemed to move through him like butter, effortlessly cutting through his skin and bones. Another finger fell. Tears cascaded down Lilith's face as she watched Silver disfigure his hand.

By the time he got to his thumb, Lilith had stopped fighting. She surrendered completely to Demetrius, to her punishment of watching her friend hurt himself. She realized then that Silver was not in control of his autonomy; he didn't mean to kill Mistress Rhodes or the others; it was all Demetrius. He never recovered from Lady Ashmore's "blessed waters." Demetrius had manipulated the darkness running through Silver's blood to make it seem like the 'cure' actually did something. There was truly nothing that could stop the darkness from spreading.

Silver was gone. It didn't matter if he was no longer aware of himself; if he was gone, he should have a peaceful death. His body should not linger and be used in such a disgraceful way.

Demetrius laughed behind her, letting his grip go and letting her fall to her knees. "You should have seen how his mother begged me to save him."

Lilith remembered either Taran or Silver telling her that Taran's dad worked with Silver's mom as guards for the king. His poor mother.

"Why are you doing this to him? What did he do to you?" Lilith's gaze was fixed on the black blood dripping from Silver's hand.

Demetrius sneered, "It should not take you this long to learn that people can seem nice, portray themselves as one thing, but then have ulterior intentions. There was more to Silver and his parents than you know. Did you not wonder why he was selected to travel with us through the ruins when there were others that could have fulfilled the job better?"

"You grew up with him. He's one of Taran's closest friends."

"He was his mother's pawn. An ambitious, vile creature that only serves herself."

"How can I trust what you're saying? Even if he's his mother's pawn, he doesn't deserve to linger in this world like this. It's cruel."

He let out a laugh, "Maybe you need to learn to be cruel to survive in this world."

Lilith felt empty. This man, this beast, felt no remorse. Would he kill her father? Her brothers? Demetrius squatted beside her and picked up a loose strand of her jet black hair. His fingers ran over the silky strands as he inhaled.

"Try me again, and I will do the same to Felicia." Demetrius stood and vanished into thin air.

Silver stood in front of her. His eyes were unblinking, as if frozen in time. She rushed to him, wiping her face off with her sleeve. "Silver. I'm so sorry. Can you hear me? Is there any part of you still there? Please, tell me what to do." She watched him for a few seconds, then noticed the blade stowed at his side. Carefully, she slipped the blade free. A precious gift that somehow was left in her grasp. Silver stood like a statue, motionless, with no care that she had stolen his dagger. What could she do with this blade? She could end her life, though no part of her wanted to go down that route.

"Please. I don't want to do this," she said as she shook his arm. "I'm so tired."

For several heartbeats, she looked at Silver, trying to find that spark in his lifeless eyes.

"I thought I could save you, that we could find a cure, and then you'd get better. Taran would have never forgiven me if I had just left you that day." Her hands clenched the hilt of the dagger so tight that her knuckles were strained white. "But would it be a kindness to end things now? Did you feel anything when you murdered them? Did you try to fight the dark, or is it truly useless?" She wished so hard that things had turned out differently for Silver. For Lady Ashmore's cure to work and for Silver to bounce back, but this person in front of her was not her friend. He was gone, and this was a shell whose only purpose was to haunt her. With her next exhale, she plunged the blade into Silver's heart. Immediate shock ricocheted through her body, and she stumbled backwards, gasping at her own actions. Black blood oozed from the site, the dagger still embedded within his chest, but he did not stir.

"Silver?" Lilith quietly called out, reaching a hand to touch his arm. Silver rolled his shoulder back and down, then grabbed the hilt of the dagger and pulled it straight out. Blood spurted across the room, an arc of black blood sprayed on Lilith's sweater. Silver neither buckled nor yelled. Nothing. Still dripping with his own black blood, he stuck the dagger in his scabbard and turned to leave.

"No, please don't leave. I don't want to be alone. Please!" begged Lilith. She clutched his arm in an attempt to restrain him, but he pulled her free and walked calmly through the room entrance. His black eyes levelled with hers one more time before he gently closed the doors.

The strength to stand escaped her, and she fell to her knees in a heap. Tears streamed down her face as she smeared black droplets across her cheek with the back of her hand. She curled up on the floor and wept for Silver, wept for Mistress Rhodes, Sir Erikson, Lady Tessa, Felicia, and the prince's sister. She wept for the constant unfairness that life had handed out to her.

The day drifted ever so slowly into the night with the sun fading over the garden. Lilith had washed and changed once more, grabbing a tunic and a fresh set of pants from the wardrobe. She had to roll the sleeves and pant cuffs several times to get them to look somewhat decent. Her eyes were puffy from crying, and her body felt heavy. All she wanted was to explore behind the wardrobe, but knowing that someone could be delivering food soon made it too dangerous to try.

She went through every nook and cranny of his room once more, emptying the wardrobe and dresser. Unlike his room at Skilheim, this was stark and minimal. No mementos or paintings of his childhood. No pile of favourite books. She had read all the books that Demetrius had given her. Although she was able to interpret more runes, she was no closer to breaking her rune curse. She had to find Andishmand or someone who could help her.

Spurred by the thought of having a book, Lilith drew out her hand and began chanting. Nothing happened. Repeating the words over, the summoning charm failed to activate. She thought about the diary and the knife she stashed in her pack.

If she could use it on the Apostles, maybe she could reach Felicia. If she had a knife, she could use it against the prince. This was the first serious time she considered acting on her thought to harm him. That thought made her cringe; something inside her hated the thought of getting her hands covered in blood. She may have thought that she could have tried to kill him and the Apostles, especially right after he took her powers, but the emotional consequences of those actions weighed heavily. Taking a life wasn't easy. She thought about the Void-infested villagers that she had blown up and winced. There could have been children in that mob, even though they were likely gone; she carried the weight of their deaths on her shoulders. She wouldn't be able to go through with stabbing Demetrius. She stared at the guard walking around the garden, the lavender glow of the sky setting in the distance, always counting and watching everyone's routine.

A gentle knock on the door made Lilith jump out of her thoughts. She waited for whoever it was to barge in, but no one did. Carefully, she opened the door and came eye level to a broad-chested Demetrius.

They entered a silent battle of who would be the first to break and say something. Arlen, Lilith's brother, had always said Lilith was as stubborn as they come.

Demetrius crossed his arms over his chest, a move that made Lilith scoff.

"Fine. What do you want?" she queried.

"You must be hungry," replied Demetrius.

"Well, you seem to limit food being delivered to this room, and I am not permitted to leave, so yes, I am hungry," quipped Lilith.

"If you want food, you'll have to eat with me," commanded Demetrius.

"Wow, how can I refuse such an offer?" Lilith's words dripped with sarcasm.

"We could skip the food and I could eat you instead," said Demetrius, smirking.

Lilith blushed. "I'd rather have the food." Her goal was to map out this palace and plan a way to get to the Temple.

"Well then." Demetrius led her to the door. "After you." Instead of leading her downstairs, he veered down towards the consorts' wing. The red textured exterior came into view, but they turned to face a massive iron and stained glass door. Two guards nodded to the prince and then opened the door. In front of them was an outdoor space that was carved entirely of white stone. Large open archways overlooked the glowing lights from the city below. Two chairs and a table set out with food were prepared under floating yellow orbs.

"This is the only spot where you can really enjoy the city." Demetrius pulled out a chair and waited for Lilith to sit. Hesitating, she crept closer to the seat. As she walked towards the balcony, she could see further down into the winding streets. Looking straight down, it was about a thirty-foot drop to the closest rooftop. The tiny windows were glowing in the evening's fading sun. People were still moving around the city, wrapping up their tasks so they could make it home before dark.

At first, it felt like there was a different kind of magic that was stirring in the air. A small, lively restaurant in the distance with patrons taking their evening meal under beautiful hanging lights, smiling merchants still making their last sales, couples holding hands as they weaved through the streets.

One could fall in love with the city life, but as she looked closer, she could spy glimpses of the rough edges hidden in the city's shadows. A quick flash of hands from two figures trying to be discreet, drabby-looking small children begging on the street, the faint smell of the excrement passing through the breeze. This is what life was like for most people struggling to survive in this world.

"You see it too, don't you?" Demetrius sat across from her, his attention pulled to the life below them. "You see the failure of this race, of these people. Who truly profits in this world?"

"Why does this matter?" Lilith unfolded her cloth napkin and draped it over her pants as she thought of what point he was trying to get at. "You've said it yourself, you don't care for these people. Why bother pointing out the underbelly of this city?"

Demetrius' eyes flashed black for a moment. "Because I intend to change things. I have been let loose, and I will show you how dark this world can fall." Several men and women came through to the balcony, holding dish after dish of steaming hot food, all under the careful supervision of two Apostles that lingered in the corners. After the plates were set down, the Apostles snapped their fingers, and the workers bowed, then filed out. Demetrius spoke once more, "Do you know what is born from destruction?"

"I'm sure you'll tell me."

"The recreation of civilization. You can burn this city down, wipe it from existence, but from its ashes only the determined will survive. Those people will rule the new world, for they have earned their right. Circumstances at the time of their birth will not dictate how they thrive."

"How can anyone survive the evil coming from the Void? If our kingdom, your kingdom, gets overtaken and everyone is turned into those mindless creatures, those that survive will not be human anymore. They won't feel anything beyond what you tell them to feel. There will not be anyone left that could thrive in such a world."

"There will always be people who are able to survive the darkness. I am one such example. The pathetic vultures of this world will be the first to die. No longer will there be arbitrary rules that place those who are born to the bottom feeders of society in positions of power."

"And what will happen to all the souls lost to your evil? What becomes of the people whose eyes turn black?"

"They are the fallen, a worthy sacrifice."

"So there's no hope for them." She thought of Silver.

"Even the gods could not bring them back to life." Demetrius ate from his plate while Lilith's hunger was driven down by her disgust.

"You need to eat, Lilith."

"I've lost my appetite."

"No, no. You need your strength for what's to come."

"Which is?"

"You are mine, and soon, you and I will be declared King and Queen of this tragic kingdom."

"I will not become your wife. I hate you, and you are fooling yourself if you think you could make me love you."

"Love has nothing to do with this. You alone are my equal in this life. A blessing ordained by the gods."

"If that is true, then it is yet another curse that I will break, along with these runes."

"You are set on being this stubborn? Can you not envision a life at my side? I will worship you day and night, give you everything you could want: your family's safety, your friends' safety–you could finally relax."

"At the cost of my freedom? This kingdom? By doing nothing, I'd be just as responsible for the deaths of all those taken by the Void. It would not be a life I'd be satisfied with. My conscience would not let me."

Demetrius stood from his seat and leaned over her, "Then I will have to rewrite your conscience, and give you a taste of what you'd be willing to sacrifice." Lilith's body instantly heated from his proximity. She waited as he leaned closer down to her face, pulling her chin up. Her eyes found his icy blues, piercing her soul, calling to her. Without thinking, she leaned in, but as his lips came closer, she snapped out of her daze.

"There are some things that are worth fighting for, and you are not it." Her words were laced with a calm venom, as she pulled her face free. "I see only a coward, willing to let others do your dirty work. You are a liar and a manipulator, and I will never stand by someone like you."

Demetrius growled, a sound that was unearthly. "Then I will break you, until you are desperate and willing." He grabbed her by the wrist, and in an instant, the twinkling city lights faded to black. Her stomach turned as his bedroom, her cage, appeared before her. She tried to turn towards him to fight, but he had already vanished.

She slept smiling, knowing that his threat to break her was a challenge, one that she was willing to endure so that she could come out victorious. His obsession would be his weakness, something for her to exploit. She would be his undoing.

Chapter 6
Seed of Uncertainty

Felicia

It felt like days had passed since she last ate. Every day, an Apostle would come and try to enter her cell, but she lay in front of the door, barricading herself from them. Her back was covered in bruises from their attempts to come in. She could hear the cries and screams from other women who had suffered punishment in her stead. Weak from starvation, she felt like she couldn't move if she wanted to. Her mana had come back, but she knew it would be too draining to attempt fighting her way out. In a nearby cell, Ivy's wet coughs had only worsened, and Felicia was worried that she was nearing her end.

The only positive thing to happen over the last day was that Lady Thalassa had stopped crying, though now Felicia was completely alone with her thoughts. Madoc had appeared in her cell on occasion, just before she slipped into oblivion. He mostly sat with her, whispering words of encouragement. Her hallucinations of her brother were not a good sign, yet she relished his presence.

Endure for another day. Just one more day. His soothing voice hugged her.

"Okay, just one more day," Felicia would reply. She crawled to the nearest wall and ran her dry tongue across the wet stone. Grit caught between her teeth became her only sustenance; she imagined that the dirt had a spicy taste.

She would die here.

Lady Thalassa had returned to her cell not long after she was taken. She was quiet, and after her whimpering stopped, Felicia tried to get information from her, but was only met with silence. The mystery of what the Apostles' punishment would be ate into her mind. Was it physical, sexual, or both? What would she have to endure in order to live? Ivy was adamant that she only suffered physical pain, though there were large periods of time during which she lost consciousness, and what happened then was unknown.

Today was not any different. The same heavy footsteps stomping down the hallway, the jingling of keys, their even-paced, calm breaths. These sounds seemed to be amplified in the dark.

From what she could tell, they stopped further than they usually did, and they had skipped their usual attempt at coming to her cell door. This was a new strategy. Leaning her head back on the door, she listened carefully. Who would be their next victim? The cries of a child pierced the silence. This child sounded young. Felicia stared at her brother's face in the corner of the dark cell. "I can't," she begged. "I can't endure this any longer." Madoc gave her a small sad smile.

"No! You want me? Right?" Felicia's voice found strength, startling her. She didn't know where this strength had come from. She looked at her fingertips and felt her connection with her mana. It had come back after a day or so and vibrated under her skin. She could try, just this once.

Footsteps approached her cell. "Are you willingly giving yourself as an exchange?" His voice was devoid of emotion.

Was she willing to hand herself over in place of a child? "Yes," she answered.

"Then move away from the door," he ordered. Felicia pushed herself to her hands and knees. They shook under her weight. Unsteadily, she crawled her way from the door. No sooner had she cleared the space, than the thick metal door flung open, almost hitting her. The Apostle held an orb in one hand. The light burned her eyes, and she shielded her face with one arm. As her vision grew accustomed to the burn, the glow illuminated the lower half of the Apostle's face, one she couldn't recognize. They were all blurring into one. As he entered her cell, that eerie smile was gone; this was going to be bad.

She braced herself for the physical assault she was sure would come, but he stayed his hand. Instead, he pulled her by the arm, stretching her limb into an uncomfortable position. She yelped and pushed her way up, forcing herself to her feet. He awkwardly shifted his arm under her breasts and dragged her out. She could see into the dark hallway. They passed so many doors. Twelve. Twelve other souls were trapped with her in this dungeon.

She was alone in her cell, but what if they had crammed more souls in the others? Ivy and Lady Thalassa had a cell to themselves, but from the sounds coming from the doors, Felicia could hear more than one body per cell in some places.

How many victims were trapped with her? How many had the Apostles taken? Her bare feet dragged along the rough stone floor, which scraped and cut the soles of her feet. She passed the cell with the sounds of a child whimpering.

"It's okay. Just keep going for one more day," she called out to them. The Apostle shook her.

"You are giving them false hope. You are all hopeless," his voice was firm and cold.

"You may have forgotten your humanity, but there is always hope," retorted Felicia. The Apostle said nothing, but she could feel his grip clench a little bit tighter.

He dragged her up a flight of stairs. He was in no rush and let her use her hand to brace herself as they ascended. The upper floors were clean and bright. Old wooden flooring, stone walls, and mounted orbs guided their way.

They stopped in front of a wooden door. It had no lock, so the Apostle just pushed it open. She saw two wooden chairs that sat on either side of a small round table. A small bell was placed in its centre. Felicia looked around. The large window had shutters closing the space, hiding her location. Ivy thought the dungeon was under the Temple, and from Felicia's time in the palace, she suspected Ivy was right. They wouldn't have transported her too far from the prince, so she knew she was still on palace grounds. She spent summers wandering around the grounds with her brother as their parents worked with the king. She was never allowed to venture close to the Temple, but one of the servants had described the inside to her, and this somewhat matched their description.

He placed her on one chair and picked up the small bell. He tilted his head, and looked at her, the sinister smile once more on his face. He shook the bell and it chimed sweetly, its ding pleasant to her ears, though she guessed the sound would soon come to haunt her. He took a seat across from her and observed her in silence. Moments later, another Apostle appeared, holding a bowl. He placed it down, put a spoon in front of her, and then left.

She looked at the steaming soup. The Apostle across from her sighed, "If you're wondering if there's a suppressant mixed in, there is."

She suspected as much; she knew the risk when she spoke up and drew attention to herself and away from the child. A choice she would make again. She tried not to look at the steaming broth.

"Do we need a little motivation?" The Apostle rang the bell. Another one of those goons brought in Ivy. Felicia immediately recognizing the familiar wet coughs. She would have been a beauty, had she not been in such a condition. Her hair was matted, the hue of red wine, with almost translucent, pearl-white skin and crisp, grey eyes. Ivy's clothes were tattered and covered in deep stains of dried blood; her arm hung at her side, limp and out of place. Her fingers were misshapen and pointed at odd angles, with several fingernails missing. Even in her state, Ivy found the strength to thrash around, seized with her wet cough.

"Eat, or this one suffers," threatened the Apostle, who sat calmly across from her.

Ivy begged Felicia. "Please. Please help me." Felicia had stored up enough mana to try and overpower the Apostle, but with Ivy here, she weighed her options. As if sensing her thoughts, the Apostle holding Ivy reared back his hand and slapped Ivy across the face. Ivy's face twisted to the side, her nose dripping with blood.

Felicia growled and picked up the spoon to stir the contents. There was no other choice. She breathed hints of herbs and spiced meat. The first sip of broth tingled against her dry mouth. An explosion of flavours hit her tongue as she scooped up more broth. She inhaled it.

Mouthful after mouthful, she shovelled more in. A deep pain surged in her stomach; she was going to vomit. She leaned to the side as the contents of her stomach lurched forward. She should have known that her stomach was no longer used to food. The rapid onslaught of substance triggered a violent cramp. Breathing heavily, she eyed the Apostle. He said nothing and waited for her to settle. He rang that cursed bell once more. The Apostle holding Ivy started beating her.

"No, stop!" Felicia picked up the spoon once more and gingerly took another spoonful. Ivy's beating stopped. After a few minutes, the Apostle rang the bell once more, letting the other one know he could take Ivy away.

Once the bowl was empty, he spoke, "Good. You've done well. Now we can start." The bell chimed once more. A grey robe came in, took the bowl and spoon, then left. Alone once more, she sat in a silent battle of wills.

She rolled her eyes, "So, what are you planning now that your master is here?"

He cocked his head to the side and then raised his hand and slapped her hard across the face. "I did not say that you are allowed to speak."

Felicia smiled, "Oh, did I hit a sensitive spot? Do you not want him to be here?" He slapped her again. She laughed. Her face felt on fire. Her expression was suddenly serious, "I remember when we first met in the throne room. I saw it." The Apostle's raised hand hovered in the air.

"Saw what?"

"I saw the way you all were surprised to see the prince. He spoke to you in your mind. You didn't even know that he was your master, which makes me wonder if you blindly followed a voice that said sweet nothings to you."

He clenched his hand into a fist and then struck. Felicia's head flew to the side, and she heard her nose break before she felt the trail of blood making its way across her lips. Adrenaline masked her pain. She rolled her neck and faced him once more, letting the blood drain down.

"Your strong will and stubbornness will not save you here. Why do you care for Lilith?"

The palms of his hands lay flat on the table. She was not in a hurry to answer him. She scrutinized his shielded face, stared at his fake smile. She memorized the tip of his nose, the curve of his lip, and the squareness of his jawline. He waited several minutes before smacking her in the face once more.

"Oh, was I allowed to talk?" She smiled at him, pushing him to see how far he would take it. He hit her again. She spat blood on the table; her lip had split open, and her eyes and cheeks were starting to swell. "You need me alive. For what?" Another hit across her face. "As a way to control her?" Hit. "Hmm. As a way to control the general." She braced herself for another strike, keeping her eyes shut, but nothing happened. She opened her eyes as much as they would allow, the swelling constricting her vision. Her adrenaline was wearing out, and she felt the overwhelming pain in her face.

"I wonder, as perceptive as you seem to be, how did you fail to notice him?" The Apostle was no longer smiling. "You will eat when we say, or we will use the others as punishment. If you try anything, or step out of line, we will do worse." He rang the bell once more as Felicia slumped into unconsciousness.

Felicia, wake up!

She pressed her hands over her face, annoyed that someone was calling for her. Around her were plain white walls, no paintings, with a set of grey curtains with a grid-like pattern. This was her bedroom.

A woman's voice called out for her once more. It sounded familiar, though she couldn't pinpoint whose it was. Padding her bare feet to the door, she opened the white door leading into the tight hallway. Immediately, the air shifted, turning from light and airy to dense and stale. All the morning sun that bathed her room had suddenly vanished, leaving her in shadows. She turned to step back into her bedroom, only to find the door was no more, and the hallway became an endless abyss.

Madoc? Felicia called out, uncertain as to who was home. An extremely tall figure appeared several yards from her, their features obscured, and her heart raced as she stared at the unknown.

"Felicia," the voice called over, melodious and commanding. *"Blood of my blood. You are so near, yet your eyes are closed."* She tried to squint, confident that this mysterious presence was not a member of her family. But, *'blood of my blood'* denoted a relative.

"Who are you?" she asked, taking a cautious step towards the figure. As her foot stepped down, the floor gave way, and she fell.

With a blink, the dark hallway transformed into a strange city. She stood in the centre of a patch of perfectly clipped grass, surrounded by smooth towers. The veil of night concealed the details of where she was, but this place was unfamiliar.

In front of her was the tall figure, closer than before, enough that Felicia could make out the silhouette of a dress, and curves that suggested this person was female.

"What is this place?" Felicia questioned, ignoring the figure and looking around.

The mysterious voice spoke, *"This is your future, should you follow my path. You could inherit everything. Do anything. However, your lack of determination and will now have you in shackles."*

Whoever this person was, Felicia disliked.

The figure sauntered closer, her body moving like a snake. With each step, the figure became smaller, shrinking until she stood head-to-head with Felicia.

Mother? Felicia stated, scrutinising the long, golden, wavy hair, similar to her own. This figure was undoubtedly her moth-

er, yet something about her movements made it seem like she was different.

"Why are you wasting your time with such vermin?" her mother said condescendingly.

Utter disbelief stirred in Felicia's mind. "What?"

Her mother glared at her. "How did you fail to notice him? You have the hand of providence and divine fortune. Use this time wisely. Taking the lives of two will put an end to the unbalanced. Fate and foresight are playing a dangerous game, and you will be caught in the crosshairs if you do not act."

A nagging sensation tugged in her mind, making Felicia look away from her mother. Around them, the walls of the towers were cascading with blood, pooling around her, unending. The blood rose steadily, the smell of copper and salt pungently filling her airways. Felicia looked back at her mother, who had shifted into the shadows. She tried to wade through the crimson liquid, unable to move.

"Mother!" Felicia yelled.

Her mother laughed, sounding like a bell chime. Felicia screamed and cried as blood flooded around her, suffocating her.

Gasping, she woke up in her cell, the cold stone soothing her sore face. The dream, though haunting, faded into the back of her mind. She could recall fleeting moments, suffocating by blood, but it felt hazy and unclear.

"How did you fail to notice him?" Those words seemed to circle again and again in her mind. Her mother had spoken it in her dream, mirroring the words of the Apostle.

But she did see him. Every time Demetrius was in the room, it was as if the air became heavier. Something inside her became more on alert, as if her mind was telling her to pay attention, but she was blinded by her friendship. There were very few people like Lilith. That determination to survive, but still compassionate. She reminded Felicia of her brother, Madoc. He was like Lilith, in that they did not lose their compassion even when they faced their darkest self. When she faced Lilith in the school tournament, she noticed it again: a kindness that existed in a world of hate.

After Lilith had left to train with Danai, part of the kindness faded. In its stead was a hint of something she had felt before. A similarity to the prince.

As they faced more challenges, Felicia placed more trust in Lilith. For once, she let someone other than Madoc into her heart, past that icy shield that covered her exterior. She was trained to be cold and calculating, but Lilith didn't notice that part of Felicia. Where the other women kept their distance, Lilith had been warm and welcoming.

Her dream flittered to the forefront of her mind. It felt like she was supposed to remember a warning, but the words were missing.

That was when her nightmares started. Her mother would torment her in the darkest hours. Images of a world unlike hers, surrounded by flame, burning into cinders. The cries of people who had lost everything, terrified of the approaching hand of death. The mysterious figure, who disguised itself like her mother, showed her what dwelled in the Void. The creature that Lilith had shown the general would be considered quite tame compared to the ones that lurked in her dreams.

'*They are coming for you,*' the ominous voice told her. It warned her not to trust Lilith. It whispered lies about their friendship, placing a seed of uncertainty in her mind. At first, she thought that voice sounded so similar to her mother, but this figure was not.

Alone with only her memories as company, Felicia dwelled in her past. She had watched silently as the prince's obsession with Lilith grew. She noticed him staring at Lilith every time they were in the same room. Every time they all gathered for Elemental Incantations, it was as if he had a predatory fixation on Lilith, yet Lilith was somewhat oblivious to how badly the prince had fallen.

Felicia had struggled with her own jealousy of others placing attention on Lilith. Taran and Silver were always quick to vie for Lilith's magnetic pull. The prince was outright snippy with others. He barked his orders, and those around him were so obedient to follow him. It had come as a shock when she learned that Taran was yet another one of the prince's tools to keep an eye on Lilith. She caught them discreetly chatting late into the evening about Lilith, but Felicia had dismissed it, thinking they were discussing the tournament. She should have paid more attention. The signs of the prince's betrayal were a clear as day, and Felicia cursed herself for being caught in his web.

She had made so many mistakes.

She'd made the mistake of trusting Silver. He would listen to her vent, but then he remained so pleasant in the prince's company. He used his sarcasm and quick wit to disarm her. She should have been more cautious of him. She should have listened to the voice.

On their journey through the Ruins of Thurndun, the prince slipped up. He knew those mines too well for someone who had only visited in passing. Felicia had her clairvoyance ring show her the way, and the prince had guided them away from their expected exit. The beast had been a conveniently timed distraction. It had been the first time Felicia spoke about her mistrust of the prince to Lilith, and Lilith had planted seeds of doubt in her mind. Maybe she had seen it wrong? Maybe she was just jealous?

She should have listened to her instinct. Madoc always said it was her special talent; she could see what others had missed. At first, she blamed Lilith for how she ended up in this dungeon, but really, she played into her own demise. Never again would she mute that intuition, that voice that seemed to guide her to the truth.

Chapter 7
Contradiction of the Heart

Lilith

The sun had set some time ago, and her room was dimly lit by the light of the full moon. Footsteps drummed on the wood flooring with faint rustling of keys. Lilith was sure no one would come. No one but him. So when she heard someone approaching from down the hall, she was ready with her plan.

She stood quietly behind the door, waiting for it to open. Her breathing was barely audible. The door slowly opened, casting a warm, bright light into the room's shadows. In reached a hand holding an orb. Lilith clenched her jaw and sprang forward, slamming the door on the person entering. She wasted no time grabbing the person's arm and pulling them to the ground. The Apostle yelped and fell into the lounging area. Lilith kept attacking, using her fists, feet, and everything she had at her disposal to strike.

Hands reached out around her from behind. She thought this Apostle had come alone, since she had heard no other footsteps as he walked to her room. That's when she smelled the familiar scent of pine. Rough hands tightened their grip around her waist. She knocked backwards, sailing her head into their face. She heard a grunt and a growl, but the hands held on. Fully energized by adrenaline, she felt her mana course through her veins. Her body was primed, full of electrifying power, one shot she'd risk for her freedom.

"I've said this before, but I like it when you play dirty, Lilith," the deep voice growled, as she struggled to get free.

"Then you'll like this." Lilith sent her electricity pulsing out of her into the prince. Immediately, his hands seized, and he dropped to the ground. The Apostle slowly got up, his hand clutching his arm as he faced her. His unsettling smile had disappeared, replaced by rage.

Lilith braced her feet apart and called to her air magic. The sudden gust of wind caused him to fly back, slamming into the wall behind him, and he fell once more to the ground. She wasted no time running through the open door, following a light down the hallway towards a set of stairs. Sprinting forwards, Lilith raced towards the consorts' wing. She knew that the Temple should be located a little beyond it. Her mana was lower than she liked, but she thought she might be able to make it, if she was lucky.

A few startled guards momentarily paused before springing into action. That slight hesitancy gave Lilith an edge. She sailed near them to close the distance, and with the help of her mana and more of her air magic, she delivered a forceful right hook on the first guard, followed by a swift kick to the face of the other. The strikes were hard enough to stun them without burning through her mana reserves. Time was not on her side, and with every passing moment, she knew she was closer to facing off with the prince once more.

The consorts' building's red textured hallways were unusually quiet. King Amadeus had filled these rooms, yet this place right now seemed oddly still. Lilith raced down the hall in the direction of the Temple, but stopped short when she heard a small voice from behind one of the doors.

"We should do something," a woman's voice whispered.

"We will get punished if he finds out we helped," said another voice.

"If we don't, then we're as good as dead anyway," replied the first voice.

Lilith heard a door behind her open, and a face appeared.

"Girl," a woman whispered, "this way."

Lilith took her chance and ran back towards the open door. Once inside, the door closed behind her, and the woman grabbed her by the wrist and started to walk. Lilith wiggled to get her wrist free, but the woman just shushed her and continued walking. They moved to an inner room where the other woman waited and closed the door behind them.

"We must move fast," said the first woman. Lilith could barely see in the dim light of a lantern, but she could have sworn one of the ladies resembled Lady Ashmore, only she had dark hair. The dark-haired beauty opened a latch, and a nearby panel on the wall unlocked.

"We can take you down, but we have to stay silent. Put this on to mask your smell." Once inside the walls, the dark-haired woman handed Lilith a dress and waited. Lilith speedily took off her borrowed pants and tunic and put on the flowy, long, deep blue dress. It smelled of a strong floral scent. The other woman took her old clothes and hurried back to the main room.

"She will distract the others with your scent to give us more time." The brunette began descending the dark staircase into the belly of the palace.

"Who are you? And why are you helping me?" Lilith whispered.

"I am who you think I am. The other ladies have been keeping me hidden since they learned of Lady Tessa's fate. Be careful of what you say here; these walls have a way of listening. I am helping you because you need to escape this place. Escape him." Lady Ashmore gracefully walked the maze of corridors, pushing hidden levers and buttons as if this place were a second home for her. It felt like a never-ending network of tunnels that led further down or maybe away from the palace. Lilith's sense of direction was disoriented.

"Wait. I can't leave. I need to find the others in the Temple. The Apostles have Felicia and likely Lady Tessa's daughter. Please, can we go there?" Lilith stopped walking, forcing Lady Ashmore to halt.

"We don't have much time. It would be a miracle just to get you out, and the risk of going towards the enemy would only end in disaster. Once you are free, you can find others and get them back here to help. Though the royals have done enough to keep this knowledge secret, this palace is filled with tunnels and passageways that can take us far beyond the city's limits. Use them to your advantage and plan an attack. It's not just your friends at the Temple that need rescuing; the consorts and their children all need your help too. It's why I can't just leave. These women are my family, and I refuse to abandon them."

Lilith nodded. Alone, she would not accomplish much. Her best chance at freeing everyone was at the encampment where she knew she had allies. She thought about the secret door behind the wardrobe that she never got to investigate. More than likely, it would have sent her somewhere near here. They moved with stealthy speed, and as they rounded another stone hallway, Lilith could see iron bars that led outwards, towards the forest.

"You are facing south; keep moving through the forest in this direction, and you'll come to the encampment in a day's time. Do not stop in town. Once you get to the encampment, you'll have to figure out who you can trust that would help us." Lady Ashmore pushed a hidden lever in the wall, and the bars lowered.

Immediately, Lilith thought of her brothers, but then she thought of the danger this would put them in. She took her first step towards her freedom into the dark forest on the outskirts of Vanguard. She turned to look back as the bars closed once more and the dim light of Lady Ashmore's lantern faded to black.

Facing the forest, Lilith took a deep breath and started walking through the trees. *How far will Demetrius go looking? How much time do I have?* Her heart raced as she kept a steady pace using the stars above as her guide. She kept herself hidden in the shadows, the moonlight illuminating her path over roots and between trees. The occasional rustling behind her made her jump and filled her with anxious energy, a part of her anticipating the prince's figure appearing before her.

Picking up her pace, she traversed her route, keeping an eye on her markers peeking through the dense leaves. With her attention focused on the stars, Lilith almost missed the sudden abyss before her. She skidded to a stop and looked for a way across. The air seemed heavier, and the more she stood still, the more she felt a dark shadow creeping swiftly through the forest. She was not alone.

Sprinting off to the left, she followed the cliff's edge downwards until she spotted an old wooden tree that had fallen and was perched as a bridge to the other side. Her legs burned as she raced over, climbing the weathered trunk. More than thirty feet in the air, she walked carefully across. *Keep moving!* her determined voice chanted as she passed the halfway point. With her next step, she heard footsteps approach behind her.

"You have gotten far, *my goddess*," said a deep, unearthly voice. Prince Demetrius stood at the end of the fallen tree. She didn't have to look back to know whose voice that was. Her focus was on just moving forward.

"It is useless to try to escape, though it seems like you had help. Nice dress," he said with a smirk.

Lilith made a rude gesture with her hand and kept walking across. Her balance was wavering with every step as her concentration was distracted by Demetrius. She heard his laughter fade into the dark. She was almost to the other side and risked a look back. Demetrius was no longer standing at the end.

"Yes, only a few more steps," the dark voice called out in front of her. His sudden appearance ahead of her made her jump, and she lost her footing and rolled to the side. Her hands clawed at the bark as she fell. Thirty feet down, she could make out the rocky ground below. If she lost her hold now, it would be a sure way to her death. The air in her lungs gave out as she let out a loud, bloody scream.

Warm hands grabbed her clammy ones, hauling her up towards the large fallen log. Demetrius pulled her into a close embrace, hugging her. Trembling, she sobbed, too stunned to move.

"Why do you run when your heart tells you to stay with me?" His voice was calm and soothing. For a moment, Lilith melted into his touch. She wanted to breathe him in, let this be her life where she could lean into him. Then reality hit her that she had failed to escape once more. Her trembling increased as she realized the punishment would be worse. *Would it be Felicia who would suffer?*

"Why do you shake? Have you realized there are consequences for your actions?" Demetrius' grip hardened as he closed his eyes and transported them back to the palace. To his room. Once inside the green-walled cage, he pushed her onto the bed.

Fear struck Lilith as the unknown weighed heavily on her conscience. She kept silent, knowing her words would only worsen her punishment. Demetrius smiled beside her, his eyes wild with energy.

"I told you before what would happen if you tried anything. Should I bring dear Felicia in?"

Lilith shook her head. Several reactions filtered through her mind: an apology, begging for forgiveness and mercy, and anger that she would never stop trying. In the end, she could only find one solution: a trade.

"I will permit you to sleep here with me."

Demetrius' smile grew wider. "Like you have any choice."

"Unless you want to sleep with one eye open, I suggest you graciously accept my offer."

"You are not in a place where you can make such an offer. I am not so desperate for mere scraps of your affection. If you offer yourself wholly, willingly, I shall accept."

Fire inside her flickered alive, "I'm more likely to cut things off accidentally if you push me. I haven't used my fire magic in a while. I almost forgot what burning flesh smells like."

Demetrius leaned on the wall behind him, watching her with amusement. "Then I give you a choice, your magic or your friend?"

"Excuse me?"

"You choose who receives your punishment. I take your magic, or your friend loses her hands."

Lilith's hands clenched the bedsheets. This was an easy choice. "Do it then, take my magic. But by doing so, you are no better than Lord Elwin."

Demetrius growled in frustration, his eyes flickering fully black. With lightning speed, he appeared above her with his hand wrapped around her throat. "No, *my goddess*. I am much worse." From seemingly nowhere, a vial with green liquid appeared in his hand. He flicked the cork off with his thumb and poured the contents between his lips. Leaning down, his soft lips grazed over Lilith's. Her pupils dilated, inhaling the sweet smell of pine. The smell triggered an image of the forest at night. Matching his scent, his lips tasted sweet. Heat thrummed under her skin with their contact; she couldn't help herself as she parted her lips. The green liquid entered her mouth along with his tongue, exploring her, driving her mad. She hated him, but craved him. She swallowed, knowing what would happen. Her powers, her mana, would be suppressed, but at least this was temporary. He didn't resort to binding the rest of her magic with ancient curses.

"You lied," she said, as he leaned back and tilted his head, watching her. "You could have made it permanent, but you chose this."

"I am not a fool. You are a force to be reckoned with, a power that will change this world. When you are set free and realize that I am not your enemy, I will enjoy every moment of it." His voice was like velvet, dark and soothing. Lilith's eyelids became heavy, but she stared deep into the dark abyss of his eyes. It was a soulless dark that called out to her, that made time stand still. She saw a reflection of herself draped in shadow. Though he said nothing, a voice entered her mind, echoing sweet words in a dialect she only knew a few words of. An ancient tongue. *Remember.*

Once more waking on the bed, Lilith immediately felt the absence of her mana. It was dark in the room as she sat up and ran her fingers along her neck. The prince watched her from the chair in the corner. His black eyes blended into the shadows.

"What should I do with you?" He leaned backwards, casually relaxing into his seat. "Hmm?" He ran his hand through his dark blue hair. She didn't dare break his eye contact. He spoke once more, his voice sultry and low, "I find it interesting. Even now, as you're shaking with fear, you are not repulsed by me." It was true, even as she stared at him like a doe watching a hunter, she still felt a pull towards him. His scent, his aura, drew her in. She felt like she was an ill-fated moth drawn to a flame. Being near him was not enough; she wanted more, wanted to touch him, make him fall apart with her touch. She wanted to consume him. At the same time, she hated him. His presence angered her, his eyes haunted her, his smile felt like a knife to her own throat.

"I could make you beg. Have you whimpering beneath my touch and shaking from need." He materialized in front of her, on his knees, crawling towards her. She froze, allowing him to come a hair's breadth away from her. Her body betrayed her as a warmth built between her legs.

"I hate you!" she yelled in his face, spit landing on his cheek.

He wiped the spit with his finger and then sucked on it. "You have yet to make your mind up on that, but one thing is for sure, you desire me. Your body calls to me."

Her body leaned into him, but with a glare, she muttered, "Just let me go."

He chuckled, "I can hear your mind. Now that you cannot shut me out, I can hear your struggle. Your words yell hate, but your mind, your soul, wants more."

"Please," she whimpered. She didn't know if this was a plea to let her go or a plea to consume her. She felt so tired of trying to fight that pull to give in to him, that small part of her that wanted to see this world burn. Every day, a new problem arose: the Apostles, the nobles, the royals, and Demetrius.

"I'm not done torturing you." He lowered his wet fingers and dragged his hand up her leg, pushing her dress higher and higher. His fingers kissed her thigh and then touched her bare core. She arched her back at his touch, feeling his fingers drag through her wetness. He circled her clit, but she would not give him the satisfaction of her moans. Her nipples hardened under her dress as he relentlessly drove her closer to her edge. His fingers retreated. "You want me inside of you. You want me to fill you. I can see it in your eyes, I can feel your arousal." He grabbed her neckline and yanked, tearing the fabric apart until he could see her breasts.

Yes, she wanted more. She wanted him, but hated herself for it. Lilith was breathing heavily, the cool air perking her nipples up.

"Gods, look at you, so beautiful." He leaned down and sucked one of her nipples. She bit her lip to stifle a moan. The prince's hands travelled back up between her legs. "I know you're denying yourself. I can hear your thoughts. I can feel your desire coating my fingers." He dipped one finger inside of her, "Tell me you want me, and I'll let you find your release."

Lilith resisted the urge to roll her hip, to tilt herself up to deepen the stretch. With her eyes closed, she turned her face away from him, giving him nothing. He halted his pursuit, removing his fingers and shifting his weight off of her.

"So be it. Just remember, you are mine. You have been made for me, and I for you. If you consider me an evil creature unworthy of your love, you should look at yourself. You have a darkness lurking within, and soon your mask will fall. I will be the one standing beside you." He faded into the shadows.

She curled up on her bed and stared upwards, looking out of the small window. It felt like she was at odds with herself. A part of her, the one she hid from everyone, wanted to join him. Wanted to be with Demetrius.

However, the rational part of her knew she would be condemning everyone else she cared for, and that was simply too much to sacrifice.

CHAPTER 8
TOO LATE FOR GENTLE ANSWERS

Felicia

How many days had it been? Felicia sat up from huddling on the icy cold, damp stone flooring. Although she felt physically less exhausted, she felt weak without her mana. Over the last few days, Felicia had mapped out a mental schedule of how the Apostles operated. Grey robes would come down, presumably in the mornings, to give the prisoners breakfast. Then there was a bit of a wait before a group of them, mixed Apostles with their little minions in tow, who would come down and preach to everyone. They would stand in the middle of the hall and provide a quite lively sermon on worshiping their master, 'The Dark King.'

Felicia barely paid attention to their ramblings, but on occasion they would throw out lines: 'Your sacrifice will heal the land,' 'You are the Gods' chosen,' and the best—'Your redemption through sacrifice will be your greatest legacy.' It was safe to assume that the prisoners were being kept as 'offerings' to the Void.

They took turns on the beatings. Lady Thalassa took the brunt of their entertainment, and they chose Felicia very seldom. Her back constantly ached from the persistent lashings with their favourite tool, the rod. Every day she was given a verse to memorize, and if she failed, she would get twelve lashings. They were never hard, but over time her skin had become sensitive. After, the Apostles would console her, apply a cooling balm while telling her this was for her own good. She wondered if any of the other women had fallen for the Apostle's words. Ivy's cough had worsened, with her pleas to help falling on deaf ears. After the beatings, they would disappear for a lengthy time, until the last prayers. Since her cooperation, they'd switched tactics with the children, spending time educating them about their rules. The children were so devoid of a loving connection, they repeated the Apostles' words, rehearsing in the dark. Their small voices whispered to each other that they were the Gods' chosen. It broke Felicia's heart.

Much of their routine was mindless. Inside her cell, she had found a bucket to do her business, so the smell of fecal matter and urine permeated the air. Once the stench became too strong, they would send grey robes to change to new buckets. The mental and psychological turmoil of their daily routine was eating at Felicia's sanity. Madoc watched from the shadowed corners of her cell. Sometimes, he would mutter phrases she had remembered from her childhood. Most times, he would just stare blankly at her. His long gold hair would change, depending on which memory would surface.

"Are you alive?" Felicia leaned her back against a wall, whispering to her delusion.

Felicia, you'll be fine. There was a pause, as if he were listening to words unspoken. *Mother had to send me. It was the King's order. She wouldn't send me in unless she knew it would be safe.* She'd heard these words before, in the last memory of seeing him alive before he ventured into the southern region. Mother was wrong. Madoc had gone into the expanding darkness as a show that someone of his status could survive. His mission was to reassure everyone that the threat of the Void was not something to panic about. Felicia let out a pained laugh. He was gone. Having gone beyond the border herself, she finally realized there was no way he could have survived.

Promise me you'll keep fighting. He smiled at her before vanishing. She rested her head against her knees, wishing she could keep her promise. They had just finished breakfast, a meagre bowl of some sort of mashed grain, when the sound of multiple footsteps came down the hall.

"The Master will be coming, so you all need to be on your best behaviour. Can't have you looking like filthy vermin. We will be taking you all to the baths. If you try anything, we will end your life on the spot. Keep in line and you will get a reward," commanded an Apostle. His voice had a slight accent, a difference that made him stand out amongst the twelve. This was the first time that Demetrius had come to the Temple; the thought made Felicia shake with fear.

The sound of keys rustled outside her door, and she stepped back further into the dark. The silhouette of a robed man made her pulse quicken. It didn't matter if they were grey-robed or white; they were evil. If anything, the grey robes were more reckless and passionate to prove their loyalty and worthiness to the main twelve. Bright light shone from an orb in their hand, making Felicia shield her eyes. The sharp sting of the light burned her eyes, her vision blurring as her eyes teared. She jumped in surprise from the strong grip of a hand clutching her bare arm, pulling her into the hallway.

They each held bright orbs, a tactic to disorient the prisoners. Not that they would try anything. Felicia shielded her eyes, trying to make out the others. She had yet to see what anyone looked like. She had only ever seen Ivy and Lady Thalassa. Blinking rapidly to clear her vision, she could make out the weakened figures in front of her. The sounds of whimpering and snivelling filled the space. No longer muffled by the wood and metal doors, these cries sounded too loud. Her senses were overpowered by the stench of the others, her ears rang from the noise, and her eyes continued to burn from the light. The robed man pulled her forward as more bodies joined the line. Felicia wondered how many were stuck with her, and as she tried to even out her breaths, she looked side-to-side, taking in the blur of tangled hair and dirt-smeared faces. She dared not speak; no one did. They knew the punishment would not be worth the effort.

Something heavy dragged along the stone; it seemed to rattle like the keys. A figure stopped in front of her, holding heavy chains.

"Raise your hands in front of you," a voice ordered. Felicia did what was asked. She had strength that many of the others did not. Her vision cleared enough to make out the features of the prisoners. To her side was Lady Thalassa, her blue hair bunched in a matted nest, while her once white dress was now a dark shade of grey and rusty red. Behind her, she could hear the weak, wet coughs of Ivy. As she raised her hands slowly, she could see the red head struggling to do as commanded. Her sickness had driven her body beyond exhaustion, and she was unable to raise her arms fully. The grey robe in front of her struck her, sending her crashing to her side. Felicia wanted to throw herself in front of Ivy, take the beatings for her, yell out, and curse the men that stood before her, but she held back. Madoc's soothing voice filled her conscience, *Stay your hand for the right opportunity. Lashing out now will not help this situation.* Felicia tilted her head to the side as her brother's voice whispered in her mind.

The grey robe pulled Ivy up and latched heavy chains around her wrists. They did the same to Felicia's outstretched arms. The heaviness of the rough metal made her arms immediately sag. Chains tethered each prisoner, as the front Apostle guided the small figure in front up the stairs. Felicia started to stumble forward as the Apostles led them upstairs. A few of the grey robes remained in the dungeon to clean up the mess. *Masking what really goes on down here?* Felicia thought. *Can't let the Master know what you've done to us?*

Her sight seemed to clear up more as they moved upstairs; she could make out more finite details of the prisoners through the blurriness. From what she could see, most had very long hair of different shades, all tangled and matted. Her own golden locks were a knotted, greasy mess. The prisoners were all slim and frail-looking from starvation, but Felicia could make out that all of the adult prisoners were women. She knew there was at least one child, from their prior cries, but to see a handful of them made her stomach turn in disgust. The youngest stood about stomach height, making them no older than seven or eight. Rage consumed her, making her blood boil. *How dare they do this?* She imagined tearing apart the Apostles, limb from limb, slowly torturing them as they did the prisoners.

The Apostles pulled the group up several flights of stairs. Stone had turned to wood, and the bright light of their orbs was drowned out by natural sunlight. The warmth soaked through her skin, providing the only comfort that she'd received since she had been there. She stretched her neck up, trying to bathe herself in light. A few of the children did the same, basking in the freshness outside of their cell. *How long had they been down there? Eight months, like Ivy?* Her thoughts turned dark at what those poor souls had suffered. For her it had only been a few weeks, for them it must have felt like a lifetime.

The Apostles pushed the line of prisoners through to a long room and told them to line up against the far wall. Everything was made from a white stone, similar to the one at the palace, but dulled and rough. Felicia looked side-to-side. From the scared expressions on everyone else's faces, this was something to fear. In front of her, Felicia could see outside a small square window, raindrops had started to smatter against the glass, the clouds obscuring the warm sun.

"We're going to remove your chains. You will strip. Try anything, and this room will be the last thing you'll see."

"If you want us to bathe, we can manage, but give us the decency of privacy. You've starved, beaten, and only gods know what else. We are too weak to try anything," an older lady spoke up. She looked to be the general's age, with a stern scowl and salt and pepper coloured hair. One of the grey-robed men marched up and struck her, sending her reeling sideways.

"We are too tired to fight back. Please, give us some privacy." Felicia could not hold back her words. The same grey robe came over, his hand raised, and it came down swiftly on her cheek. The attack left her ear ringing and her lip split. She spat out some blood on his shoes as he stepped back. He wore a look of disgust displayed on his lips as he prepared to beat her once more.

"Enough!" said an Apostle, his voice slightly raised. "You must learn to remove yourself from your human emotions. You must obey the will of the master." This Apostle had a large mole next to his nose on his right cheek. He stepped closer to the prisoners and raised his hands. She remembered this one. He was not one to serve physical punishment; instead, he was the one who tried to "educate" the children. Afterward, he would make his rounds, peering into the window of her cell door, praying over her soul.

"Show us you are able to follow directions. Show us that you accept the will of the gods into your heart, and we will allow all but one Apostle to remain while you clean." A few of the women beside Felicia eagerly nodded: it was the best deal they were going to get. The mole-marked Apostle nodded to the grey robes, who came forward to remove their chains. Felicia wrung out her wrists, massaging away the sensation of chafing from the metal and the heaviness of the chains. The Apostles and their apprentices all stepped back into a perfect line.

"Now, undress," said the Apostle, that disturbing grin on full display. This was sick, to have them all strip while they watched. Felicia clenched her hand at her side, her soul screaming at her to run and hide, but she couldn't. It was Ivy who made the first move. Removing her worn, grungy-looking skirt and blouse that were soaked with stains, she stood before them naked and unashamed. Next to her, a few other women and even the children removed their clothes. Lady Thalassa and Felicia were the last. Their hands shook as they removed the soiled, tattered nightgowns. Felicia's breath was unsteady, but she raised her head and met their eyes head-on.

The grey-robed apprentices stood smiling, not quite the same perfected smile their masters wore, but one of satisfaction. They were loving this. The moley Apostle spoke once more, "Scrub yourselves down. We will be giving you new clothes to wear, and we'll be shearing those rats' nests on your heads. Our apprentices are eager to show us their worthiness, so let that be your only warning."

In one swift motion, all but one Apostle turned to file out of the bathroom. The remaining Apostle stood with his back against the windows. The prisoners waited a few moments, then this Apostle did something unexpected: he turned to look out the window. Felicia's jaw opened at this act of kindness; it was out of character compared to the rest of his cultish friends.

The prisoners turned to face the bucket of water, a cloth, and a small shaving of soap. Felicia grabbed the cloth and dipped it into the icy cold water, then gently started scrubbing her skin. Out of the corner of her eye, she could see the deep purple bruises over Lady Thalassa's porcelain skin. The worst was near her ribs, where a large black bruise wrapped around her back.

In the other direction, she could see Ivy wincing as her deformed fingers tried to grab the cloth. Felicia moved to help her, but Ivy quickly shook her head, mouthing, *'don't.'* The older lady who had spoken out looked about, too, surveying the other women and children. Her aged eyes connected with Felicia's, and they exchanged a polite nod.

They moved in silence except for coughing and muffled groans. The soap they were given smelled too floral; it was a way to mask the smell of sickness. Felicia watched the other prisoners. The full scope of the damage was clearer now that their skin was not covered in filth. The children looked at the women for guidance, but moved slowly and quietly. She'd never seen children so well behaved. No, they were terrified and acting drained of life. Felicia wanted so badly to console them, to shield them from this nightmare.

They looked at one another, not daring to say anything, their eyes primed with fear and a sense of kinship from the shared trauma they'd experienced. This was not just a bath, but to the prisoners, this was the first time they had seen someone outside of the Apostles. They didn't have to say anything to understand the pain and suffering they all felt. This was a reprieve, a moment of delight from the dark punishment they endured every day. They were shared sisters, not by blood, but by agony.

Their slice of peace was disrupted by a new Apostle who entered carrying a bag. One of the women, the outspoken older lady who lingered around the children, must have been feeling that same urge to protect them, because she moved to stand in front of them. The rest of the women stood motionless, surprised by this small act of defiance.

The two Apostles tilted their heads at the woman. The kind Apostle spoke, "Fall in line. We will not ask twice." The old woman's body shook, but she stretched her hands out, ushering the children behind her.

"Please. Let them go. They don't deserve this. Please, we will do anything," the woman begged, her voice wavering.

Felicia had a hard time hearing her voice because her heart was beating wildly in her ears. This woman, her skin marred by abuse, had enough courage to stand between the two Apostles and the children. She was unyielding. It was obvious time had not been kind to her, but from the way she stood in defiance, Felicia could tell she was used to standing against the harshness of society. This woman had earned Felicia's respect.

"Please, I mean no disrespect. Don't do this to them. I beg you. They cannot survive like this." The woman started to cry. Felicia felt her own tears brimming.

The Apostle next to the kind one stomped forward and pulled her to the side. "Know your place. You do not tell us what to do." He pushed her to her spot, and she sank to her knees. A woman closest to the Apostle rushed up and grabbed the knife tucked into the Apostle's belt. Two things happened simultaneously: the woman lunged forward, driving the blade into the Apostle, while the kind Apostle lashed out with a burst of water magic. The blast hit the woman as the blade sank in, sending her flying back into other women, slamming them into the stone wall to their backs. They all fell in a heap.

Felicia acted purely on muscle reflex, rolling out of the way, but also closing the distance between her and the kind, mole-marked Apostle. Startled by her own actions, she rammed into the Apostle and tackled him to the ground. She had no mana, and her body was beyond exhausted, but she felt a surge of adrenaline allowing her to overpower him. They wrestled on the ground.

Felicia felt her hands wrap around the hilt of his dagger, but as she struggled to pull it free, she heard the sudden gasp leaving the Apostle. The hood of his robe had fallen back, revealing a very startled handsome young man. A man who was close in age to her. His chocolate brown eyes widened with shock as blood spurted from his mouth. It was Ivy who had grabbed the knife from the other Apostle and driven it into this one. Felicia pushed him off to the side and quickly stood. Ivy didn't wait as she removed the blade and rammed it back in. Again and again.

Two motionless Apostles lay in their own blood. Ivy, lost to a blood frenzy, and another woman on the other, both taking out their pain on the lifeless men. The others froze in a stunned moment of confusion. They had not planned this, but somehow they had attacked and killed these two Apostles.

"We don't have much time. What now?" the older woman who shielded the children spoke, her voice finding confidence.

Lady Thalassa ran to the discarded bag and freed its contents, a pile of clothes. Only quickened breaths could be heard as the women and children all hastily put on something. Felicia grabbed a sage green dress that came to her mid calf. It was a shapeless, thin fabric that was too large for her, but it allowed for freedom of movement.

"If we are in the Temple, then there should be a way into the tunnels near the stairs. We found it once before as children," said Lady Thalassa, who wore a baggy fitting, grey tunic and a long black skirt.

"Do you think you could get us there?" Felicia asked.

"I don't know. It was years ago, but I can try," she replied. Some of the women were with the kids, making sure they were okay.

Lady Thalassa watched them from the door. "We have to get them out, no matter the cost." Felicia nodded in agreement. Ivy knelt down and pulled out one of the knives as another woman pulled out the other and handed it to Felicia.

"Keep quiet, we have to move fast," Felicia whispered to the others as she opened the door. Down the hall was a grey robe. He was looking out a window, his back turned to them. Felicia moved with stealth and speed as she snuck up behind him. The song of the blade, that quiet metallic ring, was the only noise the grey robe heard before the blade met its target, sinking into his throat. Felicia smothered her hand over his mouth to muffle the gurgling, and she carefully laid him down.

Rejoining the women, they moved quietly down the stairs. Lady Thalassa motioned them to halt halfway down in front of a large tapestry—a fine weave depicting the story of the first oak tree planted in the throne room. She flipped it up, revealing a hidden panel. Pressing her hand in the upper right corner, it clicked and bounced open.

One by one, they hurried inside with Felicia covering the rear of the group. The sounds of footsteps coming from below came closer just as Felicia secured the panel behind her. They would only have mere minutes before the bodies would be found. Dread filled Felicia's body as she came to the realization that this attempt would not end well. They might be able to free the children, but at what cost?

Like mice, they moved down the hidden staircase into a concealed passage. There was barely enough room for a grown adult, but after months of starvation, the group was able to move with ease. The walls were made from dusty panels, rough wood, and dirt. Down they went, becoming one with the dark. The sounds of shouting and alarm rang through the Temple, filtering through the walls. The hunt was beginning.

Into the belly of the dark tunnels, Lady Thalassa led down every turn. If she were improvising, no one would have known. They followed her blindly until she finally turned to face them, tears trailing down her cheeks.

"I don't know where to go from here," she whispered and bit her lip to try and silence her cry.

"That's okay, my dear. We can find a way from here," spoke the older lady.

"Who are you?" Felicia asked, wanting to know this confident older woman who wasn't weighed down by the Apostles' beatings.

"I'm Beatrice Bane. I would say it is a pleasure to meet you, but considering our circumstances, it's unfortunate that we've had to meet like this." They started walking blindly into the darkness of the tunnels. Felicia kept her hand on the right side of the wall, to try and keep some sort of track on their movements.

"I'm Felicia Flavian, and this is Lady Thalassa."

"Flavian, as in General Flavian?" Beatrice asked her.

"My mother."

"I can't believe the Apostles would be bold enough to take not only a royal child, but also the feared general's daughter."

"To be fair, I highly doubt my mother would care. I'm more shocked that Lady Thalassa is here."

"Me too," Lady Thalassa muttered. "It's because my mother was so outspoken against the Apostles and the recent decisions made by the king. The prince killed her, and he sent us here."

"The prince? Prince Demetrius?" Beatrice Bane's voice sounded confused.

"Yes. We were tricked by his plight to save the kingdom, and his father, only for him to turn on us and reveal his true nature. He is one with the Void."

Beatrice didn't sound surprised. "Before my last article came out, I had heard a rumour that there was an alliance between the nobles and the Apostles. They were driven by a nameless figure, their leader. I suspected it was someone within the palace. I thought it was the king. How did this happen?"

Felicia shook her head, "I don't know. His betrayal came as a shock." She couldn't see Beatrice's face, nor read her reactions. "Please, what is happening on the outside? I was at Skilhiem before this, and news came at a delay. What is going on out there?"

"I can't say for sure how it is right now, since I think I've been here for over a month, but the Apostles have taken over Vanguard. They control the guards, they have the merchants on a leash, and they've taken over the schools."

"The schools? Why would they target the schools?" Lady Thalassa asked. The women behind them were silent, hanging on every word of this conversation.

"They have sent the ones in grey to watch over how the children are taught. Anything outside of their beliefs has been banned. They're burning books and information. Religion, history, family ledgers—you name it, they are destroying our people's history, the knowledge. The last article you read was probably the last one I released before they shut down our main operations. I secretly managed to print a flyer, and distributed them all over the realm, so that those outside of Vanguard knew of what was going on here. I had sought sanctuary deep in the city, and once they found me, they killed my team and took me here."

"Word has spread. Others must be aware of what's going on here. Those at the encampment wouldn't stay put, they have family and friends here." Lady Thalassa sounded hopeful.

"We are all living in fear. Fear of the Void, fear of the king, and now this new threat of the Apostles. There is no one coming for us. The encampment will not move against their own people, against the king. Soldiers that desert their stations will be condemned as traitors."

Felicia's eye twitched, "I doubt my mother would allow for word to spread within her ranks. She's likely controlling what information goes around the encampment. What is the point..." Felicia froze. A movement from her left had caught them by surprise. Was it over? Was this all for nothing? Felicia turned to face the Apostle.

CHAPTER 9
RIDDLES OF THE WISE

Lilith

At first, she was intentionally trying to starve herself, from sheer stubbornness and refusal to give in to the prince's demand. But after a few days, her inner fight was dying. Her mana had not returned, which was the focus of her starvation. She thought that they were coming in at night to make her take something while she was asleep, so her plan was to stay up all night to see if her hunch was right. The prince, or whatever he was, had not bothered her since the last time she had seen him. Her routine so far was to wake up, wait for an Apostle to drop off some food, stare at said food. Sit in the chair and look out the window. Everything worked in precise order, with the staff, Apostles, and guards sticking to a routine.

As predicted, an Apostle came in to take the untouched plate and replace it with another. She turned to face away from him as he left once more. The minute after the door closed, she ran over to the wardrobe and quietly pushed the clothes to the side. Over the last few days, she had ventured into the walls, down paths, and back before they noticed she was gone. It was a labyrinth of passages, one that she had no idea which path to take, but was slowly mapping out. She had ripped off an orb from the wall to use for light. This time, when she went down, she followed her markers: a torn piece of a tunic, then right down the passage towards the next marker, a small potato. She had run into a series of dead ends but luckily, no traps. Without her mana, she was truly powerless, and her senses were dulled. She never ran into the women who helped her that night. What happened to Lady Ashmore was a mystery since the prince had remained absent.

She veered left after another marker. This corridor went towards the belly of the palace, deep under the foundations of what the palace was built on top of. Her time was running out before one of the staff came in to tidy up. Feeling frustrated, the plan was to stay awake, figure out how they were suppressing her mana, or find a way out. She was just about to turn around when a whisper floated in the air. Immediately, her body tensed; someone else was down here. A pull drove her to walk closer, to find the source, taking blind turns down unknown paths until she finally saw them.

Eleven disheveled-looking women and four children. Children! They were soaking wet, wearing mismatched clothes that did not fit. The children had absent looks in their eyes. Her appearance terrified the women, but the children seemed unfazed. Then she saw two women, one with blue hair, the other golden.

"Felicia?" She barely said the words aloud before the golden-haired woman sprang forward and pushed her back. Lilith had no time to react before Felicia pulled her into a hug.

"Curse you! I hate you!" Felicia squeezed her tightly and continued, "Thank the gods." Lilith wrapped her hands around Felicia and returned the embrace. Stunned, she finally looked at the rest of the women. They were in rough shape. Most had bruises on their face, on any skin showing, and any spark in the eyes had dimmed from torture.

Lilith cursed. It came as no shock to see others as Apostles' victims, but the four children chilled her to her core. *Does he know? Does he care?* Lilith looked into the eyes of the children, who had been dealt a cruel hand, and all she could ask herself was if Demetrius was behind this. If so, was he past the point of redemption? Was he too far gone into the abyss of darkness to come back? To sink so low as to attack the most sacred members of society, children, with no remorse and no empathy, had to mean he was beyond saving.

"I take it from the look on your face, the prince had not disclosed what he and his precious Apostles were up to," Felicia said, venom-laced words of truth. Lilith really knew nothing about Demetrius. The more she found out, the uglier his world became.

"No, he didn't. Most of the time we've spent together, he's been focused on trying to keep me in his room, my cage. I'm sorry, Felicia, for the way this has ended up. Had I listened to you from the start, we would not have been placed here."

Felicia looked behind her to the line of women. "If you had listened to me, these people would still be in the dungeon as 'playthings' for the Apostles. I'm mad, yes, but we have bigger issues right now."

"Like, how to get out?" said Lilith, turning to face Lady Thalassa. "I'm lost. We are further down than I have ventured by myself. Lady Ashmore attempted to get me out, but that attempt failed. I don't know what happened to her."

"Then we figure it out as we go. How's your mana?" Lady Thalassa asked.

"Non-existent. I suspect they've been giving me something while I sleep. And yours?"

"Likewise, we've all been given daily doses of suppressant in our meals."

"Great, so we've got no way to defend ourselves."

"Except these," replied Felicia, pulling out a long dagger. One of the other women had another one.

"We need to move," stated a thin woman with matted red hair. She had a really wet-sounding cough that made her wheeze as she breathed in.

They started moving in a new direction, hopeful it was towards freedom. Lady Thalassa took up the rear, her soft voice drifting into the dark. "They were bathing us to prepare for a visit from Demetrius. Felicia negotiated privacy, then suddenly a skirmish happened, and we managed to kill two Apostles." The confidence in her voice was much different from what Felicia was used to hearing; it made her smile.

Lilith looked between the women, who had managed to subdue two Apostles without an ounce of magic. "That leaves us with ten Apostles, and a few dozen of their apprentices, the ones in grey robes." She didn't mention the one grey robe she had managed to kill herself.

"Oh, we know about those goons," Felicia smirked. "That's a title Ivy used for them."

Lilith nodded to the coughing woman with red tangled hair and stormy blue eyes. She gave her a gap-toothed smile.

"Beatrice, you need to meet Lilith." Felicia called for the older looking woman with streaks of white though her dark brown hair. She gave Lilith a polite nod.

"The reporter Beatrice?" Lilith eyed the woman.

"The Apostles have halted all information leaving the Vanguard. This is their city now." Beatrice kept an eye on the children.

Fury flashed behind Lilith's eyes. "Their rule will be a short one. We need to get you out of here. You need to head to the encampment."

"And who is there to save the people here? We don't know who is on our side and who is on the prince's," Beatrice countered.

"I can guarantee there are people there who do not stand with the ideas of the Apostles. My brothers are there. Our friends. There must be people who do not wish to see this place burn. With your voice, you can rally more people."

"I can try. Without my team, my ability to print information, I don't know how far my words can travel."

"What does Demetrius have planned for you?" Felicia turned to Lilith, who looked forlorn.

"He wants me to be his queen. His wife." Lilith hoped that she could reach her family. She was sure her brothers would help them.

"Why you?" Lady Thalassa sounded angry. "No disrespect, but you're not special."

"Well, if she had her powers, she's quite powerful." Felicia held her hand up to quiet Lady Thalassa. "Unlike most of us, she can call up any elemental magic. You should have seen her when she went through her emergence."

Lilith could feel the weight of Lady Thalassa's eye, sizing her up. "I think there's more of a connection with him beyond my powers. It's an obsession."

They stumbled into a fork in the path. Their passage had split into three. The group stood at the junction, peering into the darkness of each path. A large rodent scurried past them, going down the right pathway.

"The rats always know the way out. It may as well be a sign," said one of the women. She held onto the hands of two children and ushered them forward.

"I can't go with you," Lilith stated. "He'll be looking for me soon. I've stayed away from my room for too long. If I go with you, you'll be found, and the greatest chance of you getting out is by leading him away from you." She handed Felicia her orb.

Felicia opened her mouth to say something, but Lilith interjected. "No. You are not staying. You have to go and reach the encampment. We need allies, people we can trust, who can help bring him down." Lady Thalassa pulled on Felicia's wrist.

"We will send help if we make it," said the blue-haired royal. Felicia gave Lilith a tight hug, before taking the other women down the passage. Lilith waited until the last of the orb's light faded and then chose the left tunnel. It was so dark that she couldn't see her hand in front of her, and her pace had turned to a blind stumble forward. She kept one hand on the wall beside her and took another step. By now, Demetrius would have alerted everyone to look for her. It was useless to keep going, but she did it anyway.

After what seemed like hours, she heard a small whistling sound. The caress of a gentle breeze ruffled her hair. Squinting in the dark, she could make out a small white light bouncing in the air. *Have they found me?* She waited for the orb to reach her, its light illuminating the passageway. As it reached her, it circled around, making her think this was some sort of sentient being like the fire sprites, only this was so small that it was barely the size of her thumb. She held out her right hand, and it softly wandered over, hovering over her palm. Lilith brought the orb closer to her face, trying to make out its centre, only to realize it was made of a liquid-like substance. It zoomed off her outstretched hand back towards its original spot where she first spotted it.

Cautiously, she trailed after it. With its light, she was able to make out the dark stone passage, where the air dipped cooler and the breeze became stronger. She reached a turning point, and at the end was a door made of thick metal rods. The orb sailed through the gap, waiting for her on the other side. Lilith reached out to touch an ice-cold rod and gave it a good tug in both directions. It didn't budge. She went to one side, to feel for some sort of hinge or key, and saw a small engraving on the wall. Three runes lined up in a column. She took a step back, looking for more runes. A foot behind her, she found a small pillar of three cubes carved out of stone. Tilting her head, she touched the top stone and pushed it. As she predicted, it turned to show another face with a small rune engraving. With a smile, she matched the cube's face to mirror the engraving she had found near the rods, and it clicked. The rods lifted, revealing a stone corridor. This one was lined with dimly lit mounted orbs. Unlike the previous tunnels, this one was built from a light sandstone. She followed the floating light until it stopped in front of a large wooden door. Lilith rested her hand on the door's face, intending to push, but instead a pulse of energy emitted from the contact. It opened.

Inside the room were three bodies tethered to the walls by chains. Their arms were spread out, while they knelt on their knees, showing lines and lines of runes marking their skin, and their long hair concealed their hanging heads. The centre one had long, wavy white hair, and he wore a burgundy robe.

"Andishmand?" Lilith's voice was barely a whisper. Her hands shook as she grasped his head and lifted. His eyes were closed, his skin ashen, and his lips dry. She looked around and found a small barrel with water, with a small ladle bobbing on its surface. Quickly, she scooped some up and brought it to Andishmand's lips. Most of the water went on the ground, but his lips opened to receive a few drops. He seemed to come alive and greedily sought out more water. Lilith went back and forth, giving the men their fill. Andishmand lolled his head up, his white eyes adjusting to the surroundings, and he finally sensed the figure in front of him.

"Evelyn?" His voice was scratchy.

"No, it's Lilith. Lilith Hennan."

"Lilith," he repeated, "How are you here?"

"I found the tunnels. Please, tell me how to get you out of these chains." Lilith looked around for some sort of key.

She searched the area around them. Her hands skimmed the stone columns supporting the ceiling, but found nothing. Rushing back to Andishmand, she touched the cool metal on his wrist. A line of runes was etched into the metal.

"It's useless, these chains are bound by magic. You must leave us. Leave this place before he finds you."

"Don't worry about me. How do I free you?"

One of the other Mages leaned back, "Only a ruler can set us free. We are bound to them through rune magic."

The last Mage remained silent. He tried to say something, but as he opened his mouth, she could see that his tongue had been cut. The wound looked old, but the pain on his face told her more than enough.

"You need to leave, Lilith. Now."

"You know. You know what he is, don't you?" Lilith took a step back, preparing to leave.

"Read the journal. There are clues. Find the fallen star; her light will purify these lands. Only she can help you. Tell him nothing. There's much I wanted to tell you, you and I have crossed paths once before. Remember, only a royal can set us free."

"By blood or by marriage?" Lilith picked up what he was implying. Andishmand smiled weakly.

"You are quick. I like that about you. Either will do. Go now, before he finds you here."

Lilith backtracked through the tunnel she had come through, as the little white light danced around her, helping her.

"What are you, little light?" Lilith followed it back to her room. All the while, her mind raced as she thought of Felicia and the other prisoners. *Will they make it out?* she wondered. *Who is the fallen star?* Question after question stirred in her mind; she lost track of the turns and twists up into the palace. She soon found herself facing the panel of the wardrobe. In all this time, the prince had not found her. The little light did not pass the threshold and danced around the passageway.

"Thank you," she nodded her respect. It felt like this light was a sentient being, a creature of the tunnels. Taking a cautious step through the wardrobe, she entered her cage. A quick glance around, she relaxed as she found her room empty. The little light bounced in the air backwards, and she watched as the light faded around a corner, then replaced the back panel of the wardrobe.

Am I foolish to return? She thought it would be the best idea to give Felicia a chance. The sun was rising, and she felt the urge to surrender to sleep, but instead she waited and watched. The prince was nowhere, yet his scent lingered in the space. Her little expedition had not gone unnoticed. She sat on her bed, her pillow on her lap. Her eyelids felt heavy, and on occasion, her head would fall down only to jerk back into her semi-awake state. Doubt whispered its panicked words. *All of those prisoners are dead. Those children are dead. He found Felicia. Maybe I should have tried to escape. What now?*

It was a clear, bright morning, the sky painted in hues of gold. Her body lacked strength. A figure formed in front of the entrance to her room; as it solidified, the prince appeared, looking rather disheveled. His eyes widened at the sight of her, and he rushed towards the bed, knocking her flat on the mattress.

"You're here?" His hands frantically ran through her hair and over her skin. "I thought you slipped through my fingers. Where were you?" His voice became dark and angry. "Where did you go?"

Fire won over fear, her rage at what he'd done, who he'd hurt, yet he had the nerve to be concerned for her?

"Why did you allow children to be tortured at the hands of your Apostles? Why?" She glared at him as he pinned her down. She didn't attempt to wrestle free, and she knew that by stating such an accusation, she was admitting she found out about the prisoners, but she had to know. If he was a reflection of herself, her equal, was she capable of such actions? Would she get to the point where she would look the other way?

Demetrius frowned, straddling her while pinning her hands beside her face. The look of concern transformed into something much darker.

"Was it you who freed them?" He squeezed her wrists tighter, "Do you want to know what happened to them?"

"Did you kill them?" Lilith felt a rush of panic.

Demetrius smirked, "I could have, but no. Ms. Flavian is proving to be difficult. You'll be happy to hear that five have managed to escape. Your friend was not so lucky." Lilith narrowed her eyes. She knew it was within his power to find those that escaped, and yet he let them go.

"What will you do to her?"

"She has not lost her limbs. The Apostles are keeping an eye on her."

A mixture of relief and sadness overcame her. On one hand, Felicia was still alive, but their attempt to escape had failed.

"I want to know why you didn't stop the Apostles from kidnapping and hurting those children and women." Lilith did not back down.

Demetrius sighed, moving to sit next to her on the bed. "There are casualties in war, and I gave the Apostles permission as a reward for their loyalty, and to keep them placid. I needed them to think there was a possibility that their unwavering worship would amount to something, that their deeds and actions had the possibility of changing their doomed outcome, a hope against their madness. I fed their hope and their beliefs because in this vessel, I have limits. There is strength in blind devotion. I know what they feel, that obsession to act for something you care so deeply about. I feel it with you. For so long, you were my one hope, my shining light in an endless dark. It kills me that you don't remember–that you were given a second chance at a new life without such burdens of what was. What we were. I searched for you for years, for decades. I made these choices to use the Apostles long before you wandered back into my life. I was desperate to find you, and I'd have killed countless souls to reach this place. I would scorch this realm until you and I were the only ones standing."

"Your actions will only separate us further. By siding with them, hurting those people, I will never love you. You would burn this world, condemn it to the same darkness that you've had to endure, and in the end, it would have meant nothing. I judge you for what you've done and what you've become.

If our roles were switched, I would never have committed the atrocities that you have. What we could become depends entirely on the choices you make."

Demetrius laughed. "You think you would not act like me, yet you're dangling this false hope that if I choose to aid these people, you would love me for it. I will show you what these people are like and why their lives are not worth saving."

"You will not change my mind. I am exhausted," Lilith's voice sounded so hopeless. "I don't know how much more I can take."

He laid down, pulling her in. "Then sleep."

Lilith wished she could live a different life. One where she could be free from the weight of those trying to control her, restrain her. The heaviness of Demetrius' touch made her feel restless. Confused. She didn't fight him, not after she had managed to get away with her exploration without punishment. Instead, curled up in the bed, she waited, feeling Demetrius' breaths even out. She wished that this was all a dream, that somehow these last several months were not real.

However, denial could not save her. She had to save herself. Then when this was all done, she would leave, find a secluded place where no one would take from her, and finally rest. Until then, she would become her own master. No one would take from her anymore. Starting with the Apostles.

Chapter 10
Price of a Harmless Soul

Felicia

With the light of the orb, they were able to move much faster following the rat in hopes that it would lead them out. By luck, they had not run into anyone. *Please, let us get out!* She prayed to the old gods, to anyone who would listen.

They could smell the familiar scent of the city streets, the warm breeze carrying notes of excitement and the salt from the nearby ocean. The water had risen around them, soaking their ankles. This was it; they were almost there. From in front, a woman herding the children gave out a loud cry.

"No!" Beatrice yelled. "Somebody, help us! Please, they have taken us. We need help." She yelled and yelled until Felicia was able to push through the women and see what the fuss was about. Long horizontal bars stretched across the tunnel's path, and on the other side, she could see freedom. They were down by the docks, underneath the city.

The bars were wide enough that she could squeeze through, but it would be slow. Felicia looked at the children and knelt down. "You need to go through. Please. Go and don't look back." Behind her, the women were sobbing.

They all put on false brave faces as they encouraged the children to squeeze between the bars. The first was a small boy who had no issues climbing to the other side. He waited for the next child, unsure of what to do next. An older girl passed through next, grabbing hold of the small boy's hand.

"You vermin! Step back and repent!" the voice of an Apostle yelled from the shadows of the passage. Felicia jumped and pushed the remaining two children behind her. The next one squeezed through slowly, crying as her head got stuck. She flailed as a woman bent down to help her.

"Go, run away now!" Beatrice yelled at the three who had managed to get through. They stared at her, pale and with tears streaming down their cheeks. "Go! It'll be okay." The fourth child pressed herself between the bars, sucking in air to make herself as thin as possible. By some miracle, she was able to get through and ran after the other three.

The kneeling woman stood to join the others, standing next to Felicia. Lady Thalassa stood closest to the Apostle, her arms spread wide.

"It's just us," said Felicia, pushing her way to the front.

The Apostle was not alone. Five Apostles, plus eight of the grey robes, blocked their way forward. "You have taken the lives of two of our brothers. You must repent, and we will pray for your souls." Gone were the eerie smiles, the performed act that they usually put on. She could hear a woman trying to get through the bars. Beatrice.

"It was worth it," Lady Thalassa spoke without fear. She accepted the consequences of getting the children out.

"We control this city. In his name, we will make this world anew. Only the pure will inherit this realm, only those who are willing to sacrifice for his love. It's only a matter of time before we bring in new souls to replace the lambs that escaped."

"She's out," muttered a woman from behind. Relief coursed through Felicia, knowing Beatrice was free. She would find a way to the encampment. Felicia just had to hold out for long enough to give as many of them a chance. Her hand found Lady Thalassa's hand, who smiled at her. Ivy came up behind them and rested her hand on Lady Thalassa's shoulder, passing her a dagger. Thirteen men against ten of the remaining prisoners, without power and frail from months of torture. Whispers erupted from behind her, trying to sort out the next thinnest woman to the bars, who had the greatest chance at making it through. These women did not panic. They did not beg or wail. The last several months had taught them to push through their fear.

"You will submit to us, before the Lord. Your saviour requires obedience, and it looks like you all need to learn what that means." The closest Apostle walked forward, with his friends hot on his heels. Felicia sank down into a defensive position, one that was drilled into her from her training at Skilheim.

You did good, sis, Madoc's voice reassured her. One by one, the Apostles and their goons called upon their mana, the tang of magic filling the small tunnel.

"She's through," said a voice from behind. One more soul. Nine remained. The sun was rising behind the women, encasing them in gold light.

Felicia lunged forward, before the first Apostle could strike, sailing her dagger through the air, slashing the Apostle's chest. They had the advantage of mana, but she had the training of fighting in close quarters. He tried to blast her with his water magic, but her adrenaline was spiking, and she was able to deflect his attack off her braced arm. She collided with him, causing him to step back. Again, she slashed at him, nicking his hands. The Apostle next to him let off a small blast of fire, and it was purely thanks to her being soaked that her shoulder took the brunt of the damage, searing through the sleeve of her dress. Lady Thalassa rushed forward, roaring in challenge. She didn't have the training or knowledge on how to attack, but she lodged her dagger into the Apostle's arm. The apprentices behind him yelled in fury, unable to reach their master.

"One more," hollered a woman, letting them know their efforts were not in vain. Eight left. *Just one more.* Felicia thought as the Apostle in front of her lashed out, the blast of water hit directly in her chest, making her buckle backwards. Their magic was not strong, but she was already exhausted. Ivy caught her and picked up the fallen dagger, moving to stand in front. The Apostle shot at her with his own shards of ice, piercing her belly. Ivy let out a small gasp as she ran towards them in a last fit of fury. With her last ounce of energy, she slashed and swiped her dagger, cutting both of the closest Apostles. Lady Thalassa retreated to stand beside Felicia, transfixed on Ivy's last stand. Every moment of pain and suffering she had suffered amplified Ivy's wrath. An Apostle lashed her with his fire magic, her clothes catching flame, but she did not stop. She drove her dagger into the Apostle's stomach, then let out a roar so full of anguish as she dropped to her knees. Her whole body was consumed by fire, and she surrendered, letting out a final cry.

Felcia screamed her name, as she was powerless to intervene. The hurt Apostle was shuffled backwards with his replacement smiling at her.

"Kneel, and no one else will die in this tunnel."

"But you will kill us elsewhere. You may have beaten and broken us, but you will never own us. We will never submit to you." Lady Thalassa was shaking; she was scared, but her voice was unwavering.

"She's out," whispered a woman. Eight souls were spared and found their freedom, and Ivy's soul had found peace.

May they be spared from any more cruelty. May they live the rest of their lives for those who remained behind.

Felicia braced her hand on the tunnel wall. Her body was feeling everything, both the emotional and physical toil of this fight. A part of her readied for this next part. Her final act of defiance.

"I'll find you in the next life, Madoc," she said aloud to herself. A tear escaped as she realized that she was finally going to meet her brother. After months of trying to search for clues on his whereabouts, she knew deep down he was waiting for her on the other side. He was with her every day in her cell, watching over her. Even now, she felt his presence behind her as she faced off with the Apostles. She let out one last yell, one final roar. Behind her, she could hear the others joining her. The tunnel reverberated with the sounds of the women releasing their rage. She was sure that the whole city would have heard them. Their voices carried from the tunnels into the city streets.

Lady Thalassa sprang forward. The silhouette of the prince appeared before her. She felt the blow of magic, forcing her into the side of the tunnel, her body slamming onto the dirt at his feet.

His eyes were pure black as he sneered at the women. "Where is she?" He looked at Felicia.

Terror sank in her bones, meeting his soulless, devoid eyes. Felicia took a step back. Everyone took a step away from him, feeling the power roll off him.

"She is not with us," Felicia's voice quivered in fear.

"Did she escape?" he asked, his voice tense.

"I don't know."

"Do. Not. Lie. To. Me." he accused, his aura pulsating outwards, making Felicia's stomach turn as she fought the urge to prostrate herself before him.

"I'm not lying," she replied. She didn't want to tell him everything. He could figure it out on his own.

"Did you cross her path?" As he spoke, the Apostle behind him retreated further back. They recognized him for what he was: a lion amongst mere vermin.

Felicia didn't want to say anything and none of the other women were willing to give up any information. He and his rats had taken enough.

An Apostle broke the silence, "My liege, we did not come across her on our way down."

"Take them back to your Temple and have your apprentices search the city for her; she can't have gone far. Keep their punishment to a minimum. I need them whole and unbroken, for now. Show me you can be patient, and you will have your delayed gratification. Keep these two separated from the rest." Prince Demetrius pointed to Felicia and Lady Thalassa. He did not stay around to hear what the Apostle replied, leaving the women in the hands of the deluded monsters.

"Our Lord has spared your lives, for now. However, your sins cannot go unpunished. We will take you back to the Temple, and your journey to redemption will begin." They moved in a silent march. The Apostles had set up orbs to guide them back. The way back stretched on for a seemingly endless time. Perhaps it was the threat of what was to come, or the exhaustion taking its hold, but the women dragged their feet.

"Keep moving," urged a grey robe, pushing them forward, knocking down a woman. She let out a little cry as her hands fell forward, shredding the skin on her palms. Lady Thalassa stopped to help the woman, but before she could get near, the grey robe started beating the fallen woman senseless and without mercy. The poor woman curled herself in, trying to protect herself from the onslaught of his strikes. Only when the nearest Apostle calmly told him to 'stop' did the beating end. The woman lay, shaking in agony as the grey robe dusted off his clothes and carried on forward.

"Do not help her. She has proved herself weak both physically and spiritually. She must learn to rise on her own." They pushed the others to walk ahead, leaving the woman with an Apostle. The women shared anxious looks. The idea of leaving someone behind didn't sit right with them, not after everything they had been through. However, they'd already pushed their luck with freeing the eight souls. Only six of them were left, and by the looks in their eyes, they were all ready to meet their end, should it come, in the tunnels.

"It's okay," the injured woman spoke out, her voice just as broken as her body. The woman tried to move, but her muscles shook from effort.

"This is senseless cruelty. You have betrayed your master by hurting her. He has ordered you to keep us whole and unbroken, and even as his shadows still linger about this space, you have already failed his command," Felicia stated, her words dripping with venom.

"He has given the Apostles such orders, but our apprentices received no such command."

"You are twisting his words. Do you really believe that he is your saviour, or are you just using him to enhance your own power?"

The centre Apostle slowly walked up to stand within an inch of Felicia. He leaned in and whispered, "You see us, Felicia Flavian. It is a shame we do not let your kind amongst our ranks, but we do not want to taint our image." As he leaned back, Felicia narrowed her eyes.

"My kind?" she asked. "You mean, women?"

The Apostle smiled, "It would be easy to admit that there is an inferiority with women in general, but that is not what I meant. By 'your kind,' I was referring to those who are free thinkers, radicals that would challenge our basic nature and our way of life as it *should* be. You pose a threat to our beliefs. It is people like you who have caused us to end up in this predicament. Your kind accepted the help of those Mages. The gods wanted us to adhere to the limits of how they created us, but through people like you, we have evolved into something more dangerous. We have awakened something that should never have been awakened. We defiled what it means to be men and turned ourselves into these beasts of magic. We sought out the knowledge because the Mages forced it on us, and we turned our backs on our *true* way of life. It is time we returned to our natural state. One where man ruled the lands, one without magic, one where we understood the difference between us and the gods."

"But you just used your magic against us! I would say you're a hypocrite," Felicia boldly pointed out.

"We are not proud that we continue this habit, yet we are still trying to adapt. A learned behaviour takes time to undo, and we shall bear our own punishment, just as you will." After he finished speaking, he pushed the prisoners to continue walking.

Felicia felt a sourness at his words, that people would willingly choose to turn against seeking knowledge and instead follow blind rules because it made things easier. *Ignorance does not make life easier; it just allows them to continue to live in false comfort. The Void was the largest threat, yet there lacked action amongst people to do something about it. The rebels, lesser nobles, and the Apostles were using chaos to create power, and the common folk would turn a blind eye. If it didn't affect them directly, it wasn't their problem. Maybe the common folk recognized there was a problem? Perhaps they believed that the Apostles have given them a way out of having to sacrifice for their own comfort.*

"What is your solution to the Void?" Felicia asked the Apostle.

The Apostle leaned in close. "Why would I tell you?"

Felicia flinched, but held her ground, levelling him with a glare. "Because we deserve to know why you're putting us through this. You must have some sort of plan, or was that little speech of yours just another one of your meaningless rants to make yourself feel superior?"

The Apostles around her tensed, their smiles vanished at her words. She had indeed struck a nerve.

The usually calm Apostle grabbed Felicia by the throat, his fingers digging in ever so slightly. "For starters, we intend to give you all as sacrifices to the gods. With your lives, they will see that we wish to restore balance. We hand-selected you all as prisoners, as a representation of what is wrong with our way of life." His face turned to scan the remaining women. "We will perform a sacred ritual that will use you as vessels to filter all the mana back to the gods. Through your sacrifice, there will no longer be any magic in this realm, amongst our people."

"You found a ritual that will remove everyone's mana?" Lady Thalassa questioned, edging closer to Felicia.

"Only our ability to transform mana into elemental magic."

"How? This is insanity," uttered Felicia, struggling against the Apostle's hold.

He turned to face her, squeezing a fraction tighter before releasing. Felicia doubled over her knees, sucking in air, as the Apostle loomed over her. "The Mages were the ones who furthered our connection with magic. Does it seem too far-fetched to think they knew how to halt it?"

Felicia never thought that something like that would be possible. Then again, they could be making this all up.

"And if that doesn't work?" Lady Thalassa asked him.

"We have faith that the master will commune with the Void and provide us with direction, as he was the one who told us of such a possibility."

"And he just told you of this ritual? He just handed over that information? How do you know if it's true?" Felicia sneered, raising herself upright.

"We have faith. You have seen only a shadow of what he is capable of. He has shown us what our future would look like. He controls the Mages."

Felicia looked at him in disbelief. The only Mage she had met was Andishmand, and he did not seem like he'd be the type to let someone like Demetrius control him, nor did he seem like he was under Demetrius' influence.

"You doubt us, but in the end, it will be our faith that will transcend."

"Or you could be entirely wrong and you'll just be murdering six women for nothing."

Another Apostle pushed his way forward, interrupting their conversation, saying, "It is time we returned to the Temple." They pushed the women forward, herding them through the tunnels until they reached a doorway. Through a seemingly simple door, they were back in the Temple, in their sacred space where they worshiped.

The vaulted ceilings were surrounded by long, narrow, stone panels. It was said that the Temple predated the palace, that it was used by the people that roamed these lands. The Temple had always been a place of mystery. Its rounded architecture and stonework was unlike anything that Felicia had seen. To be inside the sacred halls, typically reserved for the highest priests, should have been an honour. However, the Apostles had misused their authority and had claimed this place as their own. Her eyes roamed the unique etching, the carved markings similar to the ones on Lilith's skin, runes. Lines of them carefully carved into the walls and the flooring. She should not be in this place. She sneered at the Apostles, huddled in discussion. They should not be in this place.

An Apostle stopped mid-sentence, catching Felicia's glare. He walked up to her, tilted his head and leaned in.

"Our Lord may have ordered us to not break your body, but we will enjoy breaking your spirit." From this angle she could see the outline of his eyes, they seemed to glow in the shadows of their hood. She knew there was nothing she could say to spare the rest of the women. She was utterly at their mercy, and the Apostles had none. He leaned back, signalling for his apprentice, and a grey robe came rushing to the call.

"Yes, my master?"

"I think it is time we remind them of their place. Bring me the muzzles." The grey robe opened a chest and pulled out six metal and leather contraptions. The Apostle pulled Felicia close. "Open your mouth."

Felicia hesitated. She had to remind herself they were not able to harm her body, and if they desired to break her spirit, they had clearly underestimated her childhood with the general. The grey robe brought the leather contraption to her mouth, making her bite onto a metal rod as he bound the strap around her face.

"You all will wear this muzzle to learn your place. You will stand as we recite our scripture, and you will not know rest until we are done. We, too, will face punishment for using the traitor's dark arts. We will all suffer retribution to atone for our sins. For it is those that are righteous who will inherit this world, for our Lord will be the divine reckoning."

The women were lined up, each muzzled, and shaking with fear. The Apostles and their apprentices all knelt before them, reaching their hands to the sky. The centre Apostle, the one across from Felicia, brought a book out from his robe, opened the cover of their sacred words, *Heart of the Abyss,* and began to read.

"The old gods have forsaken us, plagued these lands by their negligence, but he has come to restore our strength. He has come to free us, to guide us, and to give us purpose." The crowd of robed men recited these words.

"It is through our loving devotion and gospel that we will save our people, for we are the Lord's disciples. Our dark master will restore us to our former glory." They recited these words as if their voices were one. It seemed that they had organized a set of rules and interpretations of what Demetrius had shared with them, and this would become the governing structure of their new world. Usually, in her cell, when they had spoken, she ignored them. Their rambling would fade into noise. But now, facing them, she listened and judged. To her, they were so immersed in their beliefs that nothing she could do or say would persuade them to view from another's opinion. She just had to endure.

For hours she stood beside the other women, whose bodies were already exhausted, listening to these men prattle on and on. Her legs were shaking, reaching that point where her body was unable to stand any longer. Silently, she was thankful that Ivy no longer had to bear this torture. To her left, one of the women buckled and collapsed, making the head Apostle pause.

"Bind them, so they remain standing." His voice croaked from his endless chatter. "This is as hard for us as it is for you."

Felicia snorted and broke out into a muffled hysterical laughter. She would kill him. This sacred place would be filled with their blood. The Apostle ignored her, continuing his reading, as apprentices set up a rack to hold the women upright. This would be a long night.

Chapter 11
Prosperous Are Those That Conceal Their Sins

Lilith

"You've been giving me a suppressant in my sleep!" Lilith accused, throwing a pillow at Demetrius. He swatted the pillow away and leaned back in the corner chair in the bedroom, running his hand through his hair. His shirt was unkempt, and by the looks of it, he had been running his hands through his hair regularly. Three days had passed since her run-in with Felicia. Three days of pacing, in solitude, worrying about the prisoners at the Temple. Demetrius did not give her any more information, as usual. He'd only come by in the morning and give her a new book, then leave. The palace grounds had significantly increased in business. Servants that Lilith had never seen hustled through the garden, carrying various crates. Demetrius' ascension to the crown was approaching.

She risked going into the tunnels, venturing into unexplored areas for several minutes before turning around and rushing back. There was only so far that she could go before she heard a nagging inner voice reminding her of what she'd risk if she were found. The books Demetrius gave her focused more on legends than anything. Stories of mythical beasts and battles of ancient kings. She was thankful for anything to keep her mind off of hunger. No matter what she did, her magic never returned. She needed her summoning magic to get Andishmand's diary, but with every new morning was another delay in her plan.

He sighed, "You must be feeling famished. This is exhausting, Lilith, a waste of our time." It had been days since she was allowed outside of his room. Days since she started starving herself in order to manipulate him.

Lilith stood up, and the sudden motion caused her to see stars. Her hands braced on the bed as she waited for the dizziness to subside. Rough hands looped around her waist, while she heard the sounds of him breathing in her scent. She must have reeked since she hadn't bathed in a few days. Her hair felt greasy and tangled.

"A waste of time?" She couldn't string two thoughts together; she only thought about the hands touching her waist. She wanted to push him away, but didn't have the strength. "What do you hope will happen by keeping me prisoner?"

"I do not want to keep you here. I want you beside me. I want to touch you, and I want you to stop fighting me."

Lilith could easily give in. She didn't want to keep fighting, but she had been taken advantage of by him before, and she didn't want him to feel any satisfaction. "Why should I care for what you want? Look how you've treated me thus far."

"I could make you a deal. If you eat, I will grant you some freedom."

"A deal with you is what got me here. It is what killed Mistress Rhodes and probably Felicia. What about your sister? Did you kill her, too? The prisoners and the children, did you take their lives? Where are Taran and the others?"

"As I have told you before, I have sent my dear cousin to the encampment with the others. As for your friend, she is not dead. Yet. In fact, she's proving to be as stubborn as yourself. My half sister is keeping her company. I told you before their little attempt at escape proved fruitful. They have freed the children and some of the women."

"If I eat, I want them back. You must promise that you or your little followers will not harm them. I want the rest of the Apostles' prisoners released, and they are not to find replacements."

"I can persuade them not to lay a finger on the prisoners, but I'm afraid the prisoners will stay. They are, unfortunately, needed." Demetrius made for the living room. "You are quite bold to ask me to release the collateral. Knowing you three, you'll use the opportunity to escape or worse."

Lilith interrupted him, "Then you will watch me fade away. I refuse to be your puppet, and I'd rather die right here and now."

The prince groaned in frustration. "You will stop fighting me if I give you Felicia and Thalassa, and you will become my queen?" Lilith looked into his black eyes and nodded. He sighed. "I have my own conditions, a deal bound by magic. I will allow this if you promise you will not try to escape and that you'll willingly accept your role by my side."

Lilith scrunched her brows together. Escaping with Felicia was her plan. Her mind was open to him, so she had to be careful of her thoughts. "I will not fight you to leave this place. I will not try to escape from this place, as it stands. On the condition that you return my friends, Felicia and Lady Thalassa, to me, and you and the Apostles promise not to harm them or the rest of the prisoners. That goes for their apprentices as well." She held her ground, maintaining her eye contact with him. "I would also like the freedom to move about the palace."

"My coronation is approaching. We will be the new king and queen. I need to know that you will not try anything, that you will follow the ritual."

Lilith stayed silent for a while. The weight of this promise was heavy and would change her future, but also give her the power to make a change. By accepting her role as queen, she would have a chance at releasing Andishmand and the other Mages. On the other hand, she would be bound to Demetrius, not only through marriage, but also bound to his side as he ruled this kingdom. He had proven himself ruthless and untrustworthy. Yet, she was learning that she held power. No magic was needed to persuade him. She would weave herself so tightly around his mind that one slip up would cost him.

"I accept this arrangement, but I want my powers back. I want you to promise that you will not take them away. If you accept my terms, then my answer is yes." It was a risk to ask for so much, but he needed her more than she needed him and she would use that to her advantage.

The prince closed his eyes as he held her by the waist, calling up an ancient rune magic. Unlike with Lord Elwin, this magic did not burn her; it felt like silk draping along her skin. The presence of his magic coursing through her tingled like a sudden rush of coldness. It had been too long without feeling her own mana that she welcomed the intrusion. Around her wrists, she felt like there was a slight burn, an itch that she wanted to desperately scratch. Furrowing her brows, she looked at Demetrius, and his skin on his wrist and hands was giving off a faint amber glow, like hers. She stared in wonder as little markings appeared on her skin. Unlike her runes with Lord Elwin, she was able to stay conscious for this spell. The ebb and flow of mana coming from both of them made the air around them heavy. The magic gave off a sweet floral scent. Lilith tried to concentrate on the language, the chant that Demetrius was saying, but he was too quick, as if this was his mother tongue, his first language. It made Lilith pause, wondering how he had become so fluent in this speech. If this was something he was capable of, then why did he not help her with her own runes? His chanting came to an abrupt end, leaving them standing in the lingering traces of mana.

Looking at her wrist, another line of runes was inscribed below the old ones, closest to her fingers. She looked at his wrists and spied the same runes.

"You seem well-versed in rune magic. Suspiciously so," Lilith accused while glaring at him.

"A language I am familiar with, and yes, I could easily decipher your runes when we first met. Though I might add—even if I had intervened—Elwin used a powerful spell, one that even I could not undo."

"You could have told me from the start."

"If I did that, you would not have followed me here. However, I did not lie when I told you that the palace's library may hold some information on breaking rune curses."

"A library I have yet to see."

"You would have seen the library if you didn't always try to escape. I meant to take you there the first time I escorted you out, but you had other plans."

"Again, something you could have just told me. Instead of keeping secrets."

Demetrius hummed, "Yes, you're right. I guess there is no need to keep secrets from you any longer."

The way Lilith gasped, she had not expected him to admit that he was wrong. This was a spark of possible hope that he was folding.

He didn't let go of his hold on her, but enveloped them in a glowing blue mist. It felt like she was inside a cloud. She could only see his face as the mist surrounded them. She blinked, and her stomach bottomed out, then the mist dissipated.

They were in a new room. One that was much larger than her previous one. She felt hot under his gentle gaze and pulled back so that he would let go.

"Where are we?" She pried her eyes away from his face and looked around. They stood in the middle of a lounge area, two red couches flanking them on either side, as well as a table with four chairs. Behind the prince was a closed door. Behind where she stood was another closed door. It was similar in design to her own cage, the prince's room. This one had white stone flooring and cream walls with mounted orbs that lined the room.

"You'll see soon enough." He looked out the window. A soft rap of knocking interrupted Lilith's next question. A group of Apostles came in, dragging Felicia and Lady Thalassa. They were both covered in bruises, their clothes covered in grime, and they both looked exhausted.

Lilith gasped and went to stand, tripping on the chair as she stood. She fell forward, but rough hands caught her. "What have you done to them?" She reached for Felicia, angrily pulling out of Demetrius' grasp. The Apostles deposited the women on their own chairs around the table, as well as trays of food and water. Lilith clasped Felicia's hand and knelt beside her. "Felicia, can you hear me?" Felicia rested her head on her outstretched forearm. Her face was covered in a cold sweat.

"I held up my end of our deal. Now you hold up yours. Eat, Lilith." Demetrius loomed over her and pulled on her arm to stand.

"Look at them." She went to tend to her friend, but Demetrius was firm in her taking a seat. She struggled as he roughly dragged her back to her own chair.

"I don't care about them, I care about you. Now eat." They entered a silent battle of wills. Felicia let out a small whimper, causing Lilith to whip her attention to her. Lilith picked up her spoon and took a small sip of the hot broth. It tasted phenomenal. Her taste buds fired under the mixture of fine spices and herbs. She took another gulp of broth.

"Slow down. You'll make yourself sick."

Lilith didn't care. The sooner she could take care of her needs, the faster she could tend to Felicia and Lady Thalassa. She threw down her spoon and brought the bowl up to her lips, sipping the hot liquid. Her stomach felt heavy, swooshing with liquid. She went to Felcia and picked up the spoon. She gently placed spoon after spoon of broth into her mouth.

"You care so little for your sister," Lilith spoke bitterly.

"She is this vessel's half sister."

"She shares blood with you. She grew up with you. Doesn't that count for anything?"

"I spent only a blink of time with her." He pressed his lips together and went for the spoon beside Lady Thalassa's bowl. Lilith stopped, only to watch him spooning broth into his half-sister's mouth. Satisfied, she continued her care for Felicia.

"She needs medicine. They both do. They've been beaten, and their wounds will fester under their dirt. We need to bathe them and change them into clean clothes." She was trying her luck with Demetrius, but the worst he could do was deny her.

His eye was visibly twitching. "Fine." There was a sudden knock on the door, and in came an Apostle holding two small purple vials. He handed them to Demetrius and then turned his attention to the women.

"Once you are finished, I will escort you to the baths." The Apostle stepped back.

"I don't want you watching us bathe." Lilith spat at him.

"I'll take them. Please see that their wardrobes are stocked with clothes, and have more broth brought up." Demetrius uncorked one vial and tipped the contents into his half sister's mouth. He did the same with Felicia's vial. The Apostle's smile faltered for a brief second before resuming plastering the same eerie smile they all wore, and nodded. He disappeared as the women's bruising and cuts slowly faded. Felicia blinked a couple of times, as if entering her body once more.

"Lilith?" Felicia's voice was weak.

Lilith smiled and rubbed her friend's hand. "Yes. It's Lilith. Lady Thalassa is here, too." Slowly, strength returned to the ladies. Lady Thalassa looked pale and stayed quiet.

"Come." Demetrius went to lift his sister, who pushed him off. Lilith could tell from look on Tally's face that she would rather crawl than have his help, so Lilith went between Felicia and Lady Thalassa to support them both.

"Lead the way." She pointed her chin at the door and walked slowly. The bathroom was at the end of the hallway. She looked out of the windows, which overlooked a large stone court-yard surrounded by blooming pink trees. In the distance, she could see the consorts' building, which meant they were still on palace grounds. Demetrius opened up a wooden door and ushered the women inside. A large square bath was sunken into the floor, and the water was steaming. On a wall, there were robes on hooks, and on stools beside them were fluffy white towels. An adjacent wall had little spouts with small stools and barrels: the same setup as the women's bath at Skilheim.

Felicia and Lady Thalassa each took a seat on a small stool and turned to face Demetrius.

"We will not bathe with you watching." Lilith crossed her arms and stood beside an empty stool. "You can stand on the other side of the door."

Demetrius sighed and left the women. "Try anything, and they die," he hollered over his shoulder, closing the door on them.

"How did you get us out?" Feicia rounded on Lilith.

"I made a deal with him to release you both to me. The condition is that I would not try to fight him to leave, nor would I try to escape while this place stands." Lilith began removing her brown dress and sat on the stool, ready to scrub herself clean. "And I will become his queen."

"With only six of us left, they kept us in the sacred hall of the Temple, guarded by several apprentices. That night—it feels like forever ago. Lilith, we were able to free the children and a couple of the women. Beatrice was able to get out." Felicia picked up the floral soap, sniffing it in disgust. "You don't understand what it's like down there. What the Apostles did to us. I had to listen to them try to control the minds of children. We cannot stand by and let them do this."

Lilith held her finger to her lips. "We should be careful what we say and think in his presence." They glanced at the door. "Did you come out of the labyrinth of tunnels the same way you came in?" Lilith's skin was turning red from her aggressively rubbing her skin with the soap.

For the first time, Lady Thalassa spoke to them. "We entered through a panel behind a tapestry, on the landing between the third and second floor. When they found us, they escorted us to a different entrance on the main floor." Her voice dropped to barely audible. "You said you can't escape while this place stands, right?"

"Right, Lady Thalassa," said Lilith, the skin on her thighs bright red, as she kept scrubbing.

Lady Thalassa came over to her and stilled her hands. "Just call me Tally. Those who called me Tally are likely dead, and I don't want to forget." Lilith rinsed the suds as Tally continued, "I understand what you're planning, and I want to be included. I want revenge."

"We must free those held captive." Felicia gritted her teeth, lost in thought. "There's only four of them left. Ivy didn't make it out of the tunnels."

"Felicia..." Lilith wanted to apologize again for what happened. "It's my fault you're here. Really, it's my fault both of you are here. If I had not planned with the prince to come here, both of you would be safe. Tally, your mother's death..."

Tally interrupted her, "My mother's death was planned long before your involvement. An intentional move that he would have done with or without you. I need you to help me avenge her death." Lilith clenched her fingers and looked at her new line of runes.

"And we would have never known about the Apostles' prisoners," Felicia added. "I'm mad at myself for trusting the prince, but if it means we can do something about the Apostles, I'll come to terms with what happened. Eventually." Felicia and Tally washed the suds out of their hair and then headed to the bath. They stopped to watch Lilith, who was still scrubbing at her skin.

"I feel dirty. I chose to give myself to him before I knew how dangerous he could be." She rubbed her stomach raw and started to choke up. "He gave me the freedom to go through with it, and I chose wrong."

Felicia hugged her friend from behind. "We cannot change the past, but we can make amends by fighting for what's right. You are not the same person you were before this. You made a choice and it failed, but you can learn from it and choose not to let it hold you back. Felicia pulled Lilith to the bath. The steaming hot water stung Lilith's skin.

"I'm still drawn to him, pulled in by something connecting us. A spiritual tether, chaining us together. I cannot help myself, and I worry I'll lose myself by giving in to him. He told me the gods *made* me for him. If that is the case, what does that make me?" Lilith allowed herself to cry. She feared the words she said aloud.

"That makes you his temptation. He is deeply affected by you. We would not be in this bath right now if he had not given in to you and your demands. You have power over him, and you should use it not only to gain our freedom, but to get him to draw back the Void." Felicia eyed her friend.

"He doesn't control the Void. I think there's something else forcing the darkness to expand." Lilith looked nervously at the women.

"It might be true, or it could be another one of his lies. You need to find out more. Figure out what he knows. I'll work on the Apostles and how to get word out to your brothers," stated Felicia.

"As I've said before, we should be careful. Demetrius can read our minds. Without our mana, we can't protect ourselves from him. Knowing him, he's listening in on our conversation." Lilith tensed a little under the hot water. The sounds of a hushed conversation came from outside.

After a short knock, Demetrius cleared his throat declaring, "Time's up." The ladies towelled off and slipped on robes. They made their way to the door, discarding their old clothes in a pile.

Demetrius escorted them back to their room. "There are some fresh clothes in your room." Felicia and Tally went to inspect their room, leaving Lilith standing with Demetrius.

"Say your goodbyes; you are next door with me," said Demetrius, gently.

Lilith went to Felicia and gave her a quick hug. "I'll be back." The women nodded and watched as Demetrius pulled her in and enveloped them in a glowing blue mist.

Once back in his room, she headed into the bedroom, not making conversation with him. Inside her wardrobe, she found a couple of dresses, a night gown, and some underwear.

She hesitated to change, as Demetrius was watching her from the doorway. Still not speaking with him, she turned her back and slipped off her robe, quickly grabbing underwear and a silky dress. The fine pale lavender dress was cinched at the waist and flowed loosely to the ground. The sleeves were tight around the elbow and then flared out. A matching floral embroidered belt wrapped around her hips and draped to the tops of her feet.

Demetrius walked closer to her and offered her his hand. Once more the blue mist took them somewhere. She stood in front of a large set of doors, finely decorated with gilded molding.

"Another part of our deal." Demetrius pulled open the curved handle. "Access to the library." Rows upon rows of leather bound books graced dark wooden shelves. Scrolls were tucked into stone carved cubbies, with maps displayed in gold frames. Lilith craned her neck upwards, looking at the highest level of bookshelves, three levels up.

The library was teeming with people dressed in navy blue surcoats with white kirtles underneath. A leather belt hung at each waist with a set of keys dangling at their side. But what was unique were their soft, thick padded shoes. She watched as they moved around in silence, the shuffling of their feet only a whisper in the air.

A stout, cheerful man came scuttling over. "Prince Demetrius, may I be of service?"

"Lilith, this is Sir Ravanor, head librarian," the prince introduced them. Lilith couldn't help but smile at the short, jolly looking man. "So far all the recommended books on rune curses have fallen short of helpful information. Lilith has full access to any tomes that might be of use." The sounds of boots approaching from the hall made Lilith nervous. Two Apostles bowed their heads at their master, vying for his attention. "I will return to bring her back to her room." Demetrius followed the Apostles out, leaving Lilith alone with the librarian.

"If you'll follow, I'll show you our collection of books regarding runes." Sir Ravanor moved silently up one of the narrow staircases to the second level. He traveled through the maze of bookshelves, coming to an abrupt stop in front of a long row of thick leather bound books. Lilith scanned the titles, recognizing some of which she had already searched. He started pulling a few.

"These are ones that you have yet to read, ones that mention rune curses." It seemed that the prince had shared enough of Lilith's situation with Sir Ravanor.

"Do you have anything on the history of Mages?" Lilith put on her best innocent looking smile. Sir Ravenor's hand froze in front of the spine of a book. What Lilith knew about Mages was passed by word of mouth. The few texts that her father had only briefly mentioned them in relation to them passing along knowledge of magic.

"We have a vast collection written by Mages. In fact, a large portion of our magical references have been written by them."

"But are there any that discuss the history of Mages? A study of their own magic and abilities?"

Sir Ravanor's cheerful expression changed to one of nervousness. He looked around him. "There are diaries, but I am afraid those are not shared publicly. Why would my lady be in search of such texts? Maybe I could shed light on any questions you may have."

Lilith looked around her, noticing quick glances from the other librarians, and leaned in closer. "The prince has given me full access, correct?" Sir Ravanor's face flared red, sweat accumulating on his forehead.

"Yes, my lady."

"Then I've been granted permission to read all texts in this library, including those diaries."

"Y-yes." Sir Ravanor nodded, then slowly turned. Lilith trailed him up another staircase, to the furthest corner, where a large ornate gate blocked off any further access. One librarian, a slender woman with large round glasses, bowed as they approached. He placed the short stack of rune tomes on a nearby table and took his set of keys and unlocked the gate.

"This is our vault where we store our most valuable items. We are careful not to disturb these shelves and I must ask that you handle items with care." He leaned in to whisper something to the slender woman, who passed Lilith a set of crisp white gloves. "You must wear this, and only touch what I give you."

"Are there any rune books in this section?" Lilith wondered, donning the soft white gloves.

Sir Ravanor hesitated before admitting, "There are a few."

"Ones that could be useful to my search?" Lilith felt a rush of excitement as he opened the gate and stepped through. He didn't answer her last question, carefully closing the gate behind them. A familiar tang of magic fell heavy in the air around them. It was as if the books themselves leaked trails of mana. There were only a few rows of shelves, all encased in glass doors. No windows or natural light filtered into this space, only orbs of light, which burst to life as they walked past.

Lilith could see Sir Ravanor's hands trembling as he opened up a glass cabinet and pulled out a thin, black leather journal. One that was identical to Andishmand's. He handed her the diary, watching her with utmost focus.

"You may use the table to read. It cannot leave this section, and I will be here to observe." Sir Ravanor showed her to a little table and chair tucked at the end of a row of shelves, and a dimly lit orb flashed to life. Lilith tried to steady her heart racing, carefully flipping open the front cover.

Instantly, she recognized the penmanship. This was Andishmand's writing, with sharp curls making the text difficult to read.

Approximately a week after arrival (A.A.).

This place has a lightness, which makes it easy to breathe. I can feel this pull coming from the very earth beneath me. Such energy, such connection. Vast rolling hills and jagged mountains have become my new home.

I cannot recall why I'm here, why I woke up cold and alone. I feel such heaviness and imbalance. It took some time before I met another being, one that looked like me, only they felt empty to me. My feet ache, their skin blistering, bleeding and bruised. This is a first. A sensation so new, so refreshing.

The man that took me in, clothed and fed me. He said he followed a bright light that he had seen fall to the ground several nights ago.

Why does this man feel so absent of energy?

I watched as he went about his day, arduously performing his ritualistic duties, helping him haul water and tend to the dirt.

It was a shock that he could not feel the moisture hanging around him, nor could he transform the earth around him. When he saw what I could do, fear gripped his eyes. He called me names, creatures which sound familiar, but yet my memory is hazy. With time I taught him how to do as I do, how to harness the energy from the world and shape it into the elements. In secret, he shared my knowledge to his friends, to his family, and they, too, wanted more.

Four months A.A.

I was given a peculiar text. They couldn't read it, but I could. Runes. If they had this knowledge, why was it they knew nothing of Mana? I will search for more. Perhaps they were not the first to roam these lands. Perhaps there are people like me that have lived here once before.

These people are so curious, so desperate for knowledge. It was as if they, like me, didn't understand their existence. Yet, it seems the more I see of this world, I find hints of another life that once claimed these lands. Ruins overclaimed by time. The people speak of legends, but know nothing of their history.

Six months A.A.

My mind is filled with pain, a constant torment of images crashing into my memories. I remember details of my life before. Of my world, my true home. A man, whose power felt oppressive, whom I felt such a connection with, and I was his trusted friend.

Lilith devoured every page. She was completely consumed with Andishmand experiencing this world and the people that crossed his path. Word spread, village to village, of what he was teaching. He shared knowledge freely to ease the burden of people's duties. He moved freely, until he was taken to kneel in front of a man that claimed the land's authority. So began his time being used by the greed and desire for power. She felt sorry for Andishmand, whose intentions were pure. It was her kind that developed a hierarchy of magical abilities. Her people began to breed to pass down the strength of one's mana.

Andishmand went years assisting people desperate for more power, manipulating his compassion and kindness. In exchange, he gained status and riches. He became consumed with hoarding wealth and treasures. The more time he spent with her kind, the more influenced he became to develop his own desires.

For hours, Lilith flipped through each passage, muttering her feelings to Sir Ravanor, who became more and more engrossed in Lilith's excitement. As she would verbalize her disgust and annoyance, or speak her inner questions, he would give her more and more bits of information: who now were descendants of the ones that Andishmand helped rise to power, whose families had risen from poverty and, through their magical abilities, become kings and lords.

Andishmand was ageless, a mystery that fell from the sky. Towards the end of the journal, he finally found another: a being like him.

Lilith was eagerly reading one of the last diary entries when she felt a presence behind her.

"My prince." Sir Ravanor's face had become red, once again.

"I see you've managed to access the most interesting section of this library." She could feel the prince approaching and gently closed the diary, handing it back to the anxious librarian. She eyed the small row of journal spines in the glass case.

"A curious fascination." The prince followed her gaze and frowned.

"Until I came to Skilheim, I thought Mages were myths. Our own history of magic is always shrouded in mystery." Lilith nodded to Sir Ravanor and thanked him.

"Will we see you again, my lady?" Sir Ravanor smiled, walking them to the gate.

Lilith looked to the prince, who sighed. "She is permitted to come here whenever she wants." Lilith hid her smile.

Sir Ravanor scuttled off, pausing at a row of books, and quickly grabbed a thick leather tome. "My lady, I usually do not allow these books to leave, but since you are so curious about rune curses, I think you ought to read this." He handed her the worn brown book. Lilith felt a pull towards this book, as if the magic flowing from it was hers. Her fingers ran down the spine, making her hair stand up on the back of her neck. She cradled the book like it was a forbidden treasure.

"Thank you again, Sir Ravanor." Lilith gave him a genuine smile.

Once outside the library, the prince cornered her. "I feel jealous of the librarian."

"Yes, well, he doesn't pressure me to become his wife, or suppress my magic. Nor does he have a dungeon full of helpless women."

The prince let out a frustrated groan. "Lilith, you will learn to love the man I am. I can finally drop my mask and show you who lays beneath."

She scoffed, walking up the main staircase. "You let those Apostles hurt children and women. How can you allow them to do that?"

"The Apostles are a tool...but I will consider your words." He halted his steps. "Once we are united, I'll give them to you."

"You must be out of your mind if you think it would be that easy, if you think they would bow down to me." She stood on the step above him. "No. There is only one way this will end for them. If you are to make me your queen, then propose to me soaked in their blood. Offer their sacrifice to me, and I'll consider our proposal real. Free those in the dungeon, and I will stay by your side." She wanted vengeance, more than she valued her own freedom. Once she had satisfied her rage, she would reclaim everything that had been taken from her.

They walked in silence up through the queen's wing. "I want to visit Felicia and then read this book."

Demetrius smirked, while Lilith's attention drifted to the contents of the book she carried. "I have sent for food to be delivered, and I will see you tonight, *my goddess*." He tucked a strand of her hair behind her ear and then disappeared.

She closed her eyes and exhaled slowly before raising her hand to knock on Felicia's door. This world might have a chance, with her as queen.

Chapter 12
The Book

Felicia

A knock at the door had both Felicia and Tally jumping.

"It's me," Lilith's voice came through the white doors. Felicia ran over to open them, letting in an excited-looking Lilith carrying a large, brown leather book. An aura seemed to swirl around her, making Felicia take several steps back.

"What is that?" Felicia pointed to the suspicious book. It felt as if Lilith was surrounded by a cloud of dread. "Whatever it is, it's not good."

Lilith gently placed the book on a nearby side table as the women gathered around it. Felicia could see Lilith's beaming smile, while she and Tally watched with concern.

"You went to the library," Tally stated, hovering her hand over the book. "It's a relic. How did you get this?"

Lilith chuckled, "I made a friend. A kindred spirit."

Tally gaped, "Sir Ravanor?"

"He's fantastic."

"He hates me. I don't know what sort of charm you pulled over him, but I've never seen anyone leave with a relic. Unless you're the king."

Lilith smirked, her eyes locking with Tally's as she said her next words, "I'm special." She threw Tally's accusation that Lilith was nothing special in her face. Tally blushed and looked away. Felicia nodded, impressed at her retort. She scanned Lilith, feeling a change within her friend.

Lilith carefully opened the tome. The worn leather gave off a distinct aroma that left a bitter taste at the back of the throat.

Felicia could see lines of runes, surrounded by sketches. Though she could not read the ancient text, she inspected the images. A depiction of wrists with bleeding runes covering the skin caught her eye. Lilith turned page after page, muttering under her breath. Felicia looked at the various pictures, and runes making up circles, designs of magic, so similar to Lilith's summoning spell.

Lilith let out a little gasp, pushing up her own draping sleeves of her lavender dress. She explained nothing, but Felicia knew this was a significant discovery. The lines of runes closest to Lilith's hand matched the ones in the passage. Felicia's eyes went from text to Lilith's skin and back.

"This is it. This is my curse," Lilith whispered, stunned by the revelation.

"What does it say?" Tally patiently waited. Like Felicia, she inspected Lilith's runes.

Lilith huffed, ignoring Tally while she continued to read. After a few minutes, she turned the page and flipped back to the page she was on before. "It's a curse to test the wearer's worthiness."

Stand in honor, and be unshaken. For the might of the bearer shall be bound, held by the holy words. Yet when one's worth is embraced, more shall be revealed than fate hath foretold. Tread with humility. Power is not granted to those who have not mastered its weight. When the soul is made ready, the flow shall return. When the flame is made pure, the dam shall yield. Yea, the darkness doth hunger for the light. Endurance. Destruction. Metamorphosis. This is the sacred balance of all things.

Lilith impatiently flipped through the pages, skimming the text. Felicia and Tally stood together, patiently waiting until Lilith was ready to talk.

"I know all this. Andishmand had transcribed my runes in Skilhiem, but all this says is that the curse will be broken if the bearer becomes worthy of wielding their power. Who can define their own worthiness? I feel pretty worthy." Lilith let out another frustrated groan.

Felicia took a seat on the couch. "A part of you recognizes your internal conflict. Look at what you've gone through. What we've gone through. Speaking for myself, I've lost most of my compassion. I wouldn't think twice about burning this palace and everyone in it to the ground. Perhaps this curse can feel your resolve."

"But there were times where my runes felt like they were fading, and in those moments, some of my power was unleashed." Lilith looked as if she were reliving a memory. "When I attacked Bear at Skilheim, it felt like I was free."

"What was going through your mind before you attacked?"

"It felt like I was the hand of judgment. What he was doing was wrong, and I had to intervene."

Felicia leaned back, thinking aloud. "You acted, though others did not." Felicia remembered the night Lilith told her everything. Lilith had almost killed Bear to protect Verrona. "Look at your emergence. You told me, after, you felt so sure of your actions, but you lost control. Maybe it's waiting for something."

"Maybe you haven't been pushed to your breaking point," Tally interrupted. "It sounds like, in those times where your runes faded, you were defending or protecting something you feel steadfast about. There has always been something preventing you from breaking entirely. Only when that happens can you meet the singular form of your existence. Your inner purpose."

They all sat on the couch, slouched in frustration.

Felicia asked Lilith to read the text once more, mulling over the passage. "Endurance. Destruction. Metamorphosis. What if these are three requirements that must be completed? I mean, it's highlighted at the end, so clearly it's important."

"Does this," Lilith waved around her, "not count as endurance? We've gone through so much. Even if you're on to something, it seems unlikely that I would have to go through a phase of destruction."

"Endure the hardship of living without your powers, and, as you said, become the hand of judgment," Tally added.

"I'm not sure if revenge is what this curse has in mind," Felicia countered.

"Would it be a terrible thing for me to seek revenge? To see this all fall down?" Lilith lay her head back and closed her eyes, while Felicia watched her. Would it be so bad to stand by and watch Lilith unfold and embrace her darkness? She made her quiet observations. The three women, each having suffered enough for a lifetime, all of them daughters of privilege, had endured more than their share of misfortune and pain. She could help Lilith break her curse and unleash her upon the leeches who take. She had nothing to lose.

"You need to find out if there's more to this book. Find out if there's a history of people who have broken this curse." Felicia rose. "While you were away, Lady Thalassa and I came up with a plan."

"Please, drop the formalities," Tally pleaded with Felicia. "We can assume that all letters coming in and out of the palace are being monitored, if not controlled. However, my brother has greatly underestimated the consorts. They would have already established a way to reach their families outside of the palace. I can be sure of that. If we were to find them and make a bargain with them, they should be able to send word to someone we trust on the outside."

Full of excitement, Felicia interjected, "We just need a way to reach the consorts. Prince Demetrius will soon have his coronation. It would be the perfect opportunity to create alliances."

Tally talked over Felicia, "We forget that they are prisoners as well."

"We also need ears on the outside. Someone who can tell us what's going on."

"There must be some who oppose what is happening."

Lilith's eyes bounced between the two women. Felicia felt a rush of excitement. They'd already reached rock bottom. Things had to turn in their favour.

"We have nothing to lose."

CHAPTER 13
MOUTH OF THE WICKED

Lilith

Lilith woke up perfectly warm and content, and she wasn't alone. Facing away from her was Demetrius. She wanted to reach out and run her hands through his fluffy, dark blue hair; it looked incredibly soft. She caught her hand drifting over, hovering mid-air as she realized he was shirtless and also sound asleep in her bed. She could make out the scattered scars running down his back, weaving along bulges of muscle.

She wanted to push him off the bed, but also nuzzle closer to him. With a deep inhale, she breathed him in. His smell reminded her of her days under the willow tree, daydreaming with no care. She wanted to savour this scent, but hated that it reminded her of everything she'd lost, and everything he put her through. The very sight of him stirred simultaneous feelings of loathing, and of longing.

"You know, you might explode from the frantic swinging of your emotions," murmured Demetrius, rolling over to look at her.

"Why must you sleep here?" She glared at him.

"You looked so peaceful while you rested, that it made me want to join you. Sleeping next to you is much more restful," he stated, as he pulled up the covers around them and closed his eyes. To her annoyance, sleeping next to him had given her the best sleep she'd had in a long time, but he had crossed a line.

"You cannot sleep here and pretend we're okay. " She sat up and started to leave. His rough hands grabbed her wrist and gently pulled her in closer to him.

"I seem to remember that you agreed to be my queen. I refuse to sleep elsewhere."

"I seem to remember that you agreed to give me back my magic, yet here I am, powerless."

With a groan, he let out his exasperation, "You've certainly restored your sass. Fine. I have a hard time denying you. Show me that I can trust you, and then you'll earn your mana back."

"What would you have me do?" Lilith pulled her arm free. She would do anything to get an ounce of magic flowing through her veins.

"Today is the eve before my father's abdication and my ascension to the throne. As a celebration, we will be holding a ball. I want you to be there, by my side. Do this, and I will grant you *some* mana back."

"You want me to pretend to smile at all the lords and ladies? Act like I'm here willingly? You're kidding. Your father has sent thousands to the encampment. Every day, the cost of preparing soldiers to battle the darkness is rising, and our supplies are dwindling. People are struggling. Why would you think a frivolous ball would be a wise decision?" Lilith went to stand by the window. She could make out the warped tree standing at the centre of the pristine garden.

Demetrius moved off the bed and started to dress. "You are coming into the fold of my plans midway, and I'm not asking you to smile or pretend to be anything but yourself. I'll have someone get you, Felicia, and Thalassa ready." He sighed and gave her one last look before heading out of the room.

"Wait." Lilith jogged to meet him. "Why are you allowing Felicia and Tally—Lady Thalassa—to come?"

Demetrius smirked, never a good sign, as he replied, "Because separating you three has so far proven to be a headache. I'd rather have you all in my sight, and I think you all need to understand my perspective."

"What do you mean?"

"I made you a promise: to show you what people are like and why their lives are not worth saving."

An array of fresh fruit, baking, and cured meats waited in the shared space between the rooms in Felicia's and Thalassa's quarters. Lilith was casually grazing when Felicia and Tally came out. They both had gained a bit of colour since the day before.

Lilith took a sip of her juice as they sat down. "Morning. I got dropped off here. The soon-to-be king will be hosting a ball tonight, and we're expected to be there. In return, I'll be given back some mana."

"What about us? Will they return ours if we play our part tonight?" Felicia popped a ripe berry into her mouth. "This could be our chance to tell someone that we're being held here against our will."

"Yeah, and who will believe us? We're dressed as guests and we're not tied up or held hostage." Tally rolled her eyes and filled a plate, sitting next to Lilith. "We could always escape."

"You guys could, but I made a binding agreement that I have to be here," Lilith interjected. Then she really thought about the idea of them leaving. "No. Really. You both should use this opportunity to get out of here. Get to the encampment and let them know what's happening here."

Felicia grabbed a bun and relaxed on the couch near them. "First, if you think we're going to leave you here, you're out of your mind. Second, my mother will not believe a word we say. Maybe Lord Helmer, but he could be in on the whole thing. Who all is coming to this ball?"

Lilith shrugged, "I didn't think to ask. I was more preoccupied with waking up to find him in my bed."

Felicia and Tally both stopped eating. "Did he force himself on you?" Felicia asked her.

"No, he didn't touch me." Lilith looked away. "But there's a part of me that still desires him."

"Then use him. Do what you have to, to get yourself free." Felicia resumed eating. Lilith started to plan. She could seduce Demetrius, gain his trust, and restore her powers.

"Do you think they've made it out of the city?" Tally asked innocently. "The ones that escaped. Do you think those children are safe now?"

Felicia and Lilith shared a look; they were not optimistic, but Felicia set her food down and gave Tally her full attention before answering, "I hope they were able to find friends, people that would help them get safe."

Tally's hands were shaking as she spoke, "But..."

"But the people in this city can be cruel. They see a few women and children covered in filth, sharing their stories of where they were and who had them. It is unlikely that strangers would entangle themselves with their mess. For all we know, they could have had friends who would shelter them. I like to imagine the women and children somewhere far away from Vanguard," Felicia continued. "I'd like to think Beatrice is back to sharing her story and ours. She will tell others what is happening here."

"I imagine that they found safety with each other. They became a little family," Lilith spoke. They looked at her, shocked by her optimism. Was it a foolish dream? Probably, but she hoped it was true.

With a smile, Felicia agreed, "Yes. I can picture it now, the four children being looked after by the three women. Somewhere far from the city."

"And Beatrice is at the encampment. Maybe they know the truth of our situation." Lilith wondered if her father knew the truth. If they were coming to save her. However, if they came Demetrius would just use them as leverage to keep her in line. Her father was smart, he'd realize the risk of coming here. He had to.

After they had finished eating, they wandered around the room. The three of them discussed back and forth, ways to escape, forming plans, and bouncing ideas off of each other. By late morning, three women barged into their room. The ladies introduced themselves as stylists for the consorts. Lilith promptly forgot their names, and watched as a flurry of activity filled her space.

They summoned dresses and all sorts of styling products to get the girls ready. Tally was used to this pampering and relaxed under their touch. Felicia and Lilith, on the other hand, had neglected their beauty regime during their time in Skilhiem, enough to cause the stylists to gasp dramatically when the women revealed their body hair, dry skin, and unkempt nails.

The two women rolled their eyes, annoyed by the superfluous standards of beauty at the palace. Their body hair was the last thing on their minds after a day's worth of brutal training, not to mention their last few weeks of being tortured. The stylist with long lavender hair grimaced as she started with hair removal.

"I would rather run the course non-stop for a whole day than go through this torture." Felicia winced as someone pulled her long gold hair. Lilith found herself relaxing during the entire process.

"You know, I quite like this." Lilith chuckled as Felicia yelped. "Rather than how we've been treated so far, I can indulge in being pampered. I would rather wear these gorgeous dresses and head to a ball, than stay prisoner in his room." By the end, they had been waxed, scrubbed, and oiled. Running a hand down her arm, Lilith felt her smooth, soft skin and marveled at her reflection. Gone was the girl who was covered in mud after roaming the forest; in her place was a divine being with glowing skin.

Unfortunately, this pampering only enhanced the look of her runes. The stylist put her hair up in an intricately braided, half-up, half-down style with long, curled tendrils draping around her face. She was intentionally given a more royal look to match the event and her new role. The stylists tried to hide her runes with an illusory incantation, but the strength of the ancient magic was too much. Instead, they hid it with some makeup, but the faint dark markings were still noticeable.

Tally had picked out the dresses to suit their image. Felicia wore a light turquoise gown with long flowing sleeves and a rounded neckline. Her golden hair flowed in soft curls down her back. Tally selected a conservative charcoal grey dress with a draped silhouette.

They both gave Lilith a mischievous grin as she held up what would be her dress against her frame. It was a more traditionally cut, gold and deep, midnight blue dress that would hug her waist, and would then cascade to the ground. The sleeves were so long that the flowing ends lightly skimmed the floor. Lilith assessed the wide neckline, imagining herself wearing it. She could envision the exposed top of her cleavage displayed and that was a little too risqué for her comfort. Lilith brushed her thumb across the material. The fine gold embroidered detailing achieved the look of a queen. From the bottom of the skirt, it looked as if a gold tree blossomed from the ground; its branches and leaves stretched upwards towards the waistline, with scattered leaves embroidered around the skirt. Gold-feathering rose up the chest, with thick, silk gold accents lining the edges. Tally brushed her hand over the dress, commenting that it felt velvety soft. Lilith scanned the detailing up close, lost in wonder at its sheer beauty.

"Uh, I appreciate your input. This dress is stunning, but I'm not sure if this is what I'm going for. I was hoping for something more inconspicuous. Something that would not cause me to stand out so much. Couldn't I wear something like Tally's?" Lilith motioned to cover her breasts.

"Just trust us and put it on. You will be standing next to Demetrius, the future king. What you wear will define your status and role. If you want to hide, then people will see you as inferior. What you should be doing is drawing attention to yourself. Your actions and beliefs will shape this kingdom.

Only you have persuasion over the King." Tally pushed Lilith into her room.

Alone, she scowled at the dress once more before disrobing. The stylists helped them into some undergarments that would support the gowns, but this dress was more restricting than armour. Lilith wished she could hide a dagger somewhere, but the best she could do was hide a butter knife, making her think otherwise. She stretched her arm across her back awkwardly when she felt a shadow of a presence behind her, and knew that he had arrived. Large hands tugged at her dress.

"Allow me to help." His hands lightly drifted over her bare skin, shooting a thrilling sensation of desire right into her lower belly. Her cheeks blushed, turning flaming hot. Lilith willed herself to steady her breaths, calming herself with distracting thoughts of rune translations—anything to keep her mind busy. Time felt like it was moving impossibly slow, making her inwardly curse the extensive lacing this dress had.

As if Demetrius was taking his sweet time, he finally finished tying the back of the dress. Even with his hands removed, she felt a whisper of his touch along her skin. She turned to face him and heard the soft click of the lock on her door latching. He was dressed in a fine midnight blue overcoat with gold detailing, accompanied by a matching vest and pants that made him look every bit the king. Gone were his dark black eyes; instead, his icy blue eyes trailed over her body.

"We match," Lilith said flatly. "Did you spy on our thoughts?"

"I only took a glimpse at what you'd be wearing." Demetrius' palm rested against her waist. "You look beautiful, my queen." He walked her backwards until her back lightly pressed against the wall adjacent to the door.

"I'm not your queen. Yet. As for tonight, we shall be on our best behaviour if you give all of us some of our mana back." She crossed her arms in front, which only lifted her exposed cleavage. He blatantly stared at her.

"A kiss." Demetrius leaned in, breathing her in. "I will do as you ask in exchange for a kiss." Lilith took her time, having already made up her mind, but wanting him to suffer. She wanted to seduce him, use him. She slowly ran her hands down the front of his silk vest. Demetrius leaned into her touch, captivated by her. She tilted her face up and brought her lips to hover just below his. He smirked at her effort.

Just from the anticipation of feeling his lips, she had a flurry of flutters exploding at the base of her stomach. She could feel his heart beat through her fingertips, and in that moment, time seemed irrelevant. Confliction still held a grip on her rationale, and the seemingly endless reasons why she should loathe him. But, as much as she tried not to, she desired this man. This being, who seemed so willing to bend to her. He had stated he was unable to change, but given the distress he'd displayed these last few days, she'd reckon that was a lie he had told himself. This man was tormented. How often had she seen him dishevelled? How restless had he become because she was being stubborn? If she asked him to drop to his knees and worship her right now, she knew he wouldn't hesitate.

She smiled as her lips found his, and the little moan that escaped him felt ever so satisfying. With a little nibble of his lower lip, she felt his hand clench at her waist. How far could she take this? She, who has no power, held all of it. Usually, she had kept her eyes closed, but she kept her eyes on him, assessing every little twitch and furrow of his features. A dance of the tip of her tongue across that smooth skin made his brows tense. He was savouring this as much as she was.

His eyes opened, finding her amused observation. Tormenting him was almost too easy. Demetrius pulled away, his focus bouncing from her eyes to her lips in a silent question.

A pause, suspended by a mix of concern and curiosity.

One. Two. Three heartbeats.

Then, his lips crashed down on hers.

Their mouths moving as one, exploring each other in a craze of lust. All that tension she'd been carrying, every ounce of rage seemed to fizzle as he pressed his body close to hers. Lilith relished the taste of him, the feeling of his warm fingers trailing over her dress. She envisioned him taking things further, the feel of his body weighing over her, pressing into her. It took everything in her to stop from moaning. In her mind, nothing else could explain this unearthly need to be with him, as it felt like his very soul walked with hers.

His hands trailed slowly up her dress, pushing it up inch by inch. Warm fingertips left her skin tingling as he moved higher up, caressing her over her lace underwear, and then pressing his fingers over her sensitive spot. Her lace panties were soaked. She was thrilled by her imagination of what could be. What could exist between them if they found a compromise? His fingers dipped under the lace, as his tongue continued its conquest, coating them with the evidence of her reaction to him.

She wanted this and wanted him.

"Say yes to me." He ripped through the lace–a sensation that was curiously stimulating–and dipped two fingers inside her. That moan she had worked so hard to stifle escaped.

She rolled her head back as he continued to pump into her, feeling him rest his head on her chest. This felt so much more intimate than before. This was both of them, exposed and vulnerable. Her heart was beating wildly, urging her passion. For a moment, she forgot their feud and differences. She forgot her bitter resentment towards how her friends were treated. Only this mattered. His warmth feeding hers.

"Say yes, my goddess, and I will worship you." His fingers drove into her in a consistent movement. She desperately wanted to roll her hips. That pressure was building; somehow, he knew what she liked and what she needed.

The words were halfway out of her mouth, so she kept them sealed. *It would be so easy to give in to him.*

He drove her to the brink of ecstasy, a rapture so pure and divine that her eyes rolled back and her fingers dug into his shoulders. His hands widened her stance, giving him more access. She was close.

A sudden sound at the door made her jump. "Are you doing okay in there?" Tally knocked at the door.

Between pants, Lilith cleared her throat. Demetrius didn't pause in his pursuit. "I'm good. I just need a few minutes." The last word ended in a small gasp, as Demetrius kissed her neck. Her ears had to work hard to listen past the wild beats of her heart and focus on the sounds behind the door. She could hear Tally moving away.

From him, pure mana pulsed into her centre. The threads of mana sank into her bones, into her blood. He didn't pause as he restored her magic. Her body felt hot and sensitive to the invasion of unexpected magical energy, that it overwhelmed her senses. She could feel the sweat forming over her brow, and his breath on her neck. The warm sensation of her magic flowing through her pushed her over the edge, and he was greedily taking everything she gave. She bit her lip to stifle the moan that escaped her throat, her hips rolling against him, and her hands tangled through his styled hair. Energy, in its purest form flowed readily through her veins, extending from her core to the very tips of her fingers. Her pupils dilated as that feeling of pleasure crested to her release. Every muscle seemed to relax, liquifying in an explosion of bliss. For a moment, she felt complete. As if the bonds that held her back no longer existed. For a split second, she felt whole.

Her body trembled as she came down from her high. How could she feel this good? How could he make her feel this rush?

Demetrius stood upright and neatly arranged the skirt of her dress. He didn't rush to back away, but licked off his fingers with a satisfied smirk.

He watched her under his eyelashes, waiting for her to say something.

"That was more than one kiss." Her heart was beating like crazy, as she felt her magic seep into her soul once more. Immediately, she built a mental wall to protect herself.

"Absolutely ravishing. One kiss could not do justice," he replied. "Give me your hand." She placed her right hand in his, and from his overcoat, he pulled out a golden ring. Tiny golden leaves were woven into a circle with mesmerizing pink gems set between the weave. He placed the ring on her left ring finger. Immediately, she felt a hum settle over her skin.

"Is this crystal?"

"I took it from the Ruins of Thurndun. From the store. And I found this." In his palm, from that place in between, a necklace appeared with a pink crystal. Panic flared across her face for a fleeting second. Was this the necklace she had picked up? But as she looked closer, she could see it was not the same one that she had stored in her pack, the same pack that was hidden with the journal. Demetrius' brows scrunched for a second.

"It's beautiful," she said, as she opened the clasp and put it on. She looked like a royal, a queen. That hum from the crystal intensified, forming a light headache behind her eyes, and it was all she could do to ignore it.

"I am glad that you approve." He tilted his head to the side. "I can feel your magic flow through your veins, but you shut me out almost immediately after having it back."

"As you have said, 'trust is earned.' I need to protect myself from being taken advantage of again. Perhaps in time you'll be allowed in, once you show me that I can trust you."

"Ever the strategist's daughter. There are few that are as quick to adapt as you are. You will be a glorious queen. There is no one else whom I'd want by my side, as my wife." Lilith blushed at his declaration, though she kept silent in her response.

"We should get going." Demetrius forced himself to step away and unlocked the bedroom door.

"You were gone for such a long time, Lilith. I thought..." Felicia came to an abrupt stop with Tally by her side. They had finished getting ready and were busy snacking on platters of bite-sized appetizers. Both women took in the pair, Demetrius in his matching suit, with Lilith looking ever the radiant queen and bride.

"What is this?" Lilith dismissed Felicia's concerned look and picked up a small piece of stuffed mushroom.

"I had someone deliver food to keep up your strength."

Lilith was about to take a bite, but then eyed the food suspiciously. "Does this have a suppressant?"

Demetrius picked up a piece and plopped it into his mouth, slowly chewing to savour the flavour. Lilith shoved her portion in, relishing the rich complexity of the combined ingredients. She picked up a thin flute of a bubbling drink, watching Demetrius take a sip of his. Only when he had taken a sample himself did Lilith indulge. Felicia and Tally had no power themselves, so they had nothing to lose if it were compromised.

Having had his fill, Demetrius strode to the window overlooking the garden that had been transformed for the event. As they ate, Felicia came to Lilith's side and in hushed tones asked, "You have your mana back?"

Lilith nodded.

"Are you okay? Did he...?"

Lilith knew that Felicia understood the cost of re-acquiring her powers. "I'm fine," she said as she shook her head to answer her implied question.

"It's time we head over," interrupted Demetrius. He eyed the three women. "I have restored Lilith's powers and will restore yours if you abide by the rules. Do not try anything. No attempt at escape. You will not find friends amongst the crowds, so it is futile to ask for help. You are to stay with Lilith. Wander, and you will meet your end. Are we clear?"

"You said there will be no allies here. Then who will be in attendance?" replied Tally. Out of the four of them, she had grown up amongst many of the usual guests and was familiar with the typical people that frequented royal events. To say there would be no allies would mean these were not the normal crowd.

Demetrius grinned, "Some fresh blood."

"That doesn't sound good. You'll guarantee we will be safe?" Felicia asked him.

"Only if you do as you're told." He opened the entrance, where several guards stood at attention; they each held a black banner with a white oak tree on long, white, wooden spears. These banners matched the new stoles the Apostles wore, a new insignia of the approaching reckoning of the Dark King Demetrius.

With the squad, they made their way down to the throne room.

The ball displayed all manner of luxuries that the royals could afford. An elaborate assortment of food, servants pouring limitless bottles of wine, and all sorts of entertainment were stationed around the enormous throne hall. Little balls of light drifted around the glass ceiling like fireflies. The large oak tree had been decorated with soft, glowing lanterns. At its base and around the throne was a beautiful display of ivory flowers.

There was very little time to take in the stunning display when the chorus of music stilled. The very air stilled as they made their way to the entrance. The guards that escorted them down had walked further into the crowd, where the murmuring conversations still filled the air. As the guards stood at their posts, they banged their banners on the ground in rhythm, making the vibrations travel through the white stone ground and stilling all other manner of sound.

Demetrius held Lilith's hand delicately over his and walked through the crowd. At their entrance, the crowd split, forming an aisle to the throne. His face gave little emotion, which Lilith tried to mirror, but her nerves were wreaking havoc through her. She focused on walking as gracefully as possible in her ridiculous heels. So many eyes were on them. The hall was packed, shoulder to shoulder. The guests smiled at Demetrius as he glided ever so slowly, making sure that everyone had their focus on him. On her. While he received many smiles, she looked to the nearest face and received unimpressed glares. She was an unknown amongst them, a nobody. Even dressed to match Demetrius, she was held in low regard.

Ahead of her, she spied three chairs made of polished dark wood, which sat beside the throne; they contrasted with the aged white wood the throne was made from. They were still in the style of keeping for a royal, ornately carved with high backs, but there was a clear distinction between the new king and the others. King Amadeus and his queen sat on two of the dark wood chairs, as their eyes drifted stoically over the crowd, lost in a daze. Some of the guests walked over, bowing, but neither of the royals engaged in conversation. It was as if they were wearing a mask of indifference; perhaps they were unable to speak. This was the first time she had met them since they had arrived.

As a child, she had come to the palace only once, but she was never to venture far. Only once had she met King Amadeus; it was just after her mother had passed, and her memories of their meeting were as vivid as a dream. She remembered him as welcoming and kind, but for some reason, a plethora of staff hired by her father had kept her separate from the royals. She had never run into Demetrius or any of his siblings. A smile at them caused no reaction. Lilith's eyes widened as she turned to face the weight of the eyes. Would the same happen to her? A faint ringing sound started in her ears. This was too much. Too difficult to face, this crowd of judgmental people that must mean something to Demetrius. She had to make a good impression, win these people over. That panicked feeling made it feel like her chest was collapsing in on itself, and her breath came out in short bursts. *Breathe. Just breathe.*

The figures of Felicia and Tally making their way up to the front of the room became a blur to her. She could just make out them bowing to her, and as Tally stepped off to the side, Felicia hesitated.

She leaned in and whispered to Lilith, "You are more powerful than anyone here. You are by his side, not them. Make it count for those who are left in the dungeon. Give them a chance."

With a smile on her face, Felicia stepped off to the side and stood among the crowd. Demetrius didn't react to Felicia's words; he simply lowered Lilith to the chair beside him, as he faced the crowd to stand in front of the throne.

"To King Demetrius!" someone in the front yelled.

"All hail the King!" Shouts chanting their joyous devotion filled the room. While the official coronation would be held tomorrow morning, those here already pledged their allegiance.

"Thank you, everyone, for coming today." Demetrius stood to address the crowd. He kept talking through his prepared speech, but Lilith's attention focused on the attendees. Brown hair and brown eyes. Sir Prichard was here, along with other people she recognized at the failed rebel meeting back in Tilton. The thought of hanging in the basement came back to her. Who helped him? Did they recognize her? Her eyes drifted from face to face; some she remembered seeing at that restaurant on her failed trip with Danai. *Why are they here?* Green hair, grey eyes. The apothecary. She stood hand in hand with a man with long violet hair. They were both dressed in finery befitting someone above an apothecary's station. Was he a noble? The green-haired woman clearly didn't recognize her. She gave the king a hopeful smile, listening to Demetrius.

More faces that she recognized filled her view. The room was filled with nobles, but very few Lords. Lord Elwin and Lord Helmer were absent. None of the former councilmen, no consorts or family were in attendance.

"As we craft a new dawn, we will rely on our friends to set the new example. In return, you shall reap the delights that this era has to offer. May we embark on a new future, one borne of darkness, where only those who have the will to survive, inherit true power." Demetrius spoke with authority, a shepherd calming his sheep.

The crowd erupted in cheers, though Lilith viewed them with confusion. Could they not see his lies? She quickly neutralized her facial expression to one of a proud, graceful smile, one she had practiced with Felicia and Tally, until it looked almost natural.

The music roared back to life, with playful notes from flutes and stringed instruments. Kitchen staff brought out platters of expensive-looking finger foods that looked delicately refined. Smells of liquor, herbs, and something else tinted the air, something off-putting, but she couldn't quite recognize the scent.

Demetrius leaned over to his parents. With hushed tones, he pulled them to awareness. The light behind their eyes flickered to life as they blinked in their surroundings. They turned to nod at Lilith, and an unsure look of friendliness shifted on their features.

"It is a pleasure to meet you, Lilith. Our dear Demetrius has spoken highly of you." The queen's voice was elegant and soft. "We are very proud of this moment, for our son to rule with steadfast leadership. One that our people need in this uncertain time—a ruler that doesn't fear the darkness." For some reason, Lilith believed her to be harsh and unloving, but behind these rehearsed words, she could sense that the queen truly believed in her son. "Please, give him the support he needs, become that stable energy that he can depend on." The queen winced in pain, as if she were experiencing the sharp sting of a headache. There was a momentary flinch on the calm exterior that Demetrius wore; he was surely mentally lashing his mother, keeping her in line.

Quickly, Lilith smiled. "I thank you for your welcome and your wise guidance. I will do what I can for this kingdom." The queen nodded at her reply, a movement that looked like it took her entire concentration to do. King Amadeus addressed Lilith.

"You are Hennan's daughter? My, my, you look much like your mother. I hear, though, you've inherited your father's quick thinking. A useful skill. Where is your father?" Confusion shadowed his face as he searched the crowd. "Who are these peo..." His words died as his and Demetrius' mother's eyes became vacant once more.

Demetrius' jaw ticked, settling after a few moments, as he turned to face Lilith and in a whisper he spoke, "I would have liked for you to have met them prior to now, but *circumstance"*—meaning her behaviour and attempts to escape—"prevented that. They earnestly welcome you here."

Lilith's words were barely audible, "It's a bit hard for me to gather as much with them being entirely controlled by you. Their words lack conviction when they're obviously being censored."

"Noted. I will allow for proper introductions after we make it through the next couple of days."

Lilith wanted to tell him that there was no point. She couldn't trust anything they said because Demetrius thoroughly controlled them. How long had they been like this? Would her own voice become his soon? That rising panic started to flare to life again.

"Shall we dance?" She offered a necessary distraction to keep her from losing her cool. Demetrius held out his hand, helping her to stand. A few faces in the crowd focused on them once more, critically observing the new king and queen. They moved as a pair gracefully to the centre of the hall, where other couples were lost to the rhythm of the music. As Demetrius pulled her in to take the lead, Lilith smirked. She wanted to challenge him, openly defy him in some small act and let everyone watching know that she was not like them. She was not his brainwashed follower. With a squeeze of his hand, she entered a battle of wills.

The beat of the music thrummed in her heart, and with every step, she battled him to take the lead. They duelled along the white stone flooring, the light from the floating lanterns catching the iridescent cape of Lilith's dress as she swished around. Demetrius' eyes flickered with amusement as he rose to the challenge. He moved with the gracefulness expected of a master swordsman and trained warrior. Every step and twirl was poised yet agile. Lilith countered with a sharp redirect, moving her body in a fierce defiance, a quick pull out of his embrace, spinning away from him. As her fingers drifted out of his, Demetrius elegantly lunged for her hand, pulling her back in.

Onlookers gawked as they smoothly danced; the other couples had paused to watch. Every change in step flowed exquisitely, a perfect balance between their two tempers. The orchestra picked up the beat, trying to keep up with the tempo of the dance. As the music crescendoed, Demetrius gave her one last spin, then released her. Lilith arched backwards, her balance tipped awkwardly as she prepared to hit the ground.

However, as the final note sang, she felt his strong arm brace her, ending their battle in a grand pose. Applause once more erupted around them, making Lilith blush. Tiny beads of sweat covered her forehead.

As a couple, they walked back off the dance floor, making their way around the room.

"I didn't know you could dance that well," Lilith reached for a flute of alcohol from a nearby platter, but Demetrius pulled her away.

"I'm not sure if I'd call what we just did a dance, but I am surprised once more by you. You seem to be trained in all manner of things. You're an adept fighter, keen student, and graceful dancer. Did your father teach you?"

Lilith felt a blush creep along her cheeks. When he complimented her like that, she felt like she could be won over by his charm. "It was a mixture of many teachers my father hired throughout my childhood and my brother, Jasper. He would always dance with me while my other brother, Arlen, performed some musical piece. They never left me out when they were sparring or training. It's thanks to my family that I am the way I am."

Demetrius smirked and under his breath he replied, "But you've always been like this."

Lilith tilted her head in confusion. The more she talked with him, the more she noticed he would say things that insinuated he had known her from before their meeting at Skilheim, but she would remember meeting someone like him.

A staff member came by and offered Demetrius two flutes made of silver filled with some sort of drink. He handed one to Lilith, who waited for him to take the first sip. Bringing her drink to her lips, she could smell the sweet scent of fermented fruits. The first sip was a bubbly, sweet explosion along her tongue. She tipped the silver flute up and took a hefty gulp.

"This is potent, so take small sips." Demetrius worked on his, guiding them to the side. From here, Lilith could witness the full scope of the throne room. A noble was quick to come up to Demetrius and make small talk, while Lilith was lost in the spectacle.

At some point, the lights in the room had darkened, and a shift in the atmosphere changed to something more bewitching. The light and playful tunes had somehow become slow and sensual. Since their presence was no longer useful, King Amadeus and Queen Isolde had vacated their positions, and they had disappeared from the sea of people.

Just out of the corner of her eye, she could see Felicia and Tally on the opposite edge of the hall, watching the shift in people's demeanor. Dancing couples moved without elegance, shamelessly writhing with the music. Lilith took a step back as more couples engaged in provocative manners, displaying themselves with shameless abandon. It was a mixture of tongues and hands. Laughter and debauchery. That faint, off-putting smell was drifting around the air.

"What is that stench?" Lilith asked Demetrius. A small number of people were gathered around, inhaling something from small metal orbs. They blew out a yellow-tinted smoke.

"Is something the matter?" Demetrius put his empty cup down, and from the corner of his eye, he watched her take in this scene before them.

"What's going on right now? What's happened to these people?"

"This is entirely them. I have done nothing but allow them to show their true selves."

"Did you put something in the drink?"

"I guess I've earned that one, but no. I want you to watch."

Lilith returned her gaze to the crowd. To the sea of people all loose in their inhibitions. Some had removed various clothing or were in the middle of undressing one another. There was so much that caught her eye: a naked man dancing salaciously on top of a chair, a woman eating food from another woman's body, while also getting rutted by a man who was red in the face, lost in pleasure. People were gulping back the bubbling ale and more suspicious tonics being passed around. There was laughter from some women as they stripped a kitchen staff member down. Lilith clenched her teeth and began walking in their direction to break this all up, but Demetrius grabbed her arm and hauled her to the throne. He sat down and pulled her on his lap.

"Do you see? They are their own downfall. They do this to themselves because they can."

"You think you are above these people?"

"I do. I may give in to desire, but I know how to live without. I'm more interested in what you think."

"I see people who are giving in to their temptations, but that does not make them bad people. If you are trying to convince me that these people are beyond saving, then you have failed."

"Hmm." Demetrius motioned Lilith to look forward. From the entrance, four Apostles came forward with the remaining four women tethered together by chains, who looked at the crowd, stricken with terror. The Apostles unchained them and pushed them to their knees.

Lilith struggled to get to her feet, but Demetrius held on. From the sidelines, a few guards were equally struggling to hold back Tally and Felicia.

"What are you doing to them? I thought we had a deal that you would not harm the remaining prisoners."

"And *I* will not. However, I cannot speak for these guests. What do you think they'll do to them?"

"You bastard! You are responsible for their lives. They do not deserve this treatment, and by doing nothing, you are allowing others to take advantage of them. I will not allow this." She let her fire magic flare to life as she burned him, yet he laughed and held on. With a sneer, she shot her elbow to his throat, moving swiftly enough to catch him off guard. He caught her elbow in his hand and turned her to face forward. At first, the guests watched the prisoners with disdain, giving them ample space as if they couldn't stand to be in close proximity to these women. But after a few moments, a couple of them edged closer, lashing out in a quick slap or push.

"Filth!" someone yelled.

"You don't belong here."

"Whore."

"This is what you deserve."

Lilith had heard enough of these disgusting comments. She clenched her fist and exploded in a wave of pure electrifying mana. Demetrius' hand loosened, which gave Lilith just enough time to spring forward. Filled with untamed wrath, her body sailed through the air in front of the prisoners.

"The next person to touch or say anything about these women will beg for death." She turned to face an Apostle. "Take them away. Now!"

The white stone beneath her started to rattle, making the large oak tree shake above them. The glowing lanterns flickered in and out, causing an abrupt stop to the party.

"This celebration is over," Demetrius' voice boomed over everything. "We will see you tomorrow." The crowd murmured their disapproval, but gathered themselves to a respectable appearance before exiting the hall.

Lilith was lost to her own power, her rage, watching the prisoners weep before her. She was a hair away from entirely losing control.

Felicia and Tally knelt before the women, helping them up. They moved carefully, unsure of what Lilith would do. The throne room continued to shudder from Lilith's immense power, her gaze lifting to meet the Apostles.

Fear flickered across their faces. "My queen." They came to their knees.

Lilith debated killing them, but what would that make her? She wanted to preserve the light that she still felt inside, that little spark of hope that she was not a monster.

"Take the prisoners back and see to their needs." Demetrius waved them off and stood before Lilith. "My goddess, you are a stunning creature, but you need to release this energy." He nodded to the guards, who motioned for Felicia and Tally to leave. No one argued in front of Lilith. No one dared to rattle her.

That ringing tone sounded in her ear, not from panic but from the sudden absence of noise. Her body felt too hot, searing from the electrical energy flowing through her, charging the air around her. She could feel the static in the air, her hair lifting on the back of her neck.

"Go ahead," Demetrius egged her on.

Lilith didn't need any further encouragement as she sent out a pulse around her. Streaks of lightning collided with everything around her. Glass shattered from the ceiling, raining shards down on them. Demetrius moved impossibly fast and raised his hand to transform the shards into specs of sand. Immediately, she felt that drain on her mana, but she kept releasing her rage onto him. Her blast of fire ricocheted off the throne and struck the old oak tree behind it; a few of the lanterns hanging from it caught fire, and the licks of the flame spread throughout the branches. Both Lilith and Demetrius jumped back as they stood and watched the ancient tree engulfed in fire, a tree that had stood since before the age of man, destroyed by their disagreement.

Demetrius grinned, his eyes wild with energy, the pupils of his eyes fully constricted. "Can't you feel it?"

"Feel what?" she said, through gritted teeth. The urge to react, to fight, bubbling over her restraint.

"Mana is draining from around us. All because of you." Demetrius snapped his fingers, and in an instant, the fire smothered, leaving the once vibrant tree smoking in embers. The white throne chair had faint marks of soot on it. Lilith had never seen magic like his. His pure power, the ease with which he used it; no one could do that. Her power, on the other hand, had reached its pathetic limits.

The last of the false mask of politeness that she had been wearing all evening had finally crumbled. "Now you match your throne. You were supposed to be a pillar of hope for this kingdom, but behind your beautiful mask lies something gnarled and ugly. Now, when you sit upon this throne, people will see the dying tree that once held life, a mirror of what your rule will be like." She took a step back, as if shocked by her own boldness, but she couldn't hold her tongue after what she had just witnessed.

The grin on Demetrius' face faded, and his eyes shifted to black. "Do you want to know what drove me to this madness? It's only fitting on the eve of our union and our ascension that you finally understand that the very image of you standing before me both shatters me and builds me anew."

She wanted to let her feelings come crashing out, all the pent up anger and frustration of why this was how life turned out for her. She wanted to know why this was her fate and why she was his obsession. "I shouldn't care, but I do. I want to know why I am treated as such and why you are so full of hate. I want to know why you care so little for everyone around you and why you can't care for this chance at what fate has bestowed."

Demetrius held his hand out and waited patiently for Lilith to make up her mind about taking it. With her hand in his, the flecks of the falling embers of the ash tree faded into darkness, and they descended into that space between.

CHAPTER 14
MOCKER'S DELIGHT

Felicia - Several hours ago

The ballroom was a ridiculous display of the fineries the upper echelon of the kingdom was accustomed to. After Demetrius' display of welcome to these people, the guards pushed Felicia and Tally off to the side and away from the esteemed guests. As the general's daughter, Felicia had met many of King Amadeus' most notable allies, people who mutually benefited from supporting the kingdom, people with the intelligence to handle the emerging situation the kingdom faced. There were none of those faces here.

These were a different breed, with money and titles, who sought to sponge off the lower members of society to advance themselves. It didn't take much to identify the spine of these folks in their interactions with the staff and servers tonight.

At first, Felicia and Tally witnessed a few men lingering about a server, making rude remarks about how to approach people like them and how they expected a certain level of service today. They both chalked it up to these men being a few entitled nobles who thought the world catered to them, since it was not unheard of for such behaviour to come from the upper tier of society, those who inherited wealth without having to lift a finger. However, both women had met many other nobles who worked hard to build up their families' legacies, so they shook off the abhorrent men and kept watching the crowd.

Felicia took a deep inhale, smelling something bitter lingering in the air. She turned to Tally and asked, "What is that stuff that's being passed around?"

Tally leaned in next to her and, in hushed tones, replied, "It's a herb of sorts, used to relax inhibitions. It's very expensive, so only the wealthy can afford it."

"I mean, if it's a herb, you'd be able to grow it yourself."

"Not everyone wants to get their hands dirty."

"So, did Demetrius supply this stuff? Felicia was going to ask more, but heard one of the guards grumbling about her lack of use of titles.

Tally gave the guard next to them an innocent smile before turning back to Felicia, "I have no doubt this is all his arrangement. Everything we're watching has been orchestrated for a reason."

Felicia could not agree more with Tally on that opinion. The guards had made it clear that they were not allowed to wander and mingle among the guests, and the crowd had enough sense not to approach them. She looked towards Lilith, seated with Demetrius and his parents. They looked like the perfect couple, with their matching blue and gold outfits. Lilith glanced over; she was terrible at hiding the fear in her eyes.

Tally suggested, "We can make use of this night. Demetrius has given us the perfect opportunity to disappear into the sidelines of this crowd. We've heard nothing of what's going on outside, but there's no better place than here to catch up on gossip."

Felicia gaped at Tally, stunned by the cunning strategy she had come up with. She forgot that Tally had grown up surrounded by these people who only saw royals as a means to climb the social ladder. Tally knew how to play their games.

"Sure. I'm in." Felicia began looking around. They were ordered not to mingle with the guests, but they could move strategically around the ballroom. Couples were engaging in questionable acts, rather bold for a royal banquet. She shared a look with Tally, who shrugged.

"I hear this is normal for lower noble gatherings." Tally offered to scan the room. "They don't usually receive invitations here, so maybe this is how their parties go." They walked slowly with their guards trailing at a distance, quietly observing these guests' interactions.

"Did you hear?" questioned a woman wearing a flamboyant, purple feathered dress to a group of women wearing similar attire.

Felicia and Tally paused, hiding behind a large pillar.

The purple-dressed woman continued, "That woman, Bane, has written the most outlandish conspiracy. To think the Apostles would be secretly hiding women here at the palace!"

"The Apostles have cleaned up the streets, removed the trash that has burdened the city. If they want those women as a reward, they deserve them. I'll go so far as to offer my niece to them, the useless wench."

"Oh, Lady Rosthern, you cannot say such things." Another lady chuckled. "Beatrice Bane will say the wildest things to gain attention. Look at how well-behaved the children are these days, now that they are led by the Apostles."

Felicia's stomach twisted after hearing their words. She stepped further back into the shadows along the walls.

"At least we know they made it out," Tally whispered. "We know that they are controlling the children and influencing families by controlling their education."

Felicia paled, whispering, "I just don't understand how they can remain so ignorant. Why can't they see the truth?"

"Because they don't want to." Tally pulled Felicia along the wall. They needed to find out more.

"Look at him," a nobleman whispered to his friend. Their eyes lingered on the old king. "It's about time someone competent stepped up."

"Ha. You think his son will be any better? Look at who wears the real crown." His friend nudged his chin towards the Apostle who stood behind the throne. "Oh well. It gives us the opportunity to make face and move up. I personally think we should have fresh blood ruling those seats."

"The prince has married a nobody. She's not even a beauty."

Felicia was ready to step in and start a fight, but Tally pulled her away. The hate for these people festered further as they moved about the room. People were gorging themselves with food, openly engaging in sexual acts, and partaking in substances that made their eyes glaze over. They behaved like animals. Felicia was about to point them out, but then, barely audibly, she heard voices that sounded so familiar.

Three men stood slightly turned away, but Felicia recognized their features. Black hair worn in small braids, with a light brown skin that seemed to glow. It was a classmate from

Skilheim, Nero. He stood next to two inky black-haired men, one with blue eyes, the other with distinct yellow: Storm and Orin.

Several questions ran through Felicia's mind. Why were they here? *Are their families aligned with Demetrius?* Would they help her? She could see them frantically whispering while staring at Lilith. She moved in closer as her heart raced.

"I mean it was obvious there was something going on between them," Orin said, smirking while looking at the royal couple.

"But she's our age and they say they'll be wed in a few days," Nero replied, sipping on his drink.

Orin rolled his eyes as he retorted, "She has the potential to be powerful, but there are others better suited to be the next queen. He should be marrying some princess of the west, so they'd bring their forces and turn this kingdom into something respectable."

Storm shrugged. "My father says this is a ploy to win over the commoners. The royals are perceived at an all-time low. They face an all-out rebellion if they can't win over the people. But I agree, we are on the brink of extinction; now is the time for an allegiance between kingdoms."

"Really, you believe the words of that Mage? The expansion of the darkness is yet another ploy made up by them." Orin elbowed Storm. "You're just upset that you can't have her."

"Fool." Nero swatted Orin. "Don't utter such words here. You never know who's listening."

"Please. Look around you. No one is paying attention to us. Look at my father." Orin pointed to a stern-looking brute of a man, tongue deep in a flushed-looking woman.

Storm shook his head. "You'd think they'd show some concern for their sons and daughters that have been sent to die at the encampment."

"Again with this nonsense. They'll be fine." Orin looked around, making Felicia tug Tally to rush and duck behind a couple standing in front of her. She considered her choices. By the sounds of it, they were here because of their families, not that they personally had dealings with or even supported the prince.

"Those guys are classmates from school. I could try asking them for help." As Felicia talked, Tally risked bobbing her head up to get a look at the men.

"Do it!" Tally pushed Felicia forward. Felicia squared her shoulders and straightened her skirt. Her hand hovered above Orin's shoulder, but just as she was about to speak, the doors of the hall opened once more.

A sudden commotion coming from the entrance had the guards stepping forward. They reached for their weapons as the first Apostle made his way through to the centre of the crowd. Behind him were a bunch of their grey-robed goons, escorting their remaining prisoners: the women who had to remain behind because they couldn't fit through the bars to freedom. In some sort of rehearsed charade, the grey robes removed the chains from the women and pushed them into the crowd on their knees. They stood, gripping each other, as some people began to assault the poor women.

Tally grabbed Felicia's wrist, pulling her away from Orin. In a last-minute decision, she yelled his name. His face whipped in her direction, and she felt the burning gaze of his yellow eyes.

"They're lying to you!" Felicia called out to him, her words fading under the shouts of the crowd. She lost sight of him as Tally pulled her closer to the frenzy. She wanted to say more, to tell him the prince was an evil monster, but she was swallowed by the crowd.

"What is this?" Tally yelled over the commotion. Armoured hands grabbed them both from behind. The guards tracking them pulled them out of line of sight. Felicia sneered, trying to pull free from her guard's grip. This was going too far. These nobles showed no compassion and no mercy. They were just as evil as the Apostles.

Tally let out a cry of defiance, swearing and cursing those involved. Guards' hands muffled her, but before Felicia could do anything, movement from the throne had everyone clamouring backwards.

Frantically searching between the gaps of people's heads, she could make out a fiery Lilith making her way to the prisoners. A metal-plated hand pushed Felicia back against the wall, causing her to lose sight of Lilith. A voice called out, demanding they take the prisoners away. It echoed around them, shaking the glass above the throne. The ornate lanterns began to shake. Felicia could only assume that Lilith was unleashing her wrath.

The guards pushed Felicia into Tally, ushering them to move towards the exit. Felicia twisted herself to look back, locking eyes with a pair of distinct yellow ones. Orin was yelling her name, his voice lost as the crowd descended into chaos.

Half of the nobles were struggling to put their clothes back on, while the other half were not sober enough to stand. Felicia felt a mixture of fury and disbelief. This was just too ridiculous.

Demetrius' dark voice boomed over the spectacle, causing everyone to freeze. The guards pulled her back into position before hearing his words. With one last look at Lilith, she was pushed through the halls.

Rough hands pushed her and Tally up through the halls of the palace, with voices ordering them to behave. They opened up the familiar doors of their new room and shoved them in. Her knees slammed onto the hard ground.

"What's going on?" A confused Tally lay in a heap of lavender silk.

"Does it matter?" Felicia rushed to the door. "This is it. We can make it to the consorts. Quick, lie down and close your eyes." Tally quickly flopped to the ground, looking like she had fainted.

She pulled the door open, facing a menacing-looking guard who immediately went to push her back inside.

"Wait! There's something wrong with Lady Thalassa." Felicia rushed over to Tally, while the guard narrowed his eyes and cautiously approached. As he knelt to inspect Tally, Felicia backed up, reaching her hand to the side table. She wrapped her hand around one of its legs and then smashed it down over the guard. With a loud crash, the small table shattered against the guard's armour, leaving Felicia holding on to a single leg. The guard grunted, pushing his body back up.

"Now...," growled the guard. Felicia pummelled him over the head with the remaining leg, beating him into unconsciousness.

Tally sat up, watching her in shock. "Okay. I did not see that working." Felicia tossed the leg to the ground and picked up the guard's sword. It was much too heavy to hold up, so she dropped it and stole his dagger.

"Right. Let's go." Felicia brushed aside her hair, which had clung to her face, and went to open the door once more. Looking side to side, she saw no more guards stationed. Tally pushed past, mirroring Felicia's movement. "Where is everyone?"

"Probably securing the crowd. Quick, let's get going before someone comes," Tally urged, moving in a crouched jog through the hallways above the sea of chaos. Screams of people yelling echoed around them, followed by a loud bang. Whatever was happening in the throne room was keeping the guards' attention focused away from them.

By the time they had reached the consorts' wing, they could feel ripples of power and destruction shaking the ground. Felicia grinned to herself, wondering what Lilith was up to.

Tally ran to a door, knocking furiously.

"Lady Landiel, please, it's Tally."

A startled-looking lady swung the door open. Several pairs of soft hands pulled them into the room. Felicia pressed herself against the closed door, looking at a pair of twins with long dark hair.

"Meridith? Meira?" Felicia's mouth hung open. She eyed the twins standing behind a woman who could have been their elder sister.

"How do you know my daughters?" The woman spoke with authority.

"They're classmates at Skilheim," Felicia spoke as Tally ran into the arms of a tall, slender-looking woman with long blonde hair.

"We are held in the queen's wing, but they had us in the dungeon below the Temple." Tally began weeping, while Meridith and Meira suspiciously eyed Felicia.

"What are you doing here, Felicia?"

"I travelled here with Silver, Lilith, and the prince." All eyes were on her. "That was before we knew the truth about the prince's schemes. Since then, we've been separated. I was taken with Tally to the Apostles' dungeon, while Lilith was taken to the queen's wing."

"Lilith had mentioned she ran into some helping consorts, and we were hoping that offer still remained." Tally wiped her tears. The tall blonde rubbed her shoulders.

"Meridith and Meira, take these women to the haven." The tall blonde, who could only be Lady Landiel, opened up a secret passageway behind an inconspicuous panel.

"If you all know how to navigate these tunnels, why haven't you left?" Felicia wondered.

"They've taken our children. There are those who have already left, but I cannot leave my son to that monster."

Meridith pushed Felicia into the passage, while Meira pulled Tally.

"Why have you stayed?" Felicia asked Meridith.

"Our mother refuses to leave Lady Landiel, and our father is at the encampment. If we left, we would be alone. Our home has already been claimed by the Void. So we chose to stay here with our mother."

"We begged her to let us stay," Meira interrupted. "It doesn't matter, really. We either die, taken by the Void, or beside our mother, and I'd rather stay here." Meridith pulled out a small orb, which lit up the narrow tunnels.

"Orin, Storm, and Nero were at the ball. I couldn't reach them before it turned to mayhem." Felicia wondered if Orin would have helped her. He had clearly seen her, so at least someone knew she was here.

"I wouldn't trust anyone who attended the ball. We were ordered to stay in our rooms, and with them keeping the royal children hostage, we're not stepping out of line."

"Yet you're willing to help us."

"It's not our call, but my lady's."

"Do you know where they're keeping the children? We didn't see them in the dungeon," Tally asked the twins.

"We know they're close. Probably in some palace room. We've tried looking, and the children are wary of the tunnels."

They turned a corner, coming upon a wooden door. Meira pushed a lever, which opened the door, revealing a narrow staircase.

"This is as far as we can go. Follow the lights, and they will lead you to a safe place that only consorts know of. You'll find help down there. Good luck!" Meira and Meridith bid the women farewell, closing the wooden door behind them and returning to their mother.

"Your mother must have known of this place." Felicia descended the stairs, which spiralled down. Tiny orbs flickered to life, revealing a tight passageway made of brick.

Tally followed closely behind Felicia. "The palace was built on top of a ruined castle, or that's what my mother told me.

She said that the other consorts were shown this way by a former consort of my grandfather. It was a place where consorts could meet up in secret. A refuge to build alliances. She never showed me this place, but I've heard many stories about it."

"And the prince, does he know about it?"

"If he does, then this refuge will become our grave." Tally's voice sounded defeated. There were no words of comfort that Felicia could say that wouldn't just be lies. They had walked through another doorway where the narrow passage widened. On one side, little orbs hung over three large, faded paintings: a bustling depiction of a city reaching the clouds; tall grey buildings covered in nature, while small figures walked along neat paths: a crowd gathered around a giant person that shone a brilliant white, their faces stricken with awe, while some figures knelt before the giant in worship.

"What is this?" Tally moved to another painting showing a battle between people, while the giants stood off in the distance watching. Felicia leaned in closer. From this perspective, it was clearer that the common folk were not men. They had long pointed ears. They looked like Danai.

Felicia went to the next painting. It depicted a mist of fire and death. The once-tall buildings crumbled into rubble. Skeletal figures lay deep under the earth, while a small group of common folk walked above them, turning their back on the giants.

At the end of the hallway was a set of doors with rounded bronze knobs that had rusted over time. Felicia twisted the handle, pushing the door open. Inside, the orbs were already on, lighting up an enormous room supported by hundreds of thick, brick columns. The flooring was made of a large grey slab, with several cracks running along it. The air felt warm and humid, even though they were deep underground.

"Hello?" Tally called out. A figure hidden beneath a long brown cloak came rushing at them. Felicia tensed, sinking into attack position, while Tally cowered behind her.

"Lady Thalassa!" The figure ignored Felicia and bouldered into Tally, encasing her in a hug. Tally's eyes were wide, her hands flared outwards as this stranger finally retreated. Delicate white hands pulled back the hood, unveiling Lady Ashmore with dark locks. "Felicia, it is good to see you."

Lady Ashmore beamed. To Felicia, this woman seemed to put up a brave mask, but judging by her hollowed cheeks, she looked frail. Her voice carried an ethereal richness. "Lilith told me you were both in the Temple. How is it that you're down here?"

"A lot has happened." Tally continued to fill Lady Ashmore in on the current palace hubbub. They opened up to her, sharing their plans and Lilith's future as queen. Hearing the news, Lady Ashmore became more disheartened.

"I am truly sorry that you have had to endure so much. I had assumed Lilith failed to escape when I last met her. I've been here, helping the consorts as much as I can."

"Why not hide somewhere remote, away from all this?" Tally asked.

Lady Ashmore began to walk, showing them the haven of the consorts. She stopped in front of a large painting of a giant red-haired woman, with arms open wide, looking over the small group of survivors. Felicia knew this giant, or rather this goddess: Melia. She guided them to safety, a haven.

"I cannot turn my back on my friends, my people. I will help those who need a way out, bring supplies when they have none, and bring word from the outside. You must know that Demetrius holds his siblings hostage, as a way to not only control the consorts, but the consorts' families. The highest of the kingdom's elites are in the hands of that evil prince."

"King. He'll be king soon enough," Felicia added.

Lady Ashmore's face filled with disgust. "Well, a quarter of the consorts have fled, ones that have no ties here. Five consorts remain, each with a few ladies in waiting, those who chose to stay rather than flee. The six children, Demetrius' and Tally's half-siblings, are somewhere hidden in the main palace. The Apostles have secured the tunnels leading to the Temple, but they have learned of only a few of the palace's secrets. I am truly sorry that I could not reach you."

Tally held onto Lady Ashmore's arm. "It is not your fault. You are doing the best you can to help my siblings." Tally turned to Felicia. "My next younger half-sister just turned twelve, while my youngest brother is barely two. They are not capable of leaving or surviving on their own, nor would they leave their mothers."

Felicia considered Tally's situation. Her own mother had already passed, so she had no ties keeping her here. If anything, Tally could use her status as a royal child to persuade some of the elite families to take action.

"Did your mother have a family? A reason why Demetrius was keeping you?"

"My mother's family is hard to reach. They live beyond the Great Everlade Mountains, in the Red Forest, and they rarely spoke with my mother. To be honest, I don't understand why Demetrius would bother with me."

Everything Felicia had known regarding those who live in the Red Forest came from Juniper and Nym, nymph cousins who went to Skilhiem. Surely, Tally's mother was not a nymph. She suddenly recalled Lady Tessa sharing the same translucent shimmering skin as Juniper and stared at Tally.

"Are you half nymph?" Felicia thought she had only asked the question in her mind, but as soon as the words were spoken, she could see Tally flinch. She had meant to keep that question a part of her internal dialogue, only airing her suspicion once she had more proof.

Tally looked to Lady Ashmore nervously, who nodded at her. "I've been told it's a part of my family history that should remain a secret."

"Why? Is it a shame to be part Nymph?" Felicia thought of sweet Juniper, who lived with compassion and kindness.

"My father wasn't the most enthusiastic supporter of my mother's culture. To him, Nymphs were weak. Healers can be taught, and that was her people's pride. My mother's beauty is what bewitched my father." By the torment in Tally's eyes, Felicia knew Tally was reliving painful memories. Still, there was no reason that Tally should stay in the palace. This was her chance of freedom.

"Tally, you should leave with Lady Ashmore. You need to be our eyes and ears from the outside. Convince the consorts who have fled back to their families to support you. You can't stay here with Lilith and me, it's too risky for you."

"And what of the prisoners? I want to help them escape."

"When they escape, they'll need a place to go. Make that place for them. Use this as an opportunity to leave this place. Lilith and I will be your vengeance."

Tally chewed on her bottom lip, and she stared silently at the painting in front of them. "I could make a haven, a safe place for the women in the dungeon to start fresh."

"I mean, the darkness is still expanding from the Void, so even in the far corners of this world, you would eventually feel the threat, but I like your plan," Felicia smiled, teasing her friend.

"I can show her the way." Lady Ashmore moved to squeeze Tally's shoulders, then walked off once more into the belly of the haven. Stacks of crates and supplies were piled neatly along one wall, while a makeshift living room and row of beds took up another corner. Lady Ashmore opened a chest and pulled out an assortment of equipment: a small satchel, a change of clothes, and dried preserves.

"And you, Felicia?" Lady Ashmore questioned.

"I will stay with Lilith. For now, I need to send out a few letters. Will you make sure they are sent to the right people?"

She had to rush and write quickly, while Lady Ashmore readied Tally. The ink was drying on her last scroll, as she felt a hand pat her on the shoulder.

"We can't wait. It's time we leave." Tally's eyelids were puffy from crying. They had been through so much together, it almost felt wrong to be separated. Felicia pulled her into a hug.

"Don't you dare come back." Felicia felt her own tears build.

Lady Ashmore handed Felicia a small dagger with a curved hilt and a vial of purple liquid. "Be brave and trust yourself. Follow the white markers, they will take you back to the queen's wing, and keep an eye out for my white-winged friend."

She watched as Tally and Lady Ashmore disappeared, then turned to find the white marker, a white stone carved into the idol of Melia. Following a winding uphill tunnel, she used the figurines to make it to a panel door. A small latch made the door bounce open into the familiar white stoned hallway. Crouched down, she pressed herself against the walls until she found her room. Although the door was slightly ajar, the bludgeoned guard had disappeared. Panic seized her, realizing they knew she and Tally had vanished. She understood there would be consequences for her actions, but hoped Lilith would buffer the punishment. All she could do was wait.

In an effort to calm herself, she took out the curved dagger and clutched it to her chest, pressing her back against the door. If any Apostles came, she might as well take as many down as possible.

PART TWO

CHAPTER 15
TRIAL OF
DESTRUCTION

Lilith

As his mist faded, Lilith looked around. She felt soft moss under her feet, and a cool breeze played with her hair. Tall tree trunks surrounded them, with large ferns and wild flowers scattered beside her. Demetrius tugged her hand, and she followed him down a winding path towards the sound of bubbling water. Everything was cast in a strange, fluorescent blue light coming from little glowing mushrooms. The light amplified the blueness of his hair. He pushed past an over-grown bush of ferns and pulled her in close. A small waterfall cascaded down some lichen-covered stones into a large pool of water. Around the edge, little bell flowers tilted their leaves away from the steaming water. Next to the waterfall, a giant willow tree dangled its leaves close to the water.

"Where are we?" Lilith reached out to tap a finger on a glowing mushroom growing out of a nearby tree trunk.

"A place I found a long time ago. I'm glad to see it's still here." He let go of her hand and went to the pool's edge, kneeling down to swirl his hand through the waters. He patted the soft ground next to him. "Come, have a seat." Lilith looked down at her golden and blue gown; it must have cost a fortune. Demetrius sighed and shrugged off his overcoat and laid it next to him. She carefully sat down. "I have something to give you." In his fingers, he held up a tiny dark blue pearl. Inside, liquid curled slowly. Lilith picked it from him and held it up between her fingers.

"Thanks?" She twirled it between her fingers. "What is it?" Before Demetrius could answer, her thoughts quickly flitted back to the throne room. "Are we going to talk about what just happened?"

Demetrius leaned back and rolled his neck. "What happened was exactly what I had planned. I'm making a world that can coexist with what's to come."

"And what is that?"

"I believe they will make themselves known soon enough. There's no way they'll let me get away with what I'm doing."

"Who are they?"

"Your answer lies in that sphere. However, it is your choice to swallow it."

Lilith brought the tiny sphere closer to inspect it. There were too many unanswered questions.

"Will it do anything to me?"

"This was given to me by someone I trust would not harm you."

She needed to know the truth, but she'd been deceived by him too many times to blindly trust this pearl. Uncertainty clouded her judgment, as the need for her to understand outweighed her mistrust. She needed to know the reason why she was cursed, why her powers were bound, and why she was tied to Demetrius. It would all too easy for this to be a ruse, another way to subdue and pacify her. Inside the pearl, the midnight blue liquid seemed to shimmer. It looked as if someone had captured the night sky. She could easily hand it back to Demetrius and find her answers another way, but as she held her hand out, it felt like a presence was with her, soothing her. It felt as if an old friend was holding her hand, willing her to take the risk, and her body felt compelled to listen.

With caution, she placed the pearl on her tongue; it felt ice-cold. Demetrius was intensely watching her as she swallowed.

They waited for the effects to kick in, for something to happen. A sharp pain lashed through Lilith's mind, and she fell backwards, her eyes turning blind as everything faded away.

Wind whistled loudly in her ears and forced her hair to whip around her face. Her body arched backwards, and the feeling of falling rushed through her, yet she wasn't moving.

All around her was a bright white light. Beneath her, she spied a small blue crystal. She struggled to twist her body around to face it, and the wind hit her face, causing her eyes to tear.

A vision overcame her.

She was in a stable surrounded by large beasts. Gryphons. Their bodies resembled the hind of a horse, while their faces took on more bird-like features. Large feathered wings bristled as the beasts nestled in for their rest. The songs of chirping made her feel a sense of peace. In her hand was a bristle brush, while a beautiful black Gryphon stood within arm's reach. The large feathered creature nuzzled to her touch, stirring its connection with its master. Lost in thought, she swept the brush down the hind, humming a quiet tune.

'My my. How fortunate that I found this goddess here.' A voice that felt like home came from behind. A man stood just out of reach, with wild silver-white hair and iridescent blue eyes. A small scar ran over his right brow, which made his harmonious face distinctive. He was a wall of muscle, a battle-worn warrior. She felt a magnetic pull to him and an intense attraction that made her feel flustered.

Lilith's hand stilled and she closed her eyes, 'What do you want, Locke?' Her heart was beating like crazy. She imagined all the ways he could caress her. All the ways she would touch him. But that was a dream, and nothing more.

He walked up next to her and leaned on a pillar. 'Is that any way to talk to a friend?' Lilith ignored him and continued brushing her Gryphon. They had only known each other since she started serving Melia, but lately, he'd been more flirtatious. Locke reached for the reins. 'Will you be at the festival tonight?'

She tried to push his hands from the reins. The beast, sensing its master's annoyance, flared one of its wings and pushed Locke back. Lilith let out a chuckle, sweet talking her feathered companion.

"Tamer of beasts. It's no wonder why they swoon to your touch. Is that the reason you have ensnared me?"

Lilith rolled her eyes. 'Are you referring to yourself as a beast?' Her eyes trailed down his chest, giving him a sarcastic look of disappointment. 'My wiles don't work on creatures like you. I haven't decided if I'll attend the party tonight. It depends on what Melia wants. If she attends, then I have no choice but to be there to serve her.' Lilith pulled her Gryhpon's reins back and led it out of the bay, passing a smiling Locke on the way to its paddock.

'She'll be there.' Locke followed in her shadows. 'Will you serve me, too?'

Lilith scoffed, 'I only serve my master.' Her hands were busy removing the reins.

'And what if I became something more to you than your master? Would you stay by my side instead?' Locke reached for her hand, pressing himself into her back. 'What if I could free you from servitude, and offer you my hand to become my wife?'

Lilith looked over her shoulder and glared at him, 'You are not freeing me if I become your wife. I will just be exchanging one master for another, and I prefer Melia.'

Locke caressed her shoulder, slowly trailing his hand up her neck and weaving his finger through her long black hair. 'I'm sure I can convince you to prefer my touch, and my words. I can make you whimper from my commands.' Lilith leaned into him as he clenched her hair and forced her head to tilt back. 'I would *take only you, for you have marked my soul. You have tainted my desires, consumed my thoughts, and stirred something within me that I thought was impossible.' He leaned his face closer, his lips hovering over hers. She felt a surge of her own desire clouding her judgment. That pressing need to let him devour her, warming her to her core. 'If anything, you would be my master.' His fingers released their hold. She twisted to face him, pressing herself into him, stretching up to reach for his lips.*

'I would be a merciless master,' she teased him, moving out of his reach with a mischievous grin. 'Good day, Locke.' She pushed past him and left the stable, feeling a sense of satisfaction.

The vision transformed.

She was standing beside a shorter woman with long, red, wavy hair and ivory skin. Melia. Her master, but also her best friend.

'He hasn't stopped staring at you since we arrived.' Melia nudged her, eyeing up Locke, who sat across the room, drinking wine. 'He looks like he's ready to worship you.' Lilith blushed and picked up a wine jug and carefully refilled Melia's cup.

'He should stop. I'm but a lesser goddess. His attention will displease others and cause more of a headache for me.' She risked peeking a glance towards Locke. He was listening to someone beside him, but his gaze was fixed on her. Lilith felt her cheeks burning. Her feelings for Locke were only known by her and Melia. She could never act on them, nor expect any real relationship to form. He was miles above her status, and as one of the main six gods, he was expected to take one of the higher-ranking goddesses as his wife. Lilith looked around the room. Radiant power cascaded from everyone. Alda, one of the six, was with his

wife, Sif. They were conversing with Thurn and Philla. Philla's attention would occasionally drift over to Locke.

Lilith couldn't help but feel jealousy stir within her. Philla would make a suitable match with Locke, as she was his equal. She could see longing shining in Philla's eyes. Disheartened, she tried to ignore the feeling of Locke's gaze.

After the incident in the stable, she mentioned Locke's proposal to Melia, who sadly agreed that her involvement with Locke would only cause issues. However, it was Lilith's choice to get involved, and Melia would support her decision.

Lilith had always wondered why Melia took a liking to her. Others thought it strange that Melia, the most powerful goddess, the god of time, and the weaver of fates, took on a mere lesser goddess as her closest companion and faithful servant. Lilith, whose beauty was considered average, who was no enchantress and no wielder of true power, was the outlier brought to all the parties. Her appearance was always a source of gossip amongst other goddesses, especially after a certain main god started taking interest in her. Often other companions would bump into her, or say underhanded comments, to which Lilith never responded, never said harsh words, or called out for help. She took it all without losing composure.

Melia draped her arm over her shoulder and leaned in, whispering, 'Ignore them. You are worth a thousand of them. How many of their companions would turn around and stab their masters in their back if given the opportunity to rise in power? You, however, don't seek what they seek. Your only weakness is your heart, your unwavering loyalty. I see many things, hear words of betrayal yet to be spoken, but you are pure. A beacon of hope for our kind.'

'I am here for you, not them. You saved me–plucked me from a lifetime of confinement for simply existing.' Lilith thought of her first memories, cruel and lonely covered in filth. Cast out by her own mother, Lilith lived among the most deprived souls in their realm. It wasn't until Melia, her hand reaching out, with an offer to live with her, that things turned around. Life became bearable. Lilith would die for Melia because only she gave her a reason to live. 'How could I leave you, when you have given me everything?' Lilith's eyes flickered to Locke once more.

Melia smirked, reading Lilith like an open book. 'I place no judgment on the man you have chosen. Not when my own choice leaves a bitter taste in my mouth.' Lilith tried to distract Melia from focusing on the far side of the party, where her husband, Ominus, leaned back on his throne, surrounded by beauties.

The festival of light carried well into the night. The gods gorged themselves on wine and food. Women and men were brought out as entertainment. Some were playing music, others dancing, but most were busy being the playthings of the gods and goddesses. Clothes came off and bodies started writhing.

Lilith filled Melia's cup once more. 'I don't understand why you put up with him.'

Melia gulped down her drink. 'Our fate is bound to each other. I cannot exist without him and neither can he, without me. I've yet to see direction when it comes to us, but there is an opportunity for him to prove himself once more. It's a curse and a gift to see so much. I have learned to bide my time with my meddling. Patience is time's friend. Come, I need to rest my eyes.'

Melia refused to partake in such manners. She learned to turn a blind eye to her husband's wandering hands, and excused herself early from the party, which meant Lilith was allowed to *leave as well. Melia parted ways, leaving Lilith alone scowling her master's silent displeasure. Another reason why she was wary to be with one of the higher gods: she was fiercely loyal and expected loyalty in return.*

She walked through the deserted gardens, coming up to the blooming trees that shaded them in a canopy of reds and greens. She ran her hand across the bark of the old warped oak tree, when Locke came up beside her.

'You left before I could speak with you.' He stood in front of her. She breathed in his scent of pine and frost. It tingled the pleasure centre of her mind.

'Yes, well, Melia, as usual, retired early and dismissed me. You should head back. Your absence would be noticed and missed. I think Phillia was trying to get your attention.' She tried to move around him, but he stopped her once more.

'I don't care for Phillia. How many times will we circle around each other? I want you, Lilith. Only you.'

She wished it were that easy, to sink into his arms and let him claim her. 'Locke. I am not what you need. I am nothing. A nobody. You need someone who is your equal.'

'I want you. Please. I've spoken with Melia, and she will release you. Be my wife.' Locke gently wrapped his arms around her. Warmth and comfort spread through her. She could get lost just in his embrace. Every fibre of her being was screaming at her to say yes. To give in to him. She leaned back and looked into his icy blue eyes. Eyes that could pierce her soul and consume her. Just this once, she could stop resisting. Just this once, she could let her body take control. She leaned up and kissed him. He eagerly pressed her against the oak tree.

The vision rippled and changed. Flashes of memories, times with Locke where they were both lost in laughter, nights spent in bed, stolen kisses when no one was watching, disagreements that ended in passion, shared silence just enjoying each other's presence; so many memories.

Sneers from others had become normal. 'Look at her, flaunting her new status.' 'No doubt he will see the error of his choice.' 'She should have stayed with Melia. She needs to know her place.' *Voices continued to deem her unworthy of such affection from Locke. Lilith wept. It had become too hard to face them. It was too hard to listen to such pointless, vile damnation of her character because she chose to love him back. She had stopped accepting invitations to events. Not even Melia's company could elevate her spirit. Instead, she found peace in her solitude and existed only for her love. Locke's outward anger towards others had caused scene after scene. He argued with his brothers to defend his marriage, but his words only fell on deaf ears.*

The vision settled once more.

She was naked in the glowing blue waterfall, her long black hair swishing around. A man with long white hair and ice blue eyes popped up next to her. She felt elated and overjoyed to see this man. Her heart fluttered wildly, knowing what would happen next. Their bodies intertwined in a lover's embrace. 'I love you.' he whispered, as he licked her neck. His voice was dark and sultry.

That voice. She adored that voice.

'My love,' she said back. 'It has been too long.' Her hands ran through his wet hair. The man scowled, which caused her to laugh. 'Why does my husband pout?' She tried to use her thumb

to smooth the wrinkle between his brow. He wrapped his arms around her, floating in the water.

'Because, my dear, they want me to help with things happening in the underrealm. The creatures have grown restless, and they're worried they'll break through the cage. It means I'll have to leave you.'

'Then settle things quickly and come to me in one piece.' She kissed him once more.

'I won't be gone for long. Alda will be with me.' A feeling of distrust settled in her stomach, urging her to say something, but she remained silent.

Lilith returned to the white realm. The small blue dot grew larger and larger. As she fell, she realized it was not a dot, but a lake. The surface was covered in a thick layer of ice. Terror lanced through her heart, knowing that there was no way to slow herself. She would hit the ice and die. Curling her body, she braced for impact. But there was no pain. Her body broke through the barrier like a rock falling through paper. She was surrounded by endless dark water. It felt like fire was burning her body, searing her skin. Thrashing around, she released her held breath, expecting water to flood her lungs, but she only found stillness. A strange calm eased her senses.

"Lilith," a woman's voice called to her. It felt soothing to her ears. "Open your eyes." Lilith did as the voice commanded. She was lying face down on a smooth surface. Everything seemed dark, she couldn't tell if she was blind or if it was just pitch black. She blinked several times, trying to make out her surroundings. A gentle hand clasped hers. Immediately, her panic died. It was as if she were being hugged by her mother. The hand closed around her eyes. "Open your eyes, Lilith," the soft, ethereal voice commanded her. "Do not repeat the same mistakes."

Lilith focused on what was in front of her. She felt another vision invading her.

She was sitting on an open window ledge overlooking a garden, her thin blue dress draped around her. Another male voice called out to her. A beautiful man with long blonde hair casually sauntered in. Alda. He called out, 'Lilith?' Danger and distrust filled her senses. She gracefully moved off the ledge and stood to face him.

'How can I help you, Alda? Shouldn't you be with my husband? Is everything alright?'

Alda looked concerned and edged closer. 'It happened so quickly. The creatures laid a trap. They knew we were coming. My brother sacrificed himself so that we could leave. He's gone, Lilith. He's locked in the cage.'

Shock raged through her. 'Then set him free! Show me and I'll do it myself.' Alda was lying; she could tell he was hiding something.

'Lilith, he's gone.'

'I can smell your lies.' Energy coursed through her, engulfing her in hot white flame. She was poised to strike, but he was quicker. Her flames sizzled as he pressed her against a wall, pinning her wrists to her side. His lips were on her, but she would not surrender. She bit him. Alda laughed and continued his assault. Just then, she heard the voice of her love. A flash of white hair thundered towards her, gripping Alda with an unrelenting force. He hurled him through walls, raining rubble and dust.

Lilith cried out in despair, but her pleas went unanswered. Instead, several bodies came around her. A woman with long golden hair grabbed her by the hair and pushed her to her knees. 'What's going on, Sif?' Lilith questioned. 'Why are you doing this?'

Sif sneered, 'Because it was never supposed to be you. He belongs to us.' She lifted a long pink crystal dagger and drove it into Lilith's heart, again and again, an attack so vicious the tip of the crystal snapped as it lodged in her chest.

In the distance, the fighting stopped. The white haired man looked upon his dying wife and exploded, sending everyone flying back. Everything seemed to fade into darkness as Lilith reached for her love.

'Locke,' she cried weakly. The vision gave way to black.

Her vision blurred, and she found herself once more alone. The silky female voice came to her again. Melia's voice. "Melia." Lilith wept. Memories came flooding back of her time as the goddess Lilith. Melia stood in front of her and pressed her hands into Lilith's. 'My dearest Lilith. I've missed you.' Melia looked around. 'You need to find her to close the cage before it's too late. The fallen star is the key. The darkness seeks the light. You must release the Mages and unbind your curse. Time is running out. Safeguard your heart.'

Chapter 16
Tears of the Truth

Lilith

"Open your eyes, Lilith." Locke's concerned voice filled her mind. Her body felt heavy, and her mind was spinning. Slowly, she moved her head to the side and blinked her eyes open. Icy blue eyes stared at her. Locke. Only he was Demetrius.

"Locke?" she whispered his name. His pupils dilated after hearing her. He caressed her head in his arms. The smell of pine and frost filled her lungs. A scent that both tortured her and brought her another past.

"What was that?" She winced, and the feeling of a splitting migraine formed.

"Those were your memories before you died." Lilith didn't fully trust what she saw. This could be another illusion, a trick to make her surrender her guard. She needed to process what happened.

"My name was also Lilith." The goddess, Lilith. She now carried some of her memories from a lifetime ago. "And you...

You're a god!" She quickly sat up, her head spinning. "But you look so different."

"I *was* a god. As I am now, my powers are only a fraction of what they used to be. I'm much like you, with my powers stripped." Demetrius wrapped his arms around her to steady her, but Lilith leaned back, her mind reeling from all the new information. "After what happened, they forced me to marry Philla, but I refused, and they locked me in the cage."

There were still so many unanswered questions that this sphere did not reveal.

"Is the 'cage' the darkness?"

"The cage is a realm where only the most vile creatures are sent. It's a prison of sorts, created by the gods..." Demetrius opened his mouth to say something else, but Lilith held up her hand.

"I don't get it. If I were a goddess, how could I be killed? I thought gods were immortal."

"Sif used the only weapon that could kill you, the Ashen-reave. Crafted from the crystal of a sun's kiss, the product of pure celestial energy," Demetrius explained, clenching his fists. Lilith gasped and squeezed her chest; these gods thought so little of her, they committed the ultimate crime. To them she was undeserving of Locke's love.

"I just don't understand why I'm here. Why have we been given another chance?" Lilith said, looking at her fingers. "Why did they show the oracle that vision? What is the point of all of this?"

Demetrius reached out, drifting his hands up and down her back, slow and steady. "I'm not entirely sure what happened. Before I was cast into the darkness, Melia gave me the blue sphere and told me that our paths would cross again. I didn't think it would ever happen. I think Melia has been doing what she can to make things right. I believe it was her that gave the vision to the oracle, perhaps to let me know that it was our time to find each other."

"Well, it had terrible consequences. Could she not have just spoken directly with you? It's because of her that my powers are bound. Yes, she's given me another chance, but so far her intervention has only caused more issues."

"She loved you. I think she is the only other being that could understand the grief that I felt when you died. Contrary to your people's beliefs, gods are flawed and they have limits. It's not entirely her fault your powers were bound. Lord Elwin has to answer for his actions, and your father failed to protect you. Your brothers failed to protect you."

Anger at him blaming her family made her voice rise, "*You* failed to protect me. It seems to be my fate that I have to suffer at the hands of others who think that I am nothing. In this life, it is Lord Elwin and the nobles. In my past, it was the gods that deemed me insignificant." Hate and bitterness wedged themselves further into her heart, its ugliness evolving into something new, snapping her final threads of hope and optimism. She would have her revenge, but for now, she had to work out her next move.

Right now, she had to focus on her next task, freeing the Mages. Melia's words echoed in her mind, '*The fallen star is the key...You must release the Mages.*' Doubt crept up, and had her rethinking her plan. There was a possibility that this was all staged by Demetrius, that these memories were false. Everything he'd done had some sort of alternative motivation;

giving her the sphere could have played into another one of his schemes.

How long?" she asked him.

He tilted his head in confusion.

"How long did it take you to get out?" she clarified.

"There was no concept of time. However, it felt like a thousand years had passed. At first, I thought they would let me out after a period of time. But it seemed that they turned their backs on me, left me there to rot, knowing I couldn't die. And I wasn't alone. I helped force those creatures into the cage, condemned them to the same eternal punishment that I was facing. I had to fight, to survive the brutal nature of them. I became their personal guard, making sure they never escaped, while also climbing the ranks of the gods' forsaken monsters...and I became their king. I lost myself with time, driven into madness." He rubbed his thumb along her lower lip. His hands drifted lower to her throat, where he wrapped his hands around her slender neck and squeezed.

Before she could struggle, his hand let go and he grabbed her by the back of her head, tugging on her hair to force her to look at him. "I didn't think this would ever happen. I spent the first half of my life in the cage grieving for you, wishing that it was me who died. Seeing your face in the abyss, haunting me. My memory of your eyes piercing my soul, condemning me. I learned to hate you...Hate that I loved you."

His fingers wrapped in her hair gently caressed her, as he leaned in closer. "But at some point, I realized, it was my own weakness that drove me to my fate, and my love for you cursed me to this mindless existence, to become a shell of what I was. It was Melia's last words that I would find you again that gave me hope. I hate her and them. I vowed that I would find you and break you, so I could sever our bond and free myself from this madness. Without you, I wouldn't be weak, and I'd find a way to become the god I once was. I could finally seek out my revenge on those who condemned me. Just when I started to give up, somehow I found a rift, a doorway outside. Barely a blink went by, and then you wandered into my life. I knew it was you when you sat in the hall. I wanted to kill you then and there. I stared into your green eyes and I couldn't... because after everything, I still love you." He leaned his head down, resting his forehead on hers, breathing her in. "Here you are, the same as before. I thought I'd never see you again."

She wanted to reach out to him, to comfort him. There was no wonder why he carried such hate for her. A thousand years of loneliness and memories would drive anyone to the brink of madness. As sympathetic as she was to his reasoning, she still couldn't forgive him for what he'd done.

"You've changed."

"No. I changed myself for you. This was always me. Only this time, I will ensure that you are mine without compromising myself, and you will learn to love me as I am."

Lilith thought he was delusional, that his time in the cage had fractured his soul.

"You need your rest. We will ascend to our rightful place as rulers of this realm. In two short nights, we will get married and then it will be the coronation."

In the blink of an eye, they were back at the palace, standing in front of her door. As she turned to face him again, to talk things through, she found the hallway empty. This act, with him suddenly disappearing before they could talk things through and have any long, meaningful conversation, was getting old.

Annoyed, she imagined somewhere down below the Mages were hanging on the wall. She would have to face becoming queen to free them. Andishmand knew about the fallen star, he had said so himself, just like Melia. He might be able to give her more information.

She walked to the door next to hers, knocking gently to see if Tally or Felicia were still awake.

A hand burst through as someone opened the door and pulled her in. At first, Lilith only took in the golden hair and curved dagger, making her flail backwards. A flash of a memory of Sif's attack. As her eyes adjusted to the dark, she made out the terrified face of Felicia.

"What happened after the ball?" Felicia's voice sounded full of panic. Lilith held both of her arms out, trying to calm Felicia.

"I should ask you that question. It looks like you're ready to pounce on me." Lilith quickly noticed Tally's absence. Felicia dropped her knife, clutching onto Lilith for dear life.

"So much has happened, I don't know where to start. And you. We felt the rumbles of what happened right after we left, and then nothing. It was too quiet. I want to know what's going on. What was with that disgusting excuse for a ball?"

Lilith moved them to the couches, using her magic to flare the room's obs to life. "That ball was just another one of his schemes. After you left, I released what was left of my mana, which were the rumbles that you felt." She turned to Felicia, looking apologetic. "I may have accidentally burned down the ancient tree that took up most of the throne room...Actually, I may have destroyed the throne room."

Felicia grinned. "Honestly, that's probably the best news I've heard in a while."

"Yeah, I'm not sure if anyone else will look at it that way. Afterwards, Demetrius took me outside the palace, somewhere in a forest with glowing blue mushrooms. He presented me with a small sphere that could restore some memories."

"Wait. Restore memories?"

Lilith told her everything, from the memories she relived as she unveiled her true self, to the purpose of why she was alive.

Once she was done, Felicia filled her in on everything that happened to her and Tally: the paintings, the haven, the classmates who she ran into. The weight of their revelations were shared between them. Lilith clasped Felicia's hand. The friendship that was growing with Felicia felt the same as her friendship with Melia. They bared themselves open to each other and expected straightforward frankness in each other's opinions. Felicia had the opportunity to escape, but chose to stay to help Lilith tear down this sanctum of injustice and deception. Once they were done, the Temple would be a covenant of ashes.

Once they had finished their updates, no one said anything for a while.

Felicia looked once more at Lilith and narrowed her eyes, "I didn't know there was a goddess named Lilith."

"Me neither." Lilith burst out in laughter. Felicia joined in. They laughed at the absurdity of their night.

"We have to go to the library. I need Sir Ravanor's help with my curse, and we need to refresh ourselves on the old gods. We only have two nights before the wedding and then the coronation."

Lilith stayed in Felicia's room, taking Tally's bed. As soon as Felicia's head hit the pillows, she fell fast asleep. Lilith, on the other hand, watched as Felicia stirred, no doubt caught up in a nightmare. Her eyelids drifted closed, thinking of another golden-haired woman and pink crystals. Her hand hovered over her heart. She had to be careful.

In the morning, they left before breakfast. Lilith opened her mind briefly, letting Demetrius know where they were heading. He had promised to return Felicia's powers, but after last night, and with Tally's disappearance, both women thought it would be best not to press the issue.

Sir Ravanor welcomed Lilith, bowing politely to Felicia, and took them to the sacred section. Lilith wasted no time, flipping open the prized book held within her clutches, eager to show him her findings.

"So you see, it's the same curse as mine. The problem is, there's no mention of how to unbind said curse." Lilith showed off her runes, while Sir Ravanor nodded. "Do you know of any mention of curses like these being broken?"

Sir Ravanor's eyes glazed over, lost in thought. Lilith and Felicia waited patiently.

"All I can think of are the Divine Curses." He scuttled off, vanishing behind a row of shelves. They could still hear his voice. "It is said that with the divine curses, the bearer would have to endure trials." He appeared once more carrying a thick book. "A curse like yours, set in one's self-transformation, alludes to three trials: endurance, destruction and metamorphosis."

Felicia fidgeted beside Lilith. "That's what we thought as well," she interrupted him. Sir Ravanor's lips pressed into a line.

"Well, I'll give this book back to you and skim the one you have." Lilith shifted, smiling at the man. "Sir Ravanor, these sacred books are all written in the holy language. The language of the old gods."

"That is what we have assumed. This language predates our existence."

"It would seem like I need a refresher on who the old gods were. Given that most of our knowledge of them has been passed down from word of mouth, I believe that my knowledge of them is more of a variation of a story. Are there any sacred books which are believed to be the most accurate depictions of the old gods? Perhaps ones that have the gods' names, Alda and Sif."

Sir Ravanor's face lit up with excitement. Once more he vanished, only to reappear with two large books.

"Of the sacred books, I can only think of two that mention the goddess, Sif. I will let you both research them here, but please..." He gave Felicia a quick side-eye. "Make sure you handle them with care." He handed them both fresh gloves and stood further back.

Lilith was used to his presence, but Felicia kept stealing glances at him. Lilith and Felicia took a seat at the small table, and started flipping through the delicate pages.

As it turned out, there were many gods, all ranked in a hierarchy. Six categories of gods: fire, air, water, earth, light and darkness. Felicia showed Lilith the first image, a massive being with dark skin and brilliant yellow eyes: Ominus, the Dawnfather, the god of creation. On the next page was a familiar woman. Long red hair, pale white skin and eyes that looked like celestial orbs. Melia, the Weaver of Fates, and the goddess of time. A goddess of light that was the right hand of her husband, Ominus. They were the first two. Though Ominus was painted as superior, Melia was undoubtedly the most powerful.

Lilith had immediately recognized Melia, both from her own knowledge and now with the memories that Demetrius gifted her. Lilith sat up a little straighter, putting her thoughts together as she voiced them out loud, "Do you think my name now is a direct result of my mother being a Maiden of Melia? That somehow, my mother was tasked to carry me and was told to name me Lilith?"

"I mean, the coincidence is too close. I'm going to go with a hunch and say your mother knew of your fate. Did she say anything?"

"She died when I was young. I don't remember much of her or what she said. I don't really remember her voice. I mean, those who knew my mother say I look just like her, but somehow I also look like the goddess Lilith. So does that mean my mother's lineage was all preordained for my arrival at this specific point? Her blood would have to carry the reincarnated version of my old self."

Felicia began massaging her temple before responding, "Gods, this is too deep for the morning."

In contrast to them, there was the god of darkness, the Harbinger of Twilight, and the Hand of Judgement, Locke. Lilith was shocked to see the accuracy of the book's interpretation versus her memory. Stark white hair, moonlit skin, with iridescent light blue eyes. The eyes of Demetrius. He was brother to both Ominus and Alda. Next to Locke was an image of a tall blonde warrior holding a flaming sword: Alda, the Herald of Chaos. The god of fire and destruction. His wife, Sif, had wavy, long golden hair and vibrant turquoise eyes. She was known as the Blossoming Flower, an Earth goddess of fertility, nature, and fortune. Felicia chuckled.

"What's so funny?" Lilith eyed her friend.

"Don't you see the resemblance?"

"To you?" Lilith pressed, curious as to how she would answer.

"No. To my mother. They're almost the spitting image of each other." Felicia squinted closer, while Lilith looked at the image once more. Where Felicia had her father's brown eyes, her mother had the same turquoise ones as Sif. So many questions sprang to Lilith's mind. Most of them she wasn't ready to voice, but made a mental note to ask Demetrius. Surely, he would have recognized Sif, if she were disguising herself as the general.

The rest of the book was dedicated to lore surrounding each of the significant gods and goddesses, and a web of battles stemming from family arguments and conquests for realms. Aside from a brief mention of Locke's wife, there was no mention of there being a goddess named Lilith. It was as if time had erased her from memory. As for the gods themselves, they seemed to fade away from existence. Both Felicia and Sir Ravanor agreed the lack of awareness or worship towards these gods in their society was probably due to a long forgotten rift between man and creator. As well, a new hierarchy and beliefs came into play as the kingdom transformed and new alliances were established. Perhaps a king had intentionally erased knowledge of the gods to proclaim dominance.

"Why is it that the information here is not taught throughout the kingdom?" Felicia asked Sir Ravanor, who had taken a seat next to them.

"We are lucky to have the collection here at the palace. These sacred books are the remnants of what this world was like before we came. To answer why we don't teach the contents of the sacred books, that lies with the decision of the royal family. They question the benefit it would have to teach the general public about this type of history. Some of these tomes have a magic that shouldn't be taught. Look at Miss Hennan and what the power of one book has done. Could you imagine the wars that would arise to claim the knowledge of these books?"

"It's a wonder the Apostles would let this place exist without interference." Felicia inspected a nearby book. "I hear they're burning books."

Sir Ravanor leaned in, keeping his words to a whisper, "They have tried, but the king has forbidden them. I will certainly be pleased when this cult falls out of favour. Those that squander our precious knowledge deserve the harshest punishment. The Apostles are not allowed in this library." The old man smiled.

"If this place is so restricted, how did Lord Elwin know about this curse to begin with?" Lilith rubbed her runes and frowned. "Did he come here?"

Sir Ravanor scoffed. "Access to this section is prohibited, unless approved by the crown. I do not recall Lord Elwin visiting this library. It could be that he has a copy of that particular tome passed down through his ancestors. Each Lord has created their own collection. Though I hear some Lords covet this type of knowledge more than others." Lilith knew Sir Ravanor was taking a jab at Lord Helmer, and the abysmal state of Skilheim's library.

They spent another few hours skimming through the books Sir Ravanor supplied, learning very little about the Divine Curses and their trials.

Sir Ravanor returned the books and walked the ladies to the entrance. "Perhaps fate has a specific time for when you would overcome this curse and return your powers."

"Fate be damned," Lilith sneered. "I don't need fate to reach my goals."

"Sir Ravanor, have you had any contact outside of the palace? Are we alone in our hatred for them?" Felicia was bold to risk asking him such a question, but she had a feeling this would be her only chance. He pulled them off to the side, looking around to see if anyone was in earshot.

"You would be surprised how one can appear subservient, only to hide their own feelings. From what I have heard, they have few friends and have yet to learn that fear does not make lasting alliances. We have heard of your predicament. There are too many eyes within these walls, for your situation to be ignored. We hope that you could be someone deserving of our trust."

"You know of the women under the Temple." Felicia tried to keep her voice a whisper, but her rage was overwhelming. "You knew what was happening to us and yet no one has come."

"That you know of. No one speaks of the failed attempts. He seems to know everything." Sir Ravanor looked at Lilith. "It is like he can read our deepest thoughts, yet, he chooses only to punish those who act." He leaned to whisper something in her ear. "We are looking for a spark. An opportunity to change the tide of events." He leaned back, his face taking on the ever jolly, obedient librarian. "Well, if you or your friend, should ever need any more information, our doors are open for you." He squared his chest as he loudly proclaimed, "My queen."

His words rippled throughout the library. All the buzzing workers halted, fixing their gaze on Lilith as they acknowledged her role. She felt the weight of their eyes and the heaviness of holding their hope. She nodded her head to Sir Ravanor and left the library.

They walked silently, eyeing up any servants or guards that they passed, wondering who was on their side. How many were waiting for this opportunity? No sooner had the door to Lilith's room closed, than Felicia turned on her.

"Gods. I like him, but that's a lot of pressure." Felicia ran her hand through her golden locks, and slumped on the couch.

"Do you know what the marriage ritual entails?" Lilith sat beside her friend, a headache throbbing behind her eyes. "I feel like every step I take I do so blind, and he is always several steps ahead." They rested their eyes, only to hear a faint knocking on the door. Lilith cautiously opened it a sliver, her eyes dropping to the floor to see a white dove tilting its head at her. She opened the door wider and let it in. Felicia let out a little squeal of excitement as she unclasped the small scroll tied to the dove's foot.

The second is beyond the mountains. The letters have reached home. The mother is wary, but on alert.

Felicia grinned. "Tally is safe. She heads to find her family."

"And the mother is wary? What letters?"

"I sent word to my mother, your brothers, and Beatrice. I gave a brief explanation as to what is happening. My mother should be aware of the threat from the Apostles, and your brothers will know of your impending marriage."

Lilith scowled, "Why would you tell them I'm marrying him? You put them at risk. What if they come here? I'm relieved Tally is safe, she is one less person that I need to worry about. I don't want to risk my family coming here and becoming another tool to control me."

Felicia stood up, clearly defensive. "They have a right to know. I told them that if they came, they'd risk being used by him. Is that how you see me? A burden used to control you?"

"No, Felicia. That's not what I meant. I'd be lost without you. I stare at a wall of darkness, a space of my own evil, and without you, I would have long since given in. I would have become his monster if it weren't for you and Tally. I'm scared. So many people have gotten hurt because of me."

"We made a choice. It was my choice to follow you. I have found my reason to keep fighting—four souls I plan to free from the chains of the Apostles. We all have a monster dwelling beneath our skin, lurking within the darkness of our minds. I, for one, look forward to releasing her. Don't hide from what you are and what you'll become."

"And what if I become like him?"

"Maybe it takes one darkness to defeat another."

Demetrius appeared without warning, smirking as if he had heard every word.

"You had a busy morning. Walk with me?" Demetrius held out his hand. Lilith shared a look with Felicia. "Oh, Miss Flavin. My half sister has disappeared. That little mouse has scurried off without claiming her prize." A beat of silence intensified the tension. "Do you think yourself worthy to have your powers returned?" Lilith's stomach sank. Has Demetrius been listening to them all this time?

Felicia fidgeted with her dress, unable to meet his eye. Lilith could see her tremble from fear, so she stood, shielding her friend behind her.

"The night did not go as planned, though I would not call it a waste. If I had not acted as I did, then would I have the memories returned? We left the palace in chaos. Things happened." Lilith rolled her shoulders back, walking towards him with confidence. "Do you regret what happened?"

Demetrius' eyes switched to obsidian, a reminder of what he was. "I only wish it happened sooner. I regret nothing."

Lilith was pushing her luck. "Then, will you return Felicia's powers?"

Demetrius chuckled, showing a mischievous smolder. "For a price." He was staring at Lilith's lips

Lilith blushed, remembering the last price.

Demetrius laughed once more. "Both of you hold off on your schemes until the coronation."

Lilith was too quick to answer. "Only if you return her powers now."

"Done." Wisps of light danced around Felicia, who gasped at the sudden rush of magic. Lilith eyed Demetrius, wondering why he so easily gave into her. She took his hand, before he could ask for more.

"A walk?"

Demetrius took her to the garden beneath her window, holding her hand tightly.

"I assume you have questions about what is coming tomorrow?"

"The marriage ritual?" Lilith questioned back. What was known to the public was brief. The royal marriage ritual had always been a mystery, a secret kept within the family. To any normal family, marriage was just a formality, an announcement declaring a couple's shared commitment to each other, but usually there was no magic or bond involved. Thus, many forewent marriages and just lived together without formal celebration.

Demetrius pulled out a jewel crested knife. "Do you recall Sypher and Cosmo?" Lilith frowned, thinking of her classmate Cosmo and his mentor Sypher. As she could recall, she had caught them engaging in a peculiar act. They were necromancer, blood manipulators, that used a combination of blood and mana to enhance their magic.

"Do you know everyone's secrets?" Lilith asked.

"Only the dark ones."

"What does our marriage ritual have to do with blood necromancy?" Lilith also remembered Sir Hawthorne's sassy remark that it was quite sexual.

"The marriage ritual is more sanguimancy than necromancy. We're not invoking the dead, but we do use a similar blood manipulation. How would the people react if they knew that the most sacred ritual performed between their rulers was that of the most condemned magic, power through blood manipulation? All kings and their queens are bonded by blood magic."

"Why would they do that?"

"Did you know that the strength of the most prominent kings, the battles won, and the allegiances made were all possible through blood sanguimancy? Some delved into necromancy itself, raising dead armies to fight for them. It is why such a practice is frowned upon. The same people who relied on it, made it impossible for others to use."

Lilith shrugged. "To be honest, considering the things that I've learned of over the last few days, I don't find that surprising." Demetrius snickered at her reply.

"Our marriage will be sealed through blood. We tie our souls together. You will never be replaced."

Lilith snorted, "Rich, considering how many consorts your father had. His father and your forefathers all have had consorts."

"I will not. I shall take no one other than you. I seek no one else."

"Why not just use rune magic to bind us?" She looked at the line of runes she had, made from a deal between them.

"Because blood magic tethers us together. Bound by blood. Failure to adhere to the terms made between the two parties would forfeit one's life."

"Since you don't plan to follow in your ancestors' footsteps, why not do away with such a tradition?"

"Because I don't want to. I made a sacred oath to you once before, and I intend to do it again. Our souls are already intertwined, and we are bound together beyond fate. How many times have I told you, you are mine and I am yours. Not even death's hand can take that away."

Lilith blushed. When he says such things, not even she was immune to his declarations, his unfaltering love. "Tonight is my last night as Lilith Hennan. Tomorrow, I will become your wife."

"Do you not want to?" Demetrius turned to face her. His eyes looked grief stricken.

"I...I do." Lilith needed to become queen. She couldn't look into his eyes any more. She would become his wife, but too much had happened, and also she had walled off her heart. The throbbing behind her eyes intensified. "I need to rest."

Demetrius brought her back to their room, as Felicia had long since retired to hers.

"Then, you should rest. We both have a busy couple of days ahead." Demetrius kissed her hand. "I will bid you good night, my bride." He stared at her for several heartbeats, words left unspoken, before he vanished.

Lilith's face distorted first in pain, from the constant headache, but then transformed into something more disturbing. All the culminating events had taken their toll, and she had begun to enter the deep crevice of her psyche—the place she had forbidden herself to explore. She surrendered to that part of herself that wanted to burn everything to the ground, and she would be left in its centre, rejoicing.

Chapter 17

The Sacrament of a Crimson Sacrifice

Felicia

B reakfast and lunch went without trouble. Felicia came to Lilith early in the morning, where they ate, and then the stylists showed up to help them prepare for the ritual. Felicia never really understood what exactly occurred during royal rituals since the last one was between King Amadeus and Queen Isolde. Their hair was not as flamboyant as the style they had used for the ball. The stylist braided Felicia's hair in a half-up, half-down style. Lilith, on the other hand, had her hair down in soft curls. The stylist wanted to say something, her delicate hands shaking as they hovered over Lilith's hair.

Felicia wondered if they were allies. She shared a warm smile with them, which seemed to ease the tension around them.

"How does it feel to have your powers back?" Lilith picked at her fingernails; she was clearly nervous.

After they had left her alone last night, the sudden rush of magic had overwhelmed her senses. She wouldn't dare tell

Lilith that she had spent the night struggling to control the surge of energy roaring through her blood. It felt like her emergence all over again. Thankfully, her fever broke at dawn, but the lingering effects remained. Pain lashed through her aching muscles. She considered the return of Lilith's mana, how unfazed she seemed to be, as if it had been there all along. How could it be so different for her?

"I have yet to test them. My body needs time to adjust to having them back. I suppose I'll have ample time after today to practice, while you…" Felicia's insinuation was enough to make Lilith blush.

Once their hair was done, dresses were laid out for them to make their selections. Felicia waited while Lilith felt every dress, her hands running down the silky materials. The stylists bowed to the women and then left without a word. Clearly, they were ordered to do their job and nothing more. Maybe Felicia was wrong about them.

"You are absolutely useless," said Lilith to Felicia, who was just standing about waiting for her next instruction.

"Fancy dresses and balls were not really a priority with the general as my mom. It makes me feel uncomfortable dressing up to impress others."

Lilith picked up a pale peach flowing gown with layers of sheer skirts and a tight bodice, and turned to Felicia. "It's more than just impressing others; what you wear amongst these people will signify your power, your status, in comparison to others. The materials you choose, the cut of the dress, the colour, and accessories all work in harmony to give the perfect armour."

Felicia slumped on a nearby couch and sighed, "I hate this culture. This is so unnecessary considering we're all facing the impending doom of the darkness taking over. We're literally on the brink of extinction, and right now we're prioritizing a marriage celebration. We should be preparing for battle."

"I agree. We should be focused on helping those who were displaced, the crowds of common folk dying from starvation, because most of our resources are sent to the encampment. However, we do not have sway or say over what we should do. The only person that has that influence are the ones seated on the throne. I need to be the queen, so that we have a chance at changing our future."

Though Felicia knew that this was the plan, it was strange to think that Lilith would be their queen, and from this day forth, she would rule this kingdom. She watched the blood drain from Lilith's face. "Lilith? Are you okay?"

"As good as someone who is about to be married to a king who is a controlling asshole." Lilith sank to her knees, her breathing becoming ragged as she clawed at the opal stone flooring.

Felicia rushed over and knelt on her knees, clutching Lilith's arms and pulling her into her chest. She recognized a panic attack unleashing. "Breathe, Lilith. In and out. You are still in control of your life. Just focus on what is in this room, right now. Describe to me what you see." Felicia spent all of her childhood dealing with her own panic attacks, thanks to her mother.

Lilith didn't respond for a while, but eventually she spoke with a shaky voice, "I'm in a room with my best friend, Felicia.

We just had our hair done because today... Today I will be marrying Demetrius." She started panicking once more.

Felicia slowly ran her hand in small circles up and down Lilith's back. "I will be with you every step of the way." She looked over to the wardrobe. "Ultimately, this is your choice. We could try to escape. We could try to leave."

Lilith shook her head. "We tried that before, and we'd be leaving behind the Apostles' prisoners and the Mages. We need to stay. I need to stay and see this through. I choose to be a queen worthy of ruling this kingdom. I choose to pick out my dress for this ritual, to bind myself to Demetrius so that I can have the power to make the changes I want to see. I refuse to hide and cower. I refuse to let him conquer this world and plunge it into darkness," she stuttered the last part in broken sobs.

"And you won't be alone. I will be here for you, no matter what." Felicia stilled her hand. "Your next steps will be hard—the most difficult decision you'll be making in your whole life—but you will fight for us, and I will fight for you."

Lilith cradled her face in her hands. "I'm so scared."

"I am, too." Felicia embraced her until Lilith's sobs calmed. Felicia was starting to see red at the unfairness of their circumstance. "If we have the opportunity, we can try and kill Demetrius."

Lilith wiped her tears and stared at the fire raging in her friend's eyes. "Even if we managed to get weapons, we would be no match for him. The power he's shown us is only a fraction of what he is capable of. This is not the right time to show our hand. We need to be patient."

Felicia stood up. "You're right, patience is our friend. Then we focus on freeing the Mages, freeing the prisoners, and making our way to the encampment. Demetrius can't fight off an entire army."

Lilith scoffed, "The general is loyal to the king. Unless we force Demetrius to show his true self to the encampment, to her, the army won't believe us."

Lilith rose and held her hand out for Felicia. Felicia stroked Lilith's cheek. Her eyes were blotchy, but she was still beautiful.

"I'm sorry," Felicia said, as she stepped away.

"Why are you apologizing? If anything, your presence here is entirely my fault. I am the one who is sorry."

"I won't lie and say I wasn't mad at you, but I'm sorry for not being a better friend. You consider me your best friend, and yet I haven't been upfront about my life with you. I held you at a distance because I considered you competition. I should have opened myself up to you, and I am mad at myself for not seeing Demetrius' lies earlier. I should have asked you more about how you feel about him. I should have told you what I thought, but I didn't."

Lilith smiled, "I should have been more open with you, too. For me, all the challenges that kept coming up, I felt that I had to face alone. I just wanted to get through those obstacles as fast as possible and get on with my life, but I forgot to stop and take care of my friends." Felicia pulled Lilith into one more hug.

"Okay, let's get through this."

Felicia took Lilith's suggestion of wearing a periwinkle blue gown with dark silver embroidery, that was made of a buttery material. The neckline was high, and was paired with billowing, sheer sleeves and a draped skirt. The feathered silver embroidery had pearl beads stitched in, which stopped at the hip. She marveled at her own appearance.

Lilith had her own selection of three traditional-looking robes. They were all a deep midnight blue shade, the same dark blue colour of Demetrius' and Tally's hair. Though her hair was obsidian, her duty would be to continue the royal line.

Felicia came to stand beside her, critically assessing each choice. Her hands stopped over a robe with a mixture of black and gold embroidery, which almost looked like ink-like flames were trailing up the skirt. While the skirt was primarily a rich, deep midnight blue, the bodice and sleeves were entirely gold. A thick band of deep blue fabric was hung loosely off to the side, to be tied around her waist.

"You should try this one on." Felicia handed over the ensemble. Lilith nodded and started to change. While she was gone, Felicia rifled through the assorted accessories.

"Will we be allowed to watch the ritual?"

"I am not sure. I assume if you're allowed to watch, you'll be sworn to secrecy. Do you know if your mother will be in attendance for the coronation?"

"I'm sure she's been summoned, but there has been no show of our white-feathered friend. I hate that we are being kept in the dark." Felicia passed her a few gold-chained bracelets.

Lilith held up her trembling hand. "My nerves are frantic. I'm sure my father will have lost his mind with worry because I haven't sent a letter. But it's been weeks, and I haven't heard anything. Was I wrong to believe he cared more for me? I never thought I'd be marrying someone without my family being there. It feels wrong. This is all wrong. "

Felicia sighed, picking up a pink crystal necklace on a simple gold chain. "Are you sure you want to do this?"

Lilith winced as the necklace was fastened around her neck and sighed. "We've gone too far. I have to do this."

Felicia rubbed Lilith's shoulders. "Both of my parents were always too busy. When my father was around, he was pleasant and would enjoy my company, but since my brother disappeared, he's been distant. Almost as bad as my mother. I bet they believe I'm living in luxury. Even if they knew the truth, they're bound to serve the king. There's nothing they can do, and it's safer for them not to come."

Lilith wiped away a tear. She stood in front of Felicia. The gold tones of her rich olive brown skin glowed against the gold bodice.

"You look absolutely stunning." Felicia commended her, giving her an appreciative scan. "You look like a queen."

The entrance to the room opened, and the stylists rushed in to finish getting them ready.

In a final flurry of hands and brushes sweeping over their skin, they were finally ready for the ritual. The evening sun cast hues of deep oranges and pinks into the room.

They stood at the entrance, listening to the heavy footsteps making their way down the hall. All ten Apostles came in, their white robes looking fresh and perfect. Their blood red stoles looked pristine.

"My lady, are you ready to head down?" the centre Apostle asked. Felicia scanned the rest of them. There had been twelve, but after their attempted escape, two had fallen beyond saving.

She was so sure that those two would somehow recover, and it sent a thrill of satisfaction learning that ever so slowly, they were meeting their fate—their death.

"Yes. We are ready." Lilith nodded. They moved silently through the halls, down past the wrecked throne room, and outside. Felicia glanced around the royal garden, to the warped tree that stood in the middle. They walked until they reached the Temple.

The Temple was built before the palace; its style seemed out of place with the rest of the buildings. Meticulously carved stone pillars held up long stone beams. The Temple was built with multiple short levels, becoming narrower as it reached the clouds in a rounded peak.

Grey robes opened the door and bowed to Lilith as she walked through. To the right was the staircase, but in front was another set of doors, held open to reveal the inner sanctuary: a large room with dark grey walls. Though the outer perimeter of the Temple was surrounded by open windows, the inner sanctum of the Temple was dark. Thousands of tiny orbs flickering with yellow light hovered in the vaulted ceiling above, illuminating the interior. Felicia felt a shiver of cold as she entered the space. How long had it been since she had been tortured here? It felt as if there was an unseen presence watching over them. The smell of blood permeated the air. Felicia wondered if that smell was her own blood spilled here, or if it was fresh. Beneath them, four souls were still held captive. Through the silence, she tried to hear their wails, their cries for freedom. This sacred space was now tainted by innocent slaughter. She glared at the backs of the Apostles' hoods.

Patience.

This was not the time to make a move.

King Amadeus and Queen Isolde, along with the consorts and the children, all stood inside. It was the first time some of the consorts had seen their children since the Apostles arrived. The hands of the mothers clenched the clothes of their children, clinging to a desperate hope that they would be kept together. Felicia eyed the terror lacing the eyes of each child. This was not an event surrounded by blessings or by shared feelings of hope, nor was it a time of celebration. This was a sacrifice.

At the end of the room there was a sea of candles lit around crumbling, rune-carved pillars, with Demetrius standing in front of it. He wore a midnight blue robe that fell to the floor, tied at the waist with a thick gold band. It was simple compared to what Lilith wore. His eyes were that light blue, masking the evil that lurked beneath.

He grinned at Lilith as she took her place standing beside him. Felicia was pulled off to stand with the consorts. They didn't risk meeting her eyes. Some of them were trembling, while she could see the backs of King Amadeus and his queen. They stood so still.

They waited for the last Apostle to take his place next to the altar before one of them spoke.

"We are gathered here to witness the union between Lilith Hennan and Demetrius, son of King Amadeus."

Felicia looked around again at the other guests. Lilith's father and brothers were not in attendance. She could only think of how Lilith felt about getting married without her family being present. She knew it was safer for them not to be here, but it felt wrong. Lilith's eyes drifted to her; they were full of sorrow.

That inside voice spoke to her, telling her to say something, but as Felicia opened her mouth, Lilith gave a little shake of her head. Felicia scoffed so loud it was heard above the voice of the Apostle.

Felicia rolled her shoulders back. She had failed to stand up for Lilith, but not anymore. "There seems to be a few people missing at this union. Don't you think Lilith's father and brothers should be here?" She stared Demetrius down.

Demetrius took a deep breath, his eyes never leaving Lilith's as he addressed the crowd, "I sent word, but they appear not to have shown."

Felicia started to talk back, but Lilith interrupted, leaning forward to whisper, "We both know you could have done more than send word. If I am to marry you, the least you could do is have my family in attendance."

"Are you sure you want them here?" Demetrius asked Lilith. Felicia understood the hidden implication of his question. *Are you sure you want to risk your family's safety?*

Lilith frowned. "I... I need them here."

Felicia smirked, feeling proud of her friend. Demetrius stood back, vanishing into thin air. After a heartbeat, he reappeared with a very dishevelled-looking older gentleman. He rushed towards Lilith as Demetrius vanished once more.

"Lilith?" the man questioned. "What's going on?"

"This is very complicated, but I'll explain when Arlen and Jasper arrive."

Demetrius popped back in, holding the collars of Lilith's angry-looking brothers.

"What in the gods are you doing?" Jasper yelled, pulling free of Demetrius' grip. He finally took in his father and Lilith. His eyes roamed Lilith's gown, confusion written all over his face.

Lilith rushed through her explanation, blushing deeply. "Yeah, okay. I know this is very short notice, but I'm about to get married and I want you to be here."

King Amadeus and his queen made no movement. Felicia wouldn't be surprised if they didn't show any emotion to the scene that was occurring before them. The consorts, however, kept silent, but they weren't judging Lilith. The hate in their eyes lingered on Demetrius.

"Are you out of your mind?" Lilith's dad leaned in, keeping his voice low. "You cannot marry him."

"Dad. I need you to trust me. Please," Lilith begged him. Felicia saw him searching her eyes, trying to read his daughter's thoughts. Lilith nodded to him. "This is what I want. Please, just trust me."

It was enough of a plea that her father took a step back. One of the consorts, Lady Landiel, came forward and grasped Lilith's father's arm and pulled him in to stand with them.

Lilith's brothers turned to face Lilith. Arlen reached for his sister as he asked, "Are you okay, Lilith? Just tell me, and we can leave."

Felicia's heart melted hearing Arlen's words. Part of her wished Lilith would take Arlen up on his offer, but instead Lilith smiled at him.

"I'm right where I need to be," Lilith replied to him, clasping Arlen's hand. "Though I appreciate your concern."

Arlen side-eyed Demetrius, who paid him no attention and then went to stand next to his father, pulling Jasper along with him.

"May we continue, my king?" The Apostle waited for instruction. Demetrius nodded and held Lilith's hand.

"We are gathered here to witness the union between Lilith Hennan and King Demetrius; through the passing of blood, their lives will be tethered. Their marriage is sealed through the ancient words of our forefathers, through the word of the gods." The Apostle held up a dagger in a golden, gemmed scabbard. He passed it carefully over to Demetrius.

Demetrius pulled out the shining blade and held it over his own palm, saying,

"I bind my life to yours through the crimson tether of our blood. I vow to protect and keep you safe as we walk along the path that the gods have blessed us with. I offer not just my heart, but my soul and the life force that runs through my veins. Through storm and darkness, we will rise together, even as we cross into the underrealm. You are made for me, as I am for you. Together we are bound in flesh and blood. Our souls become one, shared by the unity of this marriage."

He paused to slice his palm with the dagger, and thin beads of blood pooled in his hands. He passed the blade to Lilith, who mirrored his actions and vows.

The Apostle clasped their hands together, and raised their joined hands. "Repeat after me:" He spoke in the ancient tongue. Although these words were unknown to Felicia, she could feel the rise of magic shifting around the couple. Lilith's father whispered the translation.

"With this blood, I share with you my power. From this day on, we are one. I will bear your pain as my own. I vow to love and cherish you, from this day until our last days. May these words brand our bond. May our blood be united. So it is spilled, so shall it be sealed."

Demetrius and Lilith each repeated the vow, pressing their wounded palms into each other, mixing their blood. Golden mana swirled around the two, dancing over their held palms. Felicia had never witnessed a marriage ritual and was shocked to see golden mana flowing through their hands, initiating their marriage bond.

The couple turned to face the spectators. Lilith's eyes looked glazed over, emotionless, as a round of applause burst around them, mostly from the Apostles and the grey robes. Felicia didn't join in. She didn't feel happiness for what her friend had sacrificed.

The Apostle stepped forward. "We will now let the ritual complete, if you would please head towards the palace."

Felicia stood stone still, as others were herded with Lilith's family and the consorts outside of the Temple.

"What do you mean?" Felicia asked the Apostles.

"What now?" Jasper turned to face his brother and father, mirroring Felicia's confusion.

It was Lady Landiel who answered, "Now they complete the ritual." She bowed to Lilith's father. "Sir Hennan, a pleasure seeing you. Your presence here has been sorely missed by many," she spoke, with genuine politeness. Felicia's eyes assessed Lilith's father; she had almost forgotten that he was Councilman Cyrus Hennan, now reduced to Sir Hennan.

Felicia gave him a warm smile. "Lilith has spoken very fondly of all of you. Sir Hennan, I'm sure she was very grateful that you stayed, given the circumstances of who was in attendance."

Sir Hennan blushed and shuffled on his feet. "Ah, yes. Though it seems his former highness did not even acknowledge my presence. Over a decade I have served him, yet he does not even pause to recognize me." Felicia was sure there was more to say, but they were surrounded by so many Apostles, it was for the best that some words remained unspoken. King Amadeus didn't stop to speak with any consorts, nor any of his children. He and Queen Isolde were quickly steered away by three of the Apostles and some of the grey robes.

"If you want to stay with us until the coronation, you'd be most welcome," Felicia offered, turning to face the Apostles who were clearly assigned to guard them. "We won't have a problem with that, will we?"

The Apostle closest to her kept up his facade as he replied coolly, "Sir Hennan and the others had not received an invitation to the coronation."

"Now that Lilith is united with your king, it will be in your favour to treat her family with respect. Lilith will be upset if her family is absent from the coronation. Luckily for you, the ritual was private, but the coronation will have many more spectators, and you probably don't want to redo the scene that played out earlier." Felicia weaved her arm through Lilith's father's.

The Apostle considered her words and tilted his head in the direction of the other Apostles standing next to him. Without saying anything, they nodded. The front Apostle spoke once more, "We will welcome you, Sir Hennan and the Hennan family. If you would kindly follow this Apostle, he will lead you to your private quarters."

"No need. He can come with us," Felicia insisted, smiling innocently. Her face revealed nothing.

The Apostle said nothing, but motioned for them all to follow. Just as they were leaving, one of the consorts pushed her way past a line of grey robes and clutched her child's arm.

"Please. Please let them stay with us." Another consort held her back.

"We have to let them go," the consort reassured her. "We will see them soon."

Felicia could see Sir Hennan was about to say something, so she tugged on his arm and whispered, "Stay your words. There is much you don't know."

Once inside, the Apostles deposited them in Felicia's new quarters. Usually they would leave, but this time they lingered about.

"We will see to the final preparations for the coronation. I leave the Hennan family in your hands. We will leave four of our apprentices outside, should you need any assistance. Please expect the help to arrive soon to get yourselves changed." He smiled at the group and left. Felicia shuddered at his false niceties.

Jasper looked outside the windows of the living area, while Arlen and Sir Hennan waited by the doors. After a while, Sir Hennan raised his hand and cast a silencing enchantment at the door.

Arlen approached Felicia. "Quickly, we don't have much time. Tell us what is going on. Is Lilith safe?"

Felicia rubbed her clammy palms on her dress as she spoke up, "How much do you know of what the Apostles are planning? As the former councilman, you must have knowledge of whom we are dealing with."

Lilith's father stroked the stubble forming on his cheeks while frowning. "My spies have kept me somewhat informed. I can see that they are fully in control of the palace. I am wondering if they coerced Lilith into marrying the prince, but I don't understand the benefits of doing so. Not to speak poorly of Lilith, but a marriage with her would not further any alliances. About a month ago, my contacts here went quiet. "

"I sent you a letter. The Apostles are not the ones pulling the strings. They are merely the puppets of a greater evil."

"Letter?" Jasper interrupted. "What letter?"

"Not that long ago, I sent letters to you." She pointed at Cyrus.

"Which I received."

"And to my mother and to you." She pointed to Arlen. Arlen placed his hands on his hips.

"There was no such letter."

"Well, as I explained, we have been prisoners here at the palace since our arrival. The prince betrayed us. He's evil, and those Apostles worship him. Everything that's happened—the nobles supporting the Apostles, the closing of the schools, the rules being put in place for merchants, and the push for soldiers to stay at the encampment—it has all been him." She felt tears brimming. "You have no idea what he's put us through. The pain and suffering..." Her breath came out ragged as she tried to keep her emotions from spilling out.

"What exactly happened here?" Arlen's voice was booming.

Felicia trembled from anger, from their sheer ignorance. She told them everything: every lie that was spoken from the mouth of the deceiver, every act of torment that the Apostles made her and Lilith suffer, what they've been doing to the consorts, and her suspicions about King Amadeus. It was a gamble to reveal so much, with Demetrius possibly hearing everything, so she kept the Mages and the Consort's Haven a secret.

Felicia gave them a warning. "There is more to the prince than what you have seen. Somehow, he is powered by the Void, and the Apostles worship him. Well, mostly. Their goals lie with attaining power. The being that has taken over Demetrius is a sentient evil that escaped the darkness. Lilith believes he was a god stripped of his holy power and cast into exile. She believes she was his wife from another lifetime."

Sir Hennan interrupted, "You mean to tell me, Prince Demetrius is actually a fallen god from the Void? And I just watched my daughter marry it? And don't tell me she wanted this marriage. From what I could see, she did not look like a beaming bride."

Felicia considered her next words. She had to be careful because if Demetrius learned that the Hennan family knew the truth, they would be joining the prisoners below the Temple. She turned to Arlen and Jasper, who had started pacing about the space. "If you go back to the encampment, you must tell my mother what is going on. We need numbers, people on our side, to free the people living here. I tried to tell her, but it seems like she's skeptical. Don't you think it odd that the expansion of the darkness is taking its time? In the span of a year, the south fell before the Mages were able to erect the barrier. It's been months, and the darkness has barely expanded."

"This is absolutely insane!" Arlen paused pacing and joined his father. "And Lilith?"

"She has a plan, one that requires her to stay, for now." Felicia looked nervously at Cyrus before continuing, "My concern is that now that you've heard what we've said, the Apostles, or even Demetrius, will prevent you from leaving. He's trying to keep things discreet, and now you've learned the truth."

Jasper stopped pacing. "We could kill him. If all of us attack at the same time, we could destroy the Apostles and Demetrius." He looked to Arlen for support.

"You think the four of us could somehow overpower all of the Apostles and their king?" Arlen laughed.

Jasper growled in frustration. "Then, we could head back to the encampment. Convince the general to bring forces back here." He swatted his brother's shoulder. "I told you Beatrice Bane was not some loon. She's been telling the truth." His gaze settled on Felicia. "There is discord in the encampment as well. We realize that the encroaching darkness has all but halted, conveniently outside our lines. Some believe that it is the work of Mages, but it's really the prince. The soliders just want to go home. Too long have we been stationed waiting for an evil that has yet to show its face. The soldiers are tired, hungry, and homesick. It won't take much to convince them that the true threat has already sunk its claws into their families. Amiriel has voiced his distrust of the prince. The strength of his command can persuade many to come back here."

Sir Hennan's brow furrowed. He was clearly thinking things through. "I have already let my daughter down once before. I don't want to abandon her to suffer."

"If you stay, she will only worry about you. It was Lilith's wish that you were all present for her marriage ritual, but you have to leave. She will only suffer more if you stay. He will control her by using you." She eyed up Jasper. "I suspect we will need the army on our side, not that newly appointed king. If you think there's a chance that you can inspire those in charge to fight for Lilith, then you need to go back to the encampment."

"Can't we wait until we've seen her?" Arlen asked his father.

Cyrus looked like he was dealing with a stubborn headache. "We can try."

A little knocking sound tapped on the window. Felicia spotted the friendly white bird perched on the window ledge and smiled. "I have a plan. The stylists will be here soon. How good are you at casting illusions?"

CHAPTER 18
THE SCENT OF CITRUS AND WILDFLOWERS

Lilith

Lilith blushed as the Apostles and their apprentices ushered everyone out of the Temple, leaving her alone with Demetrius, her husband. Mana circled around them, through them, and her body heated from the building energy.

Goosebumps exploded up her arms, and the hair stood upright on the back of her neck, making her shiver with a keen awareness that she was being watched.

"My wife." A deep, soothing voice came from behind her.

Pleasure shot through her at his words. Lilith had a vague understanding of marriage rituals, since many people now considered the practice outdated and avoided the ritual altogether. Her parents, however, had gone through the ritual, and their marriage was formally recognized by the crown. The aftermath of the ritual, its completion, wasn't exactly discussed with her. With Arlen's birth happening exactly nine months after, she suspected what occurred. Turning towards

Demetrius, she felt the tips of his fingers reach out and gently trail down her arms. Icy blue eyes pierced hers with a predatory focus.

It felt as if something outside of herself was compelling her to be near him and touch him. For once, she allowed her feelings for him to take over her hesitancy. She allowed that part of her that wanted to reach out and touch him, to feel his skin under her, that weight of a familiar comfort. Right now, she was carried by the memories of her previous life and the love she shared with him. With a tenderness she'd been hiding, her hands reached to him, resting on his silky chest. Every sensation felt like it was amplified a thousand fold. The weight of her gown felt too heavy, her skin felt too hot as though something burning was flowing through her veins. She fought with the desperate need to shed her clothes and bare herself freely in front of her other half.

His steady breaths slowly rose and fell. The sharp sting from her other hand made her wince. Demetrius gently picked up her injured hand and turned the palm so the slice faced him. She noticed his pupils were blown wide, and his usually calm demeanour held a disturbance. His velvety soft lips kissed her wound. The sensation made her gasp, and he opened his mouth to run his tongue across the slice, pulsing mana through the touch, spreading more warmth throughout her body and surging wetness between her legs. That sharp sting slowly faded, but he didn't stop. Licks turned to kisses that trailed up her arm. His touch seared her skin, boiling the blood in her veins. She needed him, but she hesitated.

Disbelief clouded her judgment at how tender he could be. A flash of memory crashed into the forefront of her mind, a time in her past where he kissed every inch of her.

With the next kiss, Lilith closed her palm resting on his chest, scrunching the silky fabric of his robe. A little tug brought him closer. His scent filled her nose, making her pause. A part of her once relished that scent, but now it made her nose scrunch up in disgust.

"What's wrong?" He scrutinized her every move.

"Nothing." She tried to sink back into her emotions, but scrunched her nose again as she breathed him in.

"Lilith. Tell me."

A light blush covered her cheeks, "I am not a fan of the scent of your soap. It stirs up emotions of what's happened between us lately. I'll be honest, with everything we've been through, I'm having a hard time separating this pull I have towards you from our disagreements." She took a step back, unable to meet his eyes. "I wish this were easy." She hoped for a different version of him, one that was kind and compassionate, who cared for the world and the people around them. This version of him lived through her memories, and she knew a part of that version still lingered within him. He taunted her with it at Skilheim; it's what drew her in.

A finger pulled her chin up. "Look at me," Demetrius whispered. Lilith struggled to move her eyes, frozen from anguish that she would stare into the eyes of a monster.

"Look at me," begged Demetrius.

Her eyes rose to find the hollow spot of his throat, then went upward towards his chin, the sharp tip of his nose, until they finally settled on his eyes, which spoke to her. The same eyes he shared in both lifetimes.

"I want you so desperately, it feels like there is a fire in my heart. Every breath, every move, every sound you make burns me to my core. You are the spark that has shaken my earth. My life is nothing without you. While my scent stirs your emotions, your scent leads me further into madness. That sweet, intoxicating scent of yours, which radiates from your soul, consumes my every thought and my every feeling." He pulled her into his veil that can move between the fabric of space, transporting them into his bathroom. With a flick of his hand, the water faucets sprang open. "If it's my scent that deters you, then I will change it."

Lilith held her tongue. She wanted to say, *"And if it is your plan, your actions, will you change those, too? The scent bothers me because it invokes memories of times you were cruel and wicked. You've locked me in this cage, isolated me from those I love, with only your lingering scent as my companion. I've seen a side of you that I can't love. Will you change that too?"*

She wished so desperately that he would change for her, but her circumstances were not about her alone. There were others that she had to think about. Straightening her spine, she came within an inch of him, her shaky hands rising to undo the tie of his deep blue and gold robe. Her hands reached upwards to push off the outer layer, feeling his chiselled chest under her palms. The warmth of his body seeped into her hands.

Calloused hands found hers and stopped them. "Can you feel it?"

Lilith tilted her head as Demetrius closed his eyes and brought her hands over his heart. The rhythmic thrumming of his heart beat against her hands.

"Feel how steady my heart beats for you. I will be your strength, my goddess. You don't need to be nervous. You don't need to fear me."

"'My goddess,'" Lilith repeated his little nickname. He'd been teasing her with the truth all this time.

"You are my goddess in this lifetime as well." His fingers caressed her face, leaning in. "This is taking too long." With a quick snap of his fingers, both of their clothes disappeared. Her eyes lingered on his bare chest, the light curls drifted down towards that V-shaped curve between his hips. An awareness of his eyes roaming her naked body made her blush, but her eyes drifted further south. He was standing at attention. She licked her lips and watched him take her in. Desire lingered in his eyes. The sacred energy of the ritual pulsed through them, urging for completion.

Warm steam rose from the large bath, and Demetrius held his hand out to help Lilith into the perfectly warm water. A deep sigh exhaled from Lilith's mouth as her toes dipped in. Demetrius leaned over to one side and brought over a small wicker-woven basket holding small cloths and three vials of liquid.

"I want you to select a scent that speaks to you."

Lilith hesitated. It didn't matter which scent she picked. In the end, the smell of him would trigger those memories of her time locked in their room, of every time he manipulated her, lied to her, betrayed her. No scent could cover up those memories. Without thinking, she uncorked the first vial and brought it under her nose. A refreshing burst of an aromatic herb hit her senses, with a fresh lingering tingle that felt cool and soothed her nerves. She didn't mind this perfume. It was all too similar to his own scent that there would be little difference. The second vial smelled zesty with a tangy aftertone. It was equally as refreshing as the first, but smelled so sweet she could almost taste it. The third scent hit home, quite literally. It smelled of the cottage after Arlen had cooked up his favourite fruit and was ready to can them, and a faint floral mixture that reminded her of walking through the nearby meadow. With another inhale, the scent picked up spicy tones that warmed her soul. This was the one. This would be the scent she would have chosen for the man she wanted to love, the man worthy of her love. But Demetrius had not proven himself worthy of her. She re-corked the third vial, picked up the second, and handed it to him. It would suffice for now. A clean slate that was far from the normal soap he currently favoured.

Demetrius poured the liquid on a wet cloth and lathered himself up, pausing to hand her another cloth with the vial. They lingered in the bath, in an awkward silence, until Demetrius helped them out and handed her a towel.

"I didn't expect this awkwardness between us. I know we have differences, but it's like your mind is elsewhere, rather than here." He scoffed and ran his hand through his hair. "It comes as no surprise that you are fighting the persuasion of the blood magic, our marriage ritual."

Lilith tried so hard to suppress her own thoughts and feelings for the sake of others, a knot formed in her stomach, and an acidic taste crept up her throat. "I made a promise to be your wife, and I intend to keep my word."

"But you look at me with an emptiness."

There was nothing Lilith could have said to further help this moment, so she stayed silent, her breathing turned heavy as she continued to shut herself down, and suppress the mana that was trying to overwhelm her.

Demetrius handed her a robe and donned one himself. He looked miserable. "This was not how I envisioned this going. Every time I look into your eyes, I see the words you want to say but are choosing not to. You are unhappy with how I live, but can't you see this is all for you? I wanted a world where you were safe to be with me—a world where others would see us as equals. This place, these people remind me so much of my brothers and those that betrayed me, that I feel like it's only right to transform this world into something different. I can reshape this world for us. I can make it a world that could keep you safe."

Lilith let out a breath she'd been holding. Her shoulders relaxed slightly as she spoke, "I want a world where my family and friends no longer have to live in fear. This world is far from perfect, and these people are flawed, but taking away their freedom and their lives is not the way. I don't want to live in your world of darkness with only the shadows of my loved ones haunting me. I don't need you to keep me safe because I'd rather take the risk of dying in order to help those who are too weak to fight, even if it means I'd be opening myself up for betrayal. I am trying so hard to give you what you want without having to compromise my own feelings, but it's impossible. What you want from me is impossible."

A look of pure anguish crossed over Demetrius' features. He raised his hand to reach for her, but hesitated, and gave her distance instead. "I will not force myself on you. I wanted you to come to me and make the choice to be with me as husband and wife, like we were, and I'm willing to wait for you. You are right. I have been saying that I see you as my equal, and yet I haven't been treating you as such. I want more time with you, a future with you, but I won't force your hand in this marriage.

"What are you saying?"

"We will not complete our marriage ritual tonight. I will wait until you are ready."

"But we're supposed to go through the coronation later. Don't we have to seal our marriage before that?"

"Lilith, you and I will make our own rules. What do you want?"

"You're asking me that now?" Anger rose in her, "I want you to stop the spread of the darkness. I want you to take your place as King and care for the people you rule and not see them as pieces of your plan. I want you to free us from the Apostles, to free those women who are being tortured at their hands, to let Felicia go. I want you to return Silver to who he was, to spare everyone at the encampment from having to fight a battle they cannot win. There is so much I want you to do, but you refuse to listen to me."

"I hear you. I listen to every word you say, and I will address your concerns. You want so much for others, but I'm asking you, what do you want for yourself?"

Lilith was shocked by his question. She had stopped trying to think about what she wanted for herself because she was so focused on keeping going. She'd had to keep moving forward and pushed herself to figure things out for all the challenges that she now faced, but she had lost sight of what she wanted to do with her life.

"I want to stop fighting. I want to stop having to repress my emotions, just so I can survive. I haven't stopped once to fully think about the weight of what has happened to me because something new and terrible keeps happening. You once told me I am quick to adapt, but that's not the truth. I've just bottled everything in. I've put on a brave face for so long that I forgot what I want. You know what I really want? I want to live my life without anyone trying to manipulate me. I want to wake up in the morning without that feeling of panic and dread. I want to feel all of my powers because they're mine, and have no one else threatening to take them away. I want to be with the version of you that stood up for me, the version of you that wanted to save this kingdom. I want to be with the you that laughed with me and let me choose. That is what I want."

They stood in silence, letting her words sink in. Demetrius took a tentative step closer, "I value what you want. I see you for who you are, and I'm sorry. I want to give you all those things you want. I want you by my side because you are happy to be there, but I've done so many things wrong that I don't think I can come back from the person that I am now. The coronation will happen today. I will ascend to the throne, and I had hoped you'd be there with me. But I can give you the choice. Choose to be my queen, not for everyone else, but for yourself. I will let you choose from here on."

"And this marriage ritual?"

"Can wait. You are my future, my goddess. I have waited a lifetime in darkness for you."

Lilith nodded, fighting back tears. Demetrius took her hand and led her to the couches. "Rest. The stylists will be here in a few hours. You can tell them if you want to attend the coronation or not."

Demetrius looked like he was about to leave, so Lilith grabbed him by his cuff. "Stay with me? I've been alone for so long, I want you to stay with me."

Demetrius nodded, picking her up in his arms and taking her over to the bed. She blushed as she felt the mattress dip beside her. Lilith rolled to her side and watched as he stared at the ceiling. Not once did she question his love for her; he made it abundantly clear that she was his obsession, but even now she knew he was battling his own conscience. He once claimed that he wanted to rid him of her, refusing to let her become his weakness, but his actions didn't line up with his words. If she could just persuade him to see things from her perspective, maybe this wouldn't be such a lost cause.

"Where have your thoughts drifted to?" Demetrius whispered, rolling to his side to face her.

"You are at odds with yourself." Lilith touched a stray curl of his deep blue locks. He breathed deeply, his eyes lingering on her face. "Would it be so bad to try it my way?"

"What would you have me do?" He spoke to her with such tenderness. She knew at this moment, he was completely at her mercy.

"Will you let me lead?" Lilith's hand caressed his cheek until her thumb drifted over his lips, those lips that parted at her touch; the pulse of his heart could be felt through her fingertips.

"I'm as tired as you are, and I want to spend every moment in this bed as we are now. I..." Demetrius tentatively brought his fingers over hers. "I am willing to try if you are."

Something snapped in Lilith's resolve. His eyes held no falsehood, no lies. She knew innately that he was telling her the truth.

Lilith nodded and leaned in, licking her lips as she breathed in that sweet citrus scent. His face dipped down mimicking her movements, their lips only a hair's distance away.

"Kiss me," Lilith ordered. She wanted to taste his lips on hers, to give him a reason to fight for her. She felt his hesitation, so she ordered him once more, "Kiss me, Locke."

His lips crashed onto hers with urgency, his tongue prodding at the seam of her lips. Lilith opened herself, floating her hands down his arms. He explored her, tasting her as their bodies shifted closer and closer, pressing themselves into each other. A moan escaped. She didn't know if it was hers or his, but she knew she wanted more. More of this, more of him. The effects of the blood magic she had fought so hard to ignore surged with a vengeance.

With sure hands, she undid the tie of his robe, pushing him until he was on his back and her legs straddled him. The heat between her thighs began to build, knowing that these robes were the only thing between them, and right now, she could feel his erection pressing into her. She broke their kiss and raised her head to stare into his icy blue eyes, which were almost black—only a crest of icy blue remained.

"This is for me." Lilith trailed her hands down between her breasts until they reached the tie of her own robe. She untied the sash and nudged off the soft robe. Demetrius moaned as she bared herself to him, only him. Her lips found his again as she savoured her time. He was hers, and she would fight to remind him of everything that was important.

Her hips rolled on their own, grinding on his erection. Hands pressed down on her hips, pushing her harder onto him.

"I want you inside me," Lilith moaned, between kisses. It wasn't the magic that made her desperate; it was her own truth. She desired him. She needed him, beyond reason. The energy that demanded they complete the ritual felt like a hum on her mental wall. One she could ignore if she needed to. However, locking him out felt like her soul was fracturing.

She reached between them, lifting herself up to align her soaking wet entrance to the tip of his length. Ever so slowly, she sank down, working her way inch by inch down him. Demetrius bit his lip, furrowing his brow in concentration. Her breasts bounced as she worked her way to the hilt, letting out a deep moan, and with a shift forward, she started grinding on him.

"You feel so good," Lilith mewled, shifting her hips forward and back. That building pressure was slowly rising.

"If only you could feel what I feel. Pure bliss," Demetrius said in a strained tone. He pressed her hip into her, driving himself deeper.

Lilith gasped at the fullness, making Demetrius pause to chuckle. She tightened around him, making him moan once more.

"Let me in," Demetrius begged.

She knew what he was asking. A plea she felt across her mind.

"Don't make me regret this," she warned him, as she allowed him into a space where they could share their minds freely.

Immediately, she could feel everything he was feeling—his perspective of him moving within her, her walls clenching around him, the slickness that flooded around him. Then, she was hit with the emotions that he was feeling. The seemingly endless desperation to be with her, and the need to become one. The longing. This intimacy was just the tip of what he wanted, what he longed for. There was an indescribable yearning that pained him. A hint of pieces of his shattered heart, slowly repairing.

She felt a tear spilling down her cheek, realizing that her pain was only a sliver of what he had endured. His love for her was infinite, transcending time. In this moment, he was experiencing a rebirth of something he had considered impossible. He was hers, and she was his.

"Oh my gods," she cried out as she kept riding him. That heat deep in her core was edging closer to exploding. She could feel him reaching his climax as they bared themselves open.

"Just the one god," Demetrius smirked. Her hips moved wildly as she chased the pleasure that spilled into bliss.

"I can feel you tightening around me, my goddess, I can feel you tipping over the edge. Cum for me, my love."

"Demetrius," Lilith cried out as her climax slammed into her, but he didn't slow his pace as she rode through waves of pleasure. Surprise shook her, wondering how he had not found his release. She could feel his heightened need for more.

Demetrius paused to flip her around so that she was on her hands and knees. Looking over her shoulder, Lilith excitedly waited for his next move. He spread her knees wide as he slammed into her, filling her right until his end. Over and over, he drove in and out, the slapping sounds of wet flesh hitting flesh echoed around them. Gone was the gentle relish of each other's bodies; this was unrestrained and rough.

With his mind laid bare, she was overcome with his raw emotions. He was holding himself back so that she could find her release once more. It was a different type of anguish, one that bordered on the purest of ecstasy.

He reached his hand around and started circling her most sensitive spot. She was barely down from that last high before she started to feel the chase of another climax, and she allowed him to feel her emotions. She allowed him to experience everything she felt.

With a pull of her body close to hers, her back was upright and against his chest as he continued to hammer into her. His hand paused, only to reach further up to tease her nipples. She felt the hot breath of Demetrius panting behind her, tickling her neck.

"I'm so close." He moaned as he continued driving her wild. He suddenly pulled out and flipped her to her back, widening her legs as he pushed into her once more. Emotions became less rational and more wild.

Love. She could feel his deep, unyielding love.

"Touch yourself, Lilith. I want to watch as you bring yourself to cum over me." His words came out at the same time as she felt his cock twitch inside her. Lilith reached between her legs, a blush staining her cheeks as she started to rub herself, her eyes drifting closed.

Immediately, he stopped, "Eyes on me, my love." The absence of movement was a denial of his own pleasure. One that felt like a denial of hers. It drove her mad.

She watched him through her lashes as her hand started picking up its pace. He spread her legs as wide as they could go, his eyes roaming down her body as he pounded into her at a relentless pace. It didn't take long before another climax came crashing down on her, her internal walls pulsing around him so tight that it sent him over the edge. With their minds connected, she was engulfed in each other's release, a pleasure so profound it made her consciousness dip into oblivion.

As her awareness returned, golden magic danced once more around them, coming from the fresh scars of the palms. It drifted through her, igniting her soul as they lay intertwined. She felt his soul entwining with hers. It was as if her blood stormed, and every beat of her heart became every beat of his. An immense power filled her senses, adding to her own pool of energy. His mana touched hers, bowed to hers, and eventually faded.

They were united as one.

Demetrius started moving again, this time slow and purposeful. His pupils had overtaken any traces of icy blue, and Lilith was certain hers would match. Every movement felt a thousand times more sensitive. She didn't know if it was her fingers or his that trailed up her body. She was absorbed by the feeling of tongues slipping in each other's mouths. The build of pleasure was anything but subtle, the energy moving and weaving between their bodies, coaxing out intense waves of rapture which shuddered along every nerve.

A pain etched along her hand, the one that had been sliced for the ritual. She knew this pain, a familiar sting of runes being carved into skin. They kept writhing, hands intertwined, as they watched dark runes appear on their ring fingers. A pact was sealed between them, forever tethering them to each other. They took their time, savouring each other with their touches, with every kiss, until they could no longer stand the pressure of their climax, and crested their ecstasy together.

"You are my everything," Demetrius spoke so affectionately. She understood that he was bearing his heart to her. She kissed him, recognizing his vulnerability without having returned his words. A part of her had always loved him. But she was not ready to acknowledge her feelings. Her mind was trying to catch up to the weight of her choice to be his wife. She wondered if it would always feel this way between them.

He leaned over her, breathing heavy. "I know your body so well, my love. You're wondering if it will always feel this good? Yes, my dear, it feels this good every time, even in our past, our connection was just as strong, and I'm not just referring to our physical one."

Demetrius pulled out, leaving only to get her a wet cloth. "We have enough time if you want another bath."

Lilith nodded to him, her legs feeling like they were unable to stand. "I just need a few minutes."

Demetrius came back with a warm, wet cloth and carefully cleaned her off, lifting her once more into his arms. He brought them back to the freshly warmed water, and she sank blissfully into the bath. With closed eyes, she could hear him uncorking a vial. The smell of the third vial hit her nose.

"I noticed the extra inhale you took of this one; your face hides nothing," he stated, foaming up a cloth and slowly washing her down. She relaxed completely to his touch and let him wash her off. Her breathing became deeper as she nodded off.

"Hey, don't fall asleep in the tub." Demetrius nudged her awake. He had finished cleaning both of them off and hopped out of the tub to get a fresh towel. "Here." He helped her out and wrapped her up.

Lilith was in a daze as she felt herself being tucked into bed. She could have sworn she heard a deep voice whisper, "I love you," before falling into a deeper slumber.

CHAPTER 19
REBIRTH OF THE CROWNS

Lilith

Felicia came bursting into Lilith's room, with one of the stylists following. Lilith bolted upright as her hand drifted to the empty spot next to hers. It felt like only seconds had passed in her sleep.

"You're officially wifed up," Felicia chuckled, drawing back the long drapes. "So, where is the blushing husband?"

Disappointment rocked through Lilith. She assumed that after what they had just done, Demetrius would have stayed with her. "You know, I don't know."

"Huh, well, he's got a lot to do, you know, developing a ploy to doom mankind."

Lilith turned to study Felicia. She was never this sarcastic, and although she'd always been blunt, she wasn't ever this blunt. "Are you okay? You seem a little off..."

Felicia chuckled, "Dang, here I thought I was doing a pretty good impersonation." Felicia's body turned into Jasper's. The loose-fitting dress he wore as Felicia strained against Jasper's body.

"Jasper!" Lilith shifted the covers of the bedsheets to cover her naked self. "What are you doing?" Her eyes shifted over to the stylist, who was silently glaring at her. With narrowed eyes, Lilith eyed her suspiciously. "And you are?" In her head, she was pleading for it not to be her father.

The stylist pinched the bridge of her nose, then went to the wardrobe and threw a plain dress over to Lilith. Scrambling under her sheet, Lilith scurried to pull over the long pale blue dress. She shifted off the side of her bed, and began nervously fixing her hair. From the corner of her eye, she saw the stylist return from the room's entrance, then shift into Arlen. Both of her brothers were still wearing dresses, which made for a hilarious sight. Their bulging muscles strained under the silky fabric.

"Am I still dreaming? Because there's no way this," Lilith waved down their bodies, "could be real." She was grinning like a fool, holding in her laughter. Jasper picked up a nearby pillow and hucked it at her, which she caught. "So, why have you two gone to such trouble to sneak around as a stylist and Felicia?"

Arlen fidgeted with the hem of his dress. "We're trying out Dad's illusory skills. That man continues to surprise me."

"Dad knows illusory magic? But that's a rare thing to know. I thought only royals were privy to such knowledge." She thought back to when Demetrius had turn himself into a tall blonde, 'Locke,' as they travelled through the ruins. Locke—he had used his real name. All this time he had shared little truths about who he was.

Arlen's eyes flared with emotion. A cross between anger and respect. "It looks like even dad has his secrets. It doesn't surprise me that a royal councilman specializing in strategy would use this sort of magic. Dad is a master of knowledge, after all."

"Well, you had me almost fooled, until you opened your mouth, or in your case, Arlen, acted like your usual self. So I would say his magic works."

"That's good news then, for our plan to work. If we can avoid running into people who would know us, we might be able to get out," Jasper grinned.

"What are you guys talking about?"

Jasper continued, "We're leaving before the coronation, and you should come with us. We're going to try to switch places with the stylists. They're here to get you ready, and we're going to walk out as them."

"Again, what are you talking about? Why would you leave now?"

"Since your dear husband brought us here, we're likely going to be imprisoned, much like yourself, especially since we've been talking with your friend. I like her, by the way," Jasper admitted.

Lilith groaned, realizing her mistake in wishing them here. "I'm sorry. I was caught up in the moment, and I just wanted you here while I got married." The first pangs of guilt bit into her feelings. "Is Dad mad?"

"Dad is concerned that he just watched his daughter marry a monster, so yes, he's mad. I, on the other hand, am furious. Why would you go through with it?" Arlen was using his scary, calm voice, which he had used to berate her as a child.

"You know, I never really noticed until now that your eyes bug out slightly when you use that tone." Lilith wanted to shift the conversation away from her current predicament.

"This is not the time to make jests, Lilith. Do you understand what you've just done?" Arlen held his hands on his hips.

"Yes, Arlen, I do. The barrier around the Void is about to collapse, and I know that I have to be by his side to actually make a change. Maybe I can convince Demetrius to spare those who are taken by the darkness. If I am with him, maybe I can spare everyone at the encampment. For once in my life, I have clarity as to what I should do next, so stop chiding me like I'm a child."

"Lilith, you can't be serious. Look at what he's done... who he's put in power. He is incapable of changing."

A knock at the door had the three jumping. Arlen and Jasper quickly donned their illusions with enchanted bracelets. Jasper's was a braided golden colour, while Arlen's was made from a deep red braid. In came a few grey robes, carrying a mountain of dresses. The grey robes deposited the dresses on the couches and then hurriedly left, choosing to ignore everyone in the room. Once they had left, everyone relaxed a little.

"So what's the plan? What have you done with the actual stylists?"

Jasper, dressed as Felicia, responded, "It's quite a long story. We'll head back to the other room, and we'll be right back with them in tow. Don't worry, we can trust them."

Jasper and Arlen dashed off through the doors, leaving Lilith looking puzzled. She quickly fixed the rumpled sheets, knowing her father would be coming in, and waited for them on the couch.

The real Felicia, without the bracelet, came in with the real stylists and her family. All looked quite nervous as they nodded to the four grey-robes and an Apostle stationed outside her doors.

The Apostle followed the group inside, hovering by the entrance.

Lilith glared, "You may wait outside."

The Apostle answered calmly, "Our orders were to keep an eye on all of you."

Lilith walked to inspect him. She recognized the bottom half of his face. By some luck, it was the same one who was the victim of Lilith's attempted escape, the one that Demetrius had urged her to kill. "You have no authority over who is in my room. You will wait outside. Unless you'd like me to summon my husband? Or have you forgotten that I am your master as well?" She pressed a finger on his stole, leaned in, and whispered calmly. " It must have been quite shocking to realize your worth is so little to him. Should I tell him you barged into my room and demanded to watch me, right after I had just completed the marriage ritual? What do you think he'll do? Whose words does he value more? If I were to kill you here and now, do you think I'd be reprimanded? Do you think he'd care?" She spied his usual smile falter, replaced by a thin, tight line.

She could envision the wheels turning behind his covered eyes. He was weighing his options. After a brief pause, he nodded and left. The pressure of eyes settled on her back. She turned to face the group, and most of them gaped at her.

"What was that?" Jasper gawked. He looked at her like she had sprouted a second head.

Lilith scoffed, "That was a test of my newfound authority." She eyed the three stylists, "Now tell me, what did I miss?" She settled her sights on her dad, who she was beginning to learn had more secrets than she had previously thought.

Her dad was the one who explained the situation. "We had initially planned to coerce these ladies, but Felicia took a gamble on them and asked them for help. Ladies, will you introduce yourselves?"

The little brunette's cheeks turned red, but she stepped forward, bowing to Lilith. "My name is Maxine. It is an honour to be serving you."

Lilith also blushed. Over the several times they had helped her, she had yet to ask them for an introduction. She looked not only at the brunette but also at the other two as well. "It is nice to meet you, Maxine. It's been quite a blur lately with everything going on. I apologize if I have forgotten your names."

The red-haired woman stepped forward, introducing herself as Ruby, while the lavender-haired lady introduced herself as Cece.

"My lady, we offer our help," the red-haired woman announced, her grey eyes fixed on her shoes. "We are but a few that are invisible to this palace: servants that are overlooked and remain silent as we do our job, but see much." Her eyes locked onto Lilith's. "We know the truth. We are placing our trust in you, and hope that you will be the voice of those who are too weak to fight back."

Felicia stepped to Ruby's side, interrupting her, "They despise the Apostles and the changes that are enforced in the city. The servants are scared, but they don't align with the prince's schemes. They know everything."

The short brunette spoke softly, "I have no magic myself, only a few of the servants do. We are powerless to stand against them. What can we do against a power like theirs? We wanted to free you, to free all who are held captive here, but we are inferior. How does a mouse fare against a lion?"

Cyrus patted Maxine on the shoulder. "The mouse befriends another lion to help them." Lilith teared up at the look her father was giving her. It felt as if he was seeing her for the first time, seeing her potential and her strength.

"It takes courage to step forward, and for that I am grateful." Lilith bowed her head to them. "If you're willing to risk your lives to help my family, then I am indebted to you." She faced her people. "So, what is the plan?"

Felicia cleared her throat. "The plan is to have you get ready. Our little feathered friend made an appearance, so I have enlisted help from a mutual ally. The stylists will switch appearance with your family while they make their swift exit. Then they can resume their usual appearances."

"And where will the stylists hide while they escape?" Lilith thought through Felicia's plan.

"A haven of sorts," Felicia grinned.

"Okay, I like this plan. We should get ourselves ready for the coronation." Lilith turned to face her brothers.

Arlen looked like he was about to cry. "Wait. Why can't you all just portal us home or out of here?"

Lilith didn't even consider that option. "I have tried on numerous occasions, but it seems like someone, probably Demetrius, has placed a barrier around the palace that prevents me from summoning portals. If the barrier came down, I could portal you out. As long as the rune stone is at the encampment, I can anchor a portal to it."

"We brought the rune stones with us." Jasper pulled one out of his pocket.

Lilith grimaced, "Then it's looking like this is our only option." A quiet knock came from the wardrobe. Felicia sprinted to it, opening the door to help the mutual ally inside.

Lady Ashmore wore common folk clothes, with a humble brown cape draped over her shoulders.

"Lady Ashmore!" Lilith's father greeted the woman warmly. "Thank the gods you are all right. The last I heard, you had all but vanished."

Lilith narrowed her eyes on her father. He was King Amadeus' councilman, and when he was forced out of that position, she assumed he knew nothing of what was happening here. She didn't consider that he would have people still working here, feeding him information.

"Did you know? All this time?" Lilith's heart sank at the possibility that he once again stood by, knowing what was happening to her, and chose to do nothing.

Cyrus' face pained, and he pulled Lilith closer. "I had eyes here up until a month ago, and then they went silent. Around the same time, I received a letter from you, saying that you had arrived safely and were staying at the palace to help Demetrius. At first, I wrote to you every day, and I received a short letter saying that all was well, that you were enjoying your life in the city. It said that you were busy, so you might not be able to reply as often. Weeks went by without hearing from you at school, so I assumed you were okay here. I've been investigating what happened to my contacts. Until I received a letter from one of them saying that Demetrius was working with them, I had no idea that you or your friends were held here against your will. If I did, I would have been here, trying to free you."

Anger clouded her thoughts. She remembered Demetrius telling her that he had forged her hand to pacify her father. She felt horrible that she had assumed the worst of her father. She held her face in her hands, as angry tears spilled out.

She felt her father's gentle touch pull her in for a hug. "It's okay. I'm here now. I will always be on your side. We will always be here for you." She felt more bodies wrap around her, encasing her. Her brothers rested their heads on hers.

Arlen's motherly voice soothed her. "You are more capable than you think. Just trust your instinct and don't forget it's okay to make mistakes. Forget about what everyone else thinks, and just focus on what you need to do to make it to the next day."

"I can stay with you. You don't need to carry this burden yourself," Jasper added.

Lilith wiped away her tears, looking at her family.

"I am not alone." She glanced at Felicia and at the stylists. "I am surrounded by support. This is something I must endure. I will face this without succumbing, and I will ground myself like the earth under fire. I will see this through, knowing that you have my back. You all are the tower of my strength.

However, I cannot face what's to come with the threat hanging around your necks. You have to leave."

Jasper squeezed her, "I will further your cause. We're heading to the encampment to try to convince the general to send you help here. If you need to bail and things turn south, head to the house."

They broke apart. The stylists all had red-rimmed eyes. Felicia looked absolutely stunned.

"Okay. I'm ready." Lilith turned and followed the stylists while they quickly did her hair and makeup. Felicia whispered something to Lady Ashmore, who nodded. The stylists swept Lilith's hair into an intricate updo, while hiding her tear-stained cheeks and puffy eyes with an elegant face of makeup.

Once they were done, they went to change out of their clothes and handed them to Lilith's family. Arlen kept the weaved red bracelet, while Maxine and Cece cut strands of their hair and gave them to Cyrus.

Cyrus worked quickly, braiding their strands while muttering his illusory spell. He donned the lavender one and gave the brunette strands to Jasper.

Lilith pulled Felicia to the pile of clothes.

"Wait." Felicia turned to the stylists who were now in their chemises. "Would you do the honour of selecting the gown you'd like to see your queen wearing?"

Cece bowed, inspecting the options. She pulled out a long, red and orange velvet gown. It had a skirt with a long train, embroidered with gold accents. Lilith remembered seeing old paintings of former queens, draped in blues and silver, but she refused to be like them. Gold flames trailed up the skirt, with a large embroidered piece going up the centre, until it hit the waist. Lilith would have to be laced in, as the flames highlighted her cleavage in a gentle curve, fanning out along the tight-formed sleeves. The embroidery was carefully crafted with thread that gave off a celestial shimmer. The other stylists all nodded at the piece.

"This is you. The flame of the voiceless," Ruby stated.

Lilith appreciated their choice. This dress was a bold statement. She was not a mere tool of complacency. She was wrath incarnate. A goddess of fury, and the queen of justice.

It took all three stylists to get her into the gown. Felicia walked into the room wearing a long-sleeved, silver gown, dotted with crystals. The skirt was layered with sheer fabric, and it had a deep, v-shaped neckline.

Lady Ashmore stood beside three nervous-looking stylists: Arlen, Jasper, and Lilith's father.

'Ruby' spoke with the deep voice of Arlen, "Dad thought of a possible issue. We're going to assume Demetrius will want your father and your brothers present at the coronation. Not only that, but the stylists themselves must be seen leaving the room to avoid suspicion."

"Even if we stay behind, the Apostles will check to see if we have attempted an escape," 'Cece' spoke with her father's voice.

The real Cece raised her hand. "Then we will disguise ourselves as you. We will continue the charade until the illusory magic runs out, and then we will escape ourselves."

Cyrus added, "I can cast an illusion of the stylists, but it would only last for a few minutes at best."

"That's all we need. No one pays attention to us, anyway," the real Ruby answered.

Lady Ashmore interrupted, "I will help you make it out of the city. But your families that remain here will be put in danger."

"We are each other's families. Our parents sold us to the palace as children. We have only each other," the real Maxine spoke.

Lady Ashmore passed them the sack containing Lilith's family's discarded clothes. "Then let's hope this plan works." Lilith's father was busy making more illusory bracelets. Lilith watched her father work, his fingers moving quickly as he enchanted the fibres. By the ease of which he used this magic, she gathered this was something he had practiced frequently. Why would he need to know illusory magic in the first place? She didn't have time to dwell on her thoughts as everyone bustled around her.

With everyone ready, Lady Ashmore walked through the back of the wardrobe. The real Jasper and Arlen gave Lilith another quick hug before walking through, leaving her dad last.

Cyrus, disguised as Cece, cleared his throat, "I want you to know, even though we can't stand next to you, we are fighting with you. I have so many regrets in losing your mother, that right now, I'm afraid I'm making the wrong choice."

"I have this, Dad. My relationship protects me, but I can't guarantee your safety. Not with the Apostles. You need to reach the encampment and send help."

"Oh, Lilith. My little girl." The false Cece cupped Lilith's cheek, resting her forehead on Lilith's. "You are so strong, and

I'm not just talking about your powers. Your heart and your mind are a force to be reckoned with. If you find yourself with no way out, make one. I'll be waiting for you. I love you." She placed a kiss on her forehead and took a step back. Lilith was fighting for a hold on her tears. Cyrus raised his hand, casting a bright light which settled on the floor. From it stood three very shy-looking stylists. The illusion made them slightly transparent, but it would be enough to pacify the Apostle.

"I love you too, Dad." She watched them disappear into the dark tunnels before replacing the back of the wardrobe.

With her family gone, Lilith could feel the panic setting in. There was so much happening, between the coronation, the celebration ball, and now her family's escape.

"What's wrong?" Felicia clasped Lilith's forearm.

"It's just all getting to me. Everything we have been through, and everything ahead. I'm scared and I'm exhausted."

"I understand. We've been through so much lately, and you've just been soldiering through. I can see that you're stopping yourself from fully feeling everything that's happened. I get it, I'm doing it too. There's no room to stew in our emotions, no time to dwell on how we're hurting. You've gone through so much in such a short amount of time, and I'm not just talking about our time here, but at Skilheim. Everything has been piling up, with new challenges and problems arising daily. All this stress, all your bottled-up emotions are crashing into you." Felicia tucked a strand of long black hair behind Lilith's ear. "But now is not the time to give up. You have to muster up whatever strength you possess, and we're going to do our part so your family has a chance at escaping. You have to make everyone look at you, focus on you, so that they can't see what's happening under their noses." Felicia looked at the fake versions of Lilith's family. "Ready?" They gave her a series of nervous smiles. She held the door open for Lilith.

"Are you ready to go down?" The Apostle approached her, peeking into the room to see that everyone was accounted for. The illusory stylists kept their eyes down in respect.

Lilith didn't glance back, but walked forward, waiting for the four grey robes to assume their position at her sides. "We are." She waited for the Apostle to walk in front of her, relaxing slightly as he made no comment about the stylists.

Outside of the queen's wing, they heard the guards approach, Demetrius at the centre, his eyes fixed on her.

"It's time we head down. You look radiant, my wife." Demetrius gave Lilith a kiss on the cheek and then turned to face her family. "Please, you are welcome to head with us to the throne room." The three bowed to Demetrius, saying nothing. He held his arm out for her to hold and headed down.

Lilith started to spiral as her thoughts turned dark, imagining Arlen, Jasper, and her father getting caught mid-escape. She bit the inside of her cheek, a move she reserved for when she was on the verge of losing control. She thought of the possibility that they would get caught by the Apostles, and she wouldn't know. Her panic formed a hollow ache in her stomach.

Outwardly, though, she gave off an air of refinement. Her carefully crafted expression was unwavering under pressure. Inwardly, she felt dread sinking its claws into her.

She turned her head to look outside a nearby window, the bright cloudless day beaming down. *I know you can hear me, Melia. I need your guidance. Please. I'm so lost, and I feel like*

I'm drowning. Please, help me. Lilith sent her silent prayer, hoping that her call would be answered.

"Nervous?" Demetrius asked her.

"There will be so many eyes casting their judgment on me." Lilith gave him a reasonable excuse. She could feel her palms sweating.

"Focus on me. They do not matter. You are their queen, their ruler, just as much as I am." As Demetrius spoke, a few of the Apostles' smiles faltered. Lilith glanced at the Apostle who walked them down; though he showed no emotion, she knew he had heard Demetrius' proclamation.

It seemed like everyone had assembled in the throne room, as the hallways had all been deserted by guests, except for the guards. A procession line was forming in front of the closed throne room doors. The consorts, Demetrius' half-siblings, King Amadeus and Queen Regent Isolde, all waited in a nervous silence. The former king and queen looked a bit more spunky than usual, with Amadeus chatting quietly with the only Apostles stationed outside. Just as they stood in front of the doors, Demetrius turned to Lilith's family once more.

"Why don't you head in and make yourselves comfortable. We will be starting shortly." By his words, the door opened for them. Lilith's father walked by, pulling Lilith into a quick hug. Lilith closed her eyes, imagining her real father holding her.

"Thank you, Dad." She watched as they disappeared into the sea of faces.

A slow, silky force pressed on Lilith's mind, permission for Demetrius to enter. Lilith cautiously obliged, letting him into a very contained space where her thoughts did not freely linger.

'I figured that should give them a chance to get away.' Demetrius' words startled her.

'Excuse me?' Lilith's fingers began nervously shaking.

'Relax, my love. I would not harm them. The Apostles, on the other hand, I do not trust entirely. Also, the wardrobe. Really? It's my room. You think I don't know about Lady Ashmore?'

'How did you find out?'

'Your mind is shielded like a fortress, but your brothers and the stylists, not so much. Makes you wonder: what are they teaching in Ardaven?'

'What will you do with the real stylists?'

'Right now, I'll let them make their own escape. Though I rather liked Ruby; she's the only person I trusted to cut my hair.'

Lilith's mouth hung agape as she side-eyed Demetrius.

He leaned over, smirking, "You may want to close your mouth, they're about to announce us." Lilith snapped her mouth shut and glared at him, just as a horn sounded and the enormous carved doors opened slowly to the throne room.

"And Lady Ashmore? Will you hunt her down?"

"Why would I? I have had ample opportunity to stop her. I realize the more I hurt the people you care for, the more I risk losing you. I told you, you win." His voice became silent as an Apostle called the room to stand.

The sounds of hushed murmuring came from inside, the anticipation of what was to come silencing the crowd. As a calm fell over the throne room, the rising melody of a choir began. The royals that stood in front of Lilith and Demetrius started uniformly proceeding down the aisle.

Lilith moved side to side, eagerly trying to figure out what the throne room looked like, given that she had destroyed it a few nights before. With Felicia marching with the consorts, Lilith was left standing behind Queen Isolde. Her view became much less obstructed as she marched closer to the entrance.

Somehow, the glass-paneled ceiling had been restored, likely thanks to magic that repaired most of the interior. Clear sunlight filtered through the polished glass, shining on the white stone. Where leaves and lanterns would usually accent the blooming ancient white oak tree, only the charred trunk stood in its place. The single white throne that sat before it was marred by her fire, streaks of black crawling down the back, as if a dark hand was holding the back of the throne, a contrast to the otherwise pristine environment. It seemed that not even magic was able to restore the ancient tree, whether it be immune to such effects, or was simply damaged beyond repair. If anything, the dark black bark only made the throne more prominent.

A sharp note of a soprano rang through the vaulted space, rising above the overlapping tones of the deep bass and tenors. The choir of assorted men and women all wore dark grey robes, a nod to the royal blue colour. Their song came to a close as the former rulers stood at the entrance.

'Don't smile, and when Amadeus and Isolde reach their post, you walk past them, and give them a short bow.'

'You know, a rehearsal would have been great.'

'There was a rehearsal, you were otherwise predisposed, resting after our marriage ritual.'

'Right. Well, is there anything else I should know?'

'There will be a variety of speeches made by the Apostles and King Amadeus. I will have to make a vow to serve the throne, as *will you. It's a 'repeat after me' thing, and then our crowns will be placed.'*

'Okay. Just repeat the vow and receive the crown. Got it.'

Old King Amadeus and his queen marched in time with the choir's new song as Lilith and Demetrius shuffled forward, waiting for their turn. Lilith rubbed her clammy palms on her red dress.

"You truly look stunning. This colour brings out the green of your eyes," Demetrius whispered. Then his voice filled her mind, *'Your breasts are very tempting. If I were to kneel before you, would your dress conceal me?'*

Lilith felt heat flaming her cheeks as she pictured Demetrius underneath her skirt, between her legs. *'This distraction is really not helping my nerves. I'm now flustered on top of my fretting.'*

'You'll do great, my love. You are a goddess amongst men, born to be a queen. A natural leader. Above everything, it is you that I want by my side. Only you.'

Lilith took a steady breath in, and she tried to focus on the dark blue runner below her feet. Just like the ball, she felt the gazes. The last note of the choir had come to a close. Everyone turned to look at the couple at the entrance, the new king and his queen.

With an unsteady first step, Lilith's knee buckled, but before she could fall, a hand grasped her forearm. Demetrius weaved his arm through hers, anchoring her to the present. Each step they would take would be together. Familiar faces that had attended the ball surrounded her. After her outburst at the ball, she could feel their judgment. They did not like her or want her as their queen. In defiance, she straightened further, raising her chin and her eyes. She would not cower in their presence. How dare they judge her. She hated these people, these nobles. Their smiles made her shiver in disgust.

Her ears were ringing as she took step after step down the aisle, drowning out everything else. With the white throne only a few feet away, Demetrius paused with a frown on his face. This expression was concealed from the crowd as he recomposed his features and turned them both to face the crowd.

Former King Amadeus and Queen Isolde sat to the front right, while the consorts took up the front left flank. King Amadeus looked pale and sickly, exhausted by the recent frivolities. While the consorts looked nervous, they could feel a great change transforming the royal line. They were aware of the uncertain change threatening the kingdom's way of life and its societal structures. Behind Demetrius and Lilith, the nine Apostles stood as pillars surrounding the new rulers, confining them.

The Apostle at the front lifted his hands, signalling to the crowd that they may sit. His voice echoed around them, "Today, we embark on a new dawn. Step forward, Prince Demetrius, and ascend to the throne. May..."

"Wait," Demetrius interrupted. "This will not do." He turned to face the crowd, a frown on his face.

Lilith looked at him with confusion. "What are you doing?" she whispered, staring at the curious eyes of the crowd.

"My wife is my equal. She is my one and only queen. She will rule over you, as I rule over you. She is the only woman that will be by my side, and I will take no other."

He turned to face the Apostles, raising his own hand. A warm yellow light emerged, sparks that danced above his palm.

The magic moved to the cindered tree, surrounding it. Lilith could hear Demetrius chant something under his breath in a language as ancient as time. He spoke the language of the gods, words that Lilith could now understand, thanks to her little jog in memory. The black bark began to disintegrate, its particles swirling amongst the sparks, circling next to the white throne. Gasps broke out among the crowd. This kind of magic extended beyond the normal elemental mana they were used to. This was a peek into the power of a god. This tree was sacred. She was told the tree could not be restored. No normal mana could touch its ancient bark, but he could.

Do not forget how this tree came to be in this state. I can hear your thoughts, but you have yet to realize your own magic burned this tree.

Lilith gasped at the realization. Her magic was like his, yet hers was all but a shred of what it could be. They all watched as black particles pressed tightly together, becoming a solid structure next to the once white throne. In a matter of seconds, a second throne appeared next to the original, a dark twin.

Demetrius clasped hands with Lilith, switching sides with her. The white throne would be hers, while the dark one would be his.

Once standing, Demetrius turned once more to face the crowd. Lilith's eyes trailed from Demetrius' face to the sea of witnesses. Awe and confusion mixed on their faces.

The Apostle cleared his throat, and the murmurs died. "Step forward, Prince Demetrius and his bride, his queen..."

"Our queen," Demetrius snapped.

"O-Our queen," the Apostle stuttered. "Ascend to your throne and call upon your mana. Are you ready to take the Royal Oath?"

Demetrius smoothly replied, "I am."

Lilith quickly mirrored his answer.

"Will you do your duty to uphold the laws of the Kingdom of Draydon?"

Both Demetrius and Lilith spoke, "I vow to govern and uphold the laws of my people."

"Kneel before the throne." The Apostle waited for them to kneel. "Are you willing to abide and advocate for the primary religion and swear to defend its ideals?"

From the corner of her eye, Lilith spotted a quick grimace flash across Demetrius' face as he replied, "I will do everything in my power to defend the ideas of the true religion." There was a pause as Lilith considered the vow.

"I will do everything in my power to defend the ideas of the true religion of the Kingdom of Draydon, so long as they respect and protect its people."

The Apostle frowned, but continued. "May you sign the official oaths." Another Apostle came forward, holding a long document and a long, slender knife. A dark blue wax seal was pressed at the bottom, showing the royal crest, a blooming oak tree. Demetrius cut his thumb, pressing the beads of blood beside the seal. He passed the knife to Lilith, who mirrored his movements.

The Apostle spoke once more, "May the holy one that watches over us, protect this kingdom and its faithful servants. May we glorify His name, and seek everlasting life; through the darkness we will rise. Amen."

Demetrius knelt before the throne, speaking the ancient tongue, "May I serve to protect what I hold most dear. I offer my power to restore this kingdom to a new glory. By my hand, may I create a better tomorrow. Amen."

Lilith was close enough to the Apostle that she could hear the faint growl. Clearly, Demetrius was going off script. Yet in front of all these people, the Apostle was powerless. "Present the crowns."

To Lilith's surprise, it was King Amadeus and Queen Isolde who stood. A guard opened up a wide, polished chest, and each royal reached inside to raise a crown. King Amadeus held a carved circlet of a white crystal made to look like leaves. A smaller matching one was held between the hands of Queen Isolde.

In step, they stood before Demetrius and Lilith. Demetrius bowed his head as his father placed the crown on his head. Queen Isolde edged closer, and Lilith looked to the ground, bowing her head to receive the crown. As the crown came closer, a soft tune sang to her, similar to when she was surrounded by the crystals in the Ruins of Thurndun. The drumming pulsed between her ears as the crystal touched her head; the weight was heavier than expected. In all honesty, she had expected a more luxurious-looking crown, one of gold and gems, not one made of crystal. All she could hear was the loud, ringing beat, drowning out everything around her. Demetrius shifted to stand, so she followed suit. She could see Queen Isolde's mouth move, saying something, but no sound could penetrate that noise. Demetrius tilted his head to her, a furrow between his brows as he mouthed the words, "I do." Lilith panicked, hoping that she had correctly interpreted reading his lips.

Thankfully, King Amadeus and his queen stepped back, returning to their seats. Lilith felt Demetrius enter her mind once more. She heard him speak to her, but his voice was muffled and unclear.

'I... The crown is singing so loudly in my ears, I can't hear anything! Please. I need to take it off!' Her forehead was lined with sweat in panic, and her mind was clouding from the ache between her eyes. A sudden pain lashed out in her chest. It felt like her heart was being sliced in two. *'Take it off. Take it off!'* Her hands were starting to shake, and she felt the world quake, spinning mercilessly. Black edged her vision, just as she made out hands reaching in front of her. Someone was standing in front of her, blocking her view of the spectators. Demetrius lifted the crown as the rhythmic beat slowly started to settle. He looked at her with concern and fear. Whispers filtered to her ears: *she is not worthy of the crown.* A part of her was snapping under all the pressure. A crack was forming in her soul, threatening to shatter her hope.

"This crown has been passed through many generations of Kings and Queens, but this was not the original. The first crown of man mirrored this throne, a crown made of the sacred white oak wood, and so it shall be remade anew."

Lilith could finally calm down, her eyes finding him, while her mind processed his words. She looked over her shoulder towards the new black throne and its pair. The sacred white tree was no longer.

Demetrius handed the queen's crown to a guard as he lifted his own. Disbelief traveled through the crowd, and whispers scattered among the onlookers. With the crystal crowns now handed off, Demetrius faced the throne chairs, his hands hovering above them. That same yellow mana flowed from him onto the backs of the thrones. Just a shaving off the carved wood was enough for new crowns to be born, two thin circlets, a fragile version of their crystal counterparts. One was as black as night, the other, almost pure white, except for a streak of black. He slowly strode towards Lilith, placing the white crown delicately on her head. She took a deep breath and lifted her chin. He held a hand out for her, helping her stand. While his hand weaved with hers, he gave her the black crown and knelt before her. Loud gasps trickled through the crowd.

Through his lashes, icy blue eyes shone mischievously, with a playful smirk lifting the corner of his lips. Lilith brought the black crown over his dark blue hair, her hands trailing down a few strands as the crown found its home.

"Arise, King Demetrius and Queen Lilith," the Apostle loudly declared. Demetrius stood up, offering his hand, and walked in front of the thrones. He placed Lilith on the white throne, matching her new crown, while he finally sat upon his own throne. The room was silent, as if the air had stilled. Demetrius looked upon the sea of faces with a stone-cold expression.

The Apostle waved his hands, motioning for the crowd to stand. "All hail King Demetrius and Queen Lilith, first of their name, rulers of the Kingdom of Draydon."

"Long may they reign!" a single unified voice of the crowd erupted. An unexpected feeling of excitement settled into Lilith's stomach. She was their queen, one half of the new regime. Her goal was to dismantle the very entity that placed her on this throne and destroy the Apostles. The familiar comfort of her mental shield made her smile. She would be their ruin. Only her family and her friends would be spared. Her eyes wandered over the false celebration. Her own sanity threatened to tear itself apart. She would be their villain, become an unyielding hand of righteousness, and her justice would be felt.

Chapter 20
Pursuit of Evil

Lilith

The flurry that followed had Lilith's head spinning. Scroll after scroll needed signatures, hands needed shaking, and her poised smile ached her face.

Felicia came to stand beside her, anchoring her in the present, serving as a reminder that this moment was critical to their needs. Occasionally, she felt the presence of Demetrius at the forefront of her mind, but she shut him out to preserve her sanity. She was afraid that something was going to happen, because of that nudge of unpredictability that he brought with him.

In a moment of brief peace, Demetrius leaned over. "Let me in. I am doing things your way, and in return, you will give me this."

Lilith eyed the line of procession, that carefully perfected smile never faltering. The mental door opened just for him, giving him just enough, a space created just for him.

"Yes?" Lilith mentally sighed in polite annoyance.

"We need to talk about what happened with the crown. I caught a glimpse of something while we were in the Ruins, but that... that was different."

"I'm not sure what happened. I could hear something... A strange ringing that grew louder and louder until I couldn't see or think. Then I felt a sharp pain in my heart, as if I was being stabbed. I don't understand why I'm the only one who has this reaction."

"But you are fine now? You don't feel the stabbing sensation anymore?"

"I'm completely fine now. Just exhausted. "

Demetrius nodded to the last person approaching to greet them, a noble who was ever so eager to gain favour. Lilith resumed her polite smile, nodding to the man, while Demetrius stepped to the side and flagged down the guard. The guards banged on their banners, signalling for the crowd to be silent.

"We are so pleased that you have joined us for this special day; however, it is time that we leave. Please, enjoy the refreshments, and we will see you this evening." Demetrius held his hand out for Lilith to take, which she eagerly did. With the immediate royal family assembling behind them, they strode through the crowd and back into the main palace. Demetrius paused in his steps as the consorts and his half-siblings all turned to face him to bow.

"I do appreciate that you came," Demetrius spoke, his voice tender. Some of his half-siblings smiled back, and even the consorts looked at Demetrius as if he had sprouted a second head.

They looked only to Lilith. "Long may you reign." They turned and marched towards their wing, leaving Demetrius,

Felicia, and the former king and queen behind. With the guards surrounding them, they resumed heading upstairs to the queen's room. Old King Amadeus and Queen Isolde cleared their throats.

"My son, now that you have the throne, would it not be more fitting for you both to take the king and queen's quarters?"

"Our current room will do just fine. You both may continue as you were."

"But we were thinking that now you are King, we would move into one of the outer manors."

"I'm afraid, Father, with our situation of the Void expanding, your idea will have to wait. It is not safe for you both to stray too far from the palace walls."

King Amadeus looked pained, as if something was tampering with his mind. He grabbed his head and groaned. Queen Isolde reached for her husband to console him. When she opened her mouth, pain lanced through her mind as well.

"Excuse us, we will have to retire." They followed a guard who led them to their rooms, leaving Felicia and Lilith with Demetrius. Lilith searched the sea of faces, looking for the stylists who wore her family's faces, but couldn't find them.

Felicia gave Lilith a look, one that she couldn't quite interpret. Felicia's eyes kept drifting to Demetrius as she pressed her lips together in a tight line. If only Lilith had the power of mind-reading like Demetrius, this would be so much easier.

"I am tired, I wish to go back to our room," Lilith stated, still looking at Felicia, who was shaking her head. While Demetrius turned to talk with the guard, Felicia spun her hair.

"Oh," Lilith gasped; she had forgotten to tell Felicia that Demetrius already knew about the stylists. "Yeah, he knows about the stylists, so there's no point in going along with the plan," whispered Lilith to her friend.

Felicia eye-rolled and groaned, "And the other 'stylists?'" Meaning Cyrus and Lilith's brothers.

"Demetrius allowed them to leave. It's all fine. But, our efforts were not for nothing. Although he was lenient, the Apostles would have tried something."

Felicia muttered under her breath, "Well, he should leash his dogs if they can't be controlled."

Lilith couldn't agree more and nodded. "Better yet, he should put them down."

Demetrius turned to finally face them. "To give you an update, those stylists were seen leaving the city by way of carriage. My trusted guards have been keeping an eye out. About the Apostles..." Before Demetrius could say more, the Apostles joined them on the stair landing.

"Your Highness, if you could spare a moment."

Demetrius nodded to the guards to escort the women back upstairs, while Lilith felt his presence once more at the forefront of her mind.

Stay with the others and do not go wandering. The labyrinth beneath us is not safe, and I don't mean from the guards.

Fine, she thought. She had, in fact, considered a quick visit to the Mages, but that would have to wait.

Don't change just yet; we have to make a quick appearance to the public. Demetrius rubbed Lilith's back and then strode off with the Apostles.

Lilith followed the guards, who walked them back to just outside their rooms.

One of the guards turned to face them. "You are free to move between rooms, but we will be stationed down the hall should you require anything."

"Thank you," Lilith nodded, and motioned for Felicia to enter her room. She went to the wardrobe and pulled out a long black silk dress with an image of a silver beast ascending up from the skirt.

"I'll wear this one tonight." Lilith laid the ebony dress out on her bed, looking at the fine silver scales that went to the waist, with a plunging neckline and exposed back. "It was given to me on my first day here, from them."

"It's a phoenix," Felicia stated, inspecting the silver beast. "A beast of transformation, through flame it rises from its ashes anew."

"You think it's too much?"

"No. I think it's perfect." Felicia's eyes scanned Lilith, her eyes lingering on the crown. "It was made for you."

A knock on the door had them jumping. Lilith quickly dropped the black dress and scurried to the door. As Demetrius came in, he politely nodded to Felicia. The air was a little tense, but Lilith smiled nonetheless.

"I will steal my wife for a moment." His eyes drifted to Liltih's lips.

Lilith blushed and followed him out, facing a barrage of guards posted outside. Demetrius held on to Lilith's hand as they started walking towards the throne room, but instead of heading down the stairs, they headed down a hallway towards the patio area.

"What, exactly, are we doing?" Lilith nervously started fidgeting with an embroidered gold flame on her dress.

"You don't have to worry. We're quickly making an appearance to the public, and then you are all mine until the celebration." Demetrius stroked the back of her hand in slow circles. The guards opened the door to the balcony, the bright sun beaming down on them. Lilith blinked a few times, adjusting to the harshness as the city came into view below. Seeing Vanguard in fading daylight was a whole new experience.

Tan clay rooftops swooped in every direction, with houses packed in tightly, made from a light-coloured stone. Blooming flowers grew up the sides and faces of some buildings, drifting in a light floral scent mixed with a saltiness she had missed the last time they stood on the balcony. Glistening ocean water sparkled in the distance, surrounded by a large harbour which housed a variety of sailboats. Not a single boat ventured into the waters as the people came to see the new king and queen. White and red bunting banners draped above the streets as the city went into full celebration. Dancers and performers drew in circles of spectators, wearing beaming smiles.

So many people came to see her and Demetrius, like a sea of heads waiting in anticipation. Demetrius took the first step forward, waving to the crowd. An eruption of applause and cheers sounded at his appearance. He turned and beckoned her forward. Taking a nervous stride to stand next to him, she could finally see the mass of the horde, the full scope of the people dwelling within the city walls. These were not the nobles, but faces of merchants, fishermen, families of every race and status. There were too many souls standing before her, so many people that came from other villages. No doubt there would be refugees here from the towns fallen to the darkness, people fleeing the south. How many of them now faced homelessness?

"Wave to them, my love," Demetrius encouraged.

Lilith started to wave, mimicking Demetrius, but as her eyes inspected the closer faces, she paused. These people were not in a position to act so jovially. Their faces were worn from exhaustion, and their clothes were mostly tattered, or poorly patched. She could see that they had come in their best. They had put in the effort of wearing their finest to face the new royals, to face the new king and queen that could save them. Her eyes drifted to a family, all skeletal in stature, clearly deprived of food. Everyone looked frail and starved. Her people were suffering.

"Look at them," Lilith whispered with her practiced grin fixed on her face.

"I am."

"No. I mean, look at their condition."

"I am trying to be different, make a change that would eventually end this suffering."

"But there has to be another way than feeding them to the darkness."

"As much as I'd like to continue this conversation, this is not the time to discuss such matters." Demetrius nodded to a nearby Apostle. His voice was quiet and his lips were barely moving. "I hear where you're coming from, and I'm open to your suggestions. Wait until this is over, and I will listen to what you have to say."

Lilith's grin faltered as she felt a deep connection between them flare inside her mind. A hazy memory of a feeling she once felt in a different past, where this ease between them once existed. She remembered a version of him that was always firm and possessive, but at least he was open to her opinions. Their communication was more innate, more intrinsic. She didn't have to try so hard for him to understand what she longed for. Having an honest discussion with this version of him was more of a challenge. One thing was certain: she was getting tired of fighting.

"What did the Apostles want?" Lilith questioned him, looking over her shoulder to the four stationed at the other corners, overlooking the spectators. It wasn't just a show of the new king and queen, but a display of their alliance. The royals with the Apostles. Never before had any religion claimed a spot beside the royals. Never had they appeared at an assembly of this magnitude together, standing on equal plane as the King. From below, it must appear that the Apostles held as much authority as the crown.

"Just another issue that needed my attention." Demetrius' focus was upfront on the crowd. She opened her mind to him once more.

'They should not be standing beside us. When will you tire of their claws constantly pawing at you for more power? Why do you continue to play into their hand?'

His smile faltered. *'I needed them to influence the masses, to prepare them for what's to come. However, I am in agreement. They are starting to test their power, and it's time to clip their so-called claws. Would that make you happy, my love? Would you like to do the honours?'* Demetrius' wave froze in the air.

Lilith didn't want to look down and see the happy faces wave at her, so full of joy and hope that this new reign would bring them prosperity. She knew what he had in store for them.

"We can leave now, if that is what you want." Demetrius embraced her, planting a tender kiss on her forehead in front of the masses, who revelled in this show of affection. Her wary inner voice whispered in her mind. Doubt crept into her, telling her that this was all for show.

Calloused hands found hers, hands that had seen years of training. Yet there was so much more to Demetrius than this physical body; she could see the hands of his former self, Locke. She envisioned his hands holding hers. Locke had an intimidating presence. As a god, his physical manifestation mirrored his power. Heads above everyone, a huge wall of defined muscle. She wondered if Locke would have given the Apostles this much power. But Locke was not Demetrius. Locke was defined by the strength of his power, whereas Demetrius was an immortal spirit trapped in a mortal body.

Once back in the halls of the palace, Demetrius gave the guards a signal telling them to retire. Demetrius, though tall, was so physically different from Locke. He bent down, resting his forehead on hers, basking in this private moment. A sweet and gentle energy flowed between them. A rise of power leached from him, surrounding them in a cocoon of safety, remnants of his power as a god. In an instant, they were in a study of sorts, bookshelves filled with leather books and scrolls lined one wall, while the other housed a bed and desk.

"Where are we?"

"In my study, a room that I've unfortunately been spending most of my nights in."

Those rough hands guided her to the bed as he stood before her, lifting her crown. He placed the white wooden crown on the desk and lifted his own, placing them together. With a deep sigh, he sat next to her, rolling his neck out.

"You want to change the discrepancy between the social classes, raise the lowest group of our world, so that they will not suffer. You want to close the Void," he stated, looking out the large window facing a garden.

"I want to end this suffering. The Void and the Apostles cannot go on."

"You think closing the Void will change that? This way of life is broken."

"We cannot keep going the way we are now. We are isolated and our neighbouring nations, who should be our allies, have abandoned us."

"I am open to suggestions."

"I need time to think. I alone should not make this decision; there needs to be a collective to manage the weight of this issue. We shouldn't carry this burden ourselves. You should not take it upon yourself only to fix our issues."

Demetrius lay back, sighing deeply with eyes closed. Lilith shifted to watch him. A fleeting thought drifted into her mind, that she could love this man if she let down her guard. He was trying for her.

"What would you do about the nobles and Apostles?" Ice blue eyes settled on her face.

"If it were up to me alone, I personally want to be rid of the Apostles. The nobles would likely rebel against any change that saw their own profit loss. I would not be sad to see that class dismantled. I'd like to see those who are worthy of such power given a voice."

"You want me to form a council?"

"Would that be so bad? Place people with true intentions of helping this kingdom prosper, by way of raising the lower members. Look at my father. He is a good person."

"Your father has his own secrets. To be frank, I honestly don't think that kind of person exists, but I shall look into it. People turn into different kinds of monsters when given authority. In the beginning, they might be worthy of such a task, but the seduction of power can change a person's goals. We are close to reaching the climax of my plans. It takes godly power to close the Void, and soon, their eyes will have to look our way."

"What does that mean?" Nothing annoyed Lilith more than when Demetrius spoke in riddles.

"I must pay a visit to the Void before I make up my mind." Demetirus shifted to his side, tracing a hand over Lilith's arm. "I am finding my judgment clouded by you. I told myself I would not let you change me, but, it seems you will be my undoing in this lifetime as well." He cradled her face in his hand, and she closed her eyes. "You are my wife, my queen, a goddess amongst men. Though I have made you my equal today, you will always be deserving of much more than I could offer. You are my life. I cannot exist without you."

"Sometimes it feels like the weight of your love is too heavy. Is it love? Or is it an obsession?" Lilith felt her voice was small and weak. She kept her eyes closed, for fear of facing her feelings.

He leaned forward and kissed her closed eyelids. "I have waited for you for over a millennium. Countless lives have come and gone, and still the strength of my feelings for you has not diminished. I wondered why this love was unending..." He kissed her cheeks. "Why my love for you persisted all this time, and I realized it is because you are my balance. You are my light in an endless abyss. It is not the idea of a version of you that I continue to love, but everything about you as you are." His hands tangled through her hair, pulling her in for a kiss, and probing her mouth with his tongue. He sank to his back, tugging her on top of him, so that she straddled him.

His words were snapping her resolve. They always did. Lilith let out a moan, knowing he was giving her control. She held so much tension throughout the day; she wanted a way to release that energy. Her hips started grinding on him.

"My wife is so eager. Have I told you yet that you look absolutely ravishing in this colour?" Demetrius ran his hands up and down her body, in a soft cycle. He pressed into her, raising her hips as he lifted her up and flipped her over so she was on her back. She felt his hands run down from her toes, all the way up to the tops of her thighs. Her dress was bunching up around her hips in a wild pile of deep reds and gold. "My goddess, it has been too long since I last tasted you." A thrill went up her spine as his thumbs hooked into her underwear, slowly pulling them down. Goosebumps erupted at the feeling of the soft fabric drifting down her legs. "Open your legs, my love. Let me see you." Heat seeped through her cheeks as she blushed while widening her legs. Demetrius kissed down her knees towards the tops of her thighs as his hands widened her legs further. Lilith could hardly see him as the layers of material obscured her vision, but she felt his velvety smooth tongue over her core. Another moan left her mouth, while his tongue mercilessly built that feeling inside her. She felt two of his fingers entering her, working their way slowly in and out, building momentum. That tension she'd been carrying on her shoulders slowly began to dissipate. In its stead, pleasure tightened deep within her. He increased speed, driving her close to the tipping point.

"Demetrius!" Lilith cried out in a moan, feeling her core pulsate, completely relaxing her. Demetrius rode out her waves of pleasure, and as she came down, he wiped his mouth, grinning like a fool.

"Do you want more?" He smirked at her. Lilith nodded. "I won't disintegrate this lovely dress." He held his hand out for her to take, and with a hoist, she was standing on her feet. "Turn."

Dutifully, she obeyed, spinning so that he could untie her dress. A frustrated growl breathed down her neck as his hands undid the last bind. The dress loosened and fell down her hips to the floor. She felt his lips kiss the large rune on her back. "Steadfast and true." She felt his lips trail up her runes to her shoulders, "Do you want it slow or rough?"

She went onto her hands and knees, looking over her shoulder as she ordered, "Rough."

He lined himself up and pushed all the way in, resting his hands on her hips as he quickly left, only to enter her to the hilt. Her hands clenched around the blankets as she pushed her hips back to meet him.

"Lilith, you were made for me." He was like an untamed beast, wildly pounding into her. Gone was his self-control;

this was carnal ravaging, savage and brutal. Her hands gave out as he kept her hips in the air. She moaned into the blankets. Suddenly, she felt an emptiness of him withdrawing, only to feel something not quite as wide as his shaft slowly enter her. She looked over her shoulder once more and saw Demetrius' glistening erection, his hand holding something hard as it slowly re-entered her.

"Gods, I love this magic, it's divine." Demetrius paused as he pulled the object out once more. "Coat it in your cum, my love." She spread her legs further, but upon the next exit, she felt the smooth, two-finger-wide object enter her other hole. Biting down on the blanket, she felt so full. With it in place, he lined himself up and pushed slowly in.

"Holy Gods, Demetrius." Lilith moaned as he eased to the hilt, stopping so that she could release the breath she was holding.

"Too much? Or would you like to keep going?" Demetrius stilled, waiting for her answer.

"I want...I want you to keep going." Lilith breathed, her fingers slowly circled her clit.

She heard Demetrius groan, clearly watching Lilith start to slowly move on him while rubbing herself. She felt his hands tense around her hips, his breathing becoming more laboured.

"I'm not going to last, my love, if you keep doing that." His voice sounded strained, which made Lilith smirk.

"Do what?" She answered coyly, clenching around him.

She heard him growl and felt him shift within her. "Hold on tight," the only warning he gave as he began picking up the tempo. Lilith screamed as he found that initial pace. His movements immediately brought her back to the brink of pleasure. She let out a stream of curse words, pleas, and moans. She felt him gather her hair into one hand, pulling back so she was forced to rest on her hands. Rough hands closed around her neck, giving her a light choke as her eyes rolled back.

She felt his hand around her neck relax, as she greedily sucked in air, her whole core quaking around him. Fireworks exploded in front of her as her vision started to dance. Demetrius shattered, speaking in that ancient language they once spoke, and followed her into oblivion. As they panted and breathed. side by side, Demetrius reached around and pulled the object slowly out of her.

It was polished and smooth with a wide base. Lilith studied it as it disintegrated into nothing.

"How does it always feel this good?"

Demetrius smirked, "I know your body. I know exactly what you like and what you don't. Next time, I'll be taking your ass while my copy fills your other hole."

"Such a filthy mouth."

"Says the woman that just cried out every curse word known," Demetrius smirked, bringing her in for another kiss. It tasted of her.

"Do we have to go to this celebration? We could just stay here." Her finger played along his chest.

"And miss the fun?" Demetrius heaved himself up, while Lilith looked around. This was more like his room at Skilhiem, with scrolls piled high next to an orb. The books surrounding her made her feel like she was home.

"Why don't we move here? This room feels much more homey." Her words left her mouth as she realized she'd be losing out on access to the wardrobe. Demetrius came back to her, wet cloth in hand, a mischievous look on his face.

"Are you sure? This room may not have the same luxuries as the one upstairs." He swiped the cloth over her sensitive areas, making her squirm. He went to a bookshelf and pulled it open, disappearing into another hidden room. Lilith sprang up, feeling the soreness between her legs, and winced. Demetrius came back and lifted her up, carrying her through the bookcase. Inside was a bath just big enough for the two of them. With floor to ceiling stonework, this place looked like the baths at Skilheim. She knew she wanted this room.

"Please tell me there's a secret passage here, too?"

Demetrius laughed, making Lilith beam. "I don't know. You're going to have to find out." He slowly put her in the hot water, then climbed in beside her. He let out a blissful moan.

"Turn around, so I can scrub your back," he ordered. "You are mine to take care of, and your wants become mine. I am remembering the man I used to be, before the darkness, before I was cast into the cage of the Void."

"That power you used at the coronation, I've never seen anyone use transformative magic so freely on such an ancient artifact. I thought the throne and the sacred tree could not be manipulated by mana."

"The age of the throne exists as a marker of mankind's first entrance into their realm. Before the age of man, there were others that dwelled on this plane, beings similar to Danai."

"I thought that there was only chaos before man rose up and united everyone under one banner?"

"That is what they teach you as children, but your history goes much deeper than that."

"You're telling me everything we know about our history is a lie?"

"I'm telling you that when mankind ascended as the superior race, they erased a past that they did not want to repeat."

"And why are you telling me this?"

Demetrius laughed, "You're getting me sidetracked. The magic that I used was but a fragment of my godly powers. It strained me to use what little I have retained. Before the age of mankind, my powers made me a god. I was worshiped once. Though the myths they believed were mostly built on hearsay. Thanks to the Mages, your kind has risen to us. The magic and powers that you can wield are a weaker version of my kind. You shouldn't have powers. It was a violation of the freedom we bestowed on those damned Mages."

"Without them, I would never be your equal. It's because of my power's potential that I can stand beside you." Lilith inspected her runes. "Even the way in which our capabilities have been stripped makes us similar."

"Melia must have foreseen this. Although she is the most powerful god, my kind still views Ominus as her superior. It's this arbitrary value of our worth that cursed our love. She made it possible in this lifetime for us to love freely." Demetrius ran a finger along his own runes on his finger, the runes of their marriage bond. They spent a quiet moment; no words were shared, but something between them shifted. A balance was being restored.

Demetrius used more of his mana to transfer her dress from upstairs. The black dress felt buttery against her skin, hugging her like a second skin until it cascaded like a flower from her hips. There was no room for undergarments, so she wore nothing beneath.

"What do you think?" Lilith did a slow spin in front of him. She stopped, facing him as she noticed one of his eyes twitched.

"I am at odds because you look radiant, but I am not sure if I want anyone else's eyes lingering on what's mine." She felt his eyes drift slowly up her body, focusing on her breasts. "You're not wearing undergarments?"

Lilith proudly raised her head, but blushed. "I am not." She sighed, starting to take the dress off.

"No." Hands stilled hers, "If this is what you want to wear tonight, then do so." His voice dipped into a murmur as he continued, "I'll just take the eyes of those that linger on you."

"This dress was given to me when I first came to the palace."

"Is that something you want to remember tonight?"

"I want to remember why I am here." She didn't want to forget those who lost their lives because of her. Mistress Rhodes, Sir Erikson, Tally's mother. "Is Silver still with us?" It pained her to bring him up; the last time she'd seen him, she had tried to kill him.

"Silver is seeing to the Mages."

Disappointment rocked through Lilith's body. She didn't know how to respond, knowing how the Mages were being treated. If she said something, then he would know she found them.

"Andishmand, is he here?"

"Yes. He's with the others."

"Can I see him? He helped me interpret these runes, *with no strings attached*," she said, heavy on the insinuation, since a certain prince only bargained to help, but at a cost.

"I see. I will arrange something after these events are done."

That would do for now.

"Come, if you are ready, let us face the night." He went to the desk and placed the white crown on Lilith's head, then replaced his own. "Perfect."

Gone were the rows of seats in the Throne Hall, back to its decor for the rivalries catered to the nobles.

"Welcome to the evening's celebration of his and her Highnesses' coronation." The Apostles stood in front of the thrones, with Lilith and Demetrius already seated, the picture of royalty. Lilith's eyes wandered between faces, trying to find faces she recognized.

'Looking for someone?'

'Why are the royal family and Felicia absent?'

'I decided that it would be best for them to skip this evening's festivities. They are safe in their rooms, and Felicia will be waiting for you should you want to see her after.'

'She's safe. Not in the hands of the Apostles?'

'I promised you her safety. The Apostles cannot touch her.'

Relief sagged her shoulders. She tuned out the rest of the Apostle's speech, a sermon trying to persuade their followers to remain vigilant in spreading their word. Among the nobles, most had accepted the Apostles as part of the new world, their eager faces listening to the nonsense that was spewed to their faces. However, some looked disinterested; they listened and pretended, but knew that they could not rise above their status without acknowledging the power of the Apostles. Lilith saw the ugliness of people's selfishness and greed.

Lilith recognized their pressed smiles, their tense shoulders, a mask she wore herself when facing the nobles and the Apostles alike. She smirked. They were the ones that brought the Apostles to their power, made a world they now had to pretend to enjoy. She loathed these people the most. They knew the consequences of their actions and did it nonetheless. It would be so easy if they all just went away.

Demetrius tilted his head towards her with a brief look of curiosity.

'Why do you look both amused and annoyed?'

'I really hate these people.'

Demetrius sat up straighter, his eyes drifting over the sea of faces. *'You want to save these people, do you not?'*

Lilith scowled. In that moment, after everything she'd been through, she just wanted them gone. Demetrius' smile widened. She left her thoughts open to him, asking herself if these people were worthy of being saved. If Demetrius somehow closed the Void, these nobles would only seek to further their status and drive for more power at the expense of others.

'Then this is your wedding gift.'

The Apostle's speech paused, as if he were listening to something. Lilith went between Demetrius and the hooded figures; he was telling them something. Abruptly, the Apostle smiled.

"Please, enjoy the festivities." The Apostles and the grey robes that lined the walls all turned to bow to the throne, then filed carefully out. Just as the last Apostle left, Lilith watched as his face turned from that eerie smile into something more sinister. The doors to the entrance closed. Music began, and food was brought out, with the staff hurriedly placing their platters on a long table. A few of the guests immediately tried to touch and harass the servers, playing with their hair, grabbing their clothes. Lilith's jaw clenched. These people disgusted her.

"Why are they like this?" she whispered, leaning towards him.

"Inheritance of entitlement. They have found out they can get away with behaving like this by throwing money and their position at those who try to defy them."

"You don't behave like them, nor do your siblings." She looked around, trying to find the royal family and consorts, but they too were absent. Something nagged at her mind, telling her something was wrong. "Why only invite them to this celebration?"

Demetrius leaned in closer, "Sit with me."

"I am."

"No. I mean, here," he replied, opening his arms, waiting for her to sit on his lap. She hesitated, with only a few curious glances noticing them, she took her place in his lap.

His breath played with her hair, sending a shiver up her spine. "I invited them as a gift to you."

"What do you mean?"

Demetrius nodded to the guard closest to him, trickling a wave of subtle signals through the other guards. Some found servers, relaying the message. Lilith waited and observed. A message passed through the servers, and they discreetly dismissed themselves. Several of the guards followed.

"What are you planning?" She couldn't deny the thrill and curiosity, anticipating his next move.

"I want you to decide now if they are worth saving. As my gift to you, I give you their lives. If you want, you can spare them and they will continue as they are, or I will end them here and now."

Lilith flinched. "Won't that upset your plan? Don't you need them?"

"I only needed them to get the throne and control the resources. They were the ones that were limiting the food supply. While the city starved, they hoarded everything. But they've failed to realize that if they die now, they can be replaced. A new tide of landowners and bureaucrats."

Lilith watched them in disgust as they writhed on each other, gorging themselves on food. They would never change. Something within her turned dark, that naive hopefulness lost to reality. Her eyes caught a glimpse of brown hair and brown eyes, Sir Prichard. He was here, completely engrossed in the arms of several lovers, unaware that his life was at her mercy. A mercy she had not received at their hands. She was beaten and assaulted, and now she was their queen.

"Yes." She let that rage inside her consume her thoughts, her rationale. In this moment, she wanted them gone so that she could have her vengeance. "I want them gone."

No sooner had those words escaped when the orbs surrounding them gave out, engulfing them in pitch black darkness.

Screams erupted as some guests used their fire magic to bring some light back into the hall. Only the darkness had brought new friends.

Clicking reverberated around the hall, a sound that terrified Lilith because she knew what creatures now surrounded them. The first bloody scream shook the hall as the creature of the night began the massacre. The creatures that lingered in the darkness and crawled through the Void mercilessly attacked the guests. Demetrius lifted his palm, extending it into the dark as a small sphere of light danced through the air above the slaughter.

The hall was a symphony of death.

So much blood and torn limbs scattered the darkness, mixed with explosions of magic bursting from nobles trying to fend off their attackers. One by one, the flames extinguished as the screams crescendoed, and Lilith smiled. She rolled her head from side to side, listening to the violence, to the justice. In that moment, she felt relief and comfort knowing that their deaths were less of a barrier she had to overcome. That constant headache she had been feeling dulled and became painless. It made her shudder in calmness. Not once did she feel a sense of remorse. She didn't think of the children who would no longer have their parents. She didn't dwell on the faint hope that they could change. She revelled in their deaths.

She rose from his lap, walking through the pool of blood soaking through her shoes, and staining the hem of her dress. She stood at the centre, knowing that Demetrius would protect her. The creature would not harm her. It felt like she was dipping her toes in a warm bath.

"I told you once you have darkness within you. I may be changing, but so are you." Lilith turned to face Demetrius, his eyes wholly obsidian, as he walked up to stand before her. He was right; she only felt satisfaction as she heard the screams. While he was softening, she was snapping.

The orbs along the walls flickered back to life as the last of the sobs and shrieks died. The silver beast on her skirt was drenched in the blood of the unworthy. Shredded pieces of the finest silk and material were scattered amongst their remains. Severed limbs and entrails filled the hall.

She let out a cry, not borne from frustration, but a release of the burden she had been carrying. That feeling of gloom and heaviness was leaving her shoulders. That pressure of constantly trying to be something she was not. Deep down, she had known this was where her true feelings lingered. A freedom from what was expected of her. For so long, she had repressed that part of herself. A dark madness that threatened to surface had been cracking away at the false version she had presented to everyone. In this moment, she felt alive. The creatures dared not approach her but withdrew back from where they came.

Only a handful of guards remained, unharmed. As one, they sank to their knees before Lilith and Demetrius, trembling in the might of the power before them.

"All hail the King and Queen."

Lilith stood, rolling her neck as she smiled and commanded, "Leave us." She felt numb, exhausted, mentally and emotionally drained. Her mind screamed at her, telling her enough. Enough trying to fight for those who are undeserving. Enough trying to repress her own feelings so that others could take advantage of her.

The world around them started to shake. The rattling glass of the throne's ceiling echoed around her, making ripples in the pool of blood.

"What's happening?" Lilith yelled.

Demetrius burst out into a wild laugh.

"Demetrius!" Lilith yelled once more, confused. A bright flash of lightning soared through the sky above them, followed by a deafening boom. Strike after strike, lightning hit. The clouds were circling in an ominous grey over the horizon. Lilith focused on the skies, trying to make sense of what was happening. This was coming from the barrier, in the direction of the Void.

"Are you doing this?"

Demetrius' eyes were wild with thrill. "No, my love, I am not. We have finally angered them."

"'Them' who?"

"The gods." Demetrius beamed. "They are coming."

CHAPTER 21
POWER OF THE WICKED

Felicia

Felicia nervously paced back and forth, running her hands down her casual dress. "Something doesn't feel right. I should be with Lilith," she muttered to herself. "She can handle herself. Demetrius would not harm her, and she's unreachable to the Apostles. If anything, I am in trouble being left here." She stopped pacing, still talking to herself. "What if this is part of his plan? Maybe he's separating us because he wants to manipulate Lilith." She let out a frustrated groan. "You are overthinking this. Lilith has been alone with Demetrius many times."

Before the celebration, guards came in, ordering her to stay put. No explanations. One of the palace staff brought up some food. Felicia tried to interrogate her, but the poor soul was clueless. Frustrated, she changed into something more comfortable and waited. Hours passed, and still nothing. Just as Felicia was about to resume pacing, a faint scream sounded in the distance. The sound of boots coming closer to the door made her jump. She risked opening the entrance a little, coming eye level to a guard.

"Ma'am, please stay in your room." Another faint scream rang out.

"What's going on?" Felicia demanded, furiously glaring at the guard, who was pushing her back into her room.

"Close your door. Now!" He pushed her back and slammed the door closed.

Felicia let out a string of curses. The screaming now intensified. She ran to the window to try and see if there was a disturbance. Have the Apostles finally done it? Were they trying to overthrow Demetrius? She had to think. If she could get next door, she could use the labyrinth to escape. She opened the entrance once more, staring one of the guards down.

"I'm not going to cause you trouble, I just would like to wait in Lilith's room. You were told to keep me up here and I will stay. I would feel safer waiting for Lilith there."

The guards looked at each other and nodded. "Be fast."

Felicia smiled sweetly at the guards, thanking them as she entered Lilith's room. For minutes she listened to the faint wails and pleas for mercy, until the sounds of screaming had stopped, and whatever disturbance there had been was now over.

Felicia went to a mounted orb and ripped it off the wall. She pushed apart the hanging clothes and pressed the false backing of the wardrobe. A cool breeze stirred her hair. She shook herself off and took a step into the pitch black tunnel. Moving quickly down through the narrow space, she came upon her first fork. A nagging sensation told her to go back, but instead she headed to the right. For a few minutes, she travelled through the network of dark corridors. A part of her felt hopeful that she would find a way out, the other part wondered if she had made a mistake. As she came to a halt, the tunnel started shaking.

A small pool of water started rippling at her toes. Panicked, she turned around trying to find her way back to the room. As the rumbling intensified, the stone around her groaned. She sprinted up through the wardrobe back into the room.

"Lilith?" Felicia yelled, moving from the bedroom to the main room. Lilith was not there so she ran to the bathroom, calling her name. The room was shaking violently enough to cause the orbs to flicker and the small table in the corner clattered to the ground.

She rushed to the window and saw an ominous looking cloud form to the south. The leaves of the trees shook, decorative vases in the garden below smashed, and the glass planes formed spider cracks. Felicia fell to the floor and covered her face as dust sprinkled down on her, the room groaning from the strain. A sudden flash from outside illuminated the dark skies.

Felicia got to her feet and she staggered to the entrance, surprised to see the guards had all disappeared.

Two figures materialized next to her, making her jump back. Demetrius and Lilith formed inside the room, his rough hands wrapped around her shoulders.

"Are you okay?" Lilith stepped out of Demetrius' embrace.

"I'm fine, but what's going on?"

Lilith scowled and looked at Demetrius, who was looking out the window, his eyes squinting as he focused on the ominous cloud.

Demetrius turned to look at Lilith. "Something's wrong with the barrier. I'm going to check it out, but I'll be right back."

"Wait. You can't just leave. What about the palace?" She looked at Felicia nervously. "The state of the throne room? We need you here."

Demetrius carefully took Lilith into his arms. "I'll stop at the Throne Hall and clean it up, then I'll take a quick look at the barrier. I'll be back before you miss me." Lilith scowled as he gave her a quick kiss before disappearing into nothing.

Felicia looked to the floor, at the smear of blood underneath Lilith's dress. "You're bleeding."

Lilith blushed. "It's not my blood." She went to the wardrobe and peeled off her black dress, switching to a more casual black dress.

"Not your blood?" Felicia asked, eyeing up the trail of blood smearing behind Lilith.

Lilith froze. "The nobles are gone."

"The nobles are *dead*?" Felicia needed confirmation. Her heart was racing from excitement. She should feel a sense of shock and disgust, but after everything, she felt only relief. She grinned. "Good."

Lilith grinned as well. "Good."

It took a while for the rumbling to settle with the occasional short wave of shaking interrupting their nervous pacing.

"Demetrius is still not back. Maybe this is it, our time to get to the Temple." Felicia yanked and tugged at the door to get it to open but someone had sealed it from the outside.

Lilith emerged from her dazed state. "Move back!" she ordered, as she raised her hand and sent a burst of air shooting towards the door. The door flung off of its hinges, landing in the hallway.

Running towards the entrance to the queen's wing, they passed an Apostle who came from one of the rooms.

"Hey!" he yelled at them. "Stop! You do not have permission to be out."

"I am the Queen. I don't need anyone's permission."

"Do you think that with His Highness away, you hold any power here?" The Apostle laughed.

Lilith didn't hesitate to send a ball of fire hurtling towards him. As if he was not expecting that reaction, he froze, and the fiery ball blasted into his chest. The flames fanned out, setting alight his white robes. He let out a loud howl of pain, rolling around, trying to douse the flame. Felicia took this opportunity to kick him in the balls before spewing a line of curse words at him. She felt a hand tugging her away.

"We don't have time for this," Lilith yelled. Felicia gave him one last kick to the head.

As they approached, she looked down the hallway across from them, with several closed doors. "Should we split up?"

"No. We're outnumbered and have no weapons. We'll be overpowered by them if we go at this by ourselves." Lilith's mouth opened to say more, but a loud bell rang out. Within a few seconds, several of the doors burst open, filling the hallway with Apostles and their apprentices. "We have to move." They ran towards the consorts' wing.

Both of them threw whatever they could conjure at the crowd. The rush felt intoxicating. Felicia's hands were shaking from the thrill of using her mana once more. Weeks of pent up rage boiled up to this moment, and she basked in the sensation.

"Hurry," she ordered Lilith, as they crossed the walkway. More grey robes blocked their path.

"Get back to your room!" one commanded.

"How about, no!" Lilith hit them with a large sphere of water, blasting them down. The women hopped over the grey robes. Felicia let out a laugh, relishing in this joy of defiance. She looked over to Lilith, who was beaming. To anyone else, they looked positively mad: a pair delighted as they were being hunted.

"Do you know which way to the Temple?" Lilith asked, as a dozen men chased after them. She hurled orbs of various elements behind her. Felicia hoped that it would slow them down. In return, shards of ice and fire narrowly grazed her cheek.

"I guess the order to not harm us is being ignored," Felicia grunted, dodging another spear of ice and casting her own magic. They were surrounded. Lilith rounded at the large mass of men coming from behind. She shot a bolt of lightning, hitting a couple grey robes head on. They crumpled to the ground, seizing. More and more of their apprentices closed in around them. Felicia fought in tandem with Lilith. From the corner of her eye, she could see Lilith gracefully dodging attacks while forcing her own balls of fire and daggers of ice towards the assailants. Her breathing was heavy and her forehead was lined with sweat. They were in their element. Months of training at Skilheim and pent up anger combined made them a force to be reckoned with. It was as if time moved slowly. For once, the carefully crafted smiles on the Apostles' faces had turned to furious seething. Half a dozen grey robes fell backwards in a slow trickle, colliding into their masters. Lilith chucked Felicia a dagger made of ice. Though her fingers protested the cold, she fastened her grip. They danced around each other, the sounds of gushing blood and screams creating a lovely harmony until the Apostles and their apprentices that were chasing them all lay silent on the floor.

Felicia panted, "Our mana is running out."

Lilith sprinted to a nearby consort's room, ramming the door open with a kick.

"Quick, in here." Lilith started scrambling her hands around the wall, then she let out a gasp as the panel bounced forward. Before descending into the belly of the labyrinth, Felicia pulled an orb from the wall.

"I was once in this room with Lady Ashmore. She showed me the access to the tunnels below," Lilith answered an unspoken question. For that, Felicia was grateful. They were starting to understand each other and anticipate reactions. Quickly and quietly, they descended the stairs until they hit the tunnels of the labyrinth. Lilith took the lead. "We need to keep moving until we see one of my markers, then I can figure out where to go."

"What do we need to look for?"

"I worked with what I had. It's a white cloth stuck between two stones."

"Uh. That's not much to work with, Lilith."

"I know, but we need to keep moving."

They ran steadily along the tunnels, their eyes carefully scanning the walls for any discrepancies. Felicia groaned, "This is impossible. We have no idea which way we're moving and I feel like we're moving away from the Temple."

"Please, Felicia, just trust me. We've got to make a quick pit stop before we head to the Temple."

They made it to another fork, moving deeper into unmapped territory.

"Where are you? I need you to show me the way." Lilith begged aloud, making Felicia turn to her in confusion. She was just about to say something, when a small light danced its way in the darkness of the tunnel to the left.

"Yes!" Lilith shot forward, racing after the little light. They moved more confidently snaking through the labyrinth until they hit the room.

"The Mages are up ahead!" Lilith shouted. They stumbled into the glowing room, the three figures still chained to the wall.

"Holy Gods!" Felicia clasped her hand over her mouth at the sight of the disheveled and tortured Mages.

"Andishmand! We're here!" Lilith yelled, jogging up to the middle figure. His head lolled to the side as a groan escaped.

The shimmering chains flared at Lilith's touch.

Felicia walked closer to one of the other Mages, when an ice cold hand gripped her wrist. The Mages rattled their chains, as if to warn her. She turned to face the assailant when she saw his face. Silver. She peered into his soulless eyes, frozen in disbelief. His grip tightened around her wrist and she let out a blood curdling scream. Not from pain, but from despair.

"Silver!" she cried, wrestling in his grip. "Please. How are you here? What are you doing? Let me go." Tears rolled down her cheeks. There was no light behind his eyes. No life in his face. "It's me. It's Felicia."

"He's not there, Felicia." Lilith spoke in a hollow tone. "It's not him anymore." Felicia spotted Lilith sinking into an attack position, her hands flaring into flames.

"I'm sorry, Silver," Lilith muttered under her breath, conjuring a ball of flame in her palm. Meanwhile, Felicia thrashed in his grip, clawing and elbowing with all her strength, but he didn't flinch. It was as if he felt nothing at all, his hold unyielding despite her desperate struggle.

Felicia understood at that moment, this was not Silver. "Do it, Lilith!" Felicia cried. "Now!"

Lilith hurled the flaming orb. An explosion of heat and light tore through the air, aiming for Silver, just as Felicia snapped her head back, smashing into his nose. She quickly crouched, ducking out of the way as the fireball struck its mark. Felicia and Silver were blasted apart. Flames curled around Silver, climbing his clothes and setting him ablaze. But he didn't scream or cry. He didn't even flinch. He just stood, motionless, eyes locked on the two women. As the fire consumed him, his eyes shifted from black to his usual colour. And just before the flames took him completely, he smiled at them.

"Free them!" Silver rasped, his voice breaking as the fire took his life. Then, his body collapsed to the ground.

Felicia let out a choked sob and sank to her knees, trembling. With a swift flick of her wrist, Lilith summoned a sphere of water over him, dousing the fire. Steam hissed into the air as the fire was extinguished.

Lilith turned to the three Mages. "I am Lilith, Queen of the Kingdom of Draydon. I release the Mages from their chains."

A surge of mana pulsed through the air, crackling around the bindings. Whispers of voices muttered in an ancient tongue. The chains began to glow, then shattered with a sharp *clunk*, falling away. The Mages collapsed, their bodies hitting the ground with heavy thuds.

"Gods…" Lilith gasped, rushing to Andishmand's side. She dropped to her knees and gently rolled him over, her eyes welling with tears. "Andishmand, it's me, it's Lilith. You're free."

His lips parted, whispering her name.

"Run," he breathed. "Run…now!"

"No," Lilith shook her head, her voice breaking. "I'm not leaving you."

She looked up, spotting Felicia hunched over Silver's burned body, sobbing.

"Felicia! I need your help."

"Silver...he's gone," she cried.

"I know," Lilith said softly. "He's at peace now. I'm so sorry, but we have to keep moving! Please, Felicia. I need your help." Turning back to the others, Lilith moved quickly, checking their pulses. The two remaining Mages were barely conscious, but they were alive. She gently rolled them to their sides, her expression tightening with resolve.

Felicia's mind raced, scrambling to form a plan. It would be a struggle for her and Lilith to carry one Mage, let alone three. Suddenly, Lilith stood, holding her hand out and muttering an ancient incantation. To her surprise, she saw the sparks of a magic circle form below Lilith. Lilith paused and the glowing runes faded into the stone. She could portal them out. Demetrius must have lowered the barrier before leaving. Their eyes met each other, as unspoken words passed between them, hatching their plan.

Felicia hauled one of the Mages up as Lilith knelt beside Andishmand. She could see Lilith's hands trembling as they hovered over Andishmand's chest.

"You can do it," she encouraged Lilith.

Lilith shut her eyes, forcing her breath into rhythm. Time seemed to slow. The air around them pulsed with energy, and every breath she took charged the air with more tension. Lilith's trembling fingers steadied.

The glowing orbs mounted to the walls dimmed slightly. Tiny particles of light came from them, drifting towards Andishmand, drawn in by Lilith's magic. Andishmand's breathing eased. His eyes fluttered, awareness slowly returning. But Lilith didn't stop. She poured her mana into him, transferring her strength into his battered body. The dark bruise on his one exposed wrist turned from purple to green, to yellow and then cleared. She was healing him. Anchoring him back to life.

"Lilith Hennan...how is this possible?" Andishmand's voice was dry and hoarse after sustained dehydration.

"I became Queen, to set you all free," she spoke softly.

He blinked at her, struggling to process the words. "Why?"

"Because it's the right thing to do. And if we want to survive what's coming, we need you. We need the Mages to help us one last time. You all once fought for us, gave us access to this magic—made us gods—and we have repaid you with chains. I am sorry for how they treated you. All of you. You deserved much more than what you received." She hesitated, her gaze falling for a moment. "I want to change this, change the way we live and survive. We've lived in fear of power we don't fully understand, and in doing so, we've become something worse." She paused, the image of the nobles flashing in her mind. "I've already done things I'm not ashamed of, though blood is on my hands. I won't shy away from what I want. " Her voice cracked as she reached for him, clutching at his torn, blood-stained burgundy robes. "I need your guidance. Your strength. If I'm going to make a difference, I can't do it alone. Please, Andishmand. Help me."

A slow silence followed as Andishmand considered her words.

"Such a moving speech," a voice suddenly drawled, behind them.

Lilith and Felicia jumped to stand, facing the newcomer.

The Apostles.

Nine of them stood in a semicircle, flanked by a dozen apprentices in grey robes, mana humming in the air around them like a charged storm.

"You really are a thorn in our side," the centre Apostle sneered, as he pointed his finger at Lilith. "Seize them."

Several grey robes marched forward, primed with their mana, smiles on their lips.

Felicia and Lilith were burning out. Every movement was a war against their bodies. With every swing and every spell, they felt another cry of protest. Around them, chaos howled: fire and ice clashing in violent bursts as they fought not just for survival, but for the Mages' last hope.

Andishmand forced himself upright, trembling, blood smearing his chin. With a grunt, he raised a shaking hand and uttered a string of ancient words. A glowing blue magic circle sparked to life in front of him. Then, with a flash, it exploded, releasing a storm of razor-sharp ice shards into a wave of charging apprentices.

"Take out the Mage!" an Apostle barked, voice sharp and venomous.

Another body crumpled at Felicia's feet; she was huffing, breathless. The tide of attackers wasn't slowing. Felicia's limbs felt like stone, and the fight dragged her determination down second by second. She glanced to her side. Lilith still danced through the storm, every movement deadly and elegant. This was something she was born to do.

More robes emerged from the tunnels. Lilith turned to Felicia.

"They just keep coming!" Lilith huffed, sweat clinging to her skin.

"I can't keep going." Felicia brushed sweat off her forehead, her mana was down to a trickle. "I…"

A white-robed hand lunged out of the chaos, grabbing Felicia hard.

The glint of steel flashed quickly.

"Stop or we will kill her," an Apostle ordered, his voice full of anger. He held a dagger to Felicia's throat. Felicia panicked, the cold edge biting into her skin.

Lilith's eyes narrowed, sizing up her chances. She didn't move, though the crowd of apprentices pressed closer. Felicia could feel the stillness before the strike. Lilith was calculating, coiled like a wolf preparing to pounce.

The Apostle felt it too, and added. "We care very little about her life." He dug the knife in, a bead of blood trailed down Felicia's neck.

Lilith held up her hands and backed down, the sparks of her fury still charging the air. Her voice was sharp, cold. "Aren't you worried?" she asked. "Your master will be here any moment."

The Apostle chuckled, joined by his friends.

"I doubt that very much," he said, his eyes gleaming. "You have no idea what's just happened." Then he spat on the ground between them, contempt thick in his expression. "You're alone, once more, and now we have our chance." He nodded to the apprentices.

In a rush, they all jumped on Lilith and Andishmand.

"Take them to the dungeon," commanded the Apostle.

CHAPTER 22
RISE FROM THE ASHES

Lilith

The Apostles dragged her down to the dungeon. She heard the cries of women as they dragged her past the closed wooden doors.

"You bastards, you'll never get away with this," she yelled at them. Her mana was flickering embers in her veins, but it was growing slowly.

Where is Demetrius? She needed to stall time. She could feel an occasional spasm pulsating through their shared bond. Whatever he was doing, it required all of his strength.

They dragged her into a small, windowless room. Damp air clung to the walls, and the scent of mold and rust hit her nose. Not rust, but blood. One of them conjured a glowing orb that floated to the ceiling, casting a harsh light across the small space. At the centre of the room was an odd looking chair. It was crude, cobbled together from aged wood. Its back leaned at an unnatural angle, and it had thick leather straps which dangled from the armrests and the legs.

A chill crawled up her spine. This wasn't just a chair. It was a device built for pain.

She fought them with her physical strength, pushing, biting, clawing. Anything to slow them down. An Apostle punched her in the gut, and then swung back to strike her face. The wind was knocked out of her, as she hunched in. An explosion of pain went up the left side of her face. They used the momentary lapse of her fight to wrangle her into the chair's restraints. It took six Apostles to hold her down, while two others strapped her in.

Lilith screamed and screamed, not a sound of pain, but a sound of wrath. She bared her teeth at them as the six holding her took a step back in perfect unison. *Where is Demetrius?* she thought. Surely he could feel her pain, as she could feel his.

"We have a special surprise for you," an Apostle said with unsettling cheer. "We found him among the nobles. He was *very* eager to talk to us, and he told us a peculiar tale." He leaned in. His voice dropped to a mock whisper. "Apparently, you don't handle rejection well. He said you were *jealous*... that you attacked him after seeing him with someone else. Does the king know that you are a treacherous whore? You open your legs for any man." He stood upright, the weight of his presence shadowing her. The smirk on his face deepened. "You do have a talent for making enemies, don't you? Bring him in."

The eight Apostles stepped aside in perfect unison, creating a path from the door. Footsteps echoed from down the hallway. A tall figure entered, his face cloaked in shadow. But the moment she saw the tousled blonde hair and the jagged scars crawling up his neck, her breath caught. It was Bear, the fifth year student who had attacked her classmate, Verrona. He had been punished by lashes and banished from Skilheim.

She laughed at his darkened gaze. "You fools. You do not know what you've done by bringing him here. When Demetrius finds out, you'll all be killed." Her mana was building. "When I get out, I'll take my sweet time with you."

The eerie smile of the Apostle next to her faltered. "Let's see how long you'll be laughing." He raised his hand, signalling Bear to come forward.

"I've been dreaming of this day. You took everything from me—my title, my future, my family. Now, I will take everything from you." He stood next to her face and called his ice magic. A small blade of ice formed under his palm. He dug it in her arm and sliced her, just above her line of Runes. He used the blade to tear open her sleeve to her shoulder, and then moved to tear down her chest. The tip of the blade sliced open her skin. She refused to scream out in pain. She would not give him the satisfaction. Instead, she laughed.

He paused his motion and then backhanded her across the face. A sharp throb formed above her right eye. Something wet started running down her face. He went to the open cut on her eyebrow and dug his finger into the wound. The pain was too much for her to keep up the false laugh. Beads of sweat dripped down her forehead. He grabbed her finger, which she had curled into a fist. He pulled it back until he had a firm grasp on it and then bent it further. A loud snap echoed in the room. Her mind was pushing out the pain, she dulled her senses to preserve her sanity. *He's not coming.* He grabbed the next finger and repeated the motion. The light in her eyes dulled as she worked to remove herself from her physical body. It was as if she was watching what was happening from above. *He's not coming.* She felt a sudden pain lash through her, but it was not of her. Demetrius would not be able to protect her.

Disappointment broke her heart. Just like her past life, she had to suffer alone, hoping that her husband would save her. She gritted her teeth.

No, this stops here.

Bear smiled as he broke every finger of her one hand.

I'm stronger this time.

"That is enough, for now," an Apostle demanded. Bear leaned down to lick the trail of blood running down her cheek, and then straightened. The Apostle cleared his throat. "We have time. Let her bask in this pain while we pay a visit to her friends. We will bring you back shortly." They waited for him to straighten his clothes, and then with smug delight, leave the cell.

They followed him out, and she heard boots echoing against the stone floor. The last Apostle lingered, then leaned in close, his breath hot against her ear.

"We know he lied," he whispered, almost amused. "But we brought him anyway, just to watch your face. To see what he'll do to you. When he *defiles* you." He squeezed her broken hand, slow and deliberate. She bit down on a scream.

"The King won't go near something so... tainted," he murmured, then straightened with chilling calm and slipped out the door.

She sat in silence. It was not pain, or disbelief, of how they treated her which made her laugh. Not the cruelty, nor the threat. It was their mistake.

In the frenzy, so sure of their control, they had forgotten to do one very crucial thing that would have prevented her from retaliating. She had no suppressant or rune enchanted chains. They had forgotten to suppress her mana. It flowed through her veins like a charged river waiting to break through the dam.

They hadn't cut her off. And that oversight... would cost them everything.

She waited until their footsteps vanished down the hall. Only then did she move. With her uninjured hand, she reached out, fingers trembling but steady with purpose. Closing her eyes, she inhaled deeply, and called forth her magic.

A surge of warmth grew from her centre, her chest. It spread like fire through her veins. Her mana roared to be let free. She chanted the ancient incantation, her voice low and fierce. Across the far wall, a circle of glowing runes flared to life, etched in reddish light. The air rippled.

"Arlen," she said, her voice sure and steady. "I summon you."

The red runes pulsed outwards, then a large portal tore open, swirling with glimmering shadow and magical energy. Holding it open demanded a steady flow of mana, and it flickered against her will, threatening to collapse. She gritted her teeth, forcing it wider, pouring more and more energy into it. Then, three figures stepped through. Arlen. Jasper. Amiriel. Three hulking warriors prepared for battle. Relief hit her like a wave. She was so grateful that she gave her brothers a small rune talisman before parting with them at the encampment. That one act had saved her life.

The portal slammed shut behind them, as Arlen and Jasper came running forward. Arlen took out a knife and sliced open the leather binds.

"Gods, Lilith!" Arlen sounded panicked as he took in the blood pooling down her arm, her chest, and down her face.

Jasper was on the side with her broken hand. "Holy Gods... look at her hand. Do you have any Gertwood?" He carefully lifted her broken hand and inspected the bones. "We will have to reset them before we heal them."

"Do it, quickly!" Lilith breathed in deep. "We don't have time. We need to free others. The Apostles might know of your presence, and they'll be back to suppress my powers." Amiriel exhaled, carefully nudging at the first broken finger. She gasped in pain.

"I'm so sorry, Lilith." He quickly snapped her finger back into place. The urge to scream overwhelmed her as Amiriel quickly moved to the next finger. With each snap, a bright white light burst in front of her eyes, pulling her toward unconsciousness.

Yet, her determination hardened into something sharper. Her rage festered into something new. It curdled into a new hunger: cold, precise, unstoppable. Hatred for the Apostles became a fuel that pushed past the pain. Every indignity they'd dealt her folded into a single, bright intent: she would be justice. Her thoughts narrowed on her revenge, on how they would meet their end, and the feeling of satisfaction from delivering it herself.

Amiriel worked fast, hands sure and merciful. He set her last finger with a soft curse and a practiced twist. A vial of purple liquid was brought to her lips. Rejuvenation washed through her, and the dull, burning ache in her hands eased. When he finished, she flexed the healed fingers once, feeling strength return like a promise. Somewhere inside her, the ember that had once been pain now burned with fury. Something shifted in her mind; her soul was reshaping.

Jasper removed his coat and helped Lilith into it, while Arlen and Amiriel worked on the door. Amiriel pressed his hand on the cool wooden door. Although Lilith couldn't see his face, she could feel a cool white aura radiating from him. The door warped and then blasted forward, sailing into the wall across from them. The charged air around him had a similar vibration to one that she had not felt in a very long time. This was not the time for distractions.

"We need to break them all open," Lilith hissed, as she went to the next door. Amiriel ran to the end of the hall and used his magic to blast open the door.

"You all need to stand to the side. The door will blast open." His loud voice filled the hallway. Above them, she could hear the thumping of boots rapping above her, the sounds of people coming towards them.

Lilith glared at the ceiling. This was taking too long. She turned to face down the hallway, reaching her good hand out. Her breathing slowed, in and out. Time seemed to slow with every breath. She reached out to feel the cold metal of the doors, drawing mana from her well.

She needed to release them. She would not leave these prisoners behind. Not like this. Not caged, forgotten, and used as if their lives were meaningless.

The sounds of footsteps faded into a hum, as her breath trembled. She let out a slow exhale, digging deep into the well of magic buried in her soul. If this was the end, if she died freeing them, then so be it. It would be worth it.

A sudden snap cracked through her chest, just beneath the runes etched over her heart. The force of it made her stagger back, gasping. A fullness bloomed in its place, heavy and sharp. It's sting was not painful, it was a release. Her eyes welled with tears at the sensation. She could envision invisible chains that were weighing her wrists down beginning to crumble. In her mind's eye, they flared, then turned to ash, swept away by wind and fire. The storm of magic that cracked through the chains felt like surging waves of rebirth. This feeling was accompanied by words carried by the gentle stir of air around her. Time froze completely. At first, the whispers were unintelligible, but as the words became louder, she understood what was being said. A chant in the ancient tongue engulfed her, repeating the curse that bound her magic.

Stand in honour, and be unshaken. For the might of the bearer shall be bound, held by the holy words. Yet when one's worth is embraced, more shall be revealed than fate hath foretold. Tread with humility. Power is not granted to those who have not mastered its weight. When the soul is made ready, the flow shall return. When the flame is made pure, the dam shall yield. The darkness hungers for the light. Endurance. Destruction. Metamorphosis. This is the sacred balance of all things.

These words were engraved in her mind. Yet, the whispers continued.

You stand in solemn honour, and yet your spirit does not waver. Your power has been sealed and shackled, yet you find strength through turbulence. You are ready. Your soul knows its true measure. You walk humbly, treading with caution. Without fear, you dance with your destiny. Heavy is your heart that has endured much tribulation. You have survived countless nights of raging storms. Who do you see when you face your soul? Pride has not swayed you. Fear does not guide you. Live freely as you walk hand in hand with your darkness. Such is the ancient law. Such is the sacred curse. The balance demanded its price.

And you have paid in full.

Each rune carved into her skin flared in glowing white mana. One by one, a radiant warmth entered her body, renewing her well. The reach of magic, like roots growing under her feet, demanded more. And the earth answered her. Roots of power, ancient and alive, stretched from beneath her feet, rising to meet her call. The earth fed her. Empowered her. It absorbed the mana pulsing her magic to life.

She was *made* to fulfil this purpose, and seek retribution for these women, to break these cages. She was the eyes and hands of justice. She was created to burn the old order to the ground, for every woman they silenced. For every soul condemned to oppression.

She opened her eyes and a pure white light shone from her irises. Around her, time seemed to stop. Her brothers stood frozen in shock, Amiriel's hands still half-raised in mid-spell aimed towards another door. They stared at her. The weight of their gazes beheld her, not as just a sister or friend, but something else. Something divine. The runes along her body shimmered, then faded from her skin, one by one, into nothing.

All of them disappeared, except a line of runes still circling her wrist and a single rune marking her hand, made by a different seal. Runes that tie her to this place, to the palace, along with another spell. One that tethered her, still, to Demetrius: her marriage bond. She couldn't feel the end of it, and when she called to him, only silence answered. It wasn't rejection or abandonment that she felt. She didn't need him. She would stand by herself and rise through her own strength.

She raised her hands and smiled to herself, knowing she would soon break another seal.

From her fingertips, glowing roots of mana burst forth, luminous and alive. They slithered through the air like living threads, reaching for the remaining closed doors around the dungeon. Each root spread across each door like searching fingers, finding every lock, every seam, every bolt. She felt them, as if her own hands were pressed against the worn wood and iron.

She inhaled, then pulled on the tethers. The roots surged with power, and magic thundered through her like a storm.

The doors crumpled under her magic. She drew her hand back, causing the doors to fly into each other and then slump on the stone floor. This was no rescue. This was a reckoning.

Rolling her neck, she lowered her hand and allowed time to catch up. Arlen and Jasper looked to Lilith, a vision of white, her long black hair tousled by her white roots of magic.

Her voice was unusually steady and calm as she called out to the prisoners, "We are leaving now, so if you can walk, make for the door. If you boys wouldn't mind helping those that can't move. I'm going to form a portal back to the camp."

Footsteps came down the stairs as the first Apostle reached them. Amiriel used his magic to burst him into flames. The Apostle screamed and ran towards them, giving Arlen the opportunity to rush forward with his sword and stab the Apostle through his stomach. More Apostles came down, along with their guest, Bear.

"Do not kill that one. He's mine." Lilith focused on the blonde. She reached out with her magic. It was as if a root of white light shot out towards Bear and wrapped around his throat. She moved her fingers down, sending him flying to the ground, his fingers clawing at the invisible force around his neck. Jasper disappeared into the first prison cell, while Arlen and Amiriel drew out their swords and went rushing towards the onslaught of grey robes. Amiriel raised his hand, causing those closest to him to explode into a burst of blood and entrails. Lilith sent spears of stone towards one of the Apostles, piercing his body as he flew back from the force. His body impaled into the stone wall, a show of how deadly Lilith's freed abilities were. Those in the back turned to flee.

With Arlen and Amiriel taking care of the rest, she reached her hand forward and cast a portal. Her mana barely dipped. There was nothing holding her back. Her eyes drifted to her wrist, with only a single line of runes marking them. She flexed her hand and stretched her fingers. The pure energy flowing through her felt sensational. Her fullest potential. The furthest reach of her magic swelled in her soul. She was free. Effortlessly, a portal appeared near the stairwell. Arlen and Amiriel paused to exchange impressed looks.

"You know, I'm starting to think our education may be lacking," Jasper grumbled, hauling a woman forward. A line of scared prisoners hunched behind him, cowering at the sight of the grey and white robes.

Lilith spotted dirty feet walking into her line of vision. A Mage, covered in bruises, his arm hanging at an odd angle, slowly walked up to her. His stained robe was torn and hung in tatters. He said nothing, but reached his good arm out, as if he could feel the wisps of magic swirling around him. The Mage smiled at Lilith, placing his good hand atop Lilith's.

"Spare none of them. Make them feel our pain. Make them know our suffering, and become our reckoning. You are the hand of judgment and the eyes of truth. I know who you are now."

Jasper stalked forward, breaking the moment, as he held another Mage, the one who had his tongue removed, and carried him up to the portal.

Lilith tilted her head in confusion. "What do you mean? Who do you think I am?"

"You are wrath incarnate."

Amiriel spied the two, having overheard the Mage's speech, and walked over. "Come on, you're safe. Follow me," he said, as he walked him to the portal. The frail Mage looked back to Lilith, awestruck by her.

A few more bodies walked past her. Women in various states of undress touched her shoulder as they moved towards the portal, acknowledging Lilith as their saviour. The touch of their hands seeped through her clothes, lingering on Lilith's skin. Her eyes roamed every soul that passed, but none of them were her friends. She needed to find Felicia and Andishmand. If they were not here, the Apostles must have them hidden somewhere in the Temple. Amiriel carried the last woman to the portal and paused before going through.

"Do you want help?" he said to her, a look of knowing on his face of what she had planned next.

"Can you summon a portal?" she answered.

"I can. Here, take this." He dug into his neckline, yanking on a thin leather string that held a stone rune and tossing it to her. "We will be back as soon, I'll summon a portal to you." He started to walk to the portal, but before walking through he glanced back at her. "I wish I could see what happens next. If you need us, we're just a summon away." With that, he walked through, leaving her alone. Without strain, she closed the portal and went to stand over Bear.

In the palm of her hand, she summoned a familiar blade: a glossy silver dagger that had runes running down its centre, and a white pearlescent crystal embedded at the end. Its hilt was covered in fine leather, on which Lilith had etched a singular rune. A gift from Andishmand. Without her constraints, she was able to call for *Demon's Tongue*, a shorter, single edge sword, and tied the scabbard to her waist. Now, she felt ready.

She released some of her hold on Bear, enough to keep him conscious but paralyzed. Her knee grazed his head, as she knelt beside him, the tip of her dagger slicing the skin of his forehead. She carved a singular word into his forehead, and spat on the trail of blood it formed: 'rapist.' He was squirming and trying to beg, unable to use his voice. She tore each button of his shirt off, revealing his chest, and began to carve 'unworthy' above his heart. Satisfied by her handy work, she stood. Smiling down on him as she stomped on his hand, the bones breaking under her weight. He let out a silent howl.

"I wish I could stay and play with you longer, but you're not worth the effort. If our paths cross again in the next lifetime, I'll savour torturing you." She stomped on his most beloved appendage and then walked over him. From the corner of her eye, she saw him visibly relax.

"Oh...Did you think you'd be spared?" The laugh that escaped her was ruthless. With a flick of her finger he burst into flames. His skin formed blisters as he silently screamed to his death.

She headed for the main floor, immediately spotting a handful of rebels attempting to gather items to flee. She called up her fire magic and barrelled large fireballs at them. Confused, they froze as the fire blazed through their clothes and melted their skin. She watched as they twitched, consumed by fire, their screams sending shockwaves of satisfaction down her spine. The fire spread around the rooms, engulfing the old wood furniture and plush couches. She took her time, moving down the hall, pouncing on any movement, enjoying the screams of death, savouring her wrath. A lingering thought flashed through her mind, *'This must be what Demetrius feels.'* His absence annoyed her, sparking more rage. He wasn't here to witness her bared free from restraint.

Up one floor, she heard a faint cry for help. Felicia. She glided towards the sound with unnatural speed. Her mana coursed through her blood, fuelling her muscles.

"Stand back!" she yelled as she kicked the door in, breaking the wooden door off its hinges. Felicia was tied to four posts of the bed in her underwear. Rage consumed Lilith, it ate at her conscience and devoured her mercy. She would end every last Apostle. With her blade, she freed Felicia, who eyed Lilith cautiously, sensing the change. She carefully slipped off the bed and slowly held up her hands, as if she were prey moving around a predator.

"Relax, Felicia. I won't harm you. Do you want me to send you to the camp, or would you like to join me on my hunt?" Lilith moved to a dresser, searching for clothes. She picked up a long, white, cotton dress and tossed it to Felicia.

Felicia visibly relaxed and let out a sob as she pulled on the dress. She breathed, composing herself one more. "I'm staying."

"Andishmand?" Lilith asked, the anger within her taking over. She flexed her hands beside her, blue flames dancing along her skin.

Felicia's eyes widened as she watched Lilith. "I saw them take him towards the consorts' building," she quickly answered. With a smile, Lilith stalked over to Felicia, who was frozen in fear. Lilith grabbed her arm and enveloped them in white light.

Lilith's breathing became slow and steady. Her eyes glowed white as moonlight, as she transported them to the foot of the Temple. The ground trembled beneath them. Smoke had broken through a few windows, curling to the sky.

Felicia stumbled back, descending the stone steps, as screams echoed through the blaze. The fire Lilith had ignited was quickly tearing through the Temple. From the inferno and swirling ash, a few more Apostles and grey robes came running down the main stairs towards them in a wave of desperation. Their eyes were wild and their faces streaked with soot.

Felicia ran into the clearing, while Lilith stood her ground, ready to unleash her rage. A surge of fire swirled around her. It tingled at her fingertips, and formed a crown of fire above her head.

Mana rushed into her veins like lightning, untamed and endless. The rush of limitless energy felt intoxicating. The sensation was both overwhelming and yet not enough. With a scream that rippled the sky, Lilith let go. Fire exploded outward in a tidal wave of fury and heat, which roared past her and tore into the Temple like the wrath of a forgotten god.

CHAPTER 23
UNBOUND RUNES

Felicia

Felicia feared that Lilith was no longer a mere mortal being. How could she be? Not when fire flared behind her, fanning outwards like wings of destruction.

The Temple exploded, an eruption of fire and raw energy that tore through the sky in a blinding blaze. A burst of energy pulsed outwards sending a shockwave that rippled out towards the palace.

Felicia was thrown backward and hit the ground hard. A lash of pain lanced through her hands and back as they scraped against stone. Instinct took over, and she curled into herself, covering her arms over her head, as the world screamed around her.

Above, a colossal mushroom cloud billowed where the Temple stood, black smoke churning with embers. Chunks of stone and wood shot outwards. The force of the destruction cracked the ground. The palace windows splintered, then shattered. It rained glass, fire, and ashes.

At the top of the scorched steps stood a lone figure, naked and radiant.

Lilith.

Her eyes were closed, and her arms stretched out, as if embracing the ruin of destruction. Her skin was marred with blood and soot, but she glowed faintly white, lit from within, as though the sun itself had chosen her as its vessel.

Felicia stared in awe, her breath caught in her throat. She watched as Lilith opened her eyes, and in that moment, all traces of mortality had vanished. She stood like something born of myth: not woman, not queen, but divine. Ethereal. Terrifying. A goddess draped in light and silence.

Felicia blinked, and lost sight of Lilith. Suddenly, she felt her presence standing beside her. Felicia flinched, her body locking in fear.

"Get up," Lilith spoke. Her voice sounded otherworldly. It was deep, resonant, and thrumming with power. A sound both commanding, yet seductive. Like velvet and thunder combined.

Felicia's body was shaking, and her limbs moved before her mind could catch up. Lilith turned without a word, walking up to a wall of the consorts' building. With a flick of her hand, the stones disintegrated. It was as if her magic had an invisible extension. Now exposed, a consort and her ladies cowered, trembling behind a couch that offered no protection.

"Leave," Lilith ordered.

The women bolted through the crumbling wall, their screams echoing across the smoke-filled clearing. Felicia darted into the room, and flung open a wardrobe, her heart beating wildly. Her fingers closed around the first thing they touched—a black, silky dress—and pulled it out. Peering around the corner, she saw Lilith. Casually, she sauntered down the hallway as if she hadn't just destroyed the Temple.

"Please...Let me," Felicia said breathlessly, holding up the silky dress like an offering to a god. Lilith didn't resist as Felicia slipped the gown over her soot-streaked skin. She was eerily still, like a storm that had momentarily calmed, but not passed. Lilith seemed not fully aware, as her eyes remained distant, fixed ahead, and glowing faintly with residual power.

Felicia fastened the ties on the back and took a few steps back. Lilith was a divine vision of power, tall and commanding. The gown clung to her like smoke, with the black silk gliding over her frame. Embroidered crimson-red flowers bloomed along the fabric, winding like branches up the bodice, cupping her breasts. Long, flowing sleeves fluttered with every shift of her arms.

Lilith ran her fingers over the soft material, slow and deliberate, eyes narrowing with appraisal. A glorious smile, radiant and terrifying, split across her face, her fierce eyes gleaming above it.

Drawn in by the commotion, several doors flew open. Faces peeked into the destruction, eyes of trembling ladies in waiting. After eyeing Lilith, the consorts fled, rushing past her to the breach in the wall. Felicia did a double take as she saw Meira and Meridith emerge, hands clasped tightly with an older woman. They hurried past, heads bowed, intentionally averting their eyes out of fear and respect.

Lilith floated forward again, her body gliding like shadows, every step graceful and unnerving. She tilted her head slightly and paused mid-stride. It was as if she sensed something, or someone. Like a predator catching a scent. The silence that followed was electric, as if the hallway itself held its breath.

Felicia stopped, giving Lilith some space. She watched her friend turn towards a door, and with a flick of her hand the door blasted open. Inside the room were two Apostles. They dropped to their knees as Lilith approached.

"My Queen...," one said. But his pleading fell on deaf ears. She raised her hand as if she were going to touch his cheek. Instead, the Apostles both started convulsing. Their eyes bulged as they gasped. Lilith dropped her arm and tilted her head. She beamed at them, as blood drained from their eyes, nose, and ears. The pair took one last gasp and then their heads exploded. Blood and brain matter splattered on her dress, the crimson red blending seamlessly into Lilith's embroidery.

As if she had swatted at a fly, Liltih turned and went back into the hallway. Felicia glanced behind her, at the lifeless bodies, and dry heaved.

"How many are left?" Felicia asked Lilith, her voice quivering.

"Five Apostles were killed in the temple, plus those two," Lilith said, her eyes sparkling with electricity. "Only two left. Their apprentices have deserted them." Lilith stilled as more women ran past, servants and consorts alike. They pressed themselves against the walls, giving Lilith space. Fear hung in the air.

Several grey robes were too busy trying to break into the library that they failed to notice the two women approaching. Shouts of a familiar voice, Sir Ravanor, echoed from within. Felicia charged at the men, her hands aflame, ready to strike. With a blast of flame, she sent the first two flying backwards, their robes catching fire. Her attack was nothing in comparison to Lilith's. By a soft curl of her hand, the remaining grey robes fell, paralyzed by lightning, their mouths foaming as they lay in their excrement.

"My queen, is that you?" Sir Ravanor whimpered, opening the door more.

Lilith's demeanor changed from wrath to charm, grinning at the old librarian. "Please, do not worry." Her voice was so soft. "They won't come for the Library anymore. It will be over soon." Sir Ravanor paused; he was intelligent enough to know not to ask questions. "When this is over, we will need your help." With a nod, he sealed the door shut.

As they walked past the throne room, they stopped and looked into the empty hall. Around them the panels of glass started to rattle, with little spider web cracks forming. Felicia didn't dare interrupt Lilith, as she took a step in. Underneath her feet, a large crack weaved towards the two thrones. A growing chasm was tearing, separating them, worming further back to the blackened trunk of the ancient tree. What was left, split into two, expelling whatever mystical mana it held into the hall. Lilith calmly walked beside Felicia, who wordlessly watched the hall splintered into glass and ruin.

They came to the main stairwell, and there one was: a single Apostle, surrounded by a dozen guards, their swords ready as they marched down. Step by step, they came closer. Each movement was an act of intimidation with mana building around them. Their polished armour was encased in a rising aura in hues of blues and oranges.

At once, several guards shot ice and fire at them, but their attacks met with an invisible shield, dissolving any strikes. Lilith opened up her palms and reached out. A glowing spark formed in her hands. It hovered forwards, and then flashed. Bolts of lightning erupted from the orbs, each colliding with its target, making them collapse into fits of seizures.

"Holy gods," whispered Felicia. She had never seen such raw power, or destructive mana. The Apostle turned to flee. Lilith tilted her head, her eyes stalking him. As if pulled by invisible strings, he suddenly stopped and flew backwards. By an unseen force, his body dangled in the clear space beside the stairs. The hood of his robes flopped back, revealing his face: ordinary and unassuming. Cold steel blue eyes now wide with fear. His arms stretched above his short brown hair, as he opened his mouth and violently screamed. The sounds of bones crunching became a chorus around them, a symphony of pain and suffering.

Lilith climbed the staircase, her bare feet stepping over the bodies of the fallen guards. As she stood beside the Apostle, his body disengaged from whatever hold she had on him, crashing in a heap below. A sickening thud echoed up the stairs, sending shivers up Felicia's spine.

Felicia kicked at the guard's silver armour. "Part of me is relieved to see their rule come to an end, but a part of me wishes that they suffer more."

Lilith laughed, the sound silky smooth. "How about I leave the last one for you?" She seemed completely at ease, her hand draped over the banister, her fingers caressing the old wood as she reached the top.

Felicia grinned, as she schemed. "We should save the last one for a more public execution. A visual end to their tyranny. The people of Vanguard are as much victims as we are. We all deserve to watch his death." Lilith was about to say something, when she abruptly froze. They could hear the faint sounds of someone slamming against the door.

They followed the sound to the queen's wing, to the room Felicia and Tally had once occupied. Lilith grabbed the door by the handle and gave it a slight push. The door broke and slammed to the wood floor.

"Andishmand?" Lilith called out, seeing the shocked face of the lithe Mage. His face was swollen and covered in bruises, while his hands were bound together in chains. Gone was his long white hair and long beard. They had shaved him, and by the scattered slices, they had done so roughly.

"I told you to run," Andishmand croaked, his voice breaking. Lilith ran her fingers over the metal chains which waned and cracked beneath her touch. The remnants of the chains clashed to the ground, showing a thick band of bruising along Andishmand's wrists.

"They shaved your hair, " Felicia venomously stated.

"They were desperately trying to break my will." Andishmand's eyes glinted. "Little do they realize, the kings had been trying, unsuccessfully, for years." Without his hair, there was no hiding the expansive lines of runes that covered his skin. They ran down his skull, to the back of his neck and then disappeared under his tattered burgundy robes. Felicia spied something glowing within Lilith's dress and pointed.

From across the room, the air shimmered, then a massive sky-blue magic circle blazed to life on the wall. The centre pulsed twice before morphing into a swirling, shadowy portal. Amiriel stepped through first, his eyes fixed on Lilith. Behind him glowered the stony face of Lord Helmer and Sir Tornbury, weapons drawn, ready for battle. Each of their armour was covered in weapons—blades, axes, and small shields. The two women froze, their expressions twisting into astonishment. Even the Mage, who had seen countless battles, recoiled a step. The warriors' presence was unexpected. Unnecessary.

Amiriel sheathed his sword, looking around the room. "I brought reinforcements." Lord Helmer jogged to a nearby window, looking down at the pristine gardens.

"What's the situation?" his voice held an air of suspicion.

Lilith scowled, the glow of her eyes intensifying. Felicia cleared her throat and stepped up. "The Temple has fallen. The Apostles are no more. *Her Highness* has freed us from their tyranny. She, alone, has saved us." As if realizing their mistake, the men's gaze locked onto Lilith. Sir Tornbury sank to his knees, while Lord Helmer approached the new queen.

"Pardon my rudeness." He mirrored Sir Tornbury's movements, and bowed his head in respect. "My queen."

"Enough." Lilith motioned for them to stand. The rage in her eyes subsided, and her demeanour shifted as if sated by their reverence. "We need to secure what's left of the palace. One Apostle still roams freely."

Lilith raised her hand, and the air shifted around her. A mist of warm, white light swirled around them. In the blink of an eye, they were back down by the gaping hole they came in from.

"Wait." Lilith's voice was a low whisper. White light flowed from her into Felicia and Andishmand, restoring their bodies. The bruising and swelling on the Mage's face slowly faded. Felicia stared at her hands, the cuts magically knitting themselves closed, erasing the damage caused by the Apostles.

Around them, Lord Helmer, Sir Tornbury, and Amiriel moved as if caught in a trance, taking in the wake of Lilith's destruction. The ashes of where the Temple once stood, beams had turned to embers, and the once crisp banner hung to one side, in tatters. The air around them smelled of smoke and charred flesh.

Lilith leaned towards Felicia, her eyes still luminously wild with power. "With the way I'm feeling right now, I'm tempted to destroy this place entirely. What do you think?" Lilith looked up at the large red building, the home of the consorts. The large hole looked like a wound, a gash against the red stone.

Felicia clasped Lilith's hand and gave it a little squeeze. "There could be innocents inside," she said. "Servants, consorts and their children could still be hiding. We don't need to kill needlessly. You don't kill for sport."

Lilith nodded, the wrath in her eyes softening for an instant before she perked up, something demanding her attention. In a flash, she moved towards the main palace. Her attention unexpectedly fixed on something.

"What do you sense?" Amiriel jogged beside Lilith. Felicia looked at the pair. They suited each other more than Lilith and Demetrius. Amiriel was cool and calm to Lilith's savage rage.

Lilith whipped her head side to side, "Shh. Do you hear that?" She sprinted forwards. The group ran to catch up.

"Lilith, please slow down. There's glass everywhere and we have no shoes!" Felicia yelled, waving her hand at her and Andishmand's feet. Within seconds, the glass, littering the ground shook, hovering just an inch in the air. As one, the pieces all turned to fine sand. She felt a string of white light tickle along the soles of her feet. Her whole body seemed to tingle with this intrusive magic. Andishmand released a little gasp, feeling the same strange mana. Looking at her own hands, Felicia felt a sudden rush of strength.

A troop of guards marched forward, their weapons in a defensive position.

"You there! Stand down, or we will be forced to retaliate."

"Stop!" Lord Helmer yelled. "By royal command, we're cleansing the palace of the Apostles." Several of the guards lifted their weapons, shocked by the announcement.

"We will fire, if you take one more step!" the front commander roared. He failed to notice over half of his troop standing, deciding to side with Lilith. She stood still and closed her eyes. Above her, dark clouds rolled in, summoned by her mana, her will. Then, without warning, it started to rain, crashing over them. The sudden storm struck like judgment. A few more soldiers faltered, their weapons falling from their hands as doubt gripped them.

Lilith's eyes sparked with lightning. "I'm afraid," she snapped, her voice dark and smooth, "you are *severely* outnumbered." Her words cut through the roar of the rain, carried by an ancient power, demanding authority.

"As your queen," she commanded, "I order you to stand aside." Thunder rumbled overhead, emphasizing her order, and shaking the earth beneath their feet. A jagged fork of lightning scattered along the sky, engulfing everything in a flash of white. For a heartbeat, the world seemed to freeze. The fate of Vanguard was held between surrender and ruin.

"Your death is by your choosing."

Almost all of the guards had abandoned their leader. He now stood with five others. They all aimed to strike her, casting different elements all at once. A bolt of lightning crashed to the ground. The resounding boom was deafening. Felicia and the group hunched down, covering their ears. They heard ringing.

When they looked up, the six guards were screaming on their knees, their flesh smouldering as if being burned from the inside out. Lilith continued walking in the rain. They came upon the palace garden, dark clouds continuing to rumble overhead. She stood in front of the warped, old tree.

They all eyed Lilith cautiously as Amiriel spoke, "Is she okay?" The remaining line of runes glowed against her skin and started to fade.

Felicia bit her lip. "I'm not sure... Lilith?"

Lilith raised her hand and placed it on the old bark. Sensing a shift, Felicia darted, her hand outstretched, ready to pull back her friend. Mana pulsed around them, and in an instant, Lilith vanished.

"Lilith!" Felicia shouted, her hand closing on thin air. It was too late. Felicia reached the tree first, and began clawing and tearing pieces of bark.

"Where did she go?" Amiriel searched the old bark, trying to feel for some shift.

Andishmand rested his palm on the bark, and closed his white eyes. "She is not gone. I can feel her presence still roaming this realm." The others looked at him. "She will come back to us, when fate demands it. There are many truths she has yet to learn, so her path here has not come to an end. "

CHAPTER 24
THE FALLEN STAR

Lilith

A faint ache registered around her wrists. Her mind reeled, feeling both dizzy and lucid. Part of her registered the familiar burn of the runes fading on her skin, but the majority of her focus was elsewhere. No longer was she bound to stay at the palace.

A strange song filtered through the air, an angelic voice calling to her. She walked to the large warped tree that stood at the centre of the garden, a weathered oak tree that looked much older than the one in the throne room. The light song came from within the tree. *Come closer*, it beckoned.

Felicia's voice sounded muffled, "I'm not sure... Lilith?"

She drew up her roots and extended them out to brush against the bark. The branches swayed, almost as if they were waking after a long sleep. The sweet song vibrated louder through the tree as if she were listening to the crescendo of a chorus. Louder and louder the voice rang through her mind. A circle formed on the trunk, its rune formation much different from what she used when she summoned a portal. She touched the rough bark, its cracked edges flaking under her fingers.

"Lilith!" Felicia yelled through the loud pattering of rain. Her words were lost to Lilith, for all she could hear was the mesmerizing light singing, calling to her to go touch the tree. A streak of lightning lit up the dark sky as Lilith raised her right hand and placed it on the center of the rune circle.

"Lilith!" Felicia's echoed voice faded as her body was pulled into the tree.

She landed atop a pile of sand. Stifling heat beat down on her as she gathered her gown and searched for clues as to where she was. Red stone surrounded her with small growths of spiky vegetation peppering the ground. A beam of sunlight poked through a large crack above her.

"Lilith." An otherworldly hum drifted in the hot wind. Lilith whirled around and braced herself for an attack. A light song played in the breeze. Annoyed and curious, she followed the sound. It reminded Lilith of a woman who was lost in whatever she was doing, happily singing a nondescript tune. Down through the rough red stone corridor, the tune grew louder and louder.

She entered a large opening, half concealed in shadow. Something large moved ahead; it was the source of the singing.

It flared its enormous feathered wings, spanning the width of the space as it took a step into the light. Lilith jumped back and sank into a pose to strike. Her eyes scanned the creature. Its feet were those of a large bird, with claws that ended in large talons. Gold feathers covered its curvy legs, brushing around the waist. The middle of the creature was more human-like with a narrow, curved waist made of smooth white skin. Her large breasts were covered in delicate opalescent feathers that shimmered in the light. They covered the collarbone and up to mid-neck. Her arms were shaped like those of a human, but her fingers ended in razor-sharp talons. The head was that of a beautiful woman. She had thick, curly red hair that fell to her shoulders, along with beautiful, dark grey eyes and plump, pink lips. She smiled, her teeth unnaturally white with long canines. "Lilith, there is no need to be scared." Her voice was light and airy, pleasant to the ear.

"It feels like I know you." Lilith cautiously stood from her attack position. It felt like she was meeting a friend.

The birdlike woman's grin widened, showing more sharpened teeth. "Of course, I've known you since you were a young goddess. We have lots to discuss and very little time."

"Who are you?" Lilith took a tentative step closer.

"You do not recognize me?" Her face flashed through Lilith's mind.

"Melia," Lilith gasped. "But you look so different."

"One of my many forms. I hold all knowledge of this world and others. You and I walked side by side in a distant past." Melia tilted her head. "My Lilith. Lilith Hennan. Reborn into this realm as a balance to the fading sun. You know of whom I speak, though doubt now clouds your feelings. Let me reassure you, my blessing was bestowed wisely. It was my decision to tip the tide in order to stop the coming evil. I went against the others and put in motion a new coming. The fall of the gods. They have ignored this world, up until his return. The Dark One. His mind walks the edge of madness because of what they did, and you can either join him or suffer with him."

"Isn't that the same?" Lilith interrupted.

Melia blinked and ruffled her feathers, "That is for you to choose. The powers at play are coming. Your death sparked a divide between the gods, and now they know you are reborn and that he has been freed. The stars are aligning. You have yet to find the missing key, yet you have in your possession the answers to find her. I have brought you to the start. It is your turn to find the way. Locke will not be able to come to you."

"Someone took Demetrius?" Lilith was so mad that he hadn't come back to save her. She didn't consider that there would be another who could overpower him.

"He is needed elsewhere."

"This is too cryptic. Can you give me a hint? What am I supposed to do?" A headache was forming behind her eyes, trying to decipher this message.

"You used to be good at deciphering my messages." Melia let out an exasperated sigh. "The Mage has given you an item. Look there first, and the rest should follow. You will need this." With a small burst of white magic, a round item landed in her clawed hand. She held it open for Lilith to take. Lilith walked over slowly and gently picked up the round circle. Rolling it between her hands, she felt that both sides were engraved with runes lining the outside. The crystal was an inch thick and made out of a light green stone, similar to the shade of her eyes.

"What is this?"

"You'll need this to revive tools that will help you in this battle. They've been waiting in a long-forgotten tomb for you to give life back to them. You hear their call when you're around them."

Lilith went to inspect the green stone closer. On one side, in the centre, was an engraved six-pointed star; on the other side was a symbol that she didn't recognize. It was a series of curved lines interconnected. The stone gave off a light greenish glow.

Lilith looked up to ask the creature more questions, but found the space empty. A single gold feather lay on the floor.

Kneeling down, she picked up the feather; its individual barbs shimmering in the light. She held up the stone and feather, wondering where to store the items, as an idea popped into her mind. It would be a burden to carry these items on her right now, but she had a way of storing items somewhere safe. Then she remembered Andishmand's journal. Was this the item the Mage gave her? The other possibility was the dagger, which had been tucked into her waist since travelling from the palace. She held out her hand, summoning the journal. It was wrapped in a filthy blouse, and her pack was covered in dust. Her safe place was hidden in Skilheim, an unused nook she had found in the dusty library.

This place seemed a suitable spot for her to read through the journal. Since she was told this place would be the start of her quest, she would need to venture out of this cave soon. Sitting against the wall, she used the beam of light to read the second excerpt of the journal.

Remembering the first passage, Andishmand was sent to the darkness and heard a voice calling to 'find her.' Obviously, that voice was Locke/Demetrius' and he was trying to find Lilith. The next few excerpts described Andishmand being ordered by another Mage to turn back and warn the others of the voice. What they found in the darkness was a mystery to him. He wanted to find the source, but had to follow the orders of his superior. He spoke of the creation of the barrier and the festivals that ensued in Vanguard. King Gaius had asked him what his plans were next, to which Andishmand gave a vague answer of searching the west for a way to permanently close the Void. He stayed in the kingdom for thirty-five years, roaming around, looking for answers. In that time, King Amadeus rose to power, inheriting the burden of the darkness from his father.

Lilith would have been just a small child around the time of his next entry.

I travelled far to the distant islands that lay to the west. Several of the Mages stayed at Vanguard to further consult the king. A few of us returned to the distant realms. Five of us have set out to look for some answers. I believe that the gods would not have forsaken us entirely. There must be some clues, some way to end this darkness. I've searched the nearby islands with little to no success. No one knows anything, and I have not come across anything with divine mana. Something is telling me to be here. To wait for something to arrive.

She read through more excerpts of his time on the island, how he made a home and befriended the locals. Lilith paused reading. The light above was fading. She would have to make camp here for the night and start moving tomorrow. She laid out the blanket from her pack and settled down. Luckily, she had not unpacked anything and was able to fill up her flask with her water magic. Her stomach grumbled with hunger, but she kept drinking water to fill her belly. She opened the journal once more.

I could never have imagined that the gods would answer my call. A child was born so close to my home. Her mother was close to death, and she had travelled far, all alone. I have made them as comfortable as I could, and sent a bird calling for a midwife from the nearest town. The woman has jet-black hair and vivid green eyes; her name is Evlyn. Her baby has been kissed by a fallen star. I watched as her patch of dark hair turned white like the moon. Her name is Astra. A fallen star.

The midwife has come and tended to the mother; she says she will be fine, but is weak. She may die. The baby, too, is fading. I have tried everything to keep the small child alive. I can tell her will is strong. Please let her live.

It has been two weeks since Astra and her mother made their appearance. They are both doing well. The babe is getting stronger, though she is much smaller than others that I have seen. The midwife has asked for them to be moved closer to the town. I feel apprehensive about such a request. The locals are friendly enough, but they are suspicious of my presence. I have tried my best to make myself useful to them in the last couple of weeks. A gesture to show that I mean them no harm. We will do as the mother wants. She wishes to keep herself distant. There is more to her than it seems. She is well-versed in the knowledge of the gods. I suspect she is a priestess or oracle.

Strange things have happened in town. The people are spreading rumours that the waters have been cursed. I believe the fallen stars have blessed these waters, and deep down the island dwellers know the truth. They've instilled this rumour to ward off outsiders from coming and claiming the bay. I am not sure if it is wise to stay here. The locals are growing more and more distrustful of us. We must leave.

We are travelling further west. I have found a ship that is headed to the western lands. They say the trip will be too dangerous for the mother and newborn, but I fear that if we stay, we may be in more danger. They need to survive. I am sure they are the ones. The child with silver eyes and starlight hair. She must be kept safe. Evlyn has told me that the mother priestess has sent her on this journey to hide her daughter until she is ready. Evlyn has been blessed by a god; she learned of the truth as a Maiden of Melia. She has turned her back on her family to secure the future of her daughter. They think she died. She must miss them greatly because I hear her cries in the night. Mankind is so fragile. I pity them.

The next several pages were dedicated to their travels on board the ship. A bird arrived from Vanguard with a note from a Mage. Former King Gaius' mind has been plagued by something sinister, and his body is dying. They requested Andishmand to come back to Vanguard.

Lilith thought about what she read. *Poor Andishmand. He had travelled back to Vanguard only to have his powers bound.* Then her mind drifted to Andishmand's tale of the woman and child. A fleeting suspicion drifted across her mind, but she dismissed it. Clearly, she was brought to this place to find the answers. This child, who would likely be grown, or at least her own age, should be somewhere near here. This 'Fallen Star' has the power to balance the darkness. *But why would Andishmand keep such a person secret?* She thought while flipping through the journal. *If the Void closed, what would happen to Demetrius?*

She paused to look at her smooth, clear skin in the fading sunlight. Her runes, even the ones that bound her to the palace, were gone. Only a single rune etched on her left hand ring finger remained. She couldn't feel him anymore, not even through their marriage bond. A dark thought stirred in her mind. What if he was trapped in the cage? She inspected the twisted rune, knowing that only death could make this one disappear. That realization was oddly comforting. She had to get back to the Kingdom of Draydon, and soon.

Chapter 25
A Sanctum of Ash and Ruin

Felicia

"She'll be back." Amiriel's hand stilled Felicia's desperate attempt at clawing her way into the trunk of the warped tree. "We both know this."

Felicia surrendered, letting her hands fall to her sides.

Amiriel continued, "The question is, why hasn't he returned for her?"

"Who knows," Felicia growled. "Maybe we'd still be under the Apostles' control if Demetrius had come back. I, for one, am relieved that he's away."

Andishmand nodded, "We're finally free of them."

Felicia pointed to the dark cloud in the distance. "I don't think we'll have time to celebrate. Let's make sure the palace is cleared. We've got to figure out our next move."

The chaos that ensued after Lilith obliterated the Temple and half of the palace was left to the group to sort out. The consorts and most of the serving staff fled in a panic into the streets of Vanguard. Lord Helmer and Sir Tornbury went to find any remaining soldiers and organize them enough to bar any civilians from wandering into the destroyed grounds. Several soldiers stood around one of the main gates of the palace and jumped when they saw Felicia, Andishmand, and Amiriel approach.

"We saw you with the queen." Some of the men took a step back, frantically scanning the area behind the woman as if Lilith would appear before them.

"Uhm..." Felicia pushed Amiriel next to her, feeling comfort in his overbearing presence. "The Apostles have all but been destroyed, if you hold any allegiance with them, let it die now, and you shall be spared." None of these soldiers seemed to reconsider the legitimacy of Felicia's words. So, she continued, "We need to secure the palace and make sure that civilians remain outside of these walls until the dust settles." Felicia paused to look at the area where the large temple once stood.

"We, uh, understand." One soldier nodded to the others.

"I am Amiriel, a commander of the royal army. We have been placed in charge of re-establishing order." Amiriel's voice held authority. "After you have secured our walls, there is one remaining Apostle that could still be hiding within the palace. He is considered traitorous to the kingdom. Any surviving members, including their apprentices, should be rounded up and brought to the throne hall." He took a step closer, towards the centre soldier. "I am placing you in charge of finding and organizing the remaining soldiers."

The Apostle had forced most of the royal guards to the encampment, so they expected there to be few guards left.

Andishmand cleared his throat. "Please see that the consorts and their children are found."

"What if the remaining Apostle has already fled?" a soldier asked them.

"Our focus is on securing the palace. If he has fled, then finding him will be something we deal with later on." Amiriel nodded and turned around, heading for the destroyed consorts' building. Felicia gave the soldiers a quick nod and followed him.

Out of earshot, Felicia leaned over to the other two. "So, what now?"

"Now, we organize and regroup at the encampment." Andishmand paused his cloudy eyes surveying the fallen Temple. "We need to send word to the general, and find someone who can help us organize what's left of the palace."

Felicia nodded. "Well then, we need Lady Ashmore and her bird."

Entering from the main doors to the consorts' building, they could hear that everyone had cleared out. They started room by room searching for help. They got to the highest floor and heard whispering from the end of the hall.

"Hello? It's all over," Felicia yelled, cautiously building up her mana.

"Felicia?" The soothing voice of Lady Ashmore reached them at the same time as one of the doors flew open. A tall brunette that looked like Lady Ashmore walked over to them, and pulled her in for a hug. "Thanks the gods."

"How are you here, Lady Ashmore? We thought the worst," Felicia asked. She had feared that Lady Ashmore had been taken or killed by the Apostles.

"In the chaos, a few of the consorts managed to find their children and attempt to flee using the tunnels, but we had to turn back. Some of the tunnels have collapsed."

"And the Haven?"

"Thankfully the Haven remains open."

Amiriel looked confused. "The Haven? What tunnels?"

Lady Ashmore gave Amiriel a polite smile. "The librarians here believe the palace was built on the foundations of a ruin before the age of mankind. They've mapped out most of what's down there, but there's little to no reason to venture under the palace. From what I've been told, there are tunnels leading south to the encampment and to the northern borders of Isir."

Amiriel turned to Felicia. "Wait. Do you think we could make it to the encampment? We need help. The palace is wrecked and we need reinforcements."

"What about King Amadeus or the Queen?" Andishmand asked Lady Ashmore, who responded by shaking her head in sadness.

"It looks like someone took the opportunity of the chaos to end Queen Isolde's life. An attempt was made on his Highness." Lady Ashmore pulled the group into the room where she was hiding. Several women and children were huddled in the corner. "Miss Flavian is here to help us," she announced to the others. Some of the older ladies came from their hiding spot. Felicia let out a gasp, taking in her shaved hair and bruises.

"Work of the Apostles. May the gods curse their souls." One of them spat on the floor. These women were in rough shape;

no doubt they'd had their fair share of mistreatment since the arrival of the Apostles and the rebels.

"Luckily, we may not have to worry about them any more. Queen Lilith took care of them and the rebels."

"Oh, we know. She has destroyed most of the palace. Though we are thankful to be freed from the hands of those wicked men, we are now without a home."

Felicia looked around the room. Twelve women, a mixture of consorts, ladies in waiting and a few servants looked aimless, uncertain about their future. With them were a handful of children. The youngest looked just about two, while the oldest could barely be twelve. They all had dark blue hair. King Amadeus' children. Tally was the second child of King Amadeus, but only the queen's children had direct inheritance of the throne. Demetrius was the only offspring from the union.

Right now they needed leadership. Until the new king returned. *If* he returned.

"Lady Ashmore, can you spare a moment for us?" Felicia walked back out into the hall.

"The new king has yet to return. Until then, we have no clear direction from the royals. The civilians will expect some answers about what happened, and soon. There is no denying that something happened within the palace wall, especially as consorts and palace staff fled into the streets. Unless we want them to surge against the royal line and abolish the system, we need a leader. I don't know what we should do."

"I don't either." Lady Ashmore looked at Andishmand. "What would you suggest, Mage?"

Andishmand's face turned to the door, as if he were sensing the emotions of those hidden in the room. "Before the Apostles, the king heavily relied on his councilmen, and without their guidance, we are acting on our desires alone."

"Then we assemble the councilmen. Lilith's father was one, I'm sure if I ride out and explain, he can give us advice." The wheels in Felicia's brain started turning. "We need to send out word to gather the council, let them know that we have dismantled the Apostles and are wanting their help. Maybe you'll have a few that refuse from bitterness, but I suspect most would be willing to lend us their aid."

Lady Ashmore agreed. They went back and forth fine tuning the details, but Felicia already had her mind set on heading to Lilith's home.

"I will head back to the encampment and tell the general," Amiriel announced. He turned to Andishmand. "We could use you there. In truth, the encampment is on the brink of unrest. It has been months since we have seen our families, and our resources are precariously low."

Felicia stilled at the mention of her mother. Andishmand was quiet, making her wonder what was going through the Mage's mind.

"Two Mages have been taken to the encampment already. I will have to go there, for we need to be reunited." Andishmand nodded and gave Felicia a light pat on the shoulder. He had been her least favorite teacher at Skilheim, but looking at the tired Mage, she felt sorry for him.

Before Felicia could head to the stables, a soldier knocked on the door, letting them know that the remaining Apostle and his apprentice could not be located in the palace. Lady

Ashmore stepped in to tell them to clear the labyrinth, but otherwise keep them posted. With everything planned out, Felicia made for the main palace, hoping to find the locations of the old councilmen.

The first place she would check was the library. Perhaps Sir Ravanor knew where the records were held. Navigating the hallways of the grand palace was a skill in itself. They all looked the same, with beautifully carved white stone pillars to mimic oak trees. There was a perfect blend between nature and man made elements that gave the main palace a sense of peace. She had learned to look for landmarks, special plants or unique flowers to direct her to the library. Only once had she received permission to go inside with Lilith. She had been to the palace a few times before. Her mother, a favourite general of King Amadeus, would leave her in the care of some staff. They were always kind to her, but a hindrance to their daily chores, and so Felicia was often left to play with a consort's child.

She stopped in front of a set of large white double doors. She waited a few minutes after knocking to enter. They were locked, but that hardly slowed her. Using her mana, she stepped back and filled her muscles with energy. Lifting her legs, she planned to kick the door down, but at the last second, the doors flew open.

Sir Ravanor glared at her.

"Would you kindly refrain from trying to break down my doors?" His usual cheery disposition was replaced with anger.

"I'm glad that you are safe, Sir Ravanor, but we have a problem."

"And that problem requires you to damage my library?"

"To be fair, I did knock first." She mustered up an innocent smile. "We're on a bit of a time crunch. I'm looking for information."

Sir Ravanor scanned her and let out an exasperated sigh. He opened the doorway further and motioned for her to enter. The library was just as magnificent as she remembered. Tall walls made up of floor to ceiling shelves, filled with thousands of books, circled the large interior. On either end was a set of spiral staircases that led to the floor above. The second floor balconies were lined with couches and polished furniture. There were shelves and shelves brimming with books, scrolls and maps, all neatly organized by trained staff. Not a book was out of place. When the whole palace was teeming with chaos, and Lilith was on her destructive path, the library had gone unscathed.

"Madame Bonnart?" Sir Ravanor called out.

A tall woman wearing a modest grey dress came rushing over, with a small knife in her hands. She had a wild look about her, protectively shielding the books behind her.

Throwing up her hands, Felicia shouted, "Whoa. I like your spirit, but I think you have it wrong. I'm here to find some help. I'm trying to track down some information." The woman loosened her grip on her knife after weighing Felicia's words. Sir Ravanor chuckled at the whole scene.

Felicia gave them a brief update on the situation they were in.

"What sort of information are you looking for?" Madame Bonnart asked.

"Well, we're looking to re-establish the council. We need the location of all previous councilmen to send word that they're needed here."

As if on a mission, the woman started walking to the back of the library. Felicia jogged to catch up to her. The woman looked around and started chatting, "If you're looking for those records, they'll be in the offices next door. Let me introduce you to the rest here and I'll explain what you're after. The woman looked around, seemingly searching for something, when she stopped in front of a set of bookcases. As the woman pulled back on a book, Felicia heard a small click, then the bookcase swung open, revealing an inner room that was packed full of staff all wearing the same gray uniform. Madame Bonnart quickly introduced the rest, all names Felicia immediately forgot, and explained her situation.

"So those damn Apostles are really gone?" asked a small gentleman huddled in the back.

"Almost all of them are dead," Felicia shared. The man, and almost all the others, seemed to visibly relax.

"Thank the gods," the man whispered. "We have been saved." He clutched a handful of books. By 'we,' Felicia suspected he meant the books and not the others.

"We need direction from the councilmen, so we're urgently trying to send word to them. If one of you could show me a roster of their addresses we would like to send word to them now."

A tiny woman pushed through the crowd holding up her hand.

"I can be of assistance," said the quiet woman.

"If you're reassembling the councilmen, I'd be wary of a few of them. Some were in support of the Apostles, but ultimately they all got the boot when they got forced out," another man piped up. Felicia figured there would be a few among the nine that further escalated the integration of the Apostles.

"Do you know which councilmen sided with the Apostles? We would like to avoid bringing them back." *At this moment,* Felicia thought. They would eventually have to answer for their crimes.

"It's not our place," someone tried to say, before being interrupted.

"Yes it is. We are the keepers of the kingdom's knowledge. Who this young lady contacts will be in charge of what happens next. She needs to know the truth and we have records of the meetings," the small gentleman interjected. "From what was circulating around the palace, four Councilmen supported the idea of the Apostles. The other five were against the idea: Sun, Clairepointe, Hennan, Ceraun, and Parisa."

"That's merely hearsay. You cannot go about telling this woman who to bring in by conjecture alone," someone stated.

"Then she will have to consult the manuscripts. There should be records of what went on during their meetings," another person spoke above them.

All Felicia needed was to contact Lilith's father and learn the truth from him. "Please. If you could show me the records, I'll be on my way." She motioned for the quiet woman to show the way.

The doors to the offices had been blasted open. Since she and Lilith never came down these halls during the upheaval, then it could mean that someone else had forced their way in. The office was in complete disarray. Hundreds of scrolls littered the floor, along with maps and torn books. Someone was looking for something.

"Do you know where the records for the meetings were kept?" Felicia knew the answer before asking. The small woman pointed to the broken shelf.

"Would the addresses of the councilmen be kept there as well?" Feilia toed a crushed scroll.

"They would be kept in the books over here." The small woman led Felicia through the mess and to the side. There were hundreds of books. Some had been thrown on the floor.

"Please gather anyone willing to help from the library. We need to sort out this mess and find the addresses," Felicia commanded. While the quiet woman scurried off to find others, she started searching the spines of the books. There were hundreds of books organized into volumes. 'Councilmen' had seventeen volumes. She pulled out the last volume and started flipping through pages. King Gaius went through a lot of councilmen. Every few months there would be rotation. Some left on purpose, others were cast aside. Pages and pages were filled with information about each representative: addresses, known family members, magical abilities, birthlines, social status, religious practices. Everything was noted. Felicia flipped to the very end of the book, to the last entry.

She flipped further back to the start of King Amadeus' reign. Unlike his predecessor, his councilmen stayed loyal; he saw very few changes of those that served him. She found Councilman Hennan and read dedicated pages. Listed was his graduation from Ardaven, his previous position as a scholarly apprentice, and his starting position at the palace, dated around the same time as the ascension of the King. Someone had taken time to depict his wife, a close resemblance to Lilith in her facial features. She was a former Maiden of Melia, and studied under the priesthood in the eastern kingdom. Felicia knew very little about the religions of her world. She knew the Maidens of Melia worshiped a few goddesses, but aside from Melia, she couldn't remember which ones. A note was scribbled in, using a different ink than the original lettering. An amendment was made, noting the death of his wife. Something was scratched out. Felicia brought the book closer to try to make out the text when a loud thump made her jump. Several of the library dwellers had come in to help clean up.

"What would you like us to do?" one asked her. She put the book down to direct the newcomers, telling them to put aside any recent records of meetings. It took a while for them to find a rhythm, but by the time they had figured out what to do, the sun was fading and she needed to head on the road soon.

Felicia picked up the book and found out where she had left off. She quickly jotted down the address, and took the book with her. The helpers were able to give her directions to the house, showing her a detailed map of the lands. Giving her thanks to the helpers, she waved at them and then headed for the stables.

Unfortunately, the stables had been abandoned by staff, so Felicia made use of what she could find. She saddled up an aged looking brown horse, who huffed at her when she approached, but was otherwise well tempered. She stuffed the book into a side carrier and then mounted the horse. If she rode fast, she could be there by nightfall.

She would ride through worse for this new beginning. As if ordained by the gods, perhaps just one, the stars were shining brightly. For the first time in a long while, she felt something shift in the air around her, something long promised—hope.

Just as she settled into her pace, she heard a whisper riding through the breeze. A voice that made her shiver.

"Your time is finally here, and your calling has come." Its voice was one that has haunted her, sweet yet dangerous. *"I am coming. It is time we meet."*

The air seemed to be sucked out of her, as she gripped the reigns tightly. So many issues had come from he who sits on the throne. Maybe this voice was warning her of the dawn? Maybe this voice was telling her that his time will come to an end?

Yes, she thought. *My time is here.* With a kick of her heel, the horse galloped faster, the shining night blanketing her, enveloping her in darkness.

CHAPTER 26
RISE OF A NEW DAWN

Lilith

The sand did not make for a comfortable sleep. Her body ached, and every single muscle felt stiff. By the early morning, Lilith had rummaged through her pack and changed into some very stale, wrinkled clothes. Ones that had been shoved at the bottom of her bag since they travelled through the Ruins. They reeked, but considering her alternative of a silky black and red gown, she had no other choice. She tore her beautiful dress apart to tie long strands of fabric around her feet, wincing at ruining the gown that must have cost a small fortune. The rest of the dress, she stuffed into her pack.

About halfway through wrapping her feet, her stomach grumbled, and then Lilith remembered she had her magic back. For the first time, she was able to feel the full extent of her magical capabilities. Even her emergence had not exposed her to the endless mana that now buzzed under her skin. She reached into the abundant flow of energy, which ran through her like a rushing river, infinite and intense. Similar to her emergence, her body felt feverish and sick. All she wanted to do was lie in a heap and sleep. But the warning from Melia had her stumbling to her feet.

She wondered what Demetrius was doing. No longer tethered, she couldn't feel him; their mental connection was silent. Was he safe? Was he still in this realm? Melia had mentioned he was taken by her kind, but how could a mortal exist among immortals? How can he defend himself against such power? It dawned on her that the bitter part of her feelings felt a little satisfaction that he was being challenged. This was what he wanted, for them to find him, to please his own revenge. Surely, he had a plan and could handle himself. On the other hand, she was alone, and her survival depended on herself.

Concentrating on her earth magic, she summoned roots from deep in the ground. It was as if she could feel the earth move under her feet. The very dirt she stood atop started quaking in response. Never had she felt this connected with the energy that stirred her. It was as if she could sense every particle of air, every speck of dust and debris, and the miniscule droplets of water that hung around her. Her awareness extended as far as she could feel energy; there was an end, but it stretched far.

A sprouting bud pushed through the sand, bursting into leaves. From its branches, robust berries formed. Lilith ripped them off as they ripened. She gobbled them up until the ache in her belly subsided. This magic was definitely useful, but even it had limits. She couldn't create an orchard within this cave, and subsisting on these berries alone would not last long. Her own knowledge tied her possibilities. Yes, she could make a portal, but without an anchoring rune, she couldn't bridge anywhere. She'd have to go on foot. With her pack and journal sent off to her special hiding spot, she headed further through the corridor of red stone to look for a way out.

For hours, she travelled through the network of passages; a seemingly continuous corridor appearing almost identical to her. By some miracle, she heard rushing water and focused her efforts on finding the source. She used her mana, her imaginary hand of energy, to feel for the water. Annoyed by the constant dead ends, she huffed in frustration. Cautiously, she placed her hand on the stone. If she could summon roots, surely she could transform the earth itself. Her brows furrowed in concentration. Sweat coated her skin. The rush of water seemed just within touch, so near. The hardened red stone rumbled, and from her fingertips a crack formed, splintering through the rock like lightning. A web extended, shifting the earth, as it crumbled from within, leaving a small, rough tunnel.

Lilith followed the bright light. In front of her was a short cliff; below was a wide, gentle-flowing river with crystal clear water. Around the edge grew all sorts of vegetation, mostly spiky bushes and thin trees. On the other side of the river was a wide bank and then another cliff, one that looked like it would reach the skies. Lilith saw no other option ahead. She would have to cross the river and then travel down the bank until she could get out. Now that she was no longer bound, this didn't scare her. She was alone, in an unknown place, but there was no fear lingering in her heart.

The waters of the river were cool and soaked her bound feet. At its deepest point, the river came up to her hip. She spotted tiny silver fish passing her as she sloshed across to the sandy bank. If she were not in a rush to find this mystery person, 'The Fallen Star,' this would have been a great spot to camp.

Once she made it to the opposite bank, she called upon her earth magic and formed a flat raft-like structure that was wide in the centre and tapered to a point on either end. It would have to be carved out more, so Lilith used her ingenuity and more of her handy magic to make a rudimentary axe.

She spent the better part of the morning working on her little raft, hoping it would take her upriver. A fleeting idea that she could try walking on water had crossed her mind, but this method would be faster. By the time it was done, it was pretty ugly but looked stable. In the centre, she carved a sunken portion where she would kneel, and she made a long paddle that could help her navigate the gentle waters.

She pushed her craft into the waters and hopped on. With her paddle, she was able to guide herself deeper into the river, letting the current do most of the work. The hardest part was adjusting to the oncoming rocks. She smiled at herself for her creativity. Just a day ago, she had freed herself from the Apostles, from her curse, and now she was here in this serene, magical land. The river curved along this large cliff for a while. It carried her until the sun was at its highest. At that point, the current started to pick up, and she dealt with the first dip.

Slightly panicking, Lilith started looking for an exit strategy. She was not the most confident swimmer, so falling into the rapids would not be ideal. With a steep cliff on either side, Lilith looked for some sort of rocky area that she could at least try to climb out of. She spotted a potential low spot as her raft bounced off a rock, tipping her off balance and into the river.

The fast-moving rapids pushed her under several times, and each submergence felt like she was suffocating. She screamed as the point of her raft collided with her back. This could not be how her life ended. The damn bird creature would not have sent her here just to drown in some random river.

With that mindset, she worked through her pain and swam to the bank. Smooth pebbles pushed into her nails as she clawed her way up the bank and onto safety. She lay there, still half submerged and wondered why Melia couldn't drop her off right in front of the person she needed to meet.

There must be a point to this. A test of her newfound limit. She needed this.

In front of her was a fifty-foot rock wall, her exit. Her clothes were fully soaked, and even after using more mana to force hot air through them, they still weighed on her. She removed some of the coverings from her toes and wound them around her hand. The way up did not look impossible, but the jagged rock face would make for a challenge.

The first section was not that bad. She cut a little bit of her toe trying to figure out some holds, but she was able to make it up the twenty feet to the first little landing. She bandaged her cut with her tattered dress strips and continued up the next fifteen feet to the next landing. Her body was exhausted from the swim, and her arms ached, feeling stiff. She used more of her mana to restore what she could, but given that she had not practiced, her wounds had not fully closed, and her sore body only felt minor relief. Cursing loudly, she continued upwards, as the jagged rock sliced her skin.

Making it to the second landing, she leaned forward to rest her head on the wall and opened her eyes to look down. Her stomach lurched at the forty or so feet between where she rested and the river. At least if she fell, she would end up back in the rapids.

All the possible ways she could have circumvented this climb sprang through her mind. She could have made a rune, tossed it to the top of the cliff and then portalled. She could have used her earth magic to make herself a ladder, or better yet, use a root to take her to the top. She cursed her own stupidity. Her lack of critical thinking made her weak, and she could not afford weakness.

There was maybe another fifteen feet to the top. Her head felt light and dizzy, but she continued to use her mana to heal what she could. Energy roared through her veins as she called for the earth to help her to the top. The cliff groaned as a large root, as thick as a tree trunk, split the rock apart. She grabbed it as it soared skyward, reaching past the top. She thought over and over. *No, this will not be my end.* The root sagged, crashing onto the flat ground, and Lilith gracefully hopped off, brushing away the specks of dirt off her shoulders.

This was not the time to give up. She would conquer any challenges that she faced. She would find the Fallen Star, save her family, her friends, and her kingdom. She was the spark that would free her people, create a new world—one without the Void—and then she would end those damn gods.

EPILOGUE

TIME'S EYE

DEMETRIUS

Demetrius appeared in front of the townsite of Brandy-brooke, the epicentre of the Void. The small town, mostly composed of farmland, was the first town to be claimed by the expanding darkness. The darkness claimed all towns-people, leaving none to survive. The town had been vacant since Demetrius had ordered the people and creatures to push further out. No one should venture this close to the Void. He felt his mana slowly draining.

A large black cloud rotated overhead, a new addition to the now desolate place, its centre slowly forming a tip that pointed down. The ground continued to shake; the effects were devastating. The houses were crumbling with every rumble, and glass and dust filled the air, making it hard to see. Trees cracked and smashed to the ground, while large veins expanded from the Void, creeping through the farmlands.

As if the very air stilled, everything went silent. The rumbling stopped. Leaves on the bushes and trees calmed, as if frozen in time. Even the dust, forming like a billowing veil, became unmoving. each particle suspended around Demetrius. Whatever had immobilized the environment had no effect on him. He'd never seen this kind of power.

A sound like a beating drum echoed from the centre of the darkness. Demetrius threw his hands over his ears and cast a protective spell from the sheer volume of each pulse. Its vibrations rattled his bones as he fell to his knees, unable to stand. Within the Void burst a glowing column of bright purple light. Confusion and fear filled his mind. The cage was breaking open. The rising purple light broke through the whirling black clouds. From this close, its light was blinding. He raised his left hand to shield his eyes, causing his hand to look almost translucent. Unable to do anything else, he squeezed his eyes shut and hoped this would not last.

The tiny particles of dust grazed his raised hand as time seemed to catch up. The glowing purple light dimmed to the point where it no longer burned his eyes. It continued to darken, like a black pillar connecting the sky to the surface of the world.

Impossible, he thought. Managing the creatures and the darkness while inside the Void stripped him of his strength. His godliness.

A presence emerged from the black column. A being floated gently in front of Demetrius' kneeled body.

"Locke." A voice like thunder pierced his protective shield. "Here you are. You look weak, dear brother. How pathetic." The being had long black hair and eyes so yellow, it was like looking at the sun. "I guess now your appearance matches your personality."

"Alda," Demetrius sneered. "Gods damn you." Bile rose from his stomach, making him heave. White hot anger took over his body. He shot out, sending wave after wave of furious elements. *This is your fault. You're the reason I was stuck in that cage for so long.*

In a flash of dark blue, Demetrius hit Alda square in the chest. A shockwave ignited, rebounding him across the broken ruins of the town. It was a chaos of smoke, dust and destruction.

Alda clicked his tongue, appearing before him. "That is not how you should welcome me. You behave just like those filthy humans." He raised his luminous hand, his skin shining bright yellow, its vibrancy shielded under the white armour that he wore. His palm hovered above Demetrius' head, sending a wave of pain shooting through his body. An ungodly scream ripped from his throat. A feeling of pain mixed with unrestrained terror and pure death gripped his very soul. "You are but a shell of the god that you were. It's not even amusing how pitiful you've become." Alda smiled. "What shall we do with you?"

He sent another pulse of pain, causing Demetrius to fall, his body writhing on the ground. Foam spilled from the corners of his mouth as he arched his back. Even through this, Demetrius fought back, trying to overcome Alda's attack. In the back of his mind, he could feel another sort of pain. One that wasn't his own. Lilith. Her body was being broken and whispers of her voice begging him to come. *No!* Demetrius stood to rise, adrenaline overtaking his perception of pain. He would not let her die again. Alda grinned and let out a malicious laugh. He slammed into Demetrius, body checking him through crumbling walls and glass. Blood spurted from Demertrius' mouth as he laid, feeling Lilith's pain and hopelessness.

"Enough, Alda." A light voice filled the air. With godlike speed, Alda jumped back away from Demetrius' fallen body. "He has suffered enough."

A small woman with long, wavy, light red hair and luminescent ivory skin knelt beside Demetrius, her fingers gently resting on his chest. Warmth filled him, restoring his life force. "Breathe, Locke. Come back to us." The ethereal voice summoned him back to the present.

"Melia. Of course you would take his side. Ever the doting sister to him." Alda glared at the two of them.

"Stop, Alda. You're being ridiculous. This petty feud has to end." Melia rose to her fullest height. Alda towered over her, but she held her ground. "Ominus will be joining us shortly. It's time we end this. Look at what you're doing…"

"Of course you would blame this on me. Everything he does," Alda pointed to Demetrius, "is pure and holy. Look around. This world is breaking because of him."

Demetrius laughed. "For a god, you really are an idiot. This darkness is your doing, not mine. I did not make this rift into this realm." He felt a rush of power flowing through Lilith. She had finally snapped, and her runes were breaking. However, as soon as that feeling came, he felt the link between them fade. A fear raged through him at the unknown. Yet, he knew whatever she was facing at this moment, she could handle herself.

"I did," said a deep voice, interrupting Demetrius' thoughts. A giant of a man appeared in a white light behind Melia. He was hairless, and his skin was a flawless rich deep brown. He was the first of them to rise as a god. The one that created mankind. His iridescent yellow eyes scrutinized each of them. The weight of his gaze felt as if the sun itself was judging them. Alda's superior persona faltered as Ominus' sight focused on him. "Why are you here, Alda?"

"Ominus, why have you chosen this path?" Melia faced her husband, interrupting him, looking clearly confused. For a person who saw everything, seeing her bewildered was a first for Demetrius.

"It was the only way to set him free. Locke, you will return with us." Ominus sent threads of his power into Demetrius. His body filled with energy, and an intoxicating, rich essence flowed through his veins. The familiarity of his power returned to him. It felt like a thousand years had passed since he was filled with this vitality. But there was a restraint. Something holding back the flow of this restorative spirit. Ominus looked strained.

"Ominus?" Melia gripped her husband's arm.

Ominus growled and shook off his wife, "It seems this body of his will not complete the transformation." For a flashing moment, Demetrius swore he saw the shadow of a grin pass over Alda's face.

"What will you do?" she asked innocently, looking at the dark pillar rising from the Void. "We need him to join us, otherwise we do not hold enough power to push back the cage." Ominus glared at Demetrius and Alda.

"Look at what you've done. We have felt only a brief moment of peace because you both cannot co-exist."

"Every being that roams these lands will suffer the wrath of the darkness if the cage breaks open. This whole realm will fall to them. I can feel their presence drawing closer to us," Melia whispered, her vision dazed.

Ominus shouted a line of curses, something he picked up from his time with mankind. "I shall do what I can for Locke. I will get Alda to help me..." Ominus looked around; Alda had abandoned them and vanished. He growled. "If anyone deserved to be stuck with those creatures, it should have been him."

"Then why? Why was I sent into the cage? Why did you not release me?" Demetrius looked at the couple. Thousands of years of festering hate that he had built towards the other gods for turning on him broke through his composure. The scream he unleashed was that of a god fuelled by wrath. Ominus shielded Melia with his body.

"I told you, but you did not listen." Melia glared at the back of her husband's head. Ominus turned and glared back at her and then sighed.

"There were difficulties and truths that I had to learn. We tried to open the cage, but without Alda's support and your power, we were not enough. I tried again and again, I was so desperate to set you free, but it seemed we only made a portal somewhere else." He looked at the Void. "Again, my power alone is not enough. I cannot give you your entire power back in your form, and I have no idea if such a feat would be possible." He nodded his head towards the Void. "Without the others united, we are outmatched."

Demetrius scowled. "Why do you all hide? Ashamed of what you've done?"

"Yes. We are." A look of remorse spread on Ominus' face, one that Demetrius nor Melia had ever seen before. "Please, allow me to give you part of my essence. It will not undo what I have done." He held his hand over Demetrius' chest. A flash of white transferred from Ominus to Demetrius. It felt like a rebirth. Demetrius was being reborn as Locke. His body felt stronger, and his midnight blue hair had faded to a silvery white. It was still short, but he looked more like Locke and less like a human. Ominus smiled, his hand hovering over Demetrius.

The usual attire he dressed in as Demetrius was replaced with white armour, made from the sacred ores of the holy realm. Ominus clasped his shoulder. "You will return with me, brother. I need you. You've done your part here, but we need to come up with a solution to your problem. I will not take no for an answer."

"His problem?" Melia clenched her jaw.

"Yes. Right now the return of his powers is temporary due to my essence, but we will find out how to restore you fully. He can't remain here, Melia. He doesn't belong here."

Demetrius was powerless to argue. In truth, Ominus had only spoken the truth, he did not belong here. But, with Lilith tied to this realm, this place would have to become his home.

Melia's eyes glazed over, noticing something unseen. "If you must take him with you, I need to speak with him first."

Ominus pinched the bridge of his nose, while Demetrius just stared at him. A brief thought crossed his mind: for a god, he behaved so humanly. Or was it that he made mankind like him? Ominus exhaled and nodded to his wife. He disappeared into a flash of white light, leaving the two alone.

"I sent Lilith to the west." Melia glared at him. "Isn't it ironic that she had to be rebirthed into the one creature that I hated the most? And now I'm asking you to protect not only her, but all of them." Locke had always known about the struggles of her marriage. "She will not be allowed to come back. If you choose to be with her, you must remain in this realm. By some miracle, you have been reborn, too, as their King." Melia smirked. "An almost god amongst men. I am afraid I cannot intervene much more without risking the balance of not only this realm, but all. Do well by her. Sometimes, a sacrifice is the hardest decision. She deserves so much more than we can give. Now, I'm afraid our time is up. I'm truly sorry, Demetrius." It was the first time any of the gods had called him by this name.

"You loved her. Arguably more than I did. I should be thanking you, Melia. You gave us another chance."

"You're right. Let's not screw it up this time."

Demetrius balked a laugh and blushed. "Typical." He opened his mouth to say more, but a white light surrounded him. Power that wasn't his, but Ominus'.

"I'll see you later." Melia smirked at her own joke. "Decide if you want justice or revenge."

He wanted to find Lilith. Feeling her emotions rise and fall, he knew something had happened back at home. For now, he would have to be satisfied knowing that she was alive.

What happened next would define their future. Ominus' intervention was what he was relying on. It was foolish to think he could go against the gods, but they were playing right into his plan. The white light enveloped him, basking him in warmth and comfort.

Yes. Take me back, so that I can destroy it all. Demetrius smiled.

Afterword

Acknowledgements

I could not have completed this book without my friend and editor, Sam. I am deeply grateful for the time and effort she has invested in helping me. She has been with me through thick and thin, giving me suggestions for every piece of writing, and without her, I would be an incoherent mess with a ton of commas. She has the very difficult task of dealing with my crash outs as I question all the grammatical rules, including helping me with 'forbidden' em dash. Before, they were all hyphens, and that's when I learned length does matter. There are many books that I want to write and share, and I'm very fortunate to have someone who is willing to support me both professionally and as a personal friend, so thank you, Sam.

To all my friends and family, I appreciate your support. It feels incredibly surreal to have my friends, who have known me since I was a child, cheer me on as I sell my fantasy/romance books. They never laughed when I told them I was switching careers to writing, and I feel eternally grateful that they are with me in this journey.

I would not be able to market my book without the help of my parents and my husband. I am new to the world of book markets and fairs, and my family is in the background helping me make things happen. My biggest hype lady is my daughter, and she strives to tell everyone she meets about my books. I would not be able to transform what is lurking in my brain into written words without them.

Through Bound by Runes, I met so many readers, bookstore owners, event coordinators, and other authors, and I am so thankful for their wise words and opportunities. I have been fortunate to have met such amazing people through this journey, and I am grateful to everyone who has helped me along the way. I love being a part of the community of writers and readers in Edmonton. We strive to lift each other up and celebrate each other's accomplishments, and I think that's incredibly special.

To the Beatrice Banes of this world, thank you.

Notes about the story

Tethered by Deception was the reason I wrote Bound by Runes. The trauma, especially with the Apostles of the Reckoning, was very personal. To me, this was a therapeutic outlet and a way to feel justice for my emotional and mental suffering that I experienced as a child in school.

The Apostles were those who were in charge of my education, youth pastors, and peers. They were teachers who pitted us against each other based on the strength of our faith, and omitted knowledge because it didn't fit into their ideals. They were youth pastors who preyed on the innocent children who lived in their bubble of deception and propaganda. They were the young who were fed lies from their parents, a generational manacle that continues to be handed down. They used the institution to signify status, ranking superiority over those who proved their faith. They were the ones who placed blindfolds over our eyes, dulled our brains, and made us spineless.

This is not a testament against any particular religion, but against those who use the institution to feed their deception and need for superiority.

The beauty of fantasy and sci/fi, with a dark, dystopian element, is that sometimes there is a level of truth behind the stories, a commentary on how society needs change, and a warning of what could happen if we allow the corrupt to lead. Beware of the charismatic, the overly charming, the lies told with sweet smiles.

Romance is a subplot of this story, a lovers-turned-enemies situation that is complex and mirrors real relationships. We see young love that was turned into something toxic. We explore how an obsession and infatuation became a twisted kind of love, a curse in itself.

In Bound by Runes, Lilith is naive, too trusting, and too quick to believe that everyone has good intentions. In Tethered by Deception, she is distrustful, hurt, and eventually snaps. She is vulnerable, flawed, and angry. Yet, she is maturing and learning what she wants with her second chance at life. Lilith realizes she is not defined by her relationship with Demetrius, and her worth is not reliant on him.

The final installment will further explore the complex nature of relationships, and I am excited to take you on that journey.

I hope you enjoyed Tethered by Deception.

... AND THOSE WHOSE DARKNESS BINDS THEM

www.ingramcontent.com/pod-product-compliance
Lightning Source LLC
Chambersburg PA
CBHW021221060726
47590CB00005B/1583